Q U A R

MW01138307

EACH MAN IN HIS DARKNESS

The story begins with the arrival of a young man at a small country station in the United States of America. As his origins are poor, his relatives only send a rude young coachman in a cart to fetch him and take him to his dying uncle's opulent home in Virginia. On the way, he loses a glove: an act of defiance which destiny is there to meet.

Two principal themes are the problems of Christianism and homosexuality. The characters in this book all struggle with their emotions, their sensuality, their age, their appearance, their faith and their emptiness in the earthly night which flares up at the end of the book, as if the door opened by death allows in the hope of resurrection.

This novel describes the journey of a soul which hides, which tears itself apart and saves itself, an *éducation sentimentale* in which the heart is the final arbiter when it understands that love is not just a question of sex.

The background is America – landscapes, big cities and New York, where the author confuses his memories and dreams.

JULIEN GREEN

Julien Green was born in Paris of American parents in 1900. He is bilingual and writes in French. He is the author of many novels and plays, as well as his famous *Journal*. He was elected to the Académie Française in 1971.

JULIEN GREEN

Each Man in His Darkness

Translated from the French by ANNE GREEN
With an Introduction by GIOVANNI LUCERA

QUARTET ENCOUNTERS

Quartet Books

Published in Great Britain
by Quartet Books Limited 1990
A member of the Namara Group
27/29 Goodge Street, London W1P 1FD

Originally published in French under the title
Chaque Homme dans sa Nuit by Librairie Plon 1960
Copyright © by Editions du Seuil 1986
Translation copyright © by Anne Green 1961
and © Julien Green 1979
Introduction copyright © by Giovanni Lucera 1989

British Library Cataloguing in Publication Data

Green, Julien, *1900–*
    Each man in his darkness.
    1. Title   II. Chaque homme dans sa nuit.
    English
    843.912 [F]

ISBN 0-7043-0064-8

Reproduced, printed and bound in Great Britain by
BPCC Hazell Books
Aylesbury, Bucks, England
Member of BPCC Ltd.

INTRODUCTION

'I am a Catholic and a writer, but not a Catholic writer.' One could say that the majority of Julien Green's novels are somewhat unorthodox. It is necessary to make this observation for occasionally, and with a certain obstinacy and blindness, critics avid for cut-and-dried classifications wrongly baptize certain writers Catholic novelists. In many of his books, the search for God is tacit, an inverted desire – as opposed to the flamboyance with which God is conspicuously absent from Proust's masterpiece, as Green observes in his *Journal* on 12 January 1972.

It is true, however, that some of the characters in his works are Catholics, yet there are even more Protestants, Indifferentists and agnostics. For the rare Catholics – Wilfrid in *Each Man in His Darkness*, Elisabeth in *The Enemy* and Karin at the end of *The Other One* – it is not so much the ceremonial aspect of a religion which affects them, but their bewildered search for God, the assurance that through the avatars of their existence they are chosen by Love. Julien Green is not a Catholic writer but a Catholic and a writer and there is no interplay between the two. Not one of his novels is set in a Catholic milieu.

The novel following *The Transgressor* takes us yet again to America, as does *Moira*, but this one opens up into a world of greater serenity. The book is full of deviations, cross-connecting stories, people struggling with their innermost secrets. Wilfrid is, in a sense, the meeting point of their destinies. He earns his living by selling shirts in a large shop in New York, a humble occupation considering the wealth of his family. Beyond the confines of this monotonous existence he leads a wild life. His pursuit of pleasure does nothing to stifle in him the call of a faith manifest for all to see. Here lies the drama of a man who believes, whatever his faith; but in this case he is a Christian. How can he reconcile the flesh and the spirit? Wilfrid tirelessly pursues girls and has no experience of rejection. He is twenty-four years old, unsullied and charming, and his grey, laughing eyes are irresistible. His uncle, affluent Uncle Horace, summons him to his estate, Wormsloe, in Virginia. Horace is dying. He knows that Wilfrid's faith is absolute. It is to him that he shall entrust his 'treasure', a thick envelope containing old love letters (the family scandal) and some shares which will give the young man a certain measure of independence. However, nothing in life ever happens the way one would like. Love engulfs you unexpectedly and you yourself become the source of despair to another. Wilfrid falls in love with Phoebe, the wife of his cousin, James Knight, a puritan who at a glance realizes what is happening. In the meantime, Wilfrid's cousin Angus dares not declare the love he feels for Wilfrid. To Angus, Wilfrid's love would be the only means of salvation from all the other loves submerging him. Then there is the meeting with Max when coming out of a church. This mysterious young man pursues Wilfrid, obsessed by religion yet abandoning himself to violent desire. He can escape from neither one nor the other and leads a sacrilegious life, living in a brothel and talking of God in order to seduce his companion. Ever more religious, he surrenders to the sadomasochistic games of strangers. Max wants to win Wilfrid, body and soul, to steal his faith and purity. Max is a lie; his faith has foundered due to his spiritual anguish and he takes a diabolical pleasure in returning relentlessly and with suspicious tenacity to the question of God's existence, with the aim of corrupting Wilfrid. He uses the most underhand of all weapons: 'Faith cannot survive desire,' he says, not realizing that this is the key to his own predicament.

One night Wilfrid stays with Phoebe, but by choice nothing happens. The love which unites them is pure. Wilfrid sacrifices his carnal love to a platonic passion bordering on mystical ecstasy. Phoebe's husband watches over them. Events gather speed; everyone calls on Wilfrid for help, while he misunderstands them all. Almost all gestures of love go wrong, are misconceived or are suspect. Max, in whom he would like to confide, is destined to kill him with a pistol shot after having frightened him for long minutes on a gloomy staircase. This shot is also a gesture of love. At the point of death, lying in the street, Wilfrid forgives his assassin. It is now that everything begins. Julien Green has opened a door into a shadowy world. James Knight saw Wilfrid on his deathbed at the hospital and tells Angus, who is in despair about the death of his beloved cousin:

> He was alive, he lived! . . . It seemed as though he smiled at my surprise and that he knew secrets and was keeping them to himself. As though he had played a trick on us by going, a boy's prank, and that he was watching us from afar, from a region of light, in spite of the fact that his eyelids were shut.

It is on this note of invisible happiness that the book ends. Wilfrid's act of forgiveness whilst dying has opened the doors to his paradise. Julien Green declared that this was his first optimistic novel:

> It was after having written the last word at the bottom of the final page that I questioned myself on the meaning of this long narrative, for I had to find the title, which I had not yet discovered. One of Victor Hugo's verses, in a poem which I reread by chance, seemed to me to sum up the novel: 'Each man in his darkness goes towards the light . . . ' The life of each one of us has a meaning which escapes us. It would be appropriate at this point to rediscuss the famous tapestry of which we see only the reverse side; we shall only see the right side much later on. That which appears to us today to be perplexing, obscure and confused shall reveal itself under a harmonious aspect. Each one of us, despite difficulties, vacillations and failures, moves nevertheless, through a suffocating obscurity towards peace. The day shall finally come when, as is written in the Scriptures, God shall wipe away the tears . . . Certainly, we do not know how our salvation is brought about, and our life appears to be like a novel for which we can't find a title; but God finds the title.

Green's *oeuvre* is individual and unusual. Man is at the same time his own hell and his own paradise. The attraction yet sadness of pleasure, the mystery of being, the emptiness and beauty of the visible world, the splendour of flesh and melancholy of possession: Julien Green fills a world which is strangely real and close at hand with contradictions. A novelist by instinct, possessed by his work to the point of appearing insensitive to the outside world, the paradox is that he creates a world which is recognizable and he surmounts the ageless years without losing his flesh-and-blood substance. The Germans – Hesse, Joseph Roth, Klaus Mann –

consider him to be a 'Christian Kafka' incorporating the dual meaning of mystery: man is lost at the centre of a world which he does not understand and this world inverted within him renders him incomprehensible to himself.

'However one classifies Julien Green,' wrote Gaëtan Picon, ... the proximity of his work to that of other contemporaries can only be arbitrary: his solitude is absolute.' It is for this reason that Green is misunderstood by hasty criticism, which habitually forces writers to crowd into a small scale of values, like frogs when a flood is forecast. Where can one place Green in the context of French literature? Is he an expressionistic, an Anglo-Saxon, a chimerical or a Freudian writer? The term magic-realism has been invented for him alone, although where does this leave *The Strange River*, *Another Sleep*, *The Pilgrim on the Earth* and so on? Not one single frontier is defined in his work, and all classification is debatable. This brings us back to Gaëtan Picon's assessment: ' . . . his solitude is absolute'.

Green is a novelist of violence, desire and defeat. From the first few pages, one is overcome by unease, the narrative runs towards traps in which the protagonists are snared. The themes are too rich and varied to be analysed with brevity. One can, however, retain a pivotal point at which all forces fuse: exile. Julien Green is an expatriate – this is in fact the title of Volume XIV of his *Journal*. An American from the South born in Paris, a Parisian completing his degree studies in his true fatherland, Virginia, he constantly feels himself drawn towards the other who is inside him and by the desire for that other place, which invariably translates itself either as the American South or as Paris. One can say that he is a Parisian, however one cannot make the assertion that he is French, even though *his language is his heritage*. He is, in a way, a Parisian from somewhere else. In truth man has only internal frontiers. And so, in his novels, as in his plays, one of the protagonists often comes from elsewhere. The myth of the stranger which Camus seemed to have rediscovered, found itself with greater depth and to a greater extent in Green, years before *L'Etranger*. In fact, in our century of displaced people, this very problem of identity was that of many of his characters as early as *The Pilgrim on the Earth* and well before the psychoanalysts' invasion.

Expressing Existential anxiety and delving into the unconscious, Green's *oeuvre* is more modern than those works based on social problems which so quickly become dated. An *oeuvre* which is hard to classify, maybe, but the writer is not an independent planet revolving around itself at the heart of its own miniature universe, he is part of a galaxy of ideas and emotions, and whatever the differences of milieu, of religion and of period, dream and solitude unite certain creators across space and time as if their lives form part of a vast biography of the human mind, to which each in turn contributes his own fragment. And so, a common anxiety and a similar sense of mystery grasped the hands of Hawthorne, Joyce, Maeterlinck, Kafka and Green, in their search for a personal thread in the subterranean well from which they were to extract the diamonds and the mud of the human soul.

Giovanni Lucera

PART ONE

CHAPTER I

The train had disappeared and the station was empty. Wilfred's rather worried grey eyes roamed from one end of the square to the other and at first saw nothing. His uncle's big car was not there. Perhaps there had been some mistake. Should he have gone on to the next station? No, this stop in the open fields was the right one. The letter in his pocket told him so most precisely.

Not a tree. Nothing but the immense square of beaten earth in front of the station and meadows stretching as far as the eye could reach under the sky and its heavy, wind-driven clouds. He looked around him once more, but had already understood and pretended not to see: in a corner, half concealed by a gate, waited a most commonplace gig, the caretaker's carriage, and on the seat, a young man in a red-checked shirt raised the end of his whip each time that Wilfred looked his way, but gave himself no further trouble. The boy whose father had not made a fortune was thus given a lesson in humility.

It was like a game: Wilfred turned his head with an air of shammed absent-mindedness and the youth raised the end of his whip ever so little, with a sort of indifference that seemed unfeigned, twice, thrice, as many times as you please.

Picking up his suitcase, the traveller crossed the twenty yards that separated him from the gig, in the pitiless spring light. At that moment, conscious that it raised a smile, he hated the leather suitcase, his father's suitcase, a bit too large, a trifle old-fashioned with its gaudy European labels. That kind was no longer seen in America and he had never dared to scrape off the

3

labels as he would have liked to: it was the only thing he had inherited from his father.

When he reached the carriage, he heard the boy whistling away to himself. Wilfred bit his lips in a sudden fit of rage, then, looking up, he stared at the face that towered above him. Clinging tightly to the high cheek-bones and masterful jaws, the dark skin shone like leather and the black eyes were like two great pools of shade. A few seconds went by as the young men exchanged somewhat distrustful glances, then the coachman stopped whistling.

'Mr Ingram, I believe,' he said with faintly mocking politeness.

'Yes.'

Wilfred had just lifted the suitcase, helping it up with his knee, for it was a bit heavy, when the coachman took it from him with contemptuous ease and wedged the bag under his feet. He waited until Wilfred was seated next him then, clucking his tongue, set his horse at full speed, a great bay whose rump put one in mind of an enormous chestnut, and soon they drove into a deeply rutted road. Right and left, up to the skyline enclosed by distant woods where the eye detected the first green leaves, the grass lay flat under a cold wind sprung from the depth of winter.

Without the least regard for the fine foreign labels, the coachman had planted both heels on the suitcase and it seemed to Wilfred, in spite of the shame he felt for this rather absurd object, that he himself was being trampled under foot. He furtively observed his neighbour's bony face. The insolent profile, with the small eagle nose, was topped by a mass of heavy brown hair wantonly twisted this way and that by the breeze. The young man, who was both slim and robust, seemed proud of his arms, for he had rolled up his sleeves above the elbows.

For nearly five minutes, they drove without exchanging a word

4

through bleakly majestic scenery where nothing varied but the colour of the sky as it turned from blue to grey. Great tattered clouds skimmed above their heads like sheets torn to pieces by a madman.

Wilfred would have liked to know how much longer the little journey was to last. He had not set foot in his uncle's house since the age of fifteen and so was unable to locate it exactly. He felt foreign to all this part of the country. He had been kept out of the way, in the background. When his father died, someone found him a job, first with a notary, then, as though it were not really of much importance, in a shop where he sold shirts. The family rarely remembered his existence, but this time Uncle Horace had asked to see him.

Uncle Horace was going to die, that was certain. There had been several false alarms, but this time it was true. No one loved him. He had stupidly squandered his fortune with women and had nothing much to leave but Wormsloe, his estate: a house, furniture, books that he had never read. Outside their relation-ship, only one bond existed between himself and Wilfred, a bond never mentioned without a raising of eyebrows: both were Catholics while the rest of the family belonged to the Protestant faith.

A great many questions occurred to Wilfred, questions he would have liked to ask the coachman, but this now seemed impossible. He should have entered into conversation with him at the very start. Since then, too much silence had accumulated between them, and also the lad was beginning to nod and the hands on his lap seemed already asleep. From time to time, as in a dream, they faintly pulled in the reins and consequently the horse trotted much less fast: one might have thought that an agreement had been concluded between animal and driver by which each took a little rest in his own fashion, the chief thing being to keep steadily within the rather sinuous ruts.

5

Because the young man was dozing, Wilfred had a peculiar feeling of being alone and looked around him. Little by little, the woods grew closer, crossed the meadows and came to meet the travellers. Birches with chalky white trunks shivered in the light wind and rows of firs stood shaking their heavy black sleeves.

He wondered whether he ought not to wake the youth by jolting his elbow but, finding this very simple gesture too difficult to make, remained motionless. By the side of this lad in a check shirt he looked citified in his navy-blue overcoat, hat and woollen gloves. This rustic probably thought him queerly got up. Was it just an illusion? Wilfred fancied that the coachman observed him with a hypocritical air from between half-closed lids and only pretended to doze in order to make fun of him, seeing that he was both timid and sensitive to cold. Making up his mind suddenly, Wilfred removed his gloves and laid them on his lap. He would, in the same manner, have taken off his overcoat to prove that he was manly and not afraid of the cold, but dared not.

Suddenly the coachman sat up, threw his head back and spat to one side of the road with peasant coarseness.

'Come now!' he cried. 'We aren't going to sleep here, are we?'

He cracked his whip close to the horse's ears. The bay went off at a fast trot, shaking its mane. At that moment, one of the woollen gloves slipped from Wilfred's lap and fell to the ground.

It was easy enough to tell the coachman to stop, but he did not do so. Stuffing the remaining glove into his pocket he turned and looked over his shoulder at the road where the other glove made a little dark spot. Out of sheer helplessness, he laid his hand on his breast and, looking up at his companion, was on the point of crying 'Stop!' but the word stuck in his throat and his feeling of vague uneasiness increased. He looked back several times. The glove could no longer be seen on the road and Wilfred resigned

6

himself, though he felt ashamed. Never in his life had he felt ridiculous anxiety before a human being. For the first time he was humiliated in his own eyes for no apparent reason, for no precise cause. Why? The question disturbed him because he could not answer it and once again he bit his lips as though to take vengeance on his own flesh for his cowardice.

A few minutes later, the carriage entered a wood where the light was growing dimmer. Here and there, a sunbeam shone on the bark of a tree as if to draw attention to it, for the patches of light suggested some mysterious choice. The wind dropped. The silence was only disturbed by the sound of the wheels, but when they left the wood and found themselves once more under the boundless sky, the young coachman began singing in a foreign tongue. His slightly hoarse voice had strains of sudden sweetness that were almost childlike. Wilfred saw his quivering throat and turned his eyes away. Words sprang from the open mouth with a sort of arrogant vigour and suddenly came that rather sly, rather coaxing tenderness, then a call that was like a furious shout of joy, followed by a chorus that probably made no sense, although it conveyed a feeling of uneasiness. After a while, the coachman stopped singing and cracked his whip.

'I'm getting married in two weeks!' he cried.

And he burst out laughing. Wilfred thought that he should make some comment but, finding none, tried to laugh too. He felt that his ears were growing scarlet and he fixed his eyes on the road just beyond the bay that now trotted faster.

'Did you understand what I was singing just now?' asked the young man in a voice that could be heard above the sound of the wheels and the horse's hooves. 'I bet you couldn't. It's a song from my parents' country, over there, across the ocean. The men sing it when they're going to be married.'

He turned his head toward Wilfred: 'Say, you aren't much of a talker are you!' he cried, hurling the words full in his face.

For a second or two, Wilfred looked silently at a face that was both merry and a little angry. The great black eyes were shining and deep, yet, strange as it may seem, their expression was red. It could not be described otherwise: they seemed to be gazing at a fire.

'I ask nothing better than to talk,' said Wilfred.

'Are the girls pretty in the big city?'

The question came like a blow from a fist and made Wilfred jump.

'Pretty? Yes. Some are.'

'And there're enough to go round, eh? That's not the way it is here.' Cracking his whip, he swore, then continued brusquely: 'By six tomorrow morning, I'll have quit the dump.'

'What dump?'

'Why, Wormsloe, of course! You pretty nearly die of boredom there. I'm fed up with that old man who's always sick. Your uncle, isn't he?'

'Yes, he's my uncle.'

'And Angus is your cousin?'

'Do you mean Mr Howard?'

'Mr Howard, if you like.'

'Why yes, we're cousins.'

'If you don't mind my asking, is that big black car his?'

'I can't say. I don't know the car. I haven't seen my cousin for the last four years.'

'Well, he came with his mother in a big car that hasn't got much in common with the cart we're in, let me tell you. Who owns that big car? He or his mother?'

'I don't know. Why do you ask me?'

'Oh! just for information. That cousin of yours seems to be on Easy Street.'

He stood up, feet on either side of the suitcase, and handling his whip with sudden fury lashed at the rump and sides of

8

his animal. The bay threw its head back and broke into a gallop.

At a turn in the road stood Wormsloe.

CHAPTER II

Tall and broad, the old wooden house stood out in a dark mass against the sky. It looked like a great chest. Firs and a few beeches pressed around it so closely that branches brushed softly over the walls, like hands. Wilfred remembered the coachman's phrase and could not help smiling. It really was a dump, but a gigantic and quite venerable one, for it must have gone back to the days when America was still a British colony.

The front door was ajar. He had only to push it open to find himself in a hall hung in garnet-red velvet. The first thing to meet his eye was a large and well-nigh naked woman of polished bronze who carried a torch in her fist. She stood at the foot of the stairs smiling at the visitor and he, suitcase in hand, looked at her attentively.

His thoughts perhaps led him further than he would have wished, for he did not hear someone come up to him and, turning suddenly, saw a young mulatto girl in a black dress and white muslin apron. She said his name and he took off his hat, as much from politeness as from a feeling of candid admiration for the swarthy little face and serious black eyes.

Without another word, she moved as though to take his bag, but he refused to part with it.

'It's too heavy,' he said.

'I'll show you to your room,' she said in a low voice.

9

They walked up a flight and crossed a long landing where gilt-framed engravings decorated the intervals between doors surmounted by little neo-Greek pediments, but Wilfred's room was not on that floor. In fact the maid led him up another thirty steps or so and they soon found themselves as high as they could go, at the very top of the house, in a room so small that it took only a few paces to cross it from end to end and, standing on tiptoe, the ceiling could be touched with a finger.

'The room isn't very large,' she said, smiling at Wilfred's disappointed expression, and added: 'The bell will ring five minutes before supper.'

She left at once and he looked around him, shaking his head. In a corner stood a mahogany bed covered by a white spread with a design of little blue wool tufts, and on the painted black floor a chain-stitch carpet displayed its unpretentious shades of pink, sky-blue and pale violet. A rocking-chair, a small table smothered by a moss-green velvet cover completed the furnishings.

Going up to the sash window, he leaned forward slightly and could not keep from exclaiming on seeing an immense lawn that looked like a race-course sloping gradually down to a river whose waters gleamed between the trees in the twilight. Blurred memories came back to his mind. He had walked there as a child with his father, one snowy afternoon, and for a minute he had the feeling that time had faded away, that such a thing as time no longer existed.

In the very silence of the house, he recognized the perfect fixity of things that do not change while we ourselves become each day different. He remembered his amazement on seeing the bronze woman at the foot of the staircase for the very first time. An opportune drapery concealed what should not be seen, back and front. Yet his father had said to him: 'Don't look.' Wilfred had forgotten these details and they amused him for a

10

moment, then a vague melancholy swept over him. Years had gone by and he felt old: he was twenty-four.

Taking off his overcoat, he sat in the rocking-chair and wondered what he was going to do with himself till supper-time. As he cast his eyes around him, he felt like a wild animal that had been confined in a box, and the room, in spite of its air of spick and span innocence, horrified him suddenly. It was neither a man's room nor a child's room, and every time he raised his eyes to the ceiling it seemed to have grown a little lower. His neighbours were certainly the servants. That he did not mind. He had been put there because he was of no importance. That was quite natural, but he promised himself not to spend more than one night at Wormsloe.

After a moment, he decided not to wait for the supper bell and went down to the ground floor. Once more, he examined the bronze woman. To look at her roused evil thoughts, those of which you are bound to accuse yourself, but he had had so many since his last confession that one more would make no great difference. He was up to his eyes in mortal sin, and really the woman was beautiful. She shone. Your glance as good as touched her. She probably came from Europe where Uncle Horace had travelled widely with his brother, just for pleasure, and they must have known women over there exactly like this one. As a matter of fact, the mulatto girl that he had just seen was about that colour, but her skin did not shine. Wilfred sighed. Uncle Horace was going to die, but he had had a good time. The young man looked a little longer at the perfect limbs, at all that flesh. To look meant a sort of happiness mingled with pain, with hunger, something that devastated the heart.

Reluctantly turning his head away, after some hesitation he softly opened a great door, surmounted, like those of the floor above, by a pediment of a delicate lace-like pattern. He took a step forward and found himself in a drawing-room where two

11

tall windows faced each other, one looking toward the river, the other toward the avenue that led to the entrance gate. Heavy plum-coloured velvet curtains narrowed them a little and darkened a room where everything had an air of ceremony. The last rays of twilight allowed a dim sight of heavy, faintly gleaming mahogany furniture: here a chest of drawers with brass handles writhing like flames, there a glass cabinet whose shape brought to mind a Gothic church. Two large armchairs, crouched in the semi-darkness, were like heavy persons seated opposite each other, and the more one looked at them, the more living they seemed, although motionless.

The young man's great light eyes roamed from one end of the drawing-room to the other, but he dared not move. Here, it was like being in the last century and elsewhere than in America. An enormous crystal chandelier hung from the ceiling and its hundreds of drops glistened as though it had been plunged into a lake and brought out dripping with water. Looking at it in another way, it reminded one of a fat lady picking up her skirts to dance.

Wilfred had reached this point in his meditation when the door opened and someone entered. He recognized the outline at once.

'Angus!' he cried, and holding out his hand he went toward his cousin, but the latter passed behind a table and dropped into one of the big armchairs.

'Is that you, Wilfred?' he asked in an expressionless voice. 'I don't have to ask what you're doing here. That old rake who can't make up his mind to die has made me miss an appointment.'

'Do you realize we haven't seen each other for four years?'

'Four years? I should have said less. And yet, you're right: the four years I spent at the University.'

'I'm glad to see you again,' said Wilfred, sitting down on a chair. 'Even under such circumstances . . .'

'Oh! we'll skip displays of feeling and all that, if you don't mind.'

'I don't care for them any more than you do.'

They stopped talking for a moment and a big clock that Wilfred had not noticed could be heard, ticking solemnly.

'Forgive me,' said Angus suddenly. 'I realize I'm not very agreeable, but all this gloomy business exasperates me. When I think that at this very minute someone is waiting for me, twenty-five miles away . . .'

'If it's a business appointment, that can always be fixed up.'

'Do you imagine that I'd worry about a business appointment? This is a thousand times more important than a business appointment.'

They remained silent once more and in the half-light Wilfred could see his cousin's fair hair shining.

'Why don't you turn on the light?' asked Angus. 'I hate this sinister atmosphere.'

'Where do you turn it on?'

'I see you're as smart as ever,' remarked Angus, getting up. He felt his way along the walls and suddenly the light burst from the chandelier like a great cluster of sparks. The two young men closed their eyes and opened them again. Angus looked at Wilfred in silence. 'You have changed,' he said unexpectedly.

He was the same height as Wilfred but broader in the shoulders, and his rather white face showed traces of weariness. Under his golden curls, an obstinate little brow, that of a Greek god, lent a sort of nobility to a face that was too sheerly regular, but the short nose and sulky lips lacked character.

'Oh,' said Wilfred with a laugh, 'I know my looks haven't improved.'

'I didn't say that,' answered Angus in a serious voice.

'Well, anyway,' continued Wilfred, 'you haven't changed.'

13

'You really think so? Thank you for saying that, even if it isn't quite true.'

Wilfred noticed the somewhat too obvious smartness of his cousin's black suit. It would have been impossible to dress soberly in a louder manner. He himself had the painful feeling of looking shabby in a serge suit that was becoming shiny. The one thing he felt sure of was his blue tie and even that, for the last few moments, seemed a little too bright. Angus wore a black one.

'You aren't angry with me for what happened just now, I hope,' continued Angus, coming a little closer to Wilfred. 'Now I come to think of it, that appointment wasn't really of much importance. I realized it just now, just this minute.'

'How's that?'

'Oh, it's both very simple and very difficult to explain.'

'Maybe I wouldn't understand.'

'I don't know – I don't think so.'

'That's what comes of never having studied at the University,' said Wilfred, laughing.

'I didn't mean to hurt your feelings. It's just that I hesitate to talk to you, because we've lost sight of each other for so long and I don't know how you feel about things at present. At twenty, you still looked like a very young boy and were very pious. Are you still as much of – a believer?'

Taken off his guard, Wilfred hung his head. Among all the answers that occurred to him none seemed possible. Without knowing why, he thought of the absurd bronze woman he had looked at so attentively and the dread of blushing made him blush.

'Yes,' he said, at last.

'I used to make fun of you a little,' said Angus, looking away, 'but everyone knows there are very fine Catholics, particularly in Europe. It's slightly different over here. Our Catholics are just a

14

little bit common. I'm not speaking of you, naturally. You come of a very good family and we're cousins, but it must be strange to go to church and meet your charwoman there, for instance.'

'And that never happens to you all?'

Angus gave a little well-bred laugh. 'If by "you all" you mean my mother's parish church, it doesn't,' he said. 'Charwomen at Saint Bartholomew's would create the greatest amazement, but these questions don't interest me. I go to Saint Bartholomew's to please my mother, you see. Your ideas are so out-of-date –

'Our ideas? What ideas?'

'Ah, that's where we'd differ. I mean that you wouldn't agree with me. I have become a complete agnostic.'

'In fact, you mean that you're an atheist?' asked Wilfred with a knowing air.

Angus took a cigarette from his pocket. 'It's much more subtle,' he said, snapping his silver lighter. 'I deny nothing. On the other hand, I assert nothing positively. Do you get the idea?'

Wilfred did not get the idea, but he said 'Yes' as he thrust his hands into his pockets and then looked toward the window where the chandelier was reflected in the dark panes. Wilfred felt like leaving when people talked of things that he did not understand.

'Does the smoke bother you?' asked Angus.

Wilfred shook his head and looked at his cousin. Their eyes met and for the first time since they had been together in the room, Angus smiled.

'You must admit that I've shocked you a little,' said Angus with affected jocularity. 'You think me – what? Worldly? Cynical? It isn't exactly that. At any rate, I wonder not without admiration that you should have kept your faith, even if, in another way, it disappoints me a little.'

'Disappoints you?'

'I thought that you'd shaken yourself free of all that, but

15

it matters very little. There must be trying moments in your life.'

'I really don't know what you mean.'

'Don't make yourself out more innocent than you are. You're twenty-four and have passions like everybody else, only you control them, because, for the time being, they allow themselves to be controlled.'

A sentence rose to Wilfred's lips with sudden violence. He began: 'I am –' He was about to say: 'I am impurity itself,' but the admission died away, unspoken.

'You are – what?' asked Angus. After waiting a moment, he puffed a little smoke and shrugged his shoulders slightly. 'Keep your secrets,' he said with mild contempt. 'You Catholics are the real Puritans of this country. If you were the majority, you would relax a little. And at the same time you'd be less admirable and less tiresome.'

These remarks uttered in a smooth drawing-room voice distressed Wilfred. Each word struck him like a blow in the face, for it showed him to what an extent people were misled as to his real self. He felt cheap and hypocritical. Angus turned the pages of a magazine.

Wilfred made a great effort to control himself. 'Catholics aren't saints,' he said in a voice made a little hoarse by emotion. 'That is, not all of them, of course. In convents – and elsewhere too, I suppose –' He stopped not being quite sure of what he wanted to prove.

'Now, now,' said Angus with an affable smile, 'don't take the trouble to explain these things to me. The modesty of Catholics is only equalled by their pride.'

Wilfred longed furiously to rap out some insult but checked himself.

'You have what is called a beautiful soul,' said Angus as he turned a page with feigned diligence.

'That's absolutely false. You're quite mistaken –'

16

'I never expected you to say yes,' remarked Angus as he looked up. 'Your protest is most edifying.'

Wilfred sat down. He thought to himself: 'If I try to explain, I'll get the worst of it and betray all the others. He will believe that all Catholics are like me, dissipated like me.' And then, you could not argue with Angus. Even when they were children, it was the same thing. Angus always had the advantage because he was more nimble-witted, smarter. He pondered for a moment, wondering what offensive remark he could make. 'What swine those reformers were!' he thought. But he could not voice this opinion since his cousin had just explained that he went to church to please his mother and that he no longer believed.

'Why do you go to church if you've lost your faith?' he asked suddenly.

Angus squashed his cigarette end in an ashtray and began to laugh. 'Because,' he said, detaching the syllables, 'I am a hypocrite.'

Wilfred kicked at a foot-stool.

'Don't you admire the delightful simplicity of my answer?' asked Angus.

'Indeed I don't!'

'You're angry.'

'That's none of your business.'

'You have a very interesting face when you're angry. There's something in your eyes that reminds me of wild animals. Something crazy. Young men have it, real young men, but they lose it very quickly. It's a pity.'

'Leave me alone, I don't want to hear your nonsense.'

'I teased you just now,' continued Angus, seating himself opposite Wilfred. 'I own that I was wrong. I was in a rage. Anger is a cold-blooded business with me and no one is aware of the state I'm in. I get sarcastic and say things I don't mean. I was much angrier than you were. I was disappointed.'

17

'You've already told me so.'

'You're still furious with me? Please don't bear me a grudge, Wilfred.'

'Of course I don't!' cried Wilfred in a sudden outburst of feeling. No matter how much he had been goaded to anger, he was incapable of harbouring resentment for more than a minute. He found a strange and thrilling happiness in forgiving and forgetting.

'After all,' said Angus, 'I've always been very fond of you.'

'Me too. That's why I couldn't understand just now –'

'Let's forget all that, shall we?' asked Angus, offering him a cigarette. 'You don't smoke. How right you are. With me, it's a nasty habit. I think it comes from having had to wait so often.'

'Wait?'

'Yes. Wait for what always ends by happening and what is always a disappointment. But don't let's talk about all that. How did you get here?'

'In the caretaker's gig.'

'Well, I never! To think that I could have gone for you in the car.'

'What car?'

'Why, mine, Wilfred. Why do you ask?'

'The boy who came for me at the station asked me whether the car belonged to you or to your mother.'

'Ah? That's interesting.' There was a pause and Angus seemed to be turning something over in his mind. 'How did he strike you?'

'The boy? Oh, I don't know. I've never laid eyes on him before. A little crazy. He must be a foreigner.'

'Well, you think he's a nice fellow?'

'I suppose he's all right. Wouldn't you say everyone is pretty nice at first sight?'

'No, I don't agree. I've seen too many people and I'm not as kindly as you are. Would you mind telling me what Ghéza talked about? Yes, he's called Ghéza.'

'So you know him?'

'I've talked to him a little, that's all. Did he tell you anything?'

'No – Yes, he did! He told me he was going to get married. Not that I asked him a thing.'

'Getting married. So.'

'As though it were any business of mine – Oh, listen; I lost one of my gloves on the road.' He said this like a child, because his cousin seemed pensive and because he wanted to break the silence.

'You lost a glove on the road? Where? Do you know?'

'Maybe a mile from the station. But it's not important.'

At that moment they heard a bell ring outside the house.

'We'll have supper in five minutes,' said Angus. 'Unfortunately you'll have supper alone. I have to keep my mother company. She's tired and wants to have supper in her room. I would have liked to see you after supper, but she'll never agree to my leaving her. By the way, where's your room?'

'On the top floor.'

'On the top floor! Mamma is going it a bit too strong.'

'Did she have me put up there?'

Angus hesitated before answering: 'Well, seeing the state Uncle Horace is in, she has to attend to these details. She is probably keeping the best rooms for our cousins the Knights who will be here tonight or tomorrow.'

'What about you? Where have you been put?'

'Oh,' said Angus with an embarrassed little laugh that made him look ten years younger, 'my room is next to my mother's. She was so keen on it, you see –'

'It's very natural.'

'We'll see each other tomorrow morning. I'll have several things to say to you. I'm almost sure that Uncle Horace won't

19

disturb us tonight. They're cramming him full of drugs, he's being kept asleep. You'll see, it's going to be another false alarm. Excuse me, will you, there's something I want to say to the servants.'

He stopped on the threshold and, looking at Wilfred, seemed on the point of adding something, but he changed his mind and left the room.

CHAPTER III

Left alone, Wilfred walked about the drawing-room a little and then stopped for a moment before the large mirror over the mantelpiece. Angus probably thought his tie a little too bright, a trifle vulgar. Nothing was more distinguished than black. He remembered his cousin's words about the look in young men's eyes like that of wild animals, and wondered whether this should be taken as a compliment or not. A woman had once told him that he resembled a little faun, but he was only a child at the time. 'He is better looking than I am,' he thought, flattening his hair over the top of his brow.

Some time went by. Would someone come for him? Did they know he was in the drawing-room? Walking round a large gilt rococo table, his eyes fell on the magazine scrutinized by his cousin a little while earlier. He discovered to his great surprise that it was turned upside down. Angus had pretended to look at it when he was in what he called a cold-blooded rage. But why? Such mysterious ways irritated Wilfred. Everything irritated him in this house and for the first time he missed his shabby room in the city, the store where he worked, even the store –

20

The door opened softly and a black servant told him that supper was ready. They crossed the hall together, but Wilfred carefully avoided looking at the bronze woman. He was taken to the dining-room, a gloomy, high-ceilinged place with no other lighting than the two candles that stood at one end of the table. Two rows of chairs faced each other along the walls and three valanced windows draped in plum-coloured curtains completed the sumptuously melancholy aspect of the room.

While the young man drank his soup the servant in a white coat stood three yards away. He was old and his curly hair looked like grey wool. Although he was both attentive and respectful, Wilfred was not accustomed to being waited on and it embarrassed him to be watched eating.

After the soup came a meat and vegetable course. Each time Wilfred turned his head toward the old man, the latter smiled gravely. He wore white cotton gloves and his chief concern lay in replenishing a large crystal glass and keeping it filled to the brim with clear water in which floated a small cube of ice. Wilfred suddenly pushed away his plate.

'I'm sorry,' he said, 'I've had enough.'

'Worrying has cut your appetite,' murmured the old coloured man.

'When do you think he's going to die?' asked Wilfred abruptly.

'Not tonight. The doctor said he would hold out until tomorrow evening.'

He noiselessly carried away the half-empty plate and replaced it by a dessert plate and fruit-dish full of oranges.

'Is he in pain?'

'No. They give him injections when he's in pain.'

'Does he know he's going to die?'

'He's scared of dying. Every time he falls sick, he sends for a priest, a Catholic priest.'

21

Wilfred looked at the dusky old face, seamed with innumerable wrinkles: 'Then he's very pious?'

'Yes, sir, pious when things go wrong.' He handed the fruit-dish to Wilfred, who chose an orange.

'Are you a Catholic?' asked the young man, after hesitating.

'No, sir.'

There was nothing surprising in this answer, yet Wilfred experienced a very slight shock, as though he had been put back in his place. 'I should not have asked,' he thought. It was always the same. There were days when he had the impression of being the only Catholic in the world.

'When we're dead,' continued the servant in a slow, humble voice, 'the same Lord will judge us all.' And moving back a step, as though in apology, he murmured: 'Yes, sir.'

Wilfred peeled his orange in silence. No doubt the old Negro had not meant to say anything offensive, but his sentence contained an implication. At any rate, a sensitive person could have found one. The young man lifted a small portion of orange to his lips and gazed into the distance, toward the far end of the long room. He vaguely imagined the dinners that must have been given here, the sound of footsteps, the laughter and also the pretty women with white shoulders, the play of the candle-light on their flesh. Everyone knew that Uncle Horace had lived in splendid style.

'How is it that I'm having supper in this big dining-room? Isn't there a smaller room?'

'Yes, sir.' The servant appeared to hesitate. 'Mr Angus wished you to have supper here.'

'Mr Angus?'

'He came into the pantry just now. He spoke out and gave orders as though he were in his own house. Mr Angus is bossy.'

'Where was I supposed to have supper?'

'Mrs Howard had arranged things differently, in a manner of

22

speaking, but it doesn't matter, as you've had supper here.'

'I still want to know where I was expected to have supper.'

'Well,' said the old black, lowering his voice a little, 'the table had been set for you in the pantry, if you wish to know.'

'In the pantry –'

'I don't believe Mr Horace would have allowed that, if he had known.'

Wilfred laid the bit of orange that he was about to eat on his plate. Anger strangled him, but he controlled himself. In a day or two he would have forgotten all the contempt he had been shown. It was not because he was a Catholic, it was on account of his rather humble condition and, above all, on account of his father. His father had failed, had died in poverty. Uncle Horace had done nothing to help him, but there was no good in raking up that old story.

'If you will allow me to give you a piece of advice,' said the servant, leaning slightly towards him, 'tomorrow, I would try, if I were you, to speak – yes, to speak gently to Mr Horace, nicely.'

It seemed as though he had guessed what was going on in Wilfred's mind.

'I'll do my best,' answered the latter in a toneless voice.

'He's really scared now. He's in fear of the Lord. That fear comes sooner or later, you know, Mr Wilfred. If you have it when you're young you're pretty sure of being saved. If you don't –'

Wilfred rose.

'I remember you when you came here with your father, Mr Wilfred,' continued the old man. 'You were scarcely more than a child. You can't remember me because I've changed too much. You used to play with Mr Angus. He's changed too, but he's a fine-looking young man, everybody says so, only it would be better for him to be less good-looking and to fear the Lord.'

'How can I get away?' thought Wilfred. 'He's preaching at me. I don't know how to get rid of him.' But as he did not wish to offend the old Negro, he hesitated to go and stood, resting one hand on the back of his chair.

'Mr Horace was a fine-looking man too,' pursued the old servant. 'Now that he's in his bed and his end is near, he's scared. It would be better to have been less handsome than Mr Horace used to be, less handsome than your father and less handsome than Mr Angus –'

'Yes, I think you're right,' interrupted Wilfred.

It was impossible to tell him more clearly that he was less good-looking than Uncle Horace, less good-looking than his cousin, but the old man spoke without the least malice. It occurred to Wilfred that the old dodderer wanted to save him. Black or white, all out-and-out Protestants had that mania. It was a fact that could not be resented, and in spite of himself he felt touched. He made his way slowly towards the door.

'You're young, Mr Wilfred,' continued the old man. 'The devil's an awfully smart fellow and he's going to dig pitfalls for you. I'm telling you this because I knew your father – you're like him. So I'm making free to tell you this.'

'My father did nothing wrong,' said Wilfred, his hand on the door-knob.

'Nothing wrong –' echoed the servant. 'Then he's in Heaven with the Lord, but Mr Horace, he's scared at this very moment. Lots of things have happened in this house, Mr Wilfred.'

'Yes, I know,' said Wilfred. He felt ashamed of standing there, as though he expected something to follow. He should have left at once, instead of which he continued, in a voice that rang false: 'Lots of things!' What, exactly, he would have liked to know, but dared not ask. He had been told of evening parties that had gone on till dawn, of disorderliness – what is called disorderliness in polite language. The old servant must have known all about

24

such happenings, for he had been in Uncle Horace's service for the last thirty years. It should not be difficult to make him talk. 'All sorts of things, eh?'

To his great surprise the old man merely nodded. 'It's better to forget all about it and ask God to forget about it too,' he said at last.

'The old fellow is putting me back in my place again,' thought Wilfred, but the butler's wrinkled face suddenly assumed such an air of majesty that the young man was struck with wonder. 'What do you think is going to happen to Mr Horace?' he asked awkwardly.

'Why, he's going to die, Mr Wilfred.'

'I know that, but afterwards?'

'Afterwards? That, nobody knows, but he will know it tomorrow.'

'You mean he'll know whether he's saved or lost?'

'Yes.'

'You believe he's lost?'

'I'd never say that, Mr Wilfred.'

'You must have a feeling about it.'

'A feeling, yes.'

'But you don't want to say what it is.'

'No, Mr Wilfred.'

Their conversation had lasted too long. Wilfred had been led on from question to question to say what he did not want to say. Opening his mouth, he looked at the old Negro. 'When you talk to people,' he began, 'do you sometimes have the feeling that they're lost or saved?' He would never have dared put such a question to a white man, but in his eyes all coloured people had something of wizards, Christian wizards. In this long, badly lit room where shadows fluttered over the walls, you could say certain things.

'Sometimes you can tell that they're saved,' said the Negro.

25

Their eyes met. Wilfred longed to ask a certain question, but dared not.

'I know just what you're thinking about,' said the butler, smiling. 'Don't be scared. There's nothing for you to be scared about, Mr Wilfred.'

Wilfred gave a very slight start.

'Oh, as for me –' he said, opening the door. 'Who can tell? Nobody knows.'

'I say things the way I see them. Some day, you'll remember my words, some day when you'll be looking all around you, thinking there's no hope of salvation.'

'I hope that day will never come,' said Wilfred, laughing.

He immediately regretted having laughed, cast about for something to say, but found nothing.

'I'll show you to the staircase, if you wish to go up to your room,' said the old Negro. 'Unless you'd rather return to the sitting-room.'

'Oh, no. I'd like to go upstairs.'

Leading the way, the butler took Wilfred to the end of a long passage. Its walls were hung in red and decorated with a plaster frieze where mythological subjects could be identified. Dust outlined naked bodies with bold black strokes and Wilfred would have been very glad to examine the casts a little more fully, but he followed the old Negro and could no more than glance right and left as he walked by.

When Wilfred returned to his room, it seemed neither so gay nor so small as in broad daylight. For at the moment, a small lamp scarcely lit up more than the head of the bed and a corner of the ceiling on which it cast a pale yellow circle. Everywhere else, shadows swallowed up the walls and the silence was so deep that the young man could hear the blood buzzing in his

26

ears. The sound of a door closing would have cheered him, but nothing stirred in the house.

Seating himself in the rocking-chair, he took from his pocket a novel that he had begun on the train, but the story that had interested him then now took on a different meaning. Perhaps he had chanced upon an extremely gloomy passage. So he skipped a few lines. Yet further on, the most commonplace sentences seemed alarming, with sinister implications. Having first looked around him, he closed the book.

The suitcase at his feet caught a little of the meagre light and he could see the labels that were so familiar to him. He was amused usually by their foreign names and many-coloured little pictures, but not tonight. If those paper squares really called up festive memories, pleasure trips taken by his father and Uncle Horace, there was something dismal about it all, to his mind. This was a dead man's bag and the dead man's boon companion would soon join the former, wherever he was.

The old butler's words returned to Wilfred. The Negro had known the young man's father and also knew all sorts of things. In this very house and over there, in that mysterious Europe, which Wilfred imagined in his daydreams, the dead man had had a very good time. But when all was said and done, things invariably ended on a bed of pain, with a priest bending over you. All the beds on which sensual pleasures had been enjoyed were no more than the prefiguration of this last and terrifying place of rest.

He regretted not having done violence to his pride, and not having questioned the old coloured man. As a rule, stories about women set his imagination ablaze, but his conversation with the servant had taken a turn that he did not care for. Almost all these Negroes, particularly as they grew older, were steeped in religion and always had a sermon handy. As they were usually Protestants, they did not believe in Purgatory. Either Heaven

27

or Hell awaited the dying, and if you ran after women you went to Hell.

Why had the butler given him to believe that he was saved? Obviously, the old fellow did not know. There had already been a great many women in Wilfred's life, but that, he told himself, did not show yet. The proof was that people still thought him steady and well-behaved and talked to him about religion. 'I'm young and everything can be fixed up,' he thought. Catholics knew that Purgatory existed and that things could be settled in the end, even for Uncle Horace who now stood in such terror of God.

The stillness gradually wove such a spell around Wilfred that it proved a great effort to get up and open his suitcase. The noise made by the lid as it turned on its hinges seemed strange to him and alarming, like the sound of a man yawning, and Wilfred noticed, to his shame, that his hands shook a little. The sight of the bed reassured him, however, with its unsophisticated spread, sprinkled over with blue tufts.

Having taken his pyjamas from the suitcase, he undressed as quickly as possible and slipped between the sheets, but could not bring himself to turn out the light. He wished above all to hide, but to hide from whom? In his haste to take cover under his blankets, he had neglected to say his prayers and his situation seemed all the more terrifying for that reason, but nothing in the world would have made him leave the bed into which he sank and where he felt so safe. Quite to the contrary, he drew the top of the sheet over his ears and looked at the flowered wall-paper for a moment.

There were pink ones and red ones, all smiling and gay as a garden in the sun, but after a few minutes they began to move, that was an unquestionable fact. To avoid seeing them, he lowered his head and made the sign of the cross as best he could, and this created a sort of uproar in his head, for the sheet

28

rustling around his ears sounded like a thundering waterfall. In spite of this, Wilfred said his prayers with unusual fervour, as though spurred on by the presence of death in the great house. If Angus had known of his terror how that – agnostic would have sneered! And really, how shameful it was to be so easily frightened, at twenty-four! He crossed himself once more and with a great effort, turned over and put out the light.

And now, in the dark, he waited for sleep to free him of his superstitious fears. In spite of himself, he thought of his father, on account of the odious suitcase that lay, right there, at the foot of the bed. He imagined the departed in a private room of some restaurant with a woman, and he almost fancied that he saw them both, seated at a table before glasses of champagne. The walls of the little room were hung with delicate pink velvet and decorated with mirrors. Waiters in white aprons went in and out carrying dishes, and the woman, dressed most elegantly, as though she were going to a ball, looked at Wilfred's father with an entrancing smile. Yet she was dead, just as he was. Both of them were dead and staring at each other.

Wilfred remained perfectly motionless in his bed, for fear that they might turn their glassy eyes in his direction. Strictly speaking, he rarely thought of his father, for he had known him very little, but tonight he felt him present, attracted to a house where death was lurking. Perhaps he had come to fetch his brother, as people sometimes say that it happens in the next world when the dead miss too much those that they have greatly loved or hated.

Wilfred felt a little annoyed with the relatives who had made him come to Wormsloe, and particularly with his aunt, although she had only complied with Uncle Horace's wish. He suddenly saw himself on the road, sitting by the contemptuous youth who shook the horse's reins between lazy hands . . . At that moment, Wilfred fell asleep.

A great noise wakened him and, jumping from the bed, he

29

ran to the window. What he saw made him cry out with surprise. Standing in the gig, the young coachman that he had just been thinking about was cracking his whip above his head, while with a powerful fist he curbed his horse which reared and shook its mane. The carriage lamp lit up the scene after the fashion of a vision, for outside the circle of light it was pitch dark. No sooner did the coachman catch sight of Wilfred than he called out: 'Are you coming down or will I have to come up and get you? If you go back to bed, I'll find a way of getting you up. I'll write lazy good-for-nothing on your body with this whip.' Wilfred had no idea how he dressed but suddenly he found himself next to the youth. The latter furiously lashed at the bay's rump and with a sort of leap forward they were off at a gallop into the darkness. The painful throbbing of Wilfred's heart corresponded to the sound of the horse's hooves, so that he felt as though the animal was galloping inside his breast. He saw nothing of his companion but his legs, for Ghéza had remained standing and his voice seemed to come from the sky, hoarse and rough, with sudden gentleness that made it so strange. 'Don't imagine I didn't see you, a while ago, looking at that bronze woman with eyes like an inquisitive animal! I was hiding. I'm never very far away and I've been lying in wait for you for a long time. Now we two are going out, aren't we? Just try to tell me you don't want to go on the spree with Ghéza!'

The whip slashed through the night like the sound of a fire-arm. Ghéza continued: 'Your mother should have strangled you at birth if she didn't want to see you on the road at this time of night, with Ghéza!'

'My mother is dead,' said Wilfred.

This last sentence was lost in the rumbling of wheels and crackling of hooves. On the horizon, Wilfred saw a blazing town, the walls and towers of which stood out black against the scarlet flames.

30

'You want women!' cried Ghéza. 'You'll find them over there. Pretty women, the town is full of them. You want to have a good time and so you will.'

'Stop!' cried Wilfred.

The gig stopped dead and Wilfred suddenly found himself alone on the road. At his feet, he saw the glove that he had lost and bent at once to pick it up but dared not touch it, because the glove bled like a severed hand. He cried out with fright and woke, damp with perspiration, then looked for the little lamp which he lit immediately. He remained a long time with open eyes, until the throbbing of his heart had abated.

CHAPTER IV

A few hours later, he was finishing breakfast with Angus and Mrs Howard. All three remained silent and looked toward the long avenue that could be seen through the window, as though they were expecting someone to arrive, but no one did.

Mrs Howard and her son sat side by side. It seemed as if they had set their hearts on pointing out their resemblance: the same regular classical profile, the same rather disdainful bearing, and both had the same smooth, dead white skin that set off the brightness of their dark eyes. How often had Wilfred heard that 'camellia complexion' praised as the family's mark of distinction! He alone had pink cheeks, his mother's cheeks and her rather rough hands; he looked at these with a certain amount of displeasure, whereas Angus and his mother placed long tapering fingers on the tablecloth and used them with the respect due to works of art.

31

Although unwilling to admit it, even to himself, Wilfred envied these two a little too much to feel capable of being very fond of them. Yet he wanted to love them as he loved almost everyone, but they seemed to belong to an obviously superior species and their presence humbled him. He was awkward, he was poor, he was commonplace. Quite evidently, Mrs Howard only remembered with an effort that he was there, facing her, and she seldom spoke to him. If she occasionally glanced in his direction and was kind enough to ask a question of him, it was in the gentle tone of polite condescension usually reserved for those who must be kept at a distance but whose presence cannot be completely ignored. Angus himself paid him no attention except to cast an apparently absent-minded glance in his direction. Wilfred was still so ingenuous that, in spite of himself, he admired them both: they had travelled in Europe. Their conversation was carried on in an undertone (death was so near, in the very house), and foreign names sometimes rose softly to their lips. He scarcely knew what they were talking about.

'Wilfred,' said Mrs Howard at last, with an extremely kind smile, 'I suppose you know the state your uncle is in this morning. We are afraid that he will not live through the day.'

'Yes, Aunt, I know it.'

Mrs Howard's fine eyes narrowed as though to see Wilfred more clearly from a great distance.

'He has expressed the wish to talk to you presently. You must not be frightened by his appearance or show your feelings in any way. You must listen to what he may have to say to you.'

She pushed away her plate where grapefruit rind added a brilliant touch of colour.

'In any case, you owe my brother the greatest respect,' she added in her flat, well-bred voice.

Wilfred made it clear that he was already filled with respect.

'Very well,' she said with a slight nod that signified the

32

conversation had ended, and turned to her son with an air of concern.

'All this is very tiresome,' she murmured, 'but anyway the weather is divine.'

'It reminds me of a walk we took together in Florence,' he answered, drooping his head slightly to one side.

'Cascini,' she whispered in a tone of conspiracy.

For a few moments they seemed to dream about this walk, as one would dream of a honeymoon, and they plunged into leafy groves from which Wilfred was shut out.

'What are you going to do this morning?' she finally asked Angus.

Changing his attitude abruptly, he took a packet of cigarettes from his pocket.

'I'm going to tell Ghéza to saddle me a horse,' he answered rising.

CHAPTER V

Uncle Horace's room was both lofty and spacious, and lighted by three windows, but the old-fashioned shutters had been closed to darken the place and at first Wilfred saw nothing. After a moment, he distinguished a four-poster without a tester, such as can still be found in old houses. These posts, supporting nothing, had a curiously useless appearance.

'Sit down,' said Uncle Horace.

By groping a little, Wilfred found a chair and sat down at some distance from the sick man.

'There's no reason to be frightened,' he said. 'I'm not at death's door.'

His voice was low and a trifle hollow. Wilfred had the impression that it was searching for him in the shadows.

'I'm not frightened,' he at once answered.

'The crisis is over,' said the patient. 'I slept. When I've had an injection, I'm not in pain.'

Wilfred saw him, all of a sudden. His big, round head seemed perforated by two great black holes in which the eyes shone, motionless. He had not shaved for a couple of days and a silvery stubble underlined his greedy jaw.

'Why do you look at me like that?' he asked. 'Am I such a terrifying sight? I've changed since you came here last, eh?'

'You've grown thinner, Uncle.'

'No. There's something else. Where's my sister?' he asked, changing the subject.

'I don't know.'

He kept silent.

'I can hear her walking about,' he said, after a pause. 'Listen.'

And, to be sure, a heavy step could be heard walking to and fro on the floor above.

'She's hunting about,' said Uncle Horace, as though he were talking to himself. 'She won't find a thing.'

'Am I tiring you?' asked Wilfred, hoping that he might be allowed to leave.

'No. The injection is acting very well. I want you to stay. Come a little closer.'

Wilfred got up and drew closer to the bed.

'Turn the light on,' ordered Uncle Horace.

The young man switched the little bedside lamp on.

'Lean over me, so I can look at you.'

Wilfred instinctively drew back: the semi-darkness had prevented him from noticing his uncle's complexion. The sick man's face had taken on a metallic colour, reminiscent of bronze.

34

'What are you doing? Lean over – in the light.'

With a feeling of horror, Wilfred bent his face slightly above a mask on which death seemed already at work.

'Ah,' said Uncle Horace, after a few seconds, 'you've changed too.'

He panted and Wilfred held his breath so as not to smell an exhalation that seemed to come from the grave.

'At your age, your father was better looking than you are. He was – remarkably handsome, your father was – but you're something like him – yes, indeed, you are something like him.'

He made a faint gesture and a rosary slipped over the sheet and slithered to the carpet like a snake. Wilfred stooped to pick it up.

'That's my nurse's rosary,' murmured Uncle Horace. 'Miss Gogherty comes straight from Ireland. Put it on the table. Turn the light out.'

Wilfred obeyed.

'It seems you're very pious,' remarked Uncle Horace. 'I used to be, I had moments – Now, it's different. I don't say I don't believe, no – but I ask myself questions.'

He added abruptly:

'I'm not going to die, this time. You'll see, this is going to be a false alarm.'

'Yes, Uncle.'

'Did my sister tell you I was going to die?'

Wilfred blushed in the darkness. He hated lies.

'We didn't talk about that,' he said.

'She doesn't care for me,' continued Uncle Horace in an undertone. 'I shock her.'

'Why do you say such things, Uncle? I'm sure you're mistaken.'

'You don't know, Wilfred. When she turned Protestant to marry a wealthy man, nothing obliged her to leave the Church, but in her husband's set Catholics weren't thought much of. She didn't talk to you about religion?'

35

'No.'

'She has a perfect loathing for the Church. She hates it because of me. I've led a life she doesn't approve of, but I would never have left the Church, in spite of that.'

He was silent for a moment and said:

'I give the woman her best argument against Rome and at the same time I soothe her conscience, see? You're a believer, aren't you, Wilfred?'

'Yes, Uncle.'

'You must forget what I said just now. I believe too, but by fits. I feel better. I'll be up in a couple of days, Wilfred!'

'Yes, Uncle.'

'Did you talk to Angus?'

'Yes, a little.'

'If I were you, I wouldn't get too intimate with him. He's not the right kind for you to know.'

'He and I live so far apart. There's not much chance of our meeting.'

'All right, but just the same – I'm not saying anything against him. He's very intelligent, very well-bred.'

At that moment the door opened softly and a tall woman in white stood on the threshold, then came forward a little.

'Is that Miss Gogherty?' asked Uncle Horace. 'I feel much better, Miss Gogherty. I've taken on a new lease of life.'

She came up to the foot of the bed. Of masculine build, with a long straight mouth that cut across a massive face, she wore tortoiseshell-rimmed spectacles which added to the severity of her expression. Without a word, she lit the bedside lamp and looked at the patient.

'I've taken on a new lease of life,' he repeated in an almost beseeching voice.

She turned her head toward Wilfred, who immediately rose.

'Stay,' ordered Uncle Horace. 'I still have something to say to you.'

Then Miss Gogherty's eyes met Wilfred's and, as she stared, her mouth seemed even longer and thinner.

'I'll come back, Uncle,' said Wilfred as he went out.

Behind the closed door, he heard the patient complain, but Miss Gogherty's voice simply said: 'No.'

CHAPTER VI

As Wilfred went up to his room, he met Angus leaving his. He wore a heavy dark-green cloth coat and riding boots that shone like mahogany.

'Where are you going?' he asked.

'I'm going to read in my room.'

'Do you spend your time reading?'

'Why, no.'

'You've always been so serious-minded.'

Standing on the last step of the stairs, Angus blocked the way and looked down at his cousin standing on a slightly lower level.

'Come with me,' he said suddenly.

Wilfred followed him to his room. It was bright and spacious, with a large bed canopied in goffered white linen. This detail struck Wilfred because he considered it a sign of refinement and luxury to which he was unaccustomed. On a chest of drawers between two windows, a magnificent dressing-case glittered on a white napkin. Armchairs upholstered in a flowered material invited relaxation. Angus took a few steps one way, then the other, and his boots creaked in the silence. Wilfred noticed that

37

he carried a little riding-whip with a silver handle, but almost immediately Angus, who had followed his cousin's glance, threw it on the bed.

'Are you comfortable in your little room?' he asked in a slightly impatient voice.

'Oh, it's all right. I'll be there such a little while –'

'If my mother hadn't been here, I'd have taken your room and given you this one,' said Angus very rapidly.

'Thank you. I would never have accepted.'

'Why?'

'Oh, because it wouldn't have been possible. You, at the top of the house – it's the sort of thing people wouldn't understand.'

'And yet you submit to this without a protest.'

'It's not the same where I'm concerned, it just doesn't matter.'

'You mean that it tallies with your religious views, with your ideas about Christian humility.'

Wilfred jumped as though he had been struck.

'I wasn't thinking about all that in the least,' he answered in a muffled voice.

'Forgive me. I didn't want to hurt your feelings. I hate this house. I've never been able to bear the thought of death and here we all are, waiting for that old humbug to give up the ghost. A more gruesome way of spending a Saturday can't even be imagined. A Saturday – When you think of what you could do in town –'

He dropped into an armchair.

'I thought you were going for a ride,' said Wilfred, who remained standing.

'I was, but I don't feel like it any longer. I thought about you last night.'

'About me?'

'Why don't you sit down?' (Wilfred sat on the edge of the bed.) 'Yes. I couldn't sleep. Do you mind if I speak to you frankly? I was thinking it was ridiculous for you to be working in a shop.'

'It may be ridiculous, but I have nothing else.'

'Now, don't get angry! I meant that a young man belonging to a good family like you can do better than sell shirts. It's not your fault. You didn't have enough schooling, but surely there must be something to be found for you, a job in keeping with – with your qualifications.'

'Ah? What? And where?'

'I don't know yet. Maybe in the city I live in. I have lots of friends.'

'Thank you, but I don't feel like making a change, for the moment.'

Angus bit his lips and was silent for almost a minute, then rising he went towards the chest of drawers.

'I told you I couldn't sleep last night,' he said after hesitating. 'I did something that you're going to think absolutely idiotic. I got up and went to look for your glove on the road.'

'Are you crazy?'

'Oh, as you can imagine, I didn't go there on foot! I took the car. You heard nothing?'

'Not a thing.'

'I didn't find the glove. Maybe you don't believe what I'm telling you.'

'Yes, I do.'

'I wouldn't believe it if I were you, and yet it's the truth. I don't know what I would have given to find that glove.'

There was a short silence, then Angus asked:

'Aren't you surprised?'

'Yes, a little.' And he added: 'Thank you.'

Angus gave a slight shrug and opened a drawer from which he took a pair of doeskin gloves: they were reddish-brown and apparently seamless.

39

'Would you mind trying them on?' he asked, handing them to Wilfred.

'Why?'

'Mere curiosity. I wonder if your hands are bigger than mine.'

'They're certainly bigger. And what's all this about?'

'About nothing. I'd like to know – to see for myself. Won't you try them on?'

Suddenly he looked so humble that Wilfred felt embarrassed and took the gloves. Although something in him instinctively feared luxury, he found it difficult to resist and he thought the gloves wonderful. He felt them timidly.

'Gloves aren't much in my line,' he said with a little laugh that rang false. 'Mine is shirts, collars and handkerchiefs.'

Angus paid no attention to his cousin's answer.

'I bought them in Florence,' he said as though he had not heard.

'Florence, Italy?' asked Wilfred with rather clumsy naïveté.

'That surprises you?' said his cousin gently. 'They make the best gloves in the world in Florence.'

'Really, I'm afraid they're too small,' murmured Wilfred.

His heart was beating almost as though he were about to commit some questionable action. He slipped his fingers into one of the gloves, then, after some uncertainty, his whole hand. To tell the truth, the glove was a little tight, but Wilfred was struck by the aspect his hand took on in its doeskin casing.

'Put the other one on,' said Angus in a low voice.

Wilfred took the other glove without even saying thank you. He felt awkward and flustered and the blood rose to his face.

Now, as he looked at his two gloved hands, he had the impression they were not his, but those of another man. Something undefinable spoilt his pleasure and he waited for his cousin to break a silence that continued unaccountably. 'He's not the right kind for you to know –' What had Uncle Horace meant?

40

Finally, after a minute that seemed endless, Angus whispered:

'They suit you better than they do me.'

'How's that?' asked Wilfred, venturing a glance in the mirror above the chest of drawers in which he could see himself to the waist.

'You need something to give you a well-groomed touch. I have to wear rougher gloves.'

'Ah? Why?' asked Wilfred, raising his hands a little in order to see them in the mirror.

'How do I know? It's a matter of contrast.'

'Of contrast?' repeated Wilfred absently, his eyes on his image in the looking-glass above the chest of drawers.

'Haven't you ever longed to be very smart, very well-dressed? You aren't in the least badly-dressed, mark you, only –'

'I know I'm not very well-dressed, Angus, or at any rate – not as well-dressed as you are. I can't afford it. Not yet.'

He took the gloves off slowly, almost regretfully, for their touch on his hands was like a caress.

'I could help you, if you wanted,' said Angus, in a faltering voice.

'Help me?'

Wilfred handed the gloves to his cousin.

'They are yours,' said Angus.

'Thank you! I don't want them!' cried Wilfred as he suddenly threw them down on the chest of drawers.

The look that greeted his reply allowed the young man to measure how deeply he had wounded his cousin. Amazed, he racked his brain for a few words that might have induced forgiveness, found none and, suddenly furious with himself, left the room.

CHAPTER VII

Certain details of this scene came back to him a little later,
filled with meaning. He went up to his room and looked out of
the window. The great lawn spread softly to the river whose
yellowish waters could be seen through the trees. The grass
needed cutting. No one took much care of this big garden and
an air of neglect gave it a certain wild charm.

His cousin's sentence concerning Christian virtues made
Wilfred feel wretched. It was then, he thought, that he should
have protested and protested furiously, never have allowed
the absurd and false picture of a chaste and pious Wilfred to
take shape in Angus's mind. But he had not said a word. Once
more he had lied. In a little room that had kept the sort of
innocence peculiar to houses in that part of the country, stood
a double-hearted man.

He was mad to have those gloves. How good they smelt!
How strongly they smelt! He struck the window-sill with his
fist. Truth was not in him. What was in him was the devil. He was
steeped in sin, as in a stifling mire, and Angus thought him pure.
Angus was better than he. With his elegance, wealth and cynicism
Angus, in the eyes of many Catholics, would seem a reprobate,
but the reprobate was a better man than he, Wilfred, the
believer. Angus was obviously proud of his intelligence, his
station in life, his looks, his complexion, and all that was his
reward, the reward of those who will not see God, but on earth
he was better than Wilfred, because if Angus was hypocritical,
at least he was brave enough to own it. He was disdainful, proud,

42

selfish, sensual, but made no pretence at being better than he was. Wilfred allowed people to believe what they liked, which was worse. He remained silent because he was frightened. On account of all that, he had thrown the gloves on the chest of drawers and refused a rich man's gift. And above all, he was afraid of not being loved. How confused and bewildered he felt and how eager to leave this place! As it was, he had difficulties enough in town, but in a house occupied by death something harried him from room to room.

When he grew a little calmer, he looked in his suitcase for the novel that had engaged him the night before and began reading it, near the window, but his attention wandered constantly, because his own story was not to be found in the book and it was his own story that he wanted both to forget and to live over again. He wanted to hear about himself and at the same time to have his mind taken off his worries. In his heart of hearts, he was really not quite sure what he wanted.

Closing the book, he looked at himself in a small pocket mirror. Uncle Horace was right. He was not as handsome as his father, he was not even what is called 'very good-looking'. People sometimes made fun of his large mouth. His turned-up nose did not help matters. It was impossible to look more Irish. 'The best thing about me,' he thought, 'is my complexion, my pink cheeks.' But he did not care much for his face. He would have liked to be fair with blue eyes, whereas his hair was inky black and his eyes grey. One of his eyes slanted up toward the temple and this gave him a rather odd expression. He stared at himself, secretly looking for something else in his face: did he, yes or no, give the impression of a dissipated young man? No indeed, it did not show. Not yet. That was probably the reason for so many misunderstandings. At thirteen he had longed to be a priest, but that was long before any serious offences. At present he gave the appearance of a young man who liked

43

fun and did not refuse an occasional drink, that was all. He kept a rosary in his pocket, but when he went to town to misbehave he always left it at home in a drawer, so that the little crucifix saw nothing.

His mind leapt from one subject to the other. He thought once more of those doeskin gloves and bitterly regretted not having been able to accept them; they might have helped him impress certain women that he wanted to dazzle. He would have liked to take them off casually in their presence and toss them on the corner of some table, like worthless objects. True, he had had the satisfaction of refusing them. Angus must have admired his gesture, but that was over, unfortunately, and Wilfred did not have the gloves. 'If people knew all the things that go through my mind,' he said to himself, 'I think they would take me for a lunatic, a real one, the kind that's put in a strait-jacket. All the same I'd like to see a man who is perfectly reasonable every moment of his life: maybe he would be the one to be locked up.'

CHAPTER VIII

It was a gloomy day. Angus and his mother lunched together on the second floor and Wilfred was alone in the dining-room, as he had been for supper the night before. A little later, he went into the drawing-room where he found Mrs Howard pensively shuffling cards in a corner, as she waited for Uncle Horace to die. She kept silent and, with a feeling verging on curiosity, the young man examined this prosperous woman's face: the delicate skin, the clear brow, the cheeks that seemed

44

ironed smooth by selfishness and the severe, satisfied mouth. He imagined her young, beautiful, stark naked and swooning with pleasure. At that moment, she turned and looked at him from magnificent eyes that reminded him of her son's, and asked suspiciously:

'What are you thinking about?'

He felt tempted to answer: 'Aunt, I'm thinking of your love-making that resulted in Angus.' Once her anger had spent itself, he might perhaps have obtained a truthful answer, a human answer, but he lied and she lied: it was what is called a conversation.

'I was thinking about Uncle Horace. He doesn't seem as ill as I thought he'd be.'

'People often rally at the end. He's past hope, I'm afraid. Did he say anything interesting to you just now?'

'No. The nurse came in almost immediately.'

'Poor dear Horace! He's a prey to that woman and her superstitions. I'm not saying this to offend you, but she really does go too far. She's going to send for a priest. I have nothing against that, but just think, nuns will come in afterwards.'

'That's very often done.'

'A priest, certainly. But nuns are just a theatrical touch. Can you tell me what use they'll be when he's dead?'

She looked toward the window and thinking aloud murmured:

'And all this is making me miss a bridge party.'

Wilfred, who had moved away a little, did not hear her. He was in one of his bad moods and lacked all religious feeling in circumstances in which he badly needed the fervour he experienced at other times, and then apparently uselessly; but emotions can no more be governed than love, and it happened that he could think of nothing but love, of love in its most primitive, most carnal and most violent form. His furious appetite for life was so strong that he felt as though he had filched it from

45

the dying man. Yet he heard himself answer in a quiet, patient voice, the one he kept for heretics:

'The nuns will pray for the salvation of his soul.'

'Pooh, his fate has already been settled. Rosaries reeled off by taper light won't change a thing.'

He looked at her, wondering what the soul of such an unruffled woman could be like. How terrified she would be some day, when she woke up in the other world!

'Why do you look at me so strangely?' she asked, laying out the cards.

'I look at you strangely?'

'You sometimes have the eyes of a fanatic.'

Her reply had an unpleasant effect on Wilfred, because at the very moment when it was spoken he had once more been thinking of love, tormented both by memories of past love affairs and hopes of others awaiting him in the future, the frenzied pleasure that turned him into a sort of semi-lunatic for hours on end. Did nothing of all this show in his face? Was Mrs Howard blind? She continued gently:

'I'm not averse to religion, in reasonable doses. A little is necessary, but from what I hear you take yours extremely seriously, almost tragically.'

'Almost tragically –' The words were inopportune, yet in some curious fashion they were true and a shock to Wilfred.

'Does that religion of yours make you happy?' she continued. 'Without wishing to offend you, no one would think so.'

'Her conscience is working on her, the old renegade,' he thought. But he did not feel tempted to talk of religion with a Protestant, particularly at that moment.

'I'm very happy,' he said, turning the pages of a magazine. And he tried to imitate Angus's off-hand manner.

'Really?' said Mrs Howard. 'Well, would you mind just looking at yourself?'

46

Had she guessed something, at last? Did *it* show? He had only to turn his head to catch sight of himself in a great narrow mirror between the two purple-curtained windows. He looked at his face twenty times a day, but at this moment he realized that his eyes were really those of a wild animal, as somebody had said of them so recently, and that he had the face of a fugitive. It struck him, like a revelation of himself. Lowering his eyes, he composed his features.

'I don't notice anything extraordinary, Aunt. Even if I do look a little serious, you must admit that present circumstances have a lot to do with it.'

'Circumstances? Pooh! Your uncle?'

Throwing down her cards on the little table, she rose suddenly and came up to him quickly, for a tendency to corpulence scarcely impeded her movements.

'Do you know what your uncle is?' she asked in an undertone. 'You're still very innocent, my boy. Your uncle is an old profligate. His whole life has been one long scandal that we've had endless trouble in hushing up. If my husband had not been a judge with friendly connexions in the political world –'

In spite of himself, Wilfred moved away from the woman whose face was close to his.

'Yes,' he said, 'I've heard about it.'

'Then,' she continued in a whisper, as though they were conspiring, 'you know the story about Mrs Ditmar who sold her daughter to him?'

He knew nothing of the story, yet he nodded yes.

'And do you know how old the child was?'

All of a sudden, there was something so base about the woman's mouth, her expression, that he did not recognize her. She looked ugly and it crossed his mind that, in spite of age, she had remained sensual. He could feel her breath on his skin, his brow, his eyes.

47

'Thirteen,' she said, 'just thirteen. He had to have them in their first bloom, you see, in their first bloom and pure – no mistake about that man being fond of purity. Not the way you care for it, not in the same manner' (she laughed with a knowing air that horrified the young man). 'And of course religion changed nothing in his life. He was seen at Mass. I'm not saying this to hurt your feelings, but we see religion in a different light. We want something clean, unspotted. Your father –'

He drew away abruptly and she might have fallen, as she was all but leaning on him.

'Please, Aunt!'

Standing very straight, she threw her head back and looked like a lady once more.

'I wasn't going to say anything against your father. He lived as he thought fit, but you owe what is best in you to your mother, my boy. She remained a Protestant to the end. It's not her fault that your father wished you to be brought up in the Roman Catholic faith. She believed that you would be saved, in spite of all that. You were too young to lose her.'

Her mouth half-open, she seemed on the point of adding something, but changed her mind. Her eyes softened and, moving more quietly, she went back to the little table where she picked up the cards, shuffled them again and sat down. In the silence Wilfred could hear the sound of the cards that she laid and turned over with the studious attention of a little girl, for she was playing patience, and he stared at her from a distance, as though she were a mysterious and unknown being. She had probably suffered during her life, but she was narrow-minded and made stupid by material comfort. It was impossible to argue with her. Yet Wilfred would have liked to question her about his uncle and the little Ditmar girl. His imagination was kindled and pictured for him the child nearing twenty, in the full bloom of radiant beauty. He should never have said that he knew about that affair.

'Where's Angus?' he asked after a few minutes.

'He is packing.'

'Packing? Is he going so soon?'

'He's leaving in a moment.'

'What about you, Aunt?'

'Oh, I'm staying until the end.'

After a hesitation, he ventured to question her again:

'How is it that Angus isn't staying on with you?'

'My son is in business,' she answered a little dryly. 'He came to say farewell to his uncle, who saw him after luncheon. He's paid his duty call and now he's going back to town. I'm very glad for his sake. This death-bed atmosphere is bad for him.'

'What about its being bad for me?' thought Wilfred.

She turned up a card and held it up for a second before laying it down again.

'In every way possible Angus is most exceptional,' she said finally.

Her voice trembled ever so slightly and for the first time the woman whom Wilfred judged insignificant touched him, for he guessed that she loved her son too much not to suffer from his leaving the house without her.

'I myself insisted on his going,' she said as though in answer to an objection.

She seemed on the verge of tears and Wilfred was about to praise Angus when the door opened and a man dressed in dark grey stood on the threshold. He appeared to be about fifty. He had the weary expression of people who have a disagreeable task to perform.

'Mrs. Howard,' he said.

She rose without a word and left the room with him.

CHAPTER IX

Wilfred waited a few minutes. It seemed clear that the end was near, but perhaps his presence would not be necessary, since he had seen his uncle. He envied his cousin for having been allowed to elude a painful situation. Angus had a car, he could leave. Wilfred wondered whether he would think of saying good-bye to him but, all said and done, he did not care. What he wanted was to get back to his room, his habits, the store, even the store, and his little adventures. He looked through the window at the frail, delicate trunks of young birches standing out white against a pale blue sky. All of a sudden, he felt conscious of someone in the room, behind him. It was Angus.

'How did you come in? I didn't hear you.'

Angus nodded his head toward a door concealed by a heavy curtain, after the fashion of the last century.

'I'm going,' he said. 'Did my mother tell you?'

'Yes.'

'I wanted to stay, of course. You can imagine – I wanted to leave tomorrow with her. It was she who insisted I must go right away, because she knows that certain things upset me. She made such a scene, up there, a real scene, because I didn't want to leave. I adore her, but she's frightfully domineering.'

'Ah?'

'I'll telephone in a little while. Another car will come for her tomorrow.'

'Are you going now?'

50

'Right away. My car is on the road, by the gate. Shall we walk there together?'

He fastened his big dark eyes on Wilfred's face. 'With a face like his,' thought the latter, 'he must have all the women he wants.'

'All right,' he said.

In the great avenue, Wilfred stuck his hands in his pockets and amused himself by kicking at pebbles with the tip of his shoe and sending them flying. The two young men walked slowly and in the deepest silence. When they reached the gate, Angus stopped and glanced around him before looking his cousin full in the face. Finally, he said with an effort:

'I made up my mind to speak to you, to tell you something before I got to this spot. And now I'm here, I can't. I feel that I'll never be able to.' He laughed nervously. 'Not that I'm frightened.'

'Frightened? Frightened of what?'

Angus made a gesture.

'What's the good of telling you? Talking ruins everything. I've only realized it this very moment. You're not the kind that certain things can be said to.'

Suddenly, he seized his cousin by both arms. Wilfred would never have believed him so strong, for he grasped him as one drowning man grasps another. His hands still in his pockets, the young man was too surprised to try to free himself.

'What's the matter with you?' he cried, instinctively throwing his head back.

Angus looked at him for two or three seconds, then, suddenly tearing himself from him, went to his car. Wilfred saw him get in and the door banged almost at once.

An instant later, he was alone on the road and a fresh wind

51

from the hills stirred lightly around the nape of his neck and his cheeks. Long clouds rose one above the other in the sky like snowy mountain crests, in dazzling tiers. He looked at them for a moment, pensive and still. If Angus imagined that he had not understood –

As he went back to the house, his hands still in his pockets, he began whistling under his breath.

CHAPTER X

He found his aunt in the drawing-room again and she greeted him with a smile. Her graciousness informed Wilfred in a second of what was expected of him.

'Your uncle,' said Mrs Howard with a kindly air, 'has expressed a wish to see you again. Not now. Later. He may perhaps tell you something of great interest to us all.'

'When am I to see him?'

'Oh, when the time comes,' she replied, going toward the door. 'You'll be told.'

'Will you tell me, Aunt?'

She had her hand on the brass door-knob.

'No,' she said gently. 'Not I.'

Her smooth, still face presented Wilfred with a last smile, almost a sorrowful one, and in keeping with the circumstances.

He went up to his room. He had never seen anyone die. To his mind everything should have taken place differently: the whole family gathered in an adjoining room, then finally around the death bed. But Uncle Horace had very little family. He loathed his sister and was contemptuous of Angus. As to his nephew Wilfred, he took so little interest in him, in his condition, his future – What surprised the young man was that Uncle Horace should be bent on seeing him again. The idea of another interview with the dying man horrified him. Why should this awful job be necessary? Angus was lucky, he was bowling along in his fine car to a house that Wilfred imagined as luxurious.

Of course, the Knights were still expected. Wilfred only knew them by reputation. Mr Knight was a distant cousin of Uncle Horace and had married a woman much younger than he. Wilfred knew no more.

He was in his little room. How ridiculous it seemed to him with its falsely virginal air and its big bed that had been the vehicle for filthy dreams! As to himself and his ever unsatisfied body, did he not people everywhere he went with his desires? No one knew it. He took everyone in – except God. He dreaded this thought, which now exploded in his head – there was no other way of describing it. Standing by the window, his eyes dwelling on the trees, he started as though someone had whispered in his ear.

After a while, he lay down on his bed. Perhaps emotion had wearied him. Sudden fatigue closed his eyelids and he slept about an hour. When he woke, his hand was under the pillow and his fingers were touching something that he immediately recognized: his cousin's gloves. He got up at once and held them to his face, still fascinated by their scent. It made his head swim, dazed his senses, his will. He drew the gloves over his hands, and glued his hands to his face.

'That idiot Angus!' he cried aloud, delighted and still amazed.

Without taking his eyes off his hands, he sat down, then got up, arms a-kimbo, struck attitudes, imagined the wonder of several women that he would have liked to know. If they could see him now – He imagined lots and lots of things. All of a sudden,

53

there was a rap at the door. He removed the gloves and slipped them into his pocket.

It was the old coloured man who had waited on him the night before and who bowed now, smiling.

'Mr Wilfred, they're waiting for you downstairs.'

'I know what that means,' said Wilfred.

'Don't be frightened. You're the only one he wants to see. He said so again just now.'

'But why me?'

'When things happen so, it's the Lord acting after His own mind.'

Wilfred was on the point of saying something, but thought better of it.

'Mr Angus has gone,' he remarked suddenly, trying to put off the moment when he would have to go down.

'Yes. Mrs Howard will be obliged to go home all by herself.'

He stepped aside to let the young man pass and bowed very slightly. Wilfred was not used to such marks of respect and they made him feel shy and nervous. His heart beat fast. So the time had come. He was going to see the dying man again, maybe he was even going to see him die. That was what he dreaded most. He threw a last glance at the little window. The trees bowed slowly in the wind, each branch in itself like a small tree. Now the room did not seem so absurd to him and he would have been happy to stand a moment longer by the window, but he had to go down. Why? Why must he do everything that people told him to do? He could have run away, like Angus, but Angus was determined and he, Wilfred, was not. And his cousin had a car into the bargain.

At the foot of the stairs, he found the man in dark grey who had come for Mrs Howard. It was the doctor, of course, and he talked to Wilfred in the gloomy, reasonable voice he expected; yet although he listened with every sign of attention he felt too

54

moved to understand. Finally, however, he grasped a few words that brought him back to realities: ' – a slow, progressive suffocation.'

'Is he in pain, Doctor?'

'A little. You must speak to him gently. He has insisted on seeing you. Naturally, he would be better off in a hospital.'

'Would he? Then, why –'

'I explained a moment ago that he wouldn't hear of it. He is convinced that he's done for, if he leaves the house.'

'Can't something be done to pull him round again?'

'I've told you he was bound to die. It seems to surprise you. But you won't see anything terrifying. You'll be told to leave at the right time. Don't be frightened.'

'Oh, I'm not frightened,' said Wilfred, buttoning his coat.

CHAPTER XI

A minute later, he was sitting at the foot of Uncle Horace's bed. He seemed about the same as when Wilfred had seen him only that morning, except that his eyes wandered at times.

The shutters had been opened and the room was in broad daylight although the light was that of closing day.

'I know very well how all this is going to end,' murmured Uncle Horace. 'The injections keep your strength up, but that's just a delusion. The priest has told me the truth. I'm not frightened. Do you hear me?'

'Of course, Uncle Horace.'

'Come closer. Why do you sit so far off?'

Wilfred came nearer, very little nearer, to be precise. There was something in the sick man's eyes that his nephew had never seen: eyes that could no longer look steadily at anything. Wilfred had the physical impression of this vacillating glance moving over his face, his shoulders. Uncle Horace's speech remained clear, however.

'I haven't favoured you much in my will,' said the patient, widening his lips into a smile, 'but you shall have something that I had planned to give Angus.'

He paused to recover his breath.

'His mother told me that it would give him great pleasure. I learnt later that he had a wild, an unhealthy longing for it. So I altered things a little. Do you understand?'

'Yes, Uncle.'

'There's no air in the room. It's stifling.'

'Would you like me to open the window?'

'They won't have it opened. They say it's too chilly. Come a little closer.'

Wilfred came an inch or two closer.

'The priest will be here again in a minute. Father Dolan. He told me to get ready. I insisted on seeing you first. Afterwards there will be confession and everything else. It seems impossible that all this should concern me, that the end is in sight. I don't balk at confession, but the rest – the rest seems unthinkable. It isn't that I refuse anything, but I don't want to be hustled, see? I've always done just as I wanted and now I'm being hustled –'

He waved his hands about like a child.

'I consent to confession,' he repeated, 'but in a little while, a little while. I must be given time to put my mind in order. If I have to remember everything –'

He kept his eyes closed for a moment, then murmured:

'Open the drawer in that table. You'll see some papers. Take the envelope marked *Receipted bills*.'

Wilfred opened the drawer in the bedside table and took out the envelope in question.

56

'Put it in your pocket quick,' said the patient. 'I fetched it from my safe in the bank not three weeks ago.'

The envelope was long and rather bulky.

'I had put it away for a rainy day,' continued Uncle Horace. 'I don't want your aunt to lay her hands on it. She's rich enough as it is. She's been looking around the house, here, there and everywhere, as you can imagine, but she never dared come ferreting around this room because Miss Gogherty never leaves me alone here.'

He took breath.

'Don't imagine that I'm giving you a fortune. It would seem nothing, or almost nothing, to a rich man, but it's something for a young man like you, my poor boy. I want you to remember me kindly. You'll pray for me, won't you?'

'Of course I will, Uncle.'

'There's something else in the envelope, something besides the securities.'

He suddenly interrupted himself and seemed to be turning something over in his mind.

'It is what is most precious to me in the whole world,' he continued in a low voice. 'What I couldn't bring myself to destroy. A few letters and a little likeness, a little photograph –'

'Yes, Uncle.'

There was a brief silence.

'I would have liked to take them with me,' whispered Uncle Horace, 'I would have liked these things to be put with me, close to me, so I could keep them for ever, but I know my sister and the others. Knight – They wouldn't have allowed it, they would have taken them away from me. And so you can put them aside. You can read the letters. I don't mind your doing it. I trust you. But she, and particularly the other one, Knight – The idea that they could read certain sentences –'

57

His eyes moistened and seemed to wander hesitantly to some point above Wilfred's head.

'I'm not in pain. Not very much pain,' he murmured. 'Maybe I'll go without suffering. I wish I could. If you see that things suddenly grow worse, you must run off and call Miss Gogherty. I don't want you to see – Are you still here?'

'Why, of course, Uncle.'

'Where have you put the envelope?'

'In the inside pocket of my coat.'

'I can't see you very clearly. Turn the light on.'

The young man lit the bedside lamp that shone in the twilight under the little green silk shade.

'Turn the light on,' repeated Uncle Horace.

Wilfred felt his throat go dry as he heard this simple sentence. Was *it* beginning?

'The lamp gives a very bad light,' he said.

'Yes, you can hardly see. Come closer. Listen.'

In spite of all his efforts, Wilfred was unable to have a genuinely charitable impulse for a man so near his end, but he tried to overcome his fear and disgust, and spoke gently, as one speaks to a child:

'What do you want to say to me, Uncle? I'm right here.'

'Listen. I told you that I wasn't frightened. It wasn't true. The priest, Father Dolan –'

'But, Uncle, you don't have to be frightened because the priest is here. On the contrary –'

He was about to say that extreme unction acted as a remedy in many cases, but the sick man stopped him.

'You don't understand. There's something else, Wilfred. I don't believe.'

The last sentence was said in a rush, like something that had to be got rid of quickly, and a long silence followed it. Without being quite aware of what he was doing, Wilfred rose and went

58

to a window behind the bed. He looked for an instant at the pale blue sky tinged with pink and, far away, the hills marking the horizon with a thin streak of purple. After some hesitation, he did something that he thought both low and ridiculous: drawing a small flask that contained alcohol from his pocket, he carried it to his lips and emptied it in a few swallows. He usually kept the bottle for less dismal occasions, when he was having a love affair, but at present he felt frightened and foresaw that he was about to yield to fear.

'What are you doing? Where are you?' asked Uncle Horace.

'I'm looking out of the window.'

'Did you hear what I said to you just now? I don't believe any longer. I can't. I no longer have faith –'

Wilfred let a few seconds go by, then returned to the bed. In his uncle's sightless stare he saw a rising dread of death. He leaned his shoulder against the bed-post, for he felt a trifle dizzy.

'But seeing you asked to see a priest –'

'I know, but now that no longer means anything. All my life I've run after happiness – or you might say pleasure. Yet I imagined that I had kept my faith – I didn't know where it was lodged. Somewhere in the innermost part of me – that's what I thought, what I hoped, see? I went to Mass. I don't know how I straightened things out. Maybe they got straightened out because I didn't believe –'

'Uncle,' said Wilfred, 'you're wearing yourself out talking.'

'No, I want to say what I have to say. I tried to deceive myself, but I wanted to believe. Now you have faith. I know it. I've been told so. Real faith. Tell me you have faith.'

'Yes.'

'You believe everything the Church says.'

'Yes, I do,' said the young man with sudden energy.

He felt the effects of the alcohol and at the same time an

59

intense irritation, the meaning of which escaped him. The patient gasped a little.

'Ah,' he whispered, 'to believe: what does that mean?'

'I don't know.'

'You don't know!'

'Uncle, you know you believe just as you know you're in love.'

This answer seemed so absurd to Wilfred that he tried to correct it, but his uncle did not give him time.

'That's it,' he said. 'You're sure. It's not a question of believing, you're just certain. The proof is in here.' His fist on his breast, he repeated: 'In here.' Wilfred would have been glad to leave the room because he was afraid of not being quite sure of what he was saying, but something held him there.

Slipping into the red armchair at the foot of the bed, he closed his eyes and it crossed his mind that the young housemaid he had seen the evening before had been his uncle's mistress, and in spite of himself he imagined her delicate body in the bed that he was now near enough to touch with his arm.

'No,' he said under his breath.

He never drank spirits except to misbehave, because then everything happened as in a dream and he suffered less afterwards, he could always tell himself that he had misbehaved when he was drunk; but today, by a dying man who talked about religion, it was hateful to be drunk. It was cowardice that had made him drink. That was almost always the reason for his drinking, even where women were concerned. Now it was not a question of a woman but of death. Death was wandering about in his uncle's eyes and was looking at him, Wilfred. Death was looking at him through Uncle Horace's eyes. That was why he said no.

'Are you there?' asked the patient.

'Yes indeed, I haven't budged.'

Uncle Horace did not see him, but death saw him. Death

60

takes over the eyes of those about to die as they watch the living. A full minute went by.

'I want to die with faith in my heart,' said Uncle Horace.

'But as you sent for a priest –'

'Miss Gogherty wished him to come and I didn't dare say no, but I don't believe, I can't.'

One elbow on the arm of the chair, Wilfred put his hand over his eyes to avoid seeing his uncle and said with the obstinacy of a man who has been drinking:

'But you do. When people don't believe, they refuse to see a priest.'

He realized with a strong sense of shame that his tongue was getting thick and that he was speaking less distinctly.

'I don't believe in a hereafter,' said the sick man. 'I don't believe that God is here, I don't believe He exists.'

'Hush!' cried Wilfred suddenly.

And his brow sank down on the bed, his arms foremost. He would have liked to sleep; to escape the voice that wound around his head, that pierced his ears.

'Pray,' said Uncle Horace. 'Do the asking for me.'

'The fact of your asking me to do this proves that you believe.'

'Ask for me, Wilfred. If faith is given back to me, everything will really exist and I'll be saved. Ask that God may give me a faith like yours. Ask.'

Without knowing exactly how, Wilfred straightened up and slowly rose to his feet. The room seemed gently to turn upside down and he thought: 'I'm going to sleep', but suddenly his knees bent. He heard the noise they made as they hit the floor, yet felt nothing. It seemed as though his hand went up to his brow of itself and then to his shoulders. He had the sensation that his uncle's plaintive voice brushed his cheeks and the nape of his neck:

'Pray, Wilfred, ask! Do the asking for me!'

61

Wilfred's fingers mechanically hunted in the depths of his pocket for his rosary and his lips parted, but his tongue enunciated badly and the words of the Creed were jumbled in disgraceful confusion. He remembered suddenly that he had not carried the cross to his lips. His hand was lifted, slow and heavy. He felt the cold metal on his mouth and at the same moment something scorched his heart.

'Pray aloud, so I can hear you!' begged Uncle Horace.

Then, letting the rosary slip over his forearm, Wilfred said with an effort:

'Lord, give faith to my Uncle Horace.'

There was a long silence.

'That doesn't sound like a prayer,' said Uncle Horace. 'To begin with, it's not long enough. There must be something else you could say.'

His hands fluttered like wounded birds.

'There must be,' said the young man, 'but I don't know the prayers to be said in a case like this.'

'Pray some more. Say the prayers of the Church.'

'I don't know them by heart. We ought to ask Father Dolan.'

'No, not Father Dolan. He's all right, but he's obliged to believe, he's a priest. You aren't the same. You said so yourself just now. You're like someone in love.'

'I said that?'

'Yes, you did.'

Holding his fists to his ears, Wilfred cried out suddenly:

'Lord, give me what I need to give faith to others. Make me believe.'

'Why do you say that?' asked Uncle Horace.

'I don't know what I'm saying, Uncle. I don't know how to pray.'

'You don't know how to pray?'

'No. I don't think I've ever known. I've only just found it out.'

62

His head swam. Suddenly he had the strange sensation that an inner resistance had been shattered. He felt incapable of doing anything, small and powerless, and tears rose to his eyes, tears of sadness, but above all of humiliation. A short sob escaped him.

'Why are you crying?' asked Uncle Horace. 'Is it on my account?'

'On your account and on my account. For both of us.'

Then whispering hoarsely, he said in a rush:

'Lord, give faith to both of us. Make it happen any way You please, but give us faith. We're going to die.'

'What's that you're saying, Wilfred? Speak up.'

'Oh, leave me alone!' said Wilfred. 'I'm ashamed.'

He let a few seconds go by, then in a gentler voice murmured:

'All's well.'

The words left his lips as though someone else had spoken them and so distinctly as to rouse him abruptly from lethargy. He remained kneeling for some time, sobered, his soul at peace, and for about a minute he felt himself away from the earth, but no precise idea shaped itself in his brain, except that happiness pervaded everything, a strange happiness that abolished daily life, time and the world. And yet he knew that he was in this room, at the foot of the mahogany four-poster and that through the window facing him he saw the trunks of the birches shining like silver in the twilight. Getting up at last, he looked at the poor little wizened man fluttering his fingers on his sheets.

'What are you doing?' asked Uncle Horace. 'You haven't prayed long enough. Come closer. Where's your hand?'

Wilfred gave him his right hand and the sick man clutched it avidly between his to lay it on his breast.

'Cure me,' he breathed.

'I can't cure you,' said the young man gently. 'It would take a saint to do that and I'm not a saint.'

'Yes, you are!' said Uncle Horace with sudden animation. 'Right now, you're like a saint. We all are at one moment or another of our lives. You must –'

At that instant the door opened and Miss Gogherty came up to them. She glanced at the patient and whispered in Wilfred's ear:

'Do you wish to return after his confession?'

Wilfred blushed and shook his head.

'Then say good-bye to him. The priest is waiting.'

Bending double, Wilfred overcame his disgust and pressed his lips to his uncle's damp brow. 'May this kiss wipe away lots of others,' he thought.

'I want to be loved,' said Uncle Horace with an effort that left him gasping.

CHAPTER XII

Wilfred found his aunt in the drawing-room. She was thrusting her hands into black kid gloves with the energy of a woman who has just made a decision. The young man looked silently at her, for he was still deeply moved.

'I know,' she said, casting a glance at him. 'It will all be over in an hour or two and my presence here is useless, since he hasn't expressed a desire to see me. It was you that he wanted to see, before his confession – since he's going to make his confession.' She raised her eyes to the ceiling as she said this. 'Well – did he talk to you about me or Angus?'

'No.'

'He didn't – give you anything for us?'

'No.'

64

She bit her lip.

'Very well,' she said. 'I'm off. A train leaves in an hour. I won't wait for my car to be sent. Why should I stay on? I'm no better than a stranger in this house. I must go home and look after my son. I don't want him to be alone. It depresses him.'

She seemed disturbed and pulled at her gloves.

'I have that bridge party tomorrow,' she said as though she were talking to herself.

'That bridge party –' repeated Wilfred mechanically.

'Oh, a bridge party can wait,' she said with an irritated little laugh. 'But Angus is at home all alone.'

The magnificent, stupid head she turned to Wilfred was that of a demented queen. She set her fine haggard eyes on him.

'And what about you? Are you staying on?'

'Yes, a little while longer.'

'Ah? Good. You're doing the right thing, in fact. You are his nephew, his favourite nephew, for he doesn't care for my son. Wilfred, do you –' she fingered the clasp of her bag and suddenly assumed a pleasant and somewhat embarrassed expression – 'do you need me to –'

Their eyes met.

'No, thank you, Aunt,' he answered, once he had understood.

'Very well,' she said, showing a row of teeth as white as her son's. I thought that perhaps in your situation – But I'm mistaken, aren't I? I'm really delighted to have been mistaken. If ever you happen to be anywhere near our house – you never know – it would give us great pleasure –'

She patted his forearm and went out quickly. A little while after, he saw her get into Uncle Horace's fine black car, the one he had vainly waited for at the station, and she disappeared.

He had the impression that by leaving she ceased to exist.

65

CHAPTER XIII

He was once more in his room now, sitting on a chair, his feet on
a chest of drawers, the better to think, although nothing definite
occurred to him. As a matter of fact, he did not know how to
think. He only remembered the minute when, kneeling by his
uncle's bed, he had been filled with a mysterious, inexplicable
happiness. It was due to fatigue, no doubt, and the excitement
of a trying day. 'Anyway,' he said to himself, 'I did my Easter
duty last week.' The week before, on Maundy Thursday, in fact.
Easter fell early that year, when spring had barely escaped the
clutch of winter. Wilfred preferred not to think of all that any
more – of his confession, of the *number of times* he had been
forced to admit, of the young priest's silence, then his rather
sad voice and the advice that showed such innocence. How could
prayer fight against raging temptations that swept everything
away with hurricane violence? And how did one pray at such
times? Yet Wilfred had taken that resolution of his. He had not
cheated on that score, but wouldn't his failure have made
anyone laugh? The resolution had lasted one day. A day and a
half, to be precise.

Why think of such things when he had decided not to? Why?
Perhaps on account of his uncle's confession. It must have been
a little like his, only longer. Always the same sins, but by dint
of committing them you reached death's door wondering if you
still believed in what you used to believe.

To leave this house. All he wanted at that moment could be
summed up in two words: to go. But he dared not leave until

66

Uncle Horace had breathed his last. So after those thousands and thousands of sighs of love, one came ultimately to what was called, with solemnity, the last sigh.

Only when he rose to take off his coat did he remember the envelope Uncle Horace had given him. It was a little longer than the inside coat-pocket from which he took it. His first impulse was to see what it contained, but a kind of instinctive distrust made him think better of this. Not that his uncle was dying of an infectious disease (indeed he was not), but still he was in the act of dying and for Wilfred that was reason enough; reason enough for him to wrap the envelope in half a sheet of newspaper and wash his hands afterwards in the little wash-basin. Men never behave quite so strangely as when they are alone. The envelope, in the newspaper that made it harmless in the young man's eyes, was replaced in his inside coat-pocket.

To while away the time, he put on the gloves that his cousin had given him. They were obviously handsewn and looked indefinably foreign. Where Wilfred worked, such fine gloves were not sold. Wilfred prided himself on being something of a good judge. These came from Florence, Italy. He smelt them once or twice with pleasure, then removed them, laid them on a little bedside table and, taking a sheet of paper from his suitcase, decided to write to Angus and thank him. He had never known how to turn a sentence neatly, like one in a book; now, that was his ambition when he put pen to paper. Of course, he knew how to talk, find words necessary to obtain certain things, but before a sheet of paper his mind went blank. And then, what could you say to someone as highly educated as Angus? Perhaps he would make fun of his cousin's handwriting and his style. Wilfred repeated the word 'Cascini' under his breath, taking pains to imitate his cousin's accent, and gazed at the gloves.

'*My dear Angus,*' he began at last, '*thank you for leaving me your gloves.*'

Leaving rather than *giving*, seemed rather clever; it spared his pride. He stopped. Why was it so difficult to say thank you to a rich man? After searching for an instant for the next sentence, he found this, and wrote it down at once:

'*We wear almost exactly the same size. That's funny. I wouldn't have thought it.*'

That was certainly not like the sentences in books, but he had to get on with the letter.

'*Uncle Horace is sinking, hour by hour. They say everything will be over this evening. Anyway, I'm leaving tomorrow at latest so as to be back at work on Monday—*'

Once more, he threw an admiring glance at the gloves and added:

'*I'm bored here by myself. If you were here, we could talk together a little.*'

He had a sudden outburst of feeling for Angus. After all they belonged to the same family and Angus had looked so sad as he went to his car. They had not even said good-bye.

'*It was all very silly, on the road, that time: we didn't even say good-bye, I don't know why. Maybe we'll meet again some day.*'

He hesitated greatly as to how to end the letter. *Affectionately* did not seem manly enough. Yet, between cousins – He merely signed the note with his Christian name, but a postscript followed, for after all there were those sumptuous, brand-new gloves:

'*If it didn't take three hours and a half to get to your house in the train, I'd have liked to drop in to say hello.*'

Did that sound as though he were fishing for an invitation? The idea crossed his mind, but he brushed it aside. He did not want to begin the letter over again. What he wanted was to send it off. He could think all that over later. So he slipped it into an envelope, addressed and stamped it.

Hoping for some entertainment, he turned once more to the

68

detective story that he did not seem able to finish, but now, as on the night before, every sentence hinted at something sinister and disturbing. Someone might knock at his door any moment to say that all was over and did he want to come and see – He did not want to see, but sooner or later, death would knock at his door, not his own death, but Uncle Horace's, when it had finished its work.

After a quarter of an hour, he could stand it no longer, so he got up and left the odious little room. The stairs creaked so under his feet that his heart beat, for he felt like an escaping prisoner.

However, his fears were groundless. He met no one. Once he had crossed the vast landing with its white doors surmounted by classical pediments, he reached the fine staircase whose many steps, spreading fanwise, led gently to the feet of the bronze woman who held out her torch, looking both stupid and triumphant. How many people she must have seen, how many lovely women with shoulders as bare as hers, going by in a festive hum of voices! Soon she would see the coffin.

He went out and began running across the lawn till he had reached the trees above the river. Night was falling. No one could see him and he breathed in the pure sharp air with an animal joy that made him want to cry out like a child. If Angus had been there, he thought, he would have dared him to a race in the avenue that ran along the riverside. A few minutes went by before he grew calmer. Everything around him was still and, as though he wished to break the spell of this stillness, he picked up a dead twig and snapped it in two, but the huge silence closed over the little crack, sharp as a pistol shot, enveloping his hands, his head, his shoulders and his whole being. Three yards below him, the immense river rolled water that smelt of mud to the ocean, but this evening the presence of that vast and shifting expanse could only be guessed at.

He sat on the grass and felt the trunk of one of the big maples that lined the avenue. By a trick of imagination that he often indulged in he pictured the trees as live beings who were watching over him. A delightful feeling of safety came over him and he lay down on his back. Now they could knock at the door of his room, look for him: death would not find him. Clasping his hands under his neck, he let his eyes wander far away into the sky that was visible through the rents in the foliage and suddenly it seemed to him that he was in love. With whom, he could not have said, but his heart contained so much love that there was enough there, he thought, for an entire life-time. Yet it was someone he did not know that he loved with all his might. Eyes closed, he murmured with extraordinary ardour: 'I love you!' The words seemed to free him from a mysterious burden and the little sentence hovered on his lips over and over again. He had never spoken it to anyone in that way and he had no one to say it to, but he said it and said it again with a strange, a new-found happiness. He fell asleep, unawares.

CHAPTER XIV

The freshness of the air woke him and he ran toward the house. People with lanterns were looking for him on the lawn. Still in a daze, he fled the wavering lights and hid under a fir only to emerge brusquely from its shadow. The old black butler touched his arm. Wilfred followed him to the veranda where a slim, straight man waited for him. Seen by lantern light the stranger's face seemed stern and his black eyes blazed under heavy arched eyebrows.

70

'We've never met,' said the man, 'although we're distantly connected. I'm James Knight.'

His strong, cold hand grasped Wilfred's and closed impatiently over his fingers.

'Your uncle is dead,' he went on quickly. 'Where were you?'

'I was taking a walk.'

'Did you say good-bye to him?'

'Yes.'

Knight motioned the butler away and the man went off with the lantern, leaving them in complete darkness. Knight spoke again and his precise voice seemed to probe Wilfred like a steel blade.

'Did he give you a message for me? My wife and I were delayed in town and we got here too late, unfortunately.'

'He gave me no message whatever.'

'What did he talk to you about?'

Wilfred hesitated to answer. The question was unexpected. It was repeated in a voice that detached each syllable with a sort of irritable precision.

'I'm asking you what he talked to you about.'

'Mostly about religion.'

'Religion! That old reprobate.'

His hand struck the veranda railing, then he said:

'I have a question to put. You're a Catholic, aren't you?'

'Yes.'

'Then I won't say what I think about the facilities that your church affords sinners whose lives have been nothing but one long scandal. Confession, extreme unction. Now just go and see what God thinks of him.'

The last sentence took Wilfred's breath away and left him without an answer. Mr Knight clapped his shoulder, as a policeman claps a thief's.

'Let's go there together,' he said, pushing Wilfred forward.

71

Once inside the house, they passed the bronze woman whose nakedness seemed to defy them mutely. Much against his will, the young man soon found himself in his uncle's room once more. It was dimly lit by the little bedside lamp. As he followed Mr Knight in, he saw the nurse lean over the bed and deliberately pull the sheet up, so as to conceal the dead man's face.

'Pull that sheet down,' ordered Mr Knight. 'The opportunity is seldom given to show a young man what pleasure leads to and what remains of those on whom the hand of God weighs heavily.'

Miss Gogherty came up to him.

'No,' she said in a voice that turned the monosyllable into an interminable word, and she stared straight into Mr Knight's eyes.

They confronted each other for almost a minute and neither gave in. Wilfred noticed the man's regular, obstinate profile: a perfectly straight nose continued the brow in an unbroken line and his clear-cut mouth was finely chiselled. Miss Gogherty looked ugly as she faced this man whose appearance was youthful in spite of being nearly forty, while she was like an old animal ready to bare its fangs. Yet there was something kindly in the woman's plain face while James Knight only inspired Wilfred with dislike.

'Miss Gogherty,' said Mr Knight at last, 'there is a sermon under that sheet, an eloquent and most convincing sermon. No one talks quite so well about life as death.'

'You can pull the sheet down,' remarked Wilfred at that moment. 'If I don't want to look, I just won't.'

'Oh yes, you will, my boy,' said Mr Knight. 'Curiosity is stronger than disgust, in a case like this. What you'll see is simply unforgettable. And anyway –'

He walked suddenly to the other side of the bed. Wilfred shut his eyes.

72

'Please,' said a voice quite close to them.

The doctor had just come in. He laid his hand on Mr Knight's arm.

'Come with me,' said Miss Gogherty to Wilfred.

The young man immediately left the room with her.

CHAPTER XV

In the hall, two nuns in black stood up. Their backs were turned to the statue whose torch shone over them. The nuns were coloured women, one old, the other young, and both had eyes like little girls'.

'I suppose you'll spend the night,' said Miss Gogherty after greeting them.

'Yes,' answered the elder nun.

And she added at once with an innocence and a kind of majesty that would have impressed the most cynical of men:

'He was fond of coloured people.'

Wilfred thought of the mulatto girl and felt himself blush with shame.

'I know it,' said Miss Gogherty.

'He was very good to us,' continued the old nun. 'Reverend Mother Superior chose us to pray in his room tonight.'

Wilfred could not help looking at the young nun. She was very pretty under her black veil and immediately lowered her eyes. Once more, he felt his cheeks burn.

'Wait here,' said Miss Gogherty, showing the nuns a velvet-covered bench. 'You'll be sent for in a moment.'

She went to the end of the hall with Wilfred and said to him in an undertone:

'You'll probably want to pay your uncle a last visit before leaving. You must wait a little while. He is being attended to at present.' A smile that was meant to be kind drew up the corners of her mouth slightly and only succeeded in making her look a little fiercer.

'I advise you to wait here by yourself and avoid Mr Knight. He's a bit of a fanatic, an old school Presbyterian. I thought that kind had almost disappeared, but it's plain enough that I'm mistaken. Catholics get him into the state you saw him in just now.'

After hesitating, she looked down and said:

'Your uncle talked to me about you yesterday. He thought very highly of you.'

All this embarrassed Wilfred and he wanted to cut the conversation short, without quite knowing how to go about it.

'Did he die like a good Catholic?' he asked after a moment.

'You might say that he died decently. Father Dolan will tell you about it, if you like. I believe he's in the library, but remember what I told you: Mr Knight is in the drawing-room with his wife. You'd better not go in that direction.'

Wilfred thanked her and went a roundabout way to the library, a small place gloomily lit by a brass chandelier and communicating with the dead man's room. Rows of tattered books sat forlornly on mahogany shelves, and in a corner a broken-down sofa flaunted its heavy shape with indefinable shamelessness. The mere sight of this piece of furniture reminded Wilfred of thoughts he had been trying to drive away for the last few minutes and he felt irritated and disgusted with himself. Then, hearing him enter, someone appeared in the doorway between the two rooms: a squat, swarthy man, with a quick eye. He asked Wilfred who he was and the latter told him.

'Ah, very good. I'm Father Dolan. Your uncle was most anxious to see you before his confession.'

74

His glance wandered round the room and lighted on a small black bag that lay by an armchair. Grasping it vigorously, he added:

'You'll have to excuse me. I haven't much time for talking. Is there anything you wish to ask me?'

He looked like a businessman as he said this.

'I wanted to know if he died in the Faith,' said Wilfred.

'No doubt about that. He received the Sacraments.'

'Did he really have faith?'

The priest suddenly turned his head toward Wilfred.

'Why, yes. Why do you ask?'

'Because he told me that he found it difficult to believe.'

'Those are the temptations that beset death-beds. At any rate, I can tell you that he strongly desired to put everything in order. I am speaking of his religious duties. That is sufficient. The rest is the Lord's business.'

'Please forgive me for being insistent, but how are we to know that he really believed?'

'My friend, when a traveller gets a visa for his passport and a ticket from a steamship agency, it means that he believes in the existence of the ship, the ocean he's about to cross and the port that he hopes to reach.'

The young man hesitated, then a sentence occurred to him and he spoke it almost in one breath, as though someone had prompted him:

'And supposing that once the passport is in order and the cabin engaged, he isn't really sure that there is a port at the other end of the ocean?'

'Then, my boy, the traveller makes a really deserving act of confidence and we can foresee a good crossing for him. That's all we can know from this side.'

He looked curiously at Wilfred and asked:

'What makes you ask such questions?'

75

Wilfred dared not tell him about the prayer he had made by the dying man.

'Just a doubt that went through my mind concerning my uncle,' he replied.

Father Dolan asked him where he lived and, having jotted down his address, handed him a visiting card.

'We aren't exactly neighbours,' he said, 'but we live in the same town. If ever you wish to see me, we could talk all this over.'

On the threshold, he turned brusquely, as though suddenly inspired, and ceased looking like a businessman.

'Our actions are small and limited, you know,' he said with a very kindly smile. 'We always overstep them. What we do is important, of course, but when all is said and done what counts is what we are, because what God sees in us, above all things, is what we are. Will you think this over?'

CHAPTER XVI

A few hours later, Wilfred was called from his room and he returned to the one where his uncle lay. He had the sensation, as he crossed the threshold, that someone had taken his place and was going through all the motions that he was incapable of making himself, for he had never seen death and fear gripped him by the throat. Other forms of courage were his, but not that one.

Yet there was nothing to be frightened of in a room where everything was now in perfect order. It was all very tidy, the medicine bottles had disappeared, the curtains were drawn at the windows and the lamp with the green shade shone softly by

76

the bed where Uncle Horace slumbered. Except for the little ebony cross on his breast that said all there was to be said, he might have first been thought to be deep in restful sleep. He smiled a little slyly, as though he had discovered a secret of paramount interest in his dreams, but his sleep was merely an appearance, for as Wilfred came closer he felt perspiration breaking out at the roots of his hair. He leaned against a bed-post. Had he dared, he would have run away, but he was not alone in the room. A few steps from him, the two coloured nuns knelt praying, their rosaries between their fingers.

'He's small,' he thought with horror. 'Smaller than when he was alive. He looks no bigger than a boy of fifteen.'

He thrust his hand mechanically into his pocket to bring out his rosary and his knees seemed to bend of themselves. At that moment he saw a young woman enter and walk toward him. She was beautiful in a serious, delicate way. Dressed in black and bare-headed, she scarcely looked twenty and kept the naturally ruddy complexion of early youth that owes nothing to make-up. Her smoke-grey eyes, set in a narrow face, seemed immense. Perhaps intuition made her sense the fear that gripped Wilfred, for the glance she gave him was so deeply compassionate that it verged on love. Passing behind the nuns, she knelt noiselessly on the young man's left and he saw her lips move, although she did not make the sign of the cross. As for him, he told his beads without knowing what he said, and after a moment the silence that reigned in the room seemed louder to him than thunder.

How long did it last? Wilfred could not have told, any more than he could have owned to the thoughts, some terrifying, others sensual, that drifted through his mind, but he finally noticed that the beads of his rosary no longer slipped through his fingers and that he was not praying. He then crossed himself, rose and went out.

77

It was in the hall, at the feet of the bronze statue, that the unknown young woman joined him, smiling:

'Wilfred, I'm James Knight's wife. You must call me Phoebe. You and I are cousins.'

And her lips brushed the young man's cheek, which turned very pink.

'I could see you were very much moved,' she continued. 'Maybe death frightens you, but you and I know perfectly well that death doesn't amount to anything.'

'Oh, I'm not frightened,' he said, squaring his shoulders a little and buttoning his coat.

'It's quite natural, you know. Yet we're Christians. Were you very fond of your uncle?'

'I wouldn't say I was very fond of him.'

'He talked to me about you once. He told me you were very much of a believer.'

'I'm a Catholic,' murmured Wilfred.

'Oh, I know that, but you have faith. All Catholics don't have it – well, not like you.'

He looked away. The young woman's eyes followed him, unblinking. Suddenly he had an uncontrollable fit of hysterical laughter. She looked so pretty that anything serious said by her appeared absurd, and, filled with shame, he hid his face in his hands as he tried to stifle his offensive and scandalous hilarity. Patiently and without the least sign of severity, she waited for him to calm down. Quite to the contrary, her rather full mouth half opened to show a row of small round white teeth and Wilfred noticed that her lips had a satiny sheen.

'Excuse me,' he said at last. 'I don't know what's the matter with me. You mustn't get wrong ideas into your head about me. It's not because I said a few decades of the rosary – that's always done, with us.'

'Oh,' she replied gently, 'I'm not the kind to be taken in by

78

appearances. There's something else – You don't mind my talking to you like this, do you, Wilfred?'

He felt that her eyes willed him to raise his, as for some time he could look at nothing but her little mouth and its rather full lower lip. Lifting his head ever so slightly, he fancied that her big great eyes reproached him silently.

'Let's go in here,' she said, leading the way to the drawing-room.

Wilfred was afraid of finding Mr Knight there, but the big room was empty. When they were seated at either end of the plum-coloured velvet sofa, Phoebe said, almost in one breath:

'I'm sure you must think me tactless, but then, as we're related – and also I'm so very interested in religion, not so much in the form it takes as in our own personal attitude – I mean the intercourse we can have with – why, yes, with God.'

Wilfred found her both delightful and embarrassing as she said this. Because of what she had heard about him, she touched on the only subject that he felt incapable of discussing. He crossed his legs and cupped one knee with his hand with a sort of testy vigour.

'Maybe you don't like what I'm saying,' she said with the same smile (but this time Wilfred avoided looking at her mouth). 'Of course these are such intimate subjects, the most intimate of all, I expect. All the rest is so fleeting – life, its worries, what the Gospel calls the cares of this world –'

The young man nodded. Several things pained him, the least easy to admit being that he was sitting on a sofa by a young woman whose beauty unfortunately affected him too keenly. The situation resembled what the catechism referred to as 'dangerous occasions,' those you must run away from, with this difference, that he could not run away and moreover did not want to. His embarrassment increased as the conversation proceeded and he was afraid that Phoebe might notice it, but she sat smiling, hands folded, with charming simplicity.

'I'm sure my husband could give you a wonderful talk on the subject,' she said. 'He is so much in earnest, so fervent. I'll introduce him to you by and by.'

'We've already met, a little while ago.'

'Have you? His faith is very deep, you know, Wilfred, but it's not the same kind as yours. His calling would be to convert the lukewarm. He's something of an apostle, when you come to think of it. You are too, perhaps, but in another way.'

'I don't think so.'

'Who knows? You're so young.'

She began to laugh suddenly.

'I would have liked to have a brother like you,' she said.

He blushed.

'You must think this an absurd idea,' she continued without the least embarrassment, 'but it occurred to me when your uncle was talking about you. I want you to have supper at our house. Where do you live?'

Wilfred gave her his address.

'We live just fifteen minutes away from you.'

She rose suddenly, looking at Wilfred with the eyes of a child. He got up at once, smiling.

'Oh,' she said in a voice that seemed to caress his face, 'that's the first time I've seen you smile. You laughed, a while ago, but when you smile I feel you're a different person.'

She hesitated an instant and said at last:

'My husband is to drive me to the station. I'm going home in the train but will be back for the funeral. What about you?'

'I think I will too.'

'James will be back soon. He wants to spend the night at Wormsloe to see that everything is in order.'

Having said this, she came up to him and, as she had done before, laid her lips on his cheek.

'Don't forget you're coming to the house some day. I'll write to you.'

CHAPTER XVII

There was nothing unusual about that kiss, since he and Phoebe were related, but no sooner was he alone than Wilfred raised his hand to his cheek and returning to his seat on the plum-coloured velvet sofa, lapsed into one of his customary reveries. He tried to imagine Phoebe's life with a fanatical, disagreeable husband. If they lived so near him, how was it that he had not met them sooner? Because, like the others, they had kept away from him. He remained the undeserving member of the family, the one who sold shirts and was a Catholic into the bargain. Phoebe was the only one to show him any warmth, the only one to treat him as an equal.

After a time, he heard a car leave the house. That was surely Phoebe. He went out. It had grown darker. He saw the lights of the car on the road, ran a few steps, then stopped. What was he thinking of? Did he imagine that he could overtake the car?

He returned to the house with a sigh. Certain rooms were lit up, others not, and, except in Uncle Horace's room, none of the curtains were drawn. Everything had taken on the indefinable air of places about to be forsaken.

Wilfred would have liked to go too, but how was he to get to the station? As he went back to the drawing-room, he wondered what he was going to do. His first act was to light the two lamps

81

on the mantelpiece and look at himself in the mirror. At that hour and in a house lived in by death, things came to seem weird, even the fact of looking in a mirror at a face that you knew better than any other face and one that changed gradually under the eyes of an anxious observer. He shrugged his shoulders. What was there to be frightened of? He turned on the lamp that stood on the round table in the middle of the room, then the chandelier, so that every corner was lighted up, as had happened in former days, for receptions, parties. The gilt frames shone gayly and the vast carpet seemed happy to spread out its garlands of many-coloured flowers. You could imagine a hum of voices, laughter, women sitting in the big armchairs – but tonight, silence reigned in the empty drawing-room and the light that flooded it revealed nothing but solitude and a young man who stood glancing around like someone on watch. He turned out the chandelier and it was swallowed up once more by the shadows, then the two lamps on the mantelpiece, and left the room.

Supper-time was long since over and he felt hungry. He tiptoed towards the kitchen, down the corridor with the plaster frieze and past the long, deserted dining-room, and he strained his ear but heard nothing. The pantry and kitchen were empty.

The coloured servants had apparently fled, even the old butler who waited on him at table and who was so ready to talk about religion. They had probably been frightened on hearing that their master was dead, because a dead man brings bad luck.

Wilfred wondered whether he might not be alone in the house. Not quite alone, anyway, for the two nuns were there and perhaps Miss Gogherty too. And of course, Uncle Horace was there, after a fashion. Absent and present at the same time. Had he dared, Wilfred would have returned to see him, just because this frightened him. He himself could not understand the reason for this strange wish. He felt like an animal that scents the slaughterhouse and cannot break free. The slaughterhouse not only meant the room where the dead man lay, but the universe, the whole world. Death was everywhere. He lived on a dangerous planet.

He rushed up to his room. Now he wanted to leave at any price. Opening his big suitcase, he threw into it all the things that he had brought from town, his imitation leather toilet set, his detective story, his handkerchiefs, his change of underwear, some scarves. Never mind if there was no one to drive him to the station. He would go there on foot, he would walk a couple of hours, the whole night, if necessary.

His heart was beating so loud that he was obliged to sit down, and in his anguish he began to pray, first in a whisper, then in an undertone, and the sound of his own voice soothed him a little, kept him company. A long time went by. The idea of taking a walk through the night, lugging a suitcase, was anything but pleasant and Wilfred was about to give up the plan, but he hated his little room and felt almost sure that he would be unable to sleep in that bed of his, under the same roof as a dead man. Although it was shameful, no doubt, he could not bear the thought of it. It was better to go right away, to run away.

Grasping his suitcase, he walked downstairs, and on this occasion without pausing to look at the bronze woman that he could have admired at leisure he hurried to the front door. But he did not have time to lay his hand on the brass knob. It opened and Mr Knight stood before him. His eye lighted on the suitcase.

'Where are you going?' he asked.

'I'm going to the station.'

'On foot?'

'I have to.'

'And what train do you expect to take?'

'The first one that comes along.'

Mr Knight took off his hat and the electric torch shone on his bare forehead.

'There's a train in an hour and a half. I'll drive you to the station myself in my car. Let's go and sit in the drawing-room. I want to talk to you.'

Wilfred frowned but followed Mr Knight obediently enough and both men went towards the plum-coloured velvet sofa. Somewhat uneasily, the young man saw Phoebe's husband take the seat that she had occupied an hour earlier. Then, after placing his suitcase by him, he also sat down. Mr Knight looked attentively at the bag and said at last:

'That's an awfully big suitcase.'

'It's the only one I've got.'

'You expected to stay here some time, I suppose.'

'No. A couple of days at most. It depended a little on –'

'On the turn your uncle's illness would take?'

'Yes.'

'Didn't you really expect to stay longer?'

'No. In any case, I have to be back at work Monday morning.'

'Then that's a very big suitcase for such a short stay.'

'I thought I'd told you just now –'

'I know, I know, but nevertheless – Does that suitcase lock?'

'Yes.'

'It's a kind that isn't often seen nowadays,' said Mr Knight without taking his eyes from the bag. 'And those labels tell quite a tale.'

'It was my father's suitcase,' said Wilfred in a faintly aggressive voice.

'Your father was a great traveller.'

'Yes, a great traveller.'

After a short silence, Mr Knight continued in a gentler tone:

'I must have sounded a little brusque today, my boy, but I want to help you.'

84

'I'm grateful to you for taking me to the station.'

'You're joking. I don't mean that.'

Turning his face sideways, he tried to smile.

'My wife,' he said, 'talked to me about you on our way to the station.'

'Your wife?'

'Yes. Does it surprise you?'

'A little. I scarcely know her.'

'That's exactly what I find interesting. She spoke of you as a serious, even a devout young man. Did you two talk about religion?'

'It would be more correct to say that it was she who talked about it to me.'

'And where, may I ask?'

'What's that?'

'Where did this edifying conversation take place?'

'Why – right here. Your wife sat – there, just where you are now, with me here.'

Mr Knight rose and planted himself in front of the young man.

'My boy,' he said with his hands behind his back, 'there's something about you that bothers me. You are a Catholic, I know. That should enlighten me.'

'I don't feel like talking about religion, sir.'

'I'm sure of that. You don't want to argue with a heretic, do you? Be kind enough to listen to me, however. My wife thinks you a steady, reliable young man because she lives, thank goodness, apart from the world and sees everything in an idealistic light, but I know what a man of your age is like and what lies at the back of the minds of all your generation, yourself included.'

Surprise made Wilfred open his mouth, but he remained silent. They stared at each other without a word. The young man raised his head to look up at Mr Knight and found it difficult to meet the dark, burning eyes that seemed to search his brain. An interminable minute went by, then Mr Knight asked with studied politeness:

'I suppose the existence of a place called Hell has not been concealed from you by your religion?'

'Why, no. Naturally – I don't see what –'

'You wouldn't want to go down there, in the company of –'

He nodded towards the dead man's room. Wilfred shrugged his shoulders.

'He isn't in Hell.'

'Don't be too sure of that, my boy. It's not by covering a dead man with Latin prayers that he is saved. That would be too easy, between you and me. And then, God is not mocked. Faith saves you and it is the life you've led that bears witness to your faith. He had lost his long ago.'

He walked calmly to the low mantelpiece, leaned against it and said quietly:

'He lost it in the arms of his mistresses.'

Wilfred rose.

'Mr Knight,' he said with an effort, 'I don't wish to hear what you have to say on that subject. You suggested taking me to the station.'

'We still have plenty of time. The station is only ten minutes off, in a car. Keep calm, will you, and remember what I'm going to say. Dissipation is what makes us lose our faith. Physical pleasure. It ends by stilling conscience. Oh, I know, we can imagine that we continue to believe, we can persuade ourselves of anything, but we no longer have real faith, God's faith, the one that God has given us. What we replace it with is something that we ourselves have trumped up, a sort of idol that we carry inside us and that has no more power to save us than a fetish.'

He developed this theme for several minutes with irrefutable logic and a kind of icy fury, voicing what Wilfred had never dared to admit to himself, even in his solitude, at moments before an appointment with a woman when, for instance, as he stood before a mirror and slowly tied his cravat, something or someone within himself, in his head or in his heart, said: 'How long will you keep me waiting? Don't you know I am here and that I have been looking at you unceasingly since your birth?'

Anger induced by fear seized him suddenly. He came closer to Mr Knight, who stared at him in astonishment.

'Be quiet!' cried Wilfred.

'Why should I?' asked Mr Knight without flinching. 'You've probably been told that I was a fanatic, but has it entered your head that the man who is talking to you has perhaps been sent to caution you? We are all of us sent to one another, the righteous to the wicked and the wicked to the righteous. I firmly believe this. Each one of us is no more and no less than a messenger from God, my boy. Even the executioner, even the murderer carry a message the meaning of which they don't know. Even – listen carefully – even the prostitute and the disease she passes on to you.'

Wilfred had the impression that the man had read his thoughts clearly and turned white.

'What are you leading up to?' he asked.

'To this: either you change your way of living or you'll burn in the fiery lake.'

'I firmly hope to be saved,' said Wilfred stoutly. 'I have faith, Mr Knight, real faith, the one you talked about just now, the faith of God.'

To his great astonishment, Mr Knight replied:

'I don't doubt it for a second.'

And he added:

'That's as evident as the rest, Wilfred, and you know what I mean by the rest. Come,' he continued, seeing the young man's amazement, 'let's drop the subject and go to the station. It's time to start.'

He walked quickly to the suitcase and picked it up.

'I still think it very large, but I didn't believe it would be so heavy,' he remarked as he handed it to Wilfred.

'What are you trying to insinuate, Mr Knight?'

'Oh, I'm not the kind to insinuate anything. I think there's something in the suitcase that you're carrying away from here. Something your uncle gave you.'

Wilfred's only answer was to take a little key from his pocket and hold it out to Mr Knight.

'Open the suitcase yourself,' he said.

'Why?' asked Mr Knight. 'Your word is enough and if I've been mistaken you'll forgive me, Wilfred. There are a certain number of documents in this house that it is my duty to destroy, you see, a compromising correspondence, an exchange of love letters. Your uncle's private life –'

Wilfred thought of the envelope he had in his pocket and felt guilty.

'Perhaps,' he said, putting the little key back, 'perhaps he destroyed the papers himself.'

'He burnt some of them,' replied Mr Knight gently. 'At least the ashes in his fireplace lead me to suppose so. I imagine it must have been a terrible wrench. He was strongly attached to himself, to the slightest memento of his past and, naturally, especially so to intimate ones. He battened on his lost youth. I knew the old rake. I used to tell him the truth about himself sometimes. He didn't like me. At the end, you were the only one he trusted.'

'I?'

'Yes, you. He thought you were pure.'

Wilfred blushed deeply.

'It's something to your credit to be able to blush,' remarked Mr Knight.

'Pure or not, I don't see what that has to do with all this business.'

'It has a lot to do with it, my boy. A pure man doesn't hesitate to burn impurities.'

'I don't understand you at all.'

'Yet it's quite simple. What your uncle couldn't bring himself to burn, he was convinced that you would burn for him, as he believed you to be pure. And for this reason, I was pretty sure that he had given you a packet of letters addressed to a person whose name was a little too notorious in its time. The letters were returned to him and he kept them carefully, together with the answers they had obtained. That was what he called his treasure. I doubt if he found courage enough to destroy them. He lacked courage.'

His eyes stared into Wilfred's. 'If he tries to search me,' thought the latter, 'I'll knock him down. I'm stronger than he is.'

'Shall we go?' he asked.

'We're going, but you seem in an awful hurry.'

'Why, didn't you yourself suggest that –'

'Yes.'

He looked even more attentively at the young man than before, as though he wished to burn his features into his memory for ever. 'He knows everything,' thought Wilfred. 'A servant must have listened at the door and told him everything.'

Neither of them moved. It finally became intolerable.

'Let's go,' said Wilfred limply, feeling that he had already been defeated in the silent struggle.

Suddenly he remembered what Phoebe had said to him about his smile. She had told him nothing new. Many women had said the same thing. His smile disarmed everybody. After hesitating for a few seconds, he made an effort and smiled.

There was no change in Mr Knight's face.

'If I were you,' he said at last and very slowly, 'I wouldn't smile.'

89

The remark hit Wilfred like a blow and the smile faded from his lips.

'Pick up your suitcase,' ordered Mr Knight.

A few minutes later, they were in the car and driving along without exchanging a word. When they reached the station, and as Wilfred was about to open the door of the car, Mr Knight said in a voice more courteous than his words:

'I think we've said everything we had to say. If ever you happen to go by my street and feel tempted to ring at my door, you must resist the temptation.'

'I'll resist it very easily,' replied Wilfred from the pavement.

'It will be better for you and for me,' said Mr Knight as he started the car.

PART TWO

CHAPTER XVIII

He was back again in his room, his real room, the one he usually escaped to run about the streets, he was there once more with a feeling that amounted to happiness. The dull task was over. Uncle Horace was dead, really dead this time. He lay out there at Wormsloe in his bed and he, Wilfred, was about to dive into his, worn-out but alive.

In the mirror of the little bathroom, he stared at the strong, healthy youth who smiled back at him. His hat still on his head but pushed back off a mass of untidy hair, he looked a little as though he had been out on a spree. He often looked like that. Yet, that night, he was back from a most dismal escapade.

His first act was to take the envelope his uncle had given him and drop it in a drawer which he locked carefully. Then he undressed and after saying his prayers, slipped into bed with a sigh of pleasure.

He fell asleep immediately but only for a short time and woke suddenly, as though someone had tapped him on the shoulder. He turned on the light. His room appeared in the disorder to which he was accustomed, clothes thrown here, there and everywhere, on the carpet, over the furniture. Above the bed an ivory Christ.

The room he had rented furnished on the top floor of a small brick house could not have been more ordinary. The deal desk, the two plain straight chairs, the brass bed had been used by so many people as to lose any distinguishing feature. The only thing belonging to Wilfred was the cross that had been

93

his father's. In his eyes, the rest simply did not exist.

He sat up in bed and raised both hands to his brow. Beyond all doubt, the envelope was in a drawer of the desk. That was what had woken him because he had been thinking of nothing else for hours.

It took him a long time to make up his mind. He lay down, dozed and woke up again, then rose finally as one rises to carry out a task. It was a warm night. Without even pausing to put on a dressing-gown, he opened the drawer, took out the envelope and threw it on the bed.

It was long, thick and made of maize-coloured paper. Wilfred thought that it looked sinister and a trifle repulsive. Seated on the bed, a yard removed from it, he purposely remained motionless for some time. It was half past two in the morning and the silence that buzzed in his ears was like a long, unbroken, far-away cry. He could not tear his eyes from the baleful object. The desire to open the envelope struggled with one to replace it in the drawer and go back to sleep, for he disliked touching something that a dead man had touched. However, he did what he did not want to do. His frightened fingers tore the yellow paper, then he shook the envelope.

Letters, a few photographs and another smaller envelope with a black seal scattered over the blanket with a sort of whispering sound.

He picked up a letter at random. The writing had faded, the date carried him back thirty-five years, over ten years before he was born. Uncle Horace had been having a good time with women, for this, of course, was a letter from a woman, a love letter, with sentences she had forgotten to finish and crosses to mark the places that she had kissed. Wilfred found the letter idiotic and adorable. Another, in the same hand, wrote in the same incoherent style about an appointment made for the following Thursday. The girl was probably quite young. Fearing a disappointment, Wilfred had not looked at the photographs. He hesitated, then took up one with a few words written in a masculine hand on the back: *For ever, April 7, at five o'clock in the evening.* Turning it over, the likeness of a slim, fair girl tore a cry of admiration from him, for no one could have imagined a more tender, more innocent expression than hers, although the mouth betrayed imperious greed. He held the little slip of cardboard for a long time between his fingers, never tired of gazing at features that were at the same time so pure and so sensual, at a face straining toward happiness as a flower turns eagerly to the light, till suddenly he heard his own voice whispering in the silence:

'Oh, how I would have loved you!'

The sound of his voice seemed as strange to him as if someone else had spoken, and he raised his eyes instinctively, only to lower them at once to the fascinating likeness.

The second photograph showed a young man with an unquestionably pleasing face, although too sure of himself, too mocking, too triumphant, obviously Uncle Horace, yet how different from the poor shrunken, humbled corpse that Wilfred had seen only that night. Here the pride of life exulted, together with conceit and profound self-satisfaction, all furthered by a substantial fortune and a probably admirable digestion. What scorn there was in those black eyes! At the bottom of the photograph, the same feminine hand had written: *My beloved, April 7.*

Wilfred devoured the other letters with a burning face, but envy gnawed at his heart. For he unconsciously imagined himself in place of this over-fortunate young man, this satiated gentleman to whom this artless, delightful song of love was offered with stammering gratitude.

'My treasure – that's my treasure,' Uncle Horace's old mouth had said this on his deathbed and in accents that still rang in

Wilfred's ears. He could not bring himself to destroy his treasure and so had entrusted it to Wilfred, because, Mr Knight said, he believed in his purity. He, pure! With sudden fervour, he kissed the girl's portrait, then, thinking that his dead uncle had no doubt done the same over and over again, he wiped his mouth.

Had he gone mad? Indeed, the whole scene struck him as horrible, taking place as it did on his bed, under the cross whose presence he had forgotten. He got up all of a sudden and, gathering together letters and photographs and the black-sealed envelope, he tossed them pell-mell into the drawer, which he locked. Then he dressed and went out.

CHAPTER XIX

Twenty minutes later he found himself in one of the bars in the port that stayed open all night. Cigarette smoke filtered the red lamp-light and made the eyes smart and the sound of conversation merged into a single, muffled, hoarse voice that deafened you on entering. Yet once he had crossed the threshold Wilfred felt happy, for this was the spot he dreamt of in the daytime, during long working hours. Some women were there, lots of sailors and a few young or old civilians.

In such a place, Wilfred had the impression of being himself and free of complications. His hat tilted, he stood glass in hand at the imitation mahogany bar and forgot everything with the astonishing ease inspired by this place, where life assumed such a simple and violent aspect.

Without being much of a talker, he had the gift of making

people smile, even men who would have been glad to land him a blow on the jaw and send him sprawling to the ground because women always looked at him a little more often than their admirers cared for. Glasses and smooth bands of metal shone in the pinkish light that suggested the reflected glow of a fire, but the faces never emerged from the semi-darkness that created a sort of complicity between all those present. The swing door burst open from time to time and in staggered a sailor, like a great silver statue. A woman's deliberately vulgar voice cascaded from a loud-speaker in a corner of the ceiling and meandered through a prudently obscene song.

The bar filled gradually and it was warm, but Wilfred felt very comfortable, lost in a crowd, sharing its unconcern. He knew that sooner or later he would end by not quite understanding what was said to him. Then, through the haze of cigarettes, he would make out the face of a woman smiling at him. Perhaps she would resemble the other woman whose photograph had been in his pocket for well-nigh two hours, because, strange as it might seem, it was she that he hoped to find in the bar, a place where the voice of that old conscience of his no longer spoke intelligibly.

'Yes,' he said in answer to the confused, vague sentences that buzzed in his ears.

What was said no longer mattered at that time of night. Very close at hand, someone kept repeating like a prayer: 'I've always wanted to meet you.' But Wilfred was not unconscious that he was being addressed. A young woman on his left asked insistently: 'Look, why don't you answer my question?' She gently slipped her hand in his.

'Yes,' he said, laughing like a child, 'yes.'

CHAPTER XX

At dawn, he was back within the yellow walls of his room once more and in a sort of dream he tore off his clothes and threw himself into bed. He thought of sleep as a big black hole where one ceased to exist and to remember because one part of you always tried to forget the other. And in order to live, one had to forget.

The sound of an oilcloth blind flapping against the half-open window roused him. A fresh breeze flowed like water over his cheeks and he suddenly heard the distant sound of a church bell. His body rolled up in a blanket, he opened his eyes and thought: 'Sunday.'

The unbearable ordeal was about to begin. Between sin and repentance came an interval of disgust, a disgust of the flesh and still more horrible disgust of religion. What he was about to do would be done in spite of himself: leave his bed, deluge his body with cold water that would only purify the skin, dress like an automaton and pick up a Mass book with hands that still remembered the flesh they had caressed – all this nauseated him and he recalled Mr Knight's scornful words. That was a man who saw things as they were.

'And what about me?' asked a voice in the innermost part of his being as he marked that Sunday's Mass with a ribbon. Wilfred did not reply. 'I love you', said the voice. 'There I go, imagining all sorts of things,' thought Wilfred.

Without touching the breakfast prepared the day before, he left his room, went down in the lift and slammed its door impatiently. A moment later, he was running under the elms that lined the avenue. No one could run faster than he. His toes scarcely touched the ground and he heard the faint sound they made, like that of a match striking on a box. Reaching the bus-stop just before the great red vehicle arrived, he jumped into it.

He had slipped his missal into his pocket so no one could take him for a good young man – this farce really disgusted him – and, looking rather important and a trifle insolent, he sat and yawned like a young man who had been on a spree the night before, which was exactly the case. Why, under the circumstances, did he go to church? That was a question he could not answer, but he threw himself into a contradictory situation much as you might throw yourself into a stream to swim as best you could against the current.

The church he was going to was not his parish church. It was called Saint Aloysius and only the Poles in town attended it. Ornate, heavily gilded, filled with statues of every colour in the rainbow, with great white bouquets on the altars and a pro-fusion of tapers whose little flames quivered in the air, the church carried Wilfred to a foreign country. The altar-boy's little bell rang there far more imperiously than in other churches where gentler, softer chimes were used, and all around him the young man saw faces that he found mysterious because in their eyes he could not read thoughts familiar to him. 'They're thinking in their own tongue,' he said to himself. 'They think other thoughts, with other words than ours.'

His book lay open in his hands, but he did not follow Mass very closely. In front of him were a girl in a red scarf and a boy with short fair hair whose round skull shone like a golden ball. A murmur from the priest, a clicking of rosaries could be heard. No one moved, everyone knelt, including Wilfred, but he was thinking of something the woman had said to him the night before: 'If you didn't have a good figure and one eye that

99

slanted up, no one would notice you at all.' He had been told that before. He was not handsome but he attracted women.

Closing his book, he clasped his brow in his hands. In that attitude, he looked as if he was praying and yet he could not pray. He only wanted to recover his composure, but certain things the woman had said came back to him with particular emphasis. The little bell split his brain, ringing with a sort of triumphant fury, scattering everything in his head, where pleasure attempted to live again in the shape of memories. That frenzied sound announced that the host would no longer be a mere semblance and that the Lord was to be present. To believe in such things was enough to make you lose your mind. Wilfred believed them, everyone in the church believed, but no one budged, no one cried out in amazement, happiness or terror, it was the customary miracle, the Sunday elevation, and once more the frenzied little bell rang out to tell everybody they could raise their heads.

Wilfred had not prayed. He had only whispered: 'My God, I profoundly regret –' The rest of the sentence had not passed his lips because he regretted nothing and all he found in his heart was impatience and an irritation with the tyranny of a body that unceasingly demanded pleasure. Right and left of him, people got up for Communion. They all went toward the altar, only he did not move, but stayed kneeling with his hands clasped during the loud murmuring of the *Confiteor*. They must have noticed him isolated in his pew, and the priest could see him from a distance and perhaps was thinking in strange words, Polish words: 'That man doesn't come to Communion because he has done wrong.' Wilfred got up suddenly and went to the door while the communicants were returning to their seats.

100

CHAPTER XXI

Outside, the sun shone in a sky so palely blue that it gave the impression of a limitless void. The young man gave a sigh of relief as though he had just been set free. The sharp air cleansed his cheeks that were still hot with shame. He felt better now and decided to go home via the great avenue to which the fine weather had attracted quite a crowd. Now he had left church, everything interested him – houses, trees, passers-by – and suddenly life seemed extraordinarily rich.

He had the whole day in which to come and go as he pleased and, although the state of his finances was not rosy, the few dollars he had in his pocket were sufficient to stave off boredom any way he chose. First of all, he planned to spend half an hour in the park. There, hands in pockets, head tilted back and hat over his nose, he fell asleep on a bench.

When he woke, he saw children playing around him gayly. A shabbily dressed old gentleman was throwing peanuts to the grey squirrels. Wilfred glanced at his watch. It was past noon. Usually on Sundays, he took his meals at 'Sloppy Joe's', a small restaurant in his part of town where he was sure of meeting a few friends, but that Sunday was not like other Sundays. Apart from the gnawings of hunger and the weariness incurred the day before, Wilfred felt in a light-hearted and sensual mood. He had had enough of tragedies, and wasn't he emerging from a real tragedy? His uncle's death-struggle could pass for such. And after that and on top of it, the ordeal of hearing Mass in that foreign church. After all, if he didn't have

101

some fun at twenty-four, when could he expect to have it?

He decided to lunch at the Spanish restaurant. It was situated at the other end of town in a little street lined with dark red houses, each one like its neighbour, with three white marble steps that led to the same deep green door, set off with a brass knocker: houses where rich people lived. It was of course extravagant to lunch at the Spanish restaurant, but he calculated that by skipping a meal or two during the week, he could balance his finances.

So half an hour later, he opened the door of the restaurant, crossed the room and went straight to the garden where ten or twelve small tables with fine white clothes had been set. The fact was that the so-called garden was no more than a brick-paved court, but from over the wall of a neighbouring yard a sycamore spread its branches generously so that you had the impression of greenery, and at the end of the garden, to lend a really Iberian touch, stood a small Moorish fountain with blue and white tiles. The water fell so softly into the turquoise basin that the sound could not possibly annoy anyone; on the contrary, thought Wilfred. You could really fancy yourself in Spain, in that land of beautiful, passionate ladies. That was just it – However, when he had seated himself at a table, a swarthy waiter came for his order: the man was only there for the Spanish customers and could scarcely jabber more than a few words of English. Wilfred knew all that. He was familiar with the place through having been there the summer before. He dismissed the waiter with a word and a gesture:

'Señorita,' he ordered.

The waiter understood and vanished. A moment later she appeared and Wilfred gave her his best smile. Señorita Rosa. The young lady knew English and spoke it with amazing fluency. She mouthed every sentence as if it was a single word. She was small and fair, and her ash-blonde hair had gleams of silver.

In a face scarcely larger than Wilfred's hand, eyes fringed with black lashes hesitated between green and blue, and her cheeks fined down to the mouth, forming an oval with the chin which Wilfred found beautiful. As he looked at her, the idea of a little statue or a doll immediately occurred to him. You could go over what was visible of her body and what could be guessed at without discovering a single defect, except that it was almost too tiny in its perfection and inspired a vague desire to break it. 'I could surely kill her,' he thought, 'just by hugging her tightly, the way grizzly bears do in the mountains.' But for the time being, the matter in hand was not to kill her but to order a meal, an excellent one.

'Bring me whatever you like, Señorita Rosa.'

She reeled off at a breath the names of seven or eight dishes. All the Spanish words crackled like gun-shots. 'How wonderful it would be,' thought Wilfred, 'if she could perform like that for me in that tongue some day.'

'Choose,' she said, pointing to the menu.

The more severe she looked, the more he smiled, for he liked her with that expression, even though it was discouraging.

'Help me, Señorita.'

She raised her head impatiently.

'I'll attend to my other customers. You can think your order over, meanwhile.'

How could anyone speak so distinctly and so fast? And that touch of an accent turned English into a new and delightful tongue. He watched her cross the garden and disappear into the restaurant. She took small quick steps and held herself very straight: that too surprised him. Nothing moved in the girl's body but her legs.

He remained alone in his corner for a few minutes. A lady and gentleman appeared, selected a table somewhat removed from Wilfred's and sat down. Then a young man with an

103

inquisitive air came into the garden, glanced around him as though he were looking for someone, saw Wilfred, paused a second or two and disappeared.

Wilfred watched for his Spanish girl's return. He would have liked her to prepare his meal herself, to touch it with her hands. He would have liked a great many things. She came back finally and he smiled at her again, but she continued to look serious.

'You choose for me,' he said. 'It will taste better.'

She laughed a little, from exasperation.

'I don't know what you like.'

'What I like?' he asked with such warmth that she blushed.

He guessed that she was furious, for she looked down and her lower lip quivered a little.

'Forgive me, Señorita.'

'We aren't here to chat,' she said.

And suddenly, in a gentler voice, she drew up a short menu, a very reasonable little meal.

'What about my dessert, Señorita? You aren't going to deprive me of that, are you?'

'I'll think it over,' she said gravely. 'It will be a surprise.'

A rather mysterious smile flitted over her face and she bent toward Wilfred to straighten his silver. His eyes went at once to her breast and he then noticed – how could it have escaped him? – that she wore a tiny gold cross on a thread-like chain.

He had the indefinable sensation of having been followed and caught.

'She and I believe in the same things,' he thought.

The swarthy waiter attended to him, but Wilfred took very little notice of what he ate. He was no longer hungry and his plate remained half-full. The girl returned and asked:

'Did you like it?'

'Enormously, Señorita.'

'Maybe you'd have more appetite if you weren't alone.'

104

'Why?'

She shrugged her shoulders prettily.

'Oh well, eating by yourself is a little – sad.'

How was she to guess that he had come there alone because he wanted to keep her for himself, as though she already belonged to him? Yet the whole thing began to seem a little boring to Wilfred. It was rather like seeing a play and knowing all the lines before they were spoken. All the same, the girl was very pretty and opened up conversational possibilities. He smiled mechanically and their eyes met; she looked at him unflinchingly. 'So now it's she who wants to start an affair,' he thought, 'and I'll have to go through with it.'

'I'm going to bring you a cake from my country,' she announced finally.

'Where do you come from?' He did not care.

'From Burgos.'

'Burgos?'

He hadn't the faintest idea what Burgos could be.

'If you like almond paste, you'll like this cake.'

'Oh, of course. What time do you stop working?'

The question had to be put sooner or later and he asked it a little early because he wanted to get it over.

'You're too inquisitive,' she answered with a smile that implied a secret understanding.

And off she went. The cake was brought by the waiter. Wilfred nibbled at the pastry and buried it in his pocket: he hated almond paste.

'Well?' asked Señorita Rosa, five minutes later.

He showed her his empty plate.

'See?' he said.

'Greedy,' she murmured.

'Greedy and inquisitive,' he replied laughing. 'I have a lot of faults.'

105

She smiled indulgently at him. He then asked in an undertone:
'You still won't tell me when you stop working?'

'How can I go on playing this hackneyed game,' he thought,
'knowing perfectly well how it will end?' For he was now certain
he would do whatever the girl wanted, and she knew it.

'As you're so anxious to know,' she said softly, smoothing the
tablecloth, 'I leave this establishment at eleven.'

Wilfred smiled obediently.

CHAPTER XXII

He no longer had the least desire for the Spanish girl: the game
had perhaps been won too quickly and too easily. Once more
that trick of looking like a child with a mother waiting for him
at home had worked. With certain women, he realized, it always
worked, but suddenly he felt that he had had enough of it, he
was sick of everything, of himself, of these trivial affairs. Once
he saw the cross at the girl's throat, he had ceased to want her,
but that was not on account of the cross, for he was also sick
of religion.

He left the restaurant after paying the bill brought by the
swarthy waiter. It seemed smaller than he had expected and this
he regarded in the light of a favour that amounted to an insult.
With sudden irritation, he jumped into a cruising taxi and had
himself driven home, fully determined to spend the afternoon
sleeping.

In his room, he pulled down the blind, stretched out on the
bed, but he closed his eyes in vain for he could not sleep. After
tossing and turning for a few minutes, he got up and opened
the drawer that contained his uncle's letters.

106

There was a man who had had a really good time: it showed in the mocking little smile on his thick lips, the lips of a hedonist, and then those letters, slavish letters with sentences that seemed to pant. Wilfred had never had a love letter. Women had told him that they loved him in moments when you say just anything, but they never wrote because he never gave his address, for fear of possible difficulties. He never saw the same woman twice.

Yet how glad he would have been to receive letters as bold and as compromising as those he was reading. One in particular was scarcely proper. He almost knew it by heart and, having read it over, looked for the hundredth time at the innocent face of the pretty creature who could write such things. Her name was inserted in a corner of the photograph in blue ink.

Uncle Horace had been loved by her and no doubt by a great many other women and, as he lay dying, he had still called for love because the heart is insatiable. There was also the little Ditmar girl, scarcely thirteen, but it was quite evident that Alicia had been the great love in Uncle Horace's life, since he had kept her letters to the last. Alicia must certainly have been prettier than all the others.

Wilfred looked a little longer at the girl's photograph, then, almost regretfully, put it away in the drawer with the letters. If Mr Knight imagined he was going to burn them all!

His eyes fell on the envelope with the black seal. It gave him a curious feeling of distrust, almost of repugnance. In spite of this it had to be opened, and he was reaching out to pick it up when someone knocked at the door, a couple of timid, apologetic raps. As Wilfred never had callers, he stood perfectly motionless without answering, but a moment later there came another insistent rap, as much as to say: 'I'm sure you're in.' Wilfred waited, a little puzzled. There was another knock, a very polite one. This time he opened at once.

On the landing stood a young man in a yellow waterproof that showed signs of wear. That was the first thing that struck Wilfred. 'He's going to ask me for money,' he thought, but changed his mind almost at once. The stranger's face was not that of a beggar. His long black eyes, red mouth, thin brown cheeks and high, jutting cheekbones reminded one of a gypsy and yet there was something modest and thoughtful about him. He was tall and narrow-shouldered. A grey hat concealed the top of his forehead.

'What do you want?' asked Wilfred.

'Mr Wilfred Ingram.'

Wilfred grew frightened.

'Who are you?'

'My name wouldn't mean anything to you. I've come to bring Mr Ingram something he's lost.'

'I'm Mr Ingram. I haven't lost anything.'

He was about to shut the door.

'Your Mass book,' said the man.

Wilfred instinctively put his hand to his coat pocket and through the fabric he could feel the little Spanish cake that he had refused to eat.

'My Mass book,' he said with an embarrassed smile. 'How –'

'I don't have to remind you that you wrote your name and address in the book.'

It was indeed unnecessary to remind Wilfred of this. He who never gave his address to anyone, he who was so secretive, why had he written it in his Mass book? He had been proud of it when he bought it in a moment of religious fervour. That was perhaps why he had inscribed in block letters his name, his street and the number of his house. If there were things to conceal in his life, the little black leather volume at any rate showed him to advantage, honoured its owner. He bit his lips.

'You left it at Saint Aloysius',' said the man.

He added gently:

'I was sitting behind you.'

'Why didn't you give it to me right away?' asked Wilfred thoughtlessly.

He felt disturbed by the stranger's rather too attentive gaze and spoke heedlessly.

'You left before everybody else. I myself went to the altar – with the others – and when I came back to my seat you were no longer in yours.'

His voice became more precise and betrayed a foreign intonation that had at first escaped Wilfred. He thought this conversation on the landing was becoming lengthy and a little strange.

'Well,' he asked brusquely, 'have you got the book?'

The stranger thrust his hand into the pocket of his waterproof, drew out the missal and handed it silently to Wilfred.

'Thanks,' said Wilfred. 'Many thanks. It was stupid of me.'

He began to feel less distrustful.

'Would you mind if I came in for a minute?' asked the man timidly.

'The fact is that I've got to go out in a little while,' said Wilfred with a smile that he tried to make agreeable.

'In that case –'

The stranger also smiled and turned in the direction of the lift.

'What a beast I am,' thought Wilfred. 'He went out of his way –'

'No!' he cried. 'Come in.'

After a slight hesitation, the man wheeled around and crossed the threshold. As he reached the centre of the room, he took off his hat and showed an abundance of well-groomed black hair. 'He looks most respectable,' thought Wilfred to soothe his misgivings. 'Besides, he went to Communion this morning.'

The man looked about him with a good deal of assurance that contrasted with the modest air he had worn a moment before, and his eyes fastened on the cross.

109

'You have a nice room,' he said at last.

Wilfred felt uneasy once more. 'He's going to ask me for a reward,' he said to himself. 'I wonder what is the proper amount to give.'

'It takes a good fifteen minutes to get here from Saint Aloysius',' he said aloud. 'Will you allow me –'

'You're joking,' replied the man. 'I don't want a thing. You know,' he continued, looking Wilfred in the eye, 'I could have left the book in the vestry. That's what is done as a rule. But I wanted to see you, so I took this opportunity. May I sit down ?'

Wilfred pointed to a chair.

'Oh, I won't stay long,' said the man sitting down. Laying his hat on the deal desk, he covered his knees with the folds of the waterproof. 'To begin with, someone is waiting for me.'

He lowered a long, thin, inquisitive nose. For a moment, he seemed to be turning something over in his mind, then, in a voice which the desire to sound polite made almost affected, he said :

'You're probably wondering why I wanted to see you. It's very simple. I was watching you off and on this morning, although you didn't know it. I was just behind you. You must excuse me, but how could I keep from noticing that you were the only one in the whole church not to go to Communion ?'

Wilfred was sitting on the edge of his bed. He jumped up, blushing.

'That's my business. I'll have to ask you not to talk to me about this.'

The man smiled.

'Excuse me,' he said, 'but I concluded from this that you must have great faith. I know that what I'm saying may seem paradoxical, but I'm rather familiar with the subject. Among those who thronged to the Communion table, a certain number did not believe, or only believed very faintly, others had

110

consciences that were far from clear. At any rate, a good many Communions were sacrilegious. I am very much interested in these things. You did not wish to make a sacrilegious Communion.'

'For the second time, this is none of your business.'

'Of course it isn't, but it interests me, nevertheless. You stayed in your pew while everybody else went to the altar. It may have been a difficult thing to do, particularly at your age. The fear of what people may think –'

'I don't give a rap for what people think,' said Wilfred furiously.

'Oh, I beg your pardon. I'm afraid I've gone too far. We Slavs speak out of the fullness of our hearts. We are blind to more roundabout approaches. I'm sorry to have annoyed you. My visit was most indiscreet.'

'Oh no,' said Wilfred, calming down suddenly. 'It embarrasses me to talk about religion, that's all. I'm very grateful to you for having returned my book, believe me, and without wishing to I've caused you a long journey.'

'Let's call it a walk,' said the man rising.

He bowed slightly and his ceremonious air made him seem even more foreign in Wilfred's eyes. At the door, the man smiled and for the first time showed his faultless white teeth.

'Perhaps we'll meet again,' he said.

'Not at Saint Aloysius'. I scarcely ever go to that church.'

'Not at Saint Aloysiu's. Somewhere else. Here, for instance, if you'll allow me to pay you a short call.'

'I'm hardly ever at home,' said Wilfred, panic-stricken by such insistence. 'Today is an exception.'

'Oh, I won't impose on you,' replied the man as he opened the door himself.

On the landing, he bowed again and put on his hat. Caught unprepared, Wilfred closed the door and felt like opening it again to make some courteous remark, but he was afraid

111

of appearing ridiculous and, moreover, heard the door of
the lift slam.

CHAPTER XXIII

'Who is he?' he wondered, taking up his stand at the window.
The street remained empty for an instant, then the man appeared
on the opposite pavement, walking slowly, hugging the houses,
his yellow waterproof looking dirtier than ever in the dazzling
spring light. To wear a waterproof in such magnificent weather
was strange, but everything about the man was strange and
Wilfred had no desire to see him again. Next time, he would not
open the door. To begin with, he could not tolerate a stranger
talking to him about religion, particularly in such an indiscreet,
personal way. And besides he did not care for his rather obsequious politeness. Mentally he called him 'Mr Excuse me.'
  A little before eleven that evening, he wandered around the
Spanish restaurant. Not that he really desired the young
Señorita, he only wanted to see whether she had told him the
truth. If she was there at eleven and glanced about her, it would
be rather complimentary to him, even though he did not want
her. If, on the other hand, he found her as pretty as at luncheon
they might take a short walk together. That did not pin him
down to anything. Yet, at five minutes to eleven, a sudden
resolution made him turn on his heel and go to the park, where
he sat down on a bench. The appointment had come to nothing.
Perhaps the girl was waiting for him. She would not wait long.
Spanish women are so proud. So passionate too. Wilfred had
been told that their ardour surpassed all imagining. He recalled

112

her face, her slim little neck that could almost be spanned with one hand, her throat, her white skin. Alicia's skin had probably been like hers.

He got up. What a stupid day he had spent! In the park where every shadowy nook was alive with whispering and laughter, he could see the swaying outlines of lovers gliding by, holding each other by the waist. Suddenly he regretted not having waited at the restaurant door, but he was never quite sure of what he wanted. At present, he once more desired the Señorita, and he would never have her, that was certain. She must be furious, she would never have him now, even if he begged her on his bended knees, kneeling in the street. He was ready to go down on his knees before her, in the street. 'What a fool I am!' he said under his breath and began running through the park alleys until he reached the street that led to the restaurant. Perhaps he would not be too late, after all. When he reached the door, he found it closed and the electric sign above it was out. He swore. He seldom did, but this time he swore and stamped his foot. However, as he could never take a disappointment of that sort to heart, no sooner had he reached the end of the street than he was whistling, hands in his pockets.

On returning to his room, he went to bed, turned out the light and waited vainly for sleep. Too many things were gyrating in his brain, and after an hour and a half of this he got up, lit the light, opened the desk drawer and pushed aside the love letters. What he wanted was the letter with the black seal. It was thick and heavy, and he hesitated to open it. The funereal seal awed him. If Death itself had sealed that letter, she would not have gone about it differently: the black wax was Death's mark. He threw the envelope on the desk and looked at it in disgust, then felt ashamed of his cowardice. He remembered his uncle's words: 'Don't imagine that I'm giving you a fortune –' Suddenly, while Death was looking the other way, he tore open the envelope.

113

What he saw rather disappointed him. It contained not bank-notes, but securities that had to be negotiated, a dozen of them. Wilfred knew nothing about financial transactions and it seemed evident to him that these papers were of no interest to him if his uncle's gift did not figure in his will. People would wonder how they came to belong to him. If he took them to a bank, he would certainly be questioned or even made to sign a document. As it was, Mr Knight had already insinuated something unpleasant by asking him to open his suitcase.

In spite of this, he added up the sum represented by the securities. The total made him feel slightly dizzy for, unless he was mistaken, he would have had to work almost five years in the shop to earn the same amount. It still remained to prove that the money belonged to him. He preferred not to dwell on the subject, for his dread of disease was only equalled by his dread of difficulties with the law. Putting the securities back in their place, he double-locked the drawer and went back to bed.

CHAPTER XXIV

The next morning at nine o'clock, he stood in his usual place and stood there all day. He lay down all night and stood up all day. He used to repeat the phrase to himself at times and in his mind the sentence mournfully summed up his lot. Had it not been for the nights, he would not have accepted the days. 'What young man wouldn't say the same?' he used to ask himself. And he added in his heart: 'Let's avoid philosophizing.' But he did not care much for selling shirts and underwear in a store. It seemed to him that he should have had another job and a better one.

Although no prouder than most, it humiliated him to wait on strangers from morning to night. And what future was there in it all?

The store was situated in one of the broadest and smartest streets in town. Close by, a well-known hotel reared its huge bulk and a little further on, as soon as it grew dark, blazed the lights of a movie theatre patronised by what is called the gilded youth. Shops with showy windows added to the general air of prosperity and such poor folk as strayed that way must have been under the impression that the glow from all this wealth was reflected on them, for they smiled vaguely, as though they felt less poor.

From where he stood, Wilfred could see the sky above the house-tops and in fine weather this gave him fits of sadness.

There were twelve salesmen, not counting the shopwalker, and the counters resembled all counters the world over, but the carpet was peacock-blue and at certain times Wilfred played at imagining that it was water and that the counters were wrecks floating on its surface. He was given to absent-mindedness and often had to be nudged. Yet the shopwalker, who let nothing slip where the other salesmen were concerned, turned a blind eye to Wilfred's mistakes, for in general the young man did his work thoroughly and with obvious good will. Also, people bought more from him than from the others.

That morning, in one of the twenty mirrors that endlessly reflected more mirrors and multiplied counters, salesmen and shopwalkers, he noted that he did not look any less well than usual. That reassured him: nothing showed in his face. His life was what it was, but he kept his pink cheeks. A dyspeptic friend had once said to him: 'That won't last.' Wilfred knew it.

To him, Monday was not the depressing day it is for so many other people. According to Wilfred, the tragedy, the nightmare, was Sunday, but once that day was over six remained from which

115

he could reasonably expect enjoyment. And finally, except for a few moments of weariness, he was almost always in a good temper.

He thought of all the affairs that certainly awaited him. Each week brought him one or two, sometimes more. The complete series promised to be long and wonderful. The only thing was to guard against diseases, but then he was careful. It might last for years, years of women, years of nights, and if disappointments cropped up occasionally, they were compensated for by unexpected successes.

Last night, for instance, he had not had his Spanish girl and because of this it seemed to him that fate owed him something exceptional. Tonight, perhaps the Señorita would be replaced by an equally lovely girl. He let himself daydream over the still unknown girl: she might even be longing for him unconsciously.

As a matter of fact, he thought of nothing else the livelong day but 'that', as he called it mentally. He thought about it even when his mind was busy elsewhere. Yesterday, the foreigner who had come to his room had upset everything by his indiscreet words on the forbidden subject. You did not talk about religion; religion was the core of your being, its secret. Only a foreigner would attempt to talk about certain things – only a Slav, since the man was a Slav. Wilfred gave a sigh. Anyway, he no longer had to wrestle with those complicated problems, it was Monday and on Monday he was free, rid of things. 'Rid' was the right word, but rid of what? That was simple enough: rid of Sunday.

Women scarcely ever came to the department where Wilfred worked except with their sons or husbands. That morning, however, he saw a lady coming toward him and she was alone. She wished to be shown shirts for a boy of fifteen. He brought out all sorts at all prices and strewed the counter with articles that she stared at in perplexity. Nothing appeared to suit her. She avoided looking at Wilfred, but he noticed that her lower

116

lip was trembling slightly and she told him finally that she would come back with her son. 'He's not feeling well today,' she explained. When she had gone, Wilfred remembered having seen her a few weeks before, accompanied by a sickly-looking boy, but once he had replaced the shirts in their boxes he thought no more about it.

The store was never very crowded on Mondays and he had plenty of time to dream about 'that'. Once or twice he also remembered the securities. It worried him a little to keep them in his room and he wondered whose advice he could ask concerning what to do with them. The idea of speaking to the shopwalker about it crossed his mind. The man was reliable and his liking for Wilfred was unquestionable. Of course he would have to make him think that the securities belonged to a friend, and this bothered Wilfred because he was a very bad liar.

CHAPTER XXV

The evening mail brought a note from Mrs Knight, a few lines in a delicate, precise hand, informing him that Uncle Horace's funeral would take place two days later. 'We're counting on you to come,' she added.

His first impulse was to answer that he could not attend the ceremony on account of his work, but the excuse was worthless and, on second thoughts, Wilfred felt interested in seeing Mrs Knight again, even under such unpleasant circumstances. He might also have the opportunity of exchanging a few words with Angus.

The management made no difficulties whatever and on the

following Wednesday he found himself in the wooden chapel where Mass was being celebrated. Mrs Knight was there with her husband and Angus with his mother. Self-consciousness caused Wilfred to sit at some distance from them, for he was certain that they were watching him. Apart from Mrs Knight, who knelt throughout the service, the others stood in an attitude that could be interpreted, according to fancy, as one of respect, indifference or a kind of defiance; the last conjecture was probably right where Mr Knight was concerned, for he stared disapprovingly at the altar.

It was a humble chapel, decorated with the Stations of the Cross and statues of saints whose gaudy colours Wilfred considered unfortunate. As a matter of fact he was ashamed of the setting, seeing it as he did for the first time through the eyes of people to whom the word idolatry must have constantly occurred. For this reason and for many others, he felt ill at ease. Mass seemed long to him, though in fact it was very brief, and he was obliged to own that he could not pray, even half-heartedly. He simply bent his head but looked out of the corner of his eye at Angus, whose admirably cut black suit made his handsome face and perfect features seem paler than ever.

The ceremony over, everyone left the chapel for the cemetery, and a difficulty arose: as Wilfred had no car, he was obliged to get into either Mr Knight's or his cousin's and he hesitated awkwardly. His eyes met Mrs Knight's and she smiled at him. She sat by her husband, who stared distantly just over Wilfred's head. At that moment a hand took him by the arm and he allowed his cousin to lead him to the car where Mrs Howard was already seated.

To his own amazement, Wilfred began laughing without knowing why, but no one asked for an explanation and he stopped suddenly, blushing with shame. Beside him, Angus kept his long, narrow hands on the wheel and Wilfred could not

118

help looking at them. Mrs Howard talked indefatigably from the back seat, as though to compensate for the silence she had been forced to keep in the chapel. Actually, she was talking to herself. Neither Wilfred nor Angus opened his lips and the latter kept his eyes on the dreadful hearse ahead of them.

As Uncle Horace was lowered into his grave, Wilfred thought of Alicia and her little love letters hidden in the drawer whose key he kept in his pocket. Suddenly, faced with that hole in the ground, he felt moved and a little dizzy. Angus stood by him and instinctively he touched his cousin's hand, but the hand remained unresponsive and Wilfred pulled himself together immediately.

It was decided that Angus and his mother would drive him back to town as they could pass through it without going too much out of their way. And, in any case, Mrs Howard was not sorry to be able to tell Wilfred certain things that were weighing on her mind.

He said good-bye to Mr and Mrs Knight at the cemetery gate. The former merely bared his teeth in a grin as he got into his car, but his wife behaved differently, for as her husband settled into his seat she brought her face close to Wilfred – that charming face he sometimes dreamt of – and he heard her whisper in his ear: 'Brother and sister, Wilfred!'

Surprise prevented his answering Phoebe, but he pressed his cheek against hers and they parted.

Seated once more by Angus, with Mrs Knight's sentence still ringing in his ears, he began thinking about the little creature; she was so pretty, so serious and so gauche. He would have liked to crush her body to his and for that reason did not listen to Mrs Howard's soliloquy for several minutes. Yet her speech was addressed to him and a few sentences finally reached him:

'You must understand that I'm not criticising you, but with us things are simpler – none of that muttering in Latin, nor the priest going to and fro before the altar, nor that little bell, nor

119

those painted statues. For us a few verses from the Bible are enough –'

Wilfred could see by merely glancing at his cousin that the latter was not listening very closely. From the roots of his hair to his neck, Angus's profile stood out against the sky, clear as a stroke of the pen. Wilfred felt unaccountably embarrassed. 'There isn't a woman,' he said to himself, 'who wouldn't be happy to have such a well-shaped nose, such a white skin, such small ears.' But it annoyed his cousin to be watched, no doubt, for he frowned slightly and Wilfred turned his eyes away.

'But of course,' continued Mrs Howard, 'when one has a faith like yours, one keeps it. If I mention this, it's on account of poor Horace who squandered a fortune on having a good time when he might have invested all that money for his heirs' benefit. As for the money, women devoured it long ago. And what women! Where is he now? I'm thinking of your uncle. Be that as it may, he has now been judged, believer or not.'

'He was a believer,' said Angus suddenly.

'Oh, you'd always find an excuse for him, because you're good,' replied Mrs Howard.

'No, but what you say might disturb Wilfred, whose way of thinking is not yours.'

'I can assure you that you're not upsetting me,' stammered Wilfred.

'Mamma,' said Angus, his eye on the road, 'please let's talk of something else.'

'Angus, you're an angel,' said Mrs Howard, with a well-bred display of feeling. 'My son is an angel,' she went on, turning to Wilfred.

Angus's cheeks grew pink and he gave his cousin a furtive glance as though begging him to be lenient. He was visibly ashamed of his mother's chatter, which continued to the outskirts of town where the noise of cars fortunately prevented

120

its being heard. Ten minutes later the car stopped before the house where Wilfred lived. Mrs Howard leaned out slightly to look at it.

'What floor are you on?' she asked.

'The fifth, on the street side.'

'Good,' she said condescendingly. 'Perhaps we'll meet again, one of these days.'

Wilfred thanked her and said good-bye. Then he turned to Angus. He would have liked to say something to excuse the heartlessness he had shown a few days before, but nothing came to his mind, or rather two or three sentences occurred to him, but they seemed so clumsy and tactless that he would not voice them. He shyly touched one of the hands that seemed riveted to the wheel. Then Angus turned an agonized face to him and whispered a few words that Wilfred could not catch because Mrs Howard had begun talking again. So, jumping out of the car, he slammed the door and went into the house.

CHAPTER XXVI

Later that day the store was filled with customers, which prevented him from thinking over the morning's events, but on returning to his room a fit of melancholy overwhelmed him for almost an hour. No doubt, that yawning grave had something to do with it, but, more than that, the sadness he had seen in Angus's face and, in a strange fashion, Mrs Knight's whispered sentence blended in with the rest, like a stifled cry of despair.

Throwing himself on the bed, he clasped his hands behind his neck and gazed at the crucifix with a feeling of weariness. During

121

the last few days he had begun to realize that this object disturbed him as though it were reproaching him for his way of living. On the other hand, Wilfred did not in the least repent of his sins: on the contrary, he was sure of committing others of the same kind, a great many more. That had nothing to do with faith. But why keep arguing with himself over questions that had no solution?

Fifteen minutes later, he got up and with the greatest respect imaginable gently removed the cross from the wall and shut it up in an empty drawer. It was quickly done and less difficult than he would have believed. Now he felt freer, less of a hypocrite and also more at ease to let his thoughts drift toward dissipation: he would have a rest that night but tomorrow have a look around the lower part of town. You always found what you wanted there.

It grew dark. By having supper early at a neighbouring drugstore, he could go to the movies afterwards to see a much-talked of film. He washed his face and hands, changed shirt and tie, after which, putting on a hat before the bathroom mirror, he opened the door.

On the landing stood the man in the waterproof.

'Excuse me,' he said simply.

'You!' cried Wilfred. 'It's simply not possible!'

'Yes, it is.'

His black eyes implored a word of welcome, but Wilfred was already beside himself with impatience. This bore was going to ruin his evening!

'May I come in?' asked the man.

'I'm going out, as you see.'

Then the man's eyes watered. Wilfred discovered later that he could cry at will, but at that moment his tears were rather disturbing; they ran slowly down his face.

'What's the matter with you?' asked Wilfred.

122

'Let me come in. I'll tell you. I'm only asking you for three minutes.'

He raised three fingers, like a bargaining pedlar, thought Wilfred. The man's expression was not quite the same as the first time they had met.

'Let me come in,' he repeated with a beggar's obstinacy. 'Be kind, be –'

'If he says: "Be Christian",' thought Wilfred, 'I'll kick him down the stairs and into the street.' But the man seemed to know instinctively what not to say. He paused.

'Be what?' inquired Wilfred angrily.

'Understanding.'

He ran a long bony hand over his cheek to wipe away the tears and looked at Wilfred.

'Only three minutes, you know,' said the latter, moving aside to let him in.

The man stole into the room. His eyes travelled at once to the wall above the bed, then to Wilfred, questioning him mutely. There was a short silence.

'Well?' returned the young man, one hand on his hip and his hat pushed back. His eyes blazed.

'May I sit down?'

'It's barely worth while, just for three minutes.'

'I'm very tired. Excuse me.'

Wilfred shrugged his shoulders and the man sat down on a chair in the middle of the room.

'There's been a frightful row at the office,' he said in a hollow voice. 'Maybe I'm not using quite the right term when I say office, but I don't know you well enough yet to explain. There would be so many things to explain.'

'I don't care to know. I've already told you that I am in a hurry.'

'Rest assured I have not forgotten. Everything went so badly

123

today. When everything goes very badly I think about you and about last Sunday. I threatened to leave. Won't you close the door? I really can't talk with the door open. Excuse me.'

Wilfred shut the door, keeping his eye on the man.

'Are the police after you?' he asked with a sneer.

The man raised his eyebrows.

'The police? Why no. All my papers are in order. Why do you ask? On account of the door?'

'I was joking,' replied Wilfred, a little ashamed at seeing the anxiety in the other's face.

'Oh, if you were only joking, that's fine. I like things that are said in fun, particularly when you say them. With other people, it's sometimes another matter. The police! Ha! ha!'

He laughed.

'Will you tell me why you came here?' demanded Wilfred.

'With pleasure, although it's a little difficult if you're in a hurry. I need lots of words to express myself, but I'll try to be brief. First, may I ask you a question? An object once hung from a nail above your bed – Oh, don't be impatient! Look, I'll take my question back and merely note that the object is no longer there. I understand, I understand perfectly. I understand everything. Everything can be vindicated, explained, justified. Now, you see, there's a connexion between the disappearance of the object and last Sunday.'

'I don't understand a word you're saying,' answered Wilfred, thrusting his hands in his pockets, 'but I have to go out and you're going out first.'

He nodded at the door.

'Naturally,' said the man without moving. 'First allow me to explain. The same reason that prevented you from going to Communion on Sunday made you remove the object from the wall. In both cases, I see a mark of respect, of self-effacement – well, of something more religious than certain gestures that

124

we make without believing in them. Excuse me, but you seem angry.'

'I've told you that I don't want to talk about religion,' cried Wilfred, his cheeks bright pink with rage.

The man looked attentively at him, as though he were following a play.

'I'm sorry,' he said. 'I like you so much, too much, perhaps, and there's no one else I can talk to about religion. My family do not believe. They go to church but are bored by religion and, at bottom, don't believe in it.'

'That's not my business.'

'Yes and no. You'll see in a moment. I have terrible worries. Among others, the fact that I am lost. I wanted to tell someone that.'

He paused to observe the effect of his words. Wilfred half-opened his mouth, then, after an instant, whispered:

'I don't understand.'

'Well, I go to Communion almost every Sunday. Well, all my Communions have been sacrilegious for years.'

There was a silence during which they looked at each other. Finally Wilfred stammered:

'You ought to tell things like that to a priest, not to me.'

'I can't talk to priests. I have nothing against them, but I can't talk to them. I can to you. It's strange, but that's the way it is. I don't know you and I can tell you what I've never told anybody, particularly a priest.'

He was silent once more. Wilfred took his hands from his pockets and sat on the edge of the bed.

'Doesn't it frighten you?' he asked finally.

'Frighten me?'

'Why, yes. Sacrilege –'

'I would have to have really solid faith for that, a faith like yours. I'm sometimes frightened.'

'But if you don't believe –'

'I never said I didn't believe,' said the man quickly. 'Nothing is simple, you know. There is room for twilight between complete darkness and broad daylight. At certain times I can't imagine that all that is true. Particularly that. You know what I mean – the host. At other times it seems to me as obviously true as the sun in the sky. At Communion, for instance, when I stand in the crowd, waiting for my turn to kneel, and see the priest going from one to the other with the host, I believe.'

'But then, how can you –'

'Oh, there are days when I leave without communicating. It's rather easy when a lot of people go up to the Communion table. No one notices, in a crowd. I'm going to tell you something that may perhaps shock you: I feel pity for God. You can't quite understand that, but when I see Him delivered up to just anyone, to me, completely defenceless, exactly as it was on Calvary, delivered up to the devil, then yes, indeed, I feel frightened and at the same time I have pity for Him. All this seems horrible to you, doesn't it?'

'Yes, horrible.'

'It does to me too and hurts me, but not always. It hurts me when I believe in a certain way, when I see the host or when I'm next to someone who has faith, like you. And yet I need that pain. I need Him, you understand, and that pain is what most resembles a happiness that I have never known.'

Wilfred got up.

'I would go to a priest, if I were you,' he said.

'I can't. It's a bewildering state of things: priests make me feel tongue-tied. You're not a saint, but I can talk to you.'

'I certainly am not a saint,' said Wilfred firmly, 'and I'm afraid you're completely mistaken about me. My life doesn't correspond in the least to what I believe, to my faith, in fact.'

The man raised his head and looked at him.

126

'So you imagine that I don't know it,' he asked gently. 'Others might be taken in, but not I. You haven't any idea of who I am, or what my occupation may be. I haven't been to college, but it does not take me two minutes to find out who I'm dealing with. That is probably more useful than trigonometry or literature.'

Wilfred felt himself blush and turned towards the window.

'I don't see how there could ever have been a beginning to your nasty story,' he said harshly.

'The beginning was the stupid part. A schoolboy business. We were made to go to confession every fortnight. Two of the boys had committed an offence for which they could be expelled. One of them confessed the whole thing to the priest but refused to betray his accomplice's name. I was the accomplice. I went to confession and I lied. The next day, I went to Communion with the others. I thought I would faint, for I had faith exactly as you have it now. I expected to die on the spot or to be struck down one way or the other. But nothing happened. Nothing at all happens at the time. You communicate, apparently like the others. This amazed me. I felt anxious for a few days, then I saw that nothing had changed, that nothing was different –'

'I'd rather you stopped talking to me about this,' said Wilfred.

'I've finished. I've said everything. I went on going to confession and Communion, since a point was made of it, but the whole thing was sacrilegious. You get used to it very quickly at fifteen, you know. Real uneasiness comes later, I don't know how. Perhaps from repeatedly seeing the face of those who really believe, when they come back from Communion, particularly old people. Some of them – it's not a question of radiance. There's no light, you know, but it is as though there were a light that you can't see.'

He rose.

'That's all,' he said. 'I'm going.'

127

Wilfred yielded to a sudden impulse.

'You must not communicate sacrilegiously again,' he said, standing before the door. 'If you continue that way, you'll be lost.'

'I am lost,' answered the man softly.

'That you don't know. What's your name? You've never told me.'

'What's that to you? Do you want to see me again?'

'Perhaps.'

'That may not be a very good idea. I mean that you've seen me today in a good mood, but I'm not always as I am now. My real name is hard to pronounce, so I'm called Max. Call me Max.'

'Max who?'

'Max is enough. You just have to ask for Max.'

He hesitated and added finally:

'Sherman Avenue. Number two thirteen and a half.'

'Two thirteen and a half?'

'Yes, it's one of those weird numbers to be seen in that part of town. I must tell you I don't live there. That isn't where I sleep, but you can find me there – almost always.'

'Is it your office?'

'Yes,' he said laughing, 'my office. That's what I call it, but you had better wait until I come back to see you in one of my good moods. To begin with, Sherman Avenue is the devil knows how far away, Wilfred.'

The name was spoken furtively, as a contraband article might be slipped between a couple of handkerchiefs. Wilfred blushed. He felt as though the man had touched him, and instinctively shrank back a little.

Max gave him a nod and left.

128

CHAPTER XXVII

Alone once more, Wilfred first laid his hand on his brow and discovered that drops of perspiration were beaded on the roots of his hair, then he went to the window and waited, as he had after the last visit. His heart was beating faster than usual. Why didn't the man appear in the street? Barely two minutes sufficed to leave the house and over two minutes had gone by now. Wilfred counted up to a hundred and leaned out.

On the pavement below, the man was also waiting, his head thrown back. He smiled broadly when he saw Wilfred and, touching the brim of his hat with one finger, walked off.

Wilfred darted back inside the room, furious at having been seen. Who was the man? What could it all mean – his smile, his odd manners, the whole visit and those crazy, extravagant secrets? Had Max told him all those things to shock him or to make fun of him? What an ass he had been to answer him, advise him to see a priest, talk to him about his salvation! It was really going rather far to urge someone to think about his salvation when he himself thought of nothing but women.

Shame sent the blood rushing to his face and, furious with himself, he began kicking one of the two chairs from one end of the room to the other, then he sat down on his bed. Gradually he grew calmer. Never again would he see that man Max, since he was called Max, although Wilfred preferred to call him Mr Excuse me. These ceremonious foreigners were a trifle ridiculous. What right had this one to come and talk about his faith to someone he did not know? Wilfred regretted having

129

asked him for his address. He had done so without quite knowing why, perhaps to show some interest, out of pity. But he still felt ashamed of having heard himself say: 'You should see a priest –' That pious, edifying piece of advice! And the man had replied: 'I haven't your faith – I don't believe as you do –' Oh, disgusting, disgusting!

After a while, he went to look at himself in the bathroom mirror and saw that he was quite pink, with shining eyes. Comb in hand he smoothed the locks of hair that battled round his brow and watched himself with a hostile air. The word 'hypocrite' occurred to him several times and he ended by saying it aloud in the silence of the little room.

'Hypocrite!' he repeated as he put down the comb.

He moved suddenly and spat upon the mirror.

Twenty minutes later, he walked into one of the big popular restaurants that the city boasted by dozens, where a plain but ample meal could be obtained at a modest price.

There were a great many people in the downstairs room, but on the other hand several tables were vacant on the floor above which formed a vast balcony less well lighted and a little less noisy; this projecting gallery afforded a view of the customers below. As Wilfred knew the menu by heart, he ordered the simplest dishes and looked around him. The confused hum of conversation, the clatter of crockery, the clashing of knives and forks being heaped by waiters into steel baskets, all this animation pleased him because it drew his attention away from himself. Through the great net curtains he watched the crowd in the large avenue with interest. What a lot of people and for each of these anonymous persons what a lot of problems – different from his no doubt – and what violent emotions and expectations! There must be some charming faces there, and possible intrigues. He faintly regretted not being outdoors, all the more since he had not noticed a single pretty woman in

130

the restaurant. 'If there were one, I'd have spotted her right away,' he thought. 'I have the eye of a hawk.'

His bowl of soup swallowed, he was crumbling a salt biscuit when he saw a young man coming up to him, one whose company he avoided as much as he could because they had been school-mates and Tommy – for that was his name – continued to believe him as pious as he was himself. He unconsciously exasperated Wilfred and yet the latter could not help feeling an affection for him which almost always led to telling him a little more than he intended. He was a tall boy, blond as a moth, with a pale but rather handsome face and grey eyes so limpid as to sometimes be embarrassing. His hands were delicate, better shaped than Wilfred's and narrower, less sensual. He worked in a Catholic bookshop a few steps from the big Franciscan church where Wilfred usually heard Mass.

'Are you by yourself? I'll have supper with you,' said Tommy, sitting down at the table. 'How are you?'

Wilfred felt that the young man had noticed the rings around his eyes.

'I'm tired,' he said. 'I've been worried. My uncle has died.'

'I know it. I saw the notice in the paper and was going to write you. Was he a believer?'

'Oh, I suppose so, Tommy. Anyway, he died properly. What about you? Anything new?'

'Nothing. When I've finished work I'm too tired to go out, but I can't complain. Interesting people come to the shop.'

'Laymen and priests –'

'Of course.'

'And lots of nuns, I imagine.'

'Yes,' said Tommy smiling. 'They are the most finicky cus-tomers of all. They come in with a square of paper and have to have exactly what's on their list. Laymen are much easier to direct. To begin with, they generally don't know what they want.

131

I suppose you see quite a different sort of people in your store.'

He paused to give his order: a sandwich, a large glass of milk and a slice of cake.

'It must be very strange,' he continued. 'You never know whom you're dealing with.'

'What do you mean?'

'Just an idea that came into my mind. At our place, we're pretty sure that the people who come in are Catholics.'

The artlessness of this remark annoyed Wilfred and yet he felt touched by Tommy's candour.

'All Catholics aren't interesting.'

'Of course, but –'

'And then, it's not a bad thing to see all kinds, as I do.'

'You don't think it's a little –'

'A little what?'

'I don't know,' said Tommy in sudden embarrassment. 'It would bother me, I imagine. People who come in to buy the very finest ties and shirts – Well, it's a little frivolous.'

'They don't think it the least bit frivolous, I can tell you. Everybody can't have a nunnish turn of mind.'

Tommy sat open-mouthed. The last sentence astonished him, as it had astonished Wilfred, who tried to cover it up.

'What I mean,' he said with a smile, 'is that for most rich people these unimportant trifles count enormously. I'm not saying they're right.'

'It's because they don't know,' said Tommy gravely.

'That's so.'

What was it exactly that they did not know? That the kingdom of God is not of this world? That was probably what Tommy meant. 'Although he's twenty-four,' thought Wilfred, 'he's a virgin, like so many of our boys, even in big cities. He'll see things with a different eye when he has slept with a woman.'

132

'If I were rich,' said Tommy, 'I wouldn't change a thing in my way of living.'

'Would you like to be rich?'

'I don't care one way or the other. I'm very happy. I don't need anything.'

'No temperament,' said Wilfred to himself, 'and consequently no problems. Now I need a pretty woman. And I need her right now.' It crossed his mind to say all this aloud but he did not quite dare.

'Are you going to get married some day, Tommy?'

Tommy burst out laughing and turned crimson.

'I don't know. I've never thought about it.'

'Yet you must know some girls.'

'Sure.'

'Some of them must be pretty.'

'To be pretty wouldn't be enough. I'd have to marry one that thinks as I do.'

'A Catholic?'

'Naturally.'

'The fact is, you can see perfectly lovely girls in church. Well, have I said anything extraordinary? You are looking at me as though I were the devil. There's nothing wrong about falling in love with a charming young creature and marrying her. It's been done before.'

In a flash, he imagined Tommy's marriage and the tragicomedy of his wedding night. As though he read his mind, the young man turned his childlike eyes on Wilfred.

'I don't want to,' he said.

'The works of the flesh don't appeal to you?'

'No, not in the least. If you don't mind, I'd rather talk of something else.'

'You see evil where it doesn't exist,' said Wilfred gently, 'and that's because you don't know the facts of life. You

133

spend your time in that pious bookshop of yours –'

'Oh, I'm less ignorant than you think. I've obtained permission to read a book on that very subject. It happens to be a work we always keep in stock.'

'With the *imprimatur*?'

'In our bookshop all books have the *imprimatur*. The one I'm telling you about was written by a very serious author. It's intended for young married couples,' he added, hanging his head a little.

'Is it illustrated?'

'No. I don't see the necessity for illustrations. Everything is clearly explained. Why do you ask if it's illustrated, Wilfred? It seems to me you've changed.'

'We keep changing all the time, you, me, everybody.'

'I don't know if you remember that when we were thurifers at Saint Andrew's, we wanted to become priests.'

'That's an altar-boy's dream.'

'It's not a dream. Perhaps it was God calling.'

'Even if it was God calling, we were free to respond or not. Tommy, I'd rather tell you that I'm not in the least the man you take me for. I have a good time with women and I have it often. I go from one to the other because I'm not in love with any of them. What I love is their bodies.'

Tommy stared at him, his eyes big with fright, and Wilfred paused. In the surrounding noise, they sat in a zone of silence no larger than their table. Wilfred's heart thumped. He felt both happy and appalled, like a man who has leapt over his prison walls at the risk of death.

'You don't know what physical pleasure is,' he continued. 'You're cold. The boys at school committed impurities, but not you. You've never known what it was to fight the sexual instinct; you could coddle your soul and think yourself a saint because your body never rebelled. Now, I have a body and I'm

134

not a saint. I know what that calling is, the one you talked about just now. The voice. I've heard it, and silenced it. I want it to keep quiet. I want to make love till it keeps quiet, because it disturbs and scares me. I admit it scares me. You may think me absurd telling you such things in a restaurant where women are talking about their shopping and men about their business and petty intrigues, but I didn't choose the time. It happened just like that. I didn't know I'd meet you. I'm a beast, Tommy. Tonight, in two or three hours with luck, while you're saying you're prayers, I'll be in some woman's bed, a woman whose name I don't even know yet, because I've never seen her, but I'll find her, I'll find her! Would you like me to go into details? Would you like me to tell you all about it? Maybe your book for young married people doesn't mention everything –'

'Stop!' begged Tommy.

'Why should I? You've got to know. You can tell the others I'm lost. Do you hear? I'm telling you this quite calmly, as you see. I hate theatrical attitudes. It was you who wanted to talk about religion –'

He stopped suddenly, breathless. Having talked too fast without quite knowing what he wanted to say, he had ended by repeating things that Max had said a few hours earlier. Tommy pushed away his untouched dessert and picked up the bill from the table.

'I'm going,' he said. 'I think some day you'll go back on what you've said and recover your faith.'

'I have not lost my faith.'

'Then I don't understand.'

'I know. I don't understand either. I'm sorry to have shocked you, but I don't want to act like a hypocrite.'

Tommy allowed a few seconds to go by, then said:

'We could see each other again, if you like. I know a priest –'

135

'Oh no, thank you. Things are muddled enough as they are without a priest taking a hand in them.'

Tommy hesitated, then got up and smiled. With a wave of the hand, Wilfred made a sign that he wished to be alone, but he watched him move away and an instant later saw his tall, loose-limbed silhouette making its way between the tables on the ground floor. When he reached the desk, Tommy pulled his wallet out of his pocket and opened it with a careful, old-maidish gesture. 'He's going to pray for me tonight, that's certain,' thought Wilfred, 'but it won't prevent anything happening.'

Anything, that is the delightful affairs that were awaiting him all through his youth, or what was left of it, and yet, when he went out and found himself once more in the avenue, his spirit rebelled in him and against life in general. It would have been hard for him to explain why, but the feeling was so strong and disturbed him so deeply that he felt dizzy. He would gladly have fought someone, anyone, to be rid of this excess of anger.

He decided to wander at random around Sherman Avenue, just to look about, and if he met Max he would tease him a bit and it might end in fisticuffs. That was a good way to relieve oneself. So a tram took him to Sherman Avenue. It was not far from the Polish church, in a quarter inhabited chiefly by Slavs and a handful of Finns. Not a tree to be seen along the long thoroughfare bordered by brick houses and shops; some of them squalidly poor and others next door with flashy displays in their windows. Number two thirteen and a half stood to the left of a cobbler's shop where a mountain of worn shoes could be vaguely distinguished through a dirty glass pane, while on its right, a 'Five and Ten' offered the passers-by toilet requisites, toys, and in one corner a mound of soft toffees.

Wilfred raised his head and looked at the house. It was narrow, black and five storeys high. Among all the others, a

136

single window on the third floor showed a pale yellow rectangle of light in the surrounding darkness.

The avenue was almost empty at that time of night. He stuck his hands in his pockets, irresolute. A few minutes went by, then he whistled. There was no reply.

'Hey, Max!' he called.

A man and a young woman walked slowly by him as he paced up and down the sidewalk. The woman's small face was arrogantly ugly, yet attractive all the same, thought Wilfred. As they went by, the great hulking fellow leaned over her; she probably exhausted him. When they had gone past, Wilfred was about to call Max again and looked up.

Someone was standing in the window, a stocky broad silhouette, a bald skull, a short neck belonging to a round-shouldered vigorous old man. He watched Wilfred for an instant, then his voice reached the young man, tinged with suspicion but quiet:

'Max is out.'

'When will he be back?'

'I don't know.'

'Is he here as a rule?'

'Sometimes.'

'When?'

'I don't know.'

'Where does he live?'

'I don't know.'

Wilfred suddenly felt irritated and, as he searched his mind for something to say, the old man asked:

'Who are you?'

'I don't know!' cried Wilfred.

The man gave a jeering laugh and, turning towards the interior of the room, rapped out a few words in a foreign tongue.

137

CHAPTER XXVIII

On reaching home, he found a letter from Angus in his mail-box. It was written on beautiful paper that Wilfred admired a little grudgingly, and without troubling to remove his hat he sat on his bed and began to read:

'*Dear Wilfred,*

'*I'm not quite sure what I'm going to say in this letter. Anyway it will surprise you, I think, because I feel I'll be led to admit what would best be kept to myself, no doubt.*

'*It is late. My mother is asleep. The house is steeped in silence and the air from the open window smells of trees and wet earth. It has just rained and great drops pelted noisily over the leaves of the sycamores; the darkness is less oppressive now. If you were here, I could talk to you more easily than I can write, but you'll never come here.*

'*I received your letter. I have it here before me and could reel it off to you by heart. It doesn't say much, but what counts is that you wrote it and so, at least, you made a gesture that blots out the other. Do you remember what happened on the road when I left you at Wormsloe? I believe it would have been better if you had struck me in the face, but you couldn't act otherwise than you did: you're the kind that stands aside from evil – or what you call evil.*'

At that point, Wilfred laid the letter on his knee and pushed his hat back. 'That cousin of mine is awfully simple,' he thought. After two or three seconds, he went on reading:

'*I don't feel very happy at present. It's not your fault, but you shouldn't have touched my hand in the car on the way back to town after the funeral. No matter how safe you are from physical passions, you must have noticed the power you unintentionally exercise over others. It is hard to remain indifferent to your looks. That is what I didn't want to say and what I am saying nevertheless. I am three years older than you. Wisdom and the most elementary self-respect should oblige me to be silent, but why should I, since I am never going to see you again? This letter makes it impossible.*

'*That is exactly why I am writing to you: we must not meet again. I don't share your views on religion but wonder sadly that you can be so faithful to them, and I would never do anything to turn you away from your beliefs. As regards my inclinations, don't judge me hastily, don't judge me at all. Leave that to the One in whom you trust. Perhaps He will forgive us all. Man's judgement has never disturbed me much, for I know what it is worth. Yours would be the only one that could wound me, because you are chaste.*'

' "Chaste"!' cried Wilfred.

The letter told him nothing that he had not guessed long before, but it harrowed him. It crossed his mind that Angus might be laying a trap for him, was begging for a protest, an admission. But if Angus was sincere, he was mistaken, to say the least: he was prostrating himself before someone who existed only in his imagination. Wilfred went on with the letter:

'*Things would be no better if I told you about my feelings, but it pains me to write a letter that will drive you away from me for ever. It's a sort of ending, a death that I must accept. I think that my grief will abate, with the help of time, because I wish it to. I have a great many weaknesses but I am not really a pleasure-loving person and there are days when my loathing for the flesh equals yours. This comes, I suppose, from our common heredity. You are a little what I would have liked to have been myself. It may surprise you to hear that when I was very young I had yearnings toward some vague ideal. I longed passionately for perfection, not to be subjected to passions, and I believed, I believed in God. The discovery of*

*pleasure did away with all that. Personal sanctity is perhaps not
an idle dream, but it seems inaccessible to natures like mine. I am
probably too sensitive to physical beauty, whereas you are neither
like me, nor like the mass of men. The small amount of respect
I still have for myself would disappear if I tried to make you love
me. And then, there would be something monstrous –'*

The letter dropped on the carpet as Wilfred got up and went
to the open window, where he leaned on his elbows. Wafted
in by the fresh, clear night air, the noise of the city reached him
like an animal growling in the distance. He wondered what all
this meant. The letter was really amazing. It forced him to face
himself. His cousin could have had no idea of what he was doing,
writing such things. All of a sudden, Wilfred pitied him deeply.

'Poor fellow!' he murmured.

Then with secret satisfaction he added in an even lower tone:
'Anyway, I'm not like him.'

At that moment, an inner voice asked: 'What makes you so
sure that he isn't better than you?'

Deeply ashamed, he picked up the letter and sat on a chair
in the middle of the room to finish it.

*'– something monstrous about it, on account of the ideas you
have, I feel sure, about attachments of this kind. Yet I could have
helped you. I don't think you know yourself any too well, because
you are frightened of yourself, like so many very pious young men.
What's more, your present situation is not at all the sort you
deserve: you lead a mean, uninteresting life. I could have improved
a good many things for you, but you probably scorn happiness.
Rest assured however that I will always be there to help you, if
necessary. The one favour I ask of you is that you never attempt
to see me again. You can write, if you have to.'*

There followed a few words that had been crossed out and
that Wilfred was unable to decipher, then the signature. As
he folded the letter to place it in his wallet, the idea came to

140

him that this was the first love letter he had ever received and for a whole hour he could think of nothing else.

In the bathroom, where he went to run a comb through his hair, he attempted to see his face as Angus saw it. What was so special about his features? Try as he might, he could not see himself as good-looking. A woman had once said to him: 'You're irresistible and I wonder why.' A great sigh escaped him, then he suddenly burst out laughing.

'What a fool!' he cried.

CHAPTER XXIX

Leaving the house, he walked towards the park that skirted the quarter where he lived. He needed to stroll under trees and to think everything over. How could anyone, in the middle of the present century, imagine that a young man of his age could have stayed chaste? What was going on in his cousin's mind? Was he, by any chance, making fun of him? He would soon receive an answer to that letter of his –

The darkness smelt of the first summer dust and couples were strolling down the long avenue, between two rows of elms and maples. The lighting was subdued but distinct enough to make any flagrant misconduct difficult. There was a tender dreaminess in the air and Wilfred felt its effects although he suffered in his pride from being subjected to these relentless laws. Everywhere on the surface of the globe, millions of men experienced, as he did, the gnawing of this animal hunger, a persistent, humiliating hunger, yes, humiliating because one always yielded to it. So Angus imagined or pretended to believe that his less fortunate

141

cousin was a steady, decent young man and pious into the bargain. Chaste –

'Really, what a fool he is! he cried out in sudden anger.

A doubtful-looking and solitary passer-by turned and came in his direction with an indefinable air of concern. Wilfred turned back towards one of the park wickets.

How should he answer his cousin – for he had to answer – and what kind of letter was he to write? An indignant letter would be ridiculous. To begin with, he felt no indignation whatever and, besides, who was he to pose as a champion of virtue? Should he tell the truth, then, his truth?

He sat down on a bench. The truth could not be told. At all events, he, Wilfred Ingram, could not tell it. Angus had told it, in spite of everything, with an honesty and pluck that Wilfred lacked totally. 'I'd be brave enough to fight, but I'm not brave enough to speak the truth,' he thought. Yet, only a moment ago he had told it to Tommy; but Tommy did not count for much in his eyes, whereas he did not wish to go down in Angus's estimation.

Why? He rose and went home through little empty streets where you might have thought yourself miles away from the great city, for low-roofed houses dating from over a century before lent the quarter an old-fashioned, trim appearance. Each house had a flight of small white steps that contrasted sharply with its brown stone front, and behind every front lay a riddle: love, cupidity, vice, ambition.

'My face is also a front,' he said to himself. He wanted to be loved and that was why the letter hurt him so deeply. He was loved with a love to which he could not respond. And for this reason he did not wish to tell his cousin the truth. Far better, to his mind, that Angus should believe his nonsense and keep his love. Now he was certain that the letter was no trap. It was sincere. It was too compromising, to begin with, not to be sincere.

Once home, he felt a great weight of fatigue on his shoulders. The whole business made him ill. He took a bath and in the tepid water thought over the answer he wished to make. As he looked at his arms, legs, the whole of his white body, he tried to imagine the suffering it could bring to his cousin's heart, and as he drifted into a day-dream a thought floated up from his childhood with all the mystery and dread that attended it: 'Your body is the temple of the Holy Ghost.' He believed it, but not with his flesh; he believed, but his body did not.

It was an effort to tear himself away from the thoughts going through his mind, and to leave a bath-tub where the water was gradually turning cold. After drying himself, he put on a dressing-gown and sat at the table to write the following letter:

'*Angus, I'm not the man you imagine me to be and you think me better than I am.*' (Angus could put that down to humility and believe more than ever in Wilfred's virtue; the latter would have at least voiced this feeble protest.)

Having written the sentence, he put down his pen and, elbows on the table, grasped his head in both hands. What could he say? What could he find to say? He did not wish to hurt his cousin's feelings. Did Angus's letter really require an answer? All of a sudden, he took up his pen and continued:

'*I can't understand how a man could feel the way you do about me, but if anyone is to have such sentiments and admit them, then I would rather it were you. Coming from anybody else, the letter I have by me would be simply intolerable. There is only one thing to do, and that is to let the whole thing fade from our memory.*'

Reading this over, he wondered whether his letter was really like a letter. What he feared above all was appearing ridiculous. The idea that he had, to a certain extent, imitated his cousin's style never entered his mind, but it took him a good five minutes to bring himself to write the word 'affectionately' under these few lines. 'Affectionately' was going a long way, even between cousins. Angus could turn the adverb over and over in his wretched mind and read unintended meanings into it. 'Never mind,' thought Wilfred as he signed his name, 'I can't help it, I'm sick of it.'

He was sick of others as well as of himself, sick of physical love and the extravagant nonsense it made you talk, the crazy things it made you do. To fall in love with a woman he had never seen, a woman met by chance who would love him silently, that was what he wanted. The Spanish girl no longer existed in his eyes. He had thought too much about her and she had lost all mystery. Through a weird trick of memory, he remembered Uncle Horace's securities just as he drifted into sleep.

CHAPTER XXX

Next morning, before leaving for work, he made sure that his securities were still in the drawer with his uncle's love letters and Alicia's photographs. What should he do with them all? It was a strange treasure. As for the securities, he felt undecided and anxious, wishing neither to keep nor to destroy them, but the letters in Alicia's hand still made his heart beat a little as though they had been addressed to him. Instead of which, it was a man who wrote letters to him –

The weather that day was magnificent and the houses visible from the store where Wilfred worked looked black under the bright blue sky. There was something wrong with the world, he thought, if a healthy, loving young man was obliged to earn his living standing at a counter selling shirts and underwear. Even religion could not make him accept a situation that suddenly

144

appeared monstrous to him. He had never thought much about money, but that morning he had to have it, he wanted to be free.

Brusquely leaving his place, he went up to the shop walker. He was a man of about fifty, stout and dignified, his face wreathed in a professional smile which was intended for customers but remained glued to his lips even when the store was free of them. He was called Mr Schoenhals, and Wilfred used to speculate about the meaning of the name.

'What is it, my boy?' asked Mr Schoenhals, his hands behind his back.

'I need some information, Mr Schoenhals. A friend I saw yesterday owns some securities that he wants to negotiate and asked me how to go about it.'

'So you've come into a legacy?' asked the shopwalker.

The creases in his pink cheeks deepened a little around the thin lips stretched in a universal smile. Wilfred blushed.

'A legacy, me?'

'What about that uncle you buried last week?'

'Oh, this has nothing to do with him – or with me.'

'Go back to your place, Wilfred. If you feel like talking to me, let it be outside working hours.'

He obeyed. What else could he do? As he passed by a mirror, he saw his eyes sparkling with anger. He had been clumsy, naïve. His story did not hold water and Mr Schoenhals had made fun of him in a kindly way. Yet, fifteen minutes later, the shopwalker came up to him and said, running a thumb over his chin:

'If I can help you with some advice, don't hesitate to ask me, you know.'

Wilfred thanked him. Mr Schoenhals had always been particularly nice to him. That day, as usual, he noticed that the fat man smelt of lavender and puffed a little as he spoke. His sea-green eyes stood out between little black lashes.

'I was joking, just now,' he said. 'All your friend has to do is to

145

go to a bank with his securities. He'll be given all necessary information there. Are the securities registered or payable to the bearer?'

'To the bearer, I think.'

'Then it's a very simple transaction.'

'You have to give your name and address, of course.'

'Usually you go to a bank where you have an account. They know who they're dealing with there. Why do you ask?'

'My friend wanted to know.'

Mr Schoenhals turned his glaucous eyes on Wilfred.

'I hope your friend is reliable,' he murmured.

He gave a nod to indicate the arrival of a customer.

Looking very undecided, a young man was making his way towards them, and as Wilfred went up to him Mr Schoenhals moved away, hands behind his back. The customer was so humbly dressed that it was difficult to understand his presence in the store and Wilfred was so flustered by Mr Schoenhals's last sentence that for a moment he could not grasp what was being asked of him. His uneasiness must have been communicated to the stranger, for he repeated his question in a stammer:

'Could I see a white silk shirt?'

His request seemed all the more singular for his wearing of a leather jacket; his sunburnt face too was that of a farm-hand.

'What size in collars do you wear?'

'Oh,' said the youth with a strained laugh, 'I've grown fatter this winter. You'd better take my measurement.'

Saying this, he opened his shirt collar and Wilfred slipped his tape measure over a full, strong neck which the name of Schoenhals suited far better than the shopwalker. He laughed again, like a child, when he felt the salesman's fingers on his skin. His ruddy complexion, his red lips, everything about him denoted vigour and open-air country life and the childlike innocence of his slightly drawling voice compelled affection, but Wilfred only felt a sudden and violent embarrassment and,

146

moving away as soon as he had taken his measurements, quickly showed him several kinds of shirts.

The youth ran his brown hands over the silk that he dared not finger and said all of a sudden:

'I don't know what I want. You choose for me.'

He looked up at Wilfred for the first time and his nut-brown eyes threw a disarmingly honest glance.

'I've never treated myself to a silk shirt before,' he added.

Wilfred advised him to take a shirt that was slightly less expensive than the others. Drawing a bundle of banknotes from his pocket, the lad said:

'I'll leave it to you. Give me three of them.'

And in a more confidential tone, he murmured:

'I should tell you that I'm getting married. I'll need them for the wedding parties. This is the first time I've ever come to the big city and Lord knows when I'll be back.'

'Where do you come from?' asked Wilfred, wrapping up the shirts.

He named a small town a few miles from the Canadian border and asked Wilfred if he ever went that way.

'No, never.'

'Too bad. I'd be so glad if you did. I could have introduced you to my girl. We're going to have a little farm.'

Wilfred could not help smiling.

'A little farmhouse with a barn twice its size and painted red, I bet.'

The boy stared at him open-mouthed as he would have looked at a conjurer who had brought off a sleight-of-hand.

'Well, I never! How on earth did you guess?'

'Oh, people down here know a lot of things,' said Wilfred as he knotted the string, and for the first time he laughed too.

The parcel was ready and once more the customer held out his dollars.

147

'At the desk,' said Wilfred with a nod.

'My name is Joe Lovejoy,' said the lad offering his outstretched hand.

Wilfred took it nervously, hoping that Mr Schoenhals would not notice this and, because he could not do otherwise, he gave his name but turned red.

'Can I write to you here?' asked Joe Lovejoy.

'Why do you want to write to me?'

'I have a surprise for you.'

'A surprise?'

'Oh, you don't have to be scared about it,' said the youth and as he smiled his brown cheeks dimpled. 'Can I write, yes or no?'

'Yes,' said Wilfred in an undertone.

He went to the desk with his young customer, who paid, then handed him the parcel, not without fearing that he might attempt to resume their conversation. But merely waving his hand, the boy disappeared.

The cashier, an affable old lady whom Wilfred suspected of being a little false, threw him a grandmotherly glance from behind her spectacles.

'So you've just made a friend,' she said.

'Oh, he's one of those country boys who shake hands with everybody.'

'Still –'

He went round his counter and sat on a stool reserved for customers. It was against the rules to sit down, but he felt tired. A minute or two went by, then Mr Schoenhals's grave and unctuous voice made him start. He was standing right behind Wilfred.

'Anything the matter?'

'Not a thing.'

The shop walker laid his hand on Wilfred's shoulder as he was about to get up.

148

'Stay where you are,' said the voice above the young man's head. 'Do you know that customer?'

'No, not at all.'

'He shook hands with you.'

'Yes. He comes from the country.'

'Those boys are awfully nice,' said Mr Schoenhals gently.

Wilfred did not reply and heard him breathing heavily. A few seconds passed. Mr Schoenhals in a fatherly voice advised him to rest a little longer, then his shoes creaked on the carpet as he carried his majestic person away.

The young man was perplexed, for, although nothing very extraordinary had happened, he did not feel the same as a few moments ago. Before a lad as simple and as transparent as Joe Lovejoy, he had had the feeling of being fundamentally dishonest. He cheated from morning till night; that lad did not. It seemed ridiculous to say so, but Joe loved him, loved him in his way, without realizing what this meant. Now Wilfred was incapable of such love, although he wanted to love someone, but there was no one to love. Dissipation was killing his faculty for love. His heart was impotent, but the presence of love moved him deeply.

After a moment he got up, stood by his counter again and for the first time saw his life in the light of a disaster. The big ground glass globes lighting the store suddenly looked like so many hostile objects. There were twelve of these luminous spheres, and Wilfred would have shattered them with pleasure. Even when the sun shone in the sky as it did at present, those lights never went out; they stared at salesmen and customers with an indifference that destroyed the joy of life.

'I'm not made to sell shirts,' he thought. People took him for a good fellow because he smiled at one and all, but right now his heart was near to bursting with sadness and anger. However, he had to stick things out, accept them. He remembered what

149

his cousin had written: '...I could have helped you...' Wilfred had posted his answer to that letter just before coming to work; perhaps he should have thought matters over a little longer before writing. There were certainly other things to be said to Angus. And once more he remembered his securities.

CHAPTER XXXI

On reaching home that day, he found a package at his door, together with a letter. He opened the package first and his surprise was only equalled by his disappointment, for he loved presents and a package addressed to him could only mean a present. Indeed, it was one: two little books of devotion, the *Imitation* and the *Spiritual Combat*, both volumes in bad condition. The letter was from Max:

'*Dear Wilfred,*' he wrote, '*so you may not think me worse than I really am, allow me to present you with two little books that I often used to read. I don't any longer, because it's enough for me to open them to hear the cry of lost souls that have dashed themselves to pieces against the crystal wall of perfection. But you might try the experience.*

'*When shall we meet? Tonight?*

'*Yours,*

MAX.'

'*P.S. – Was it you who came yesterday? The old dog who answered from the window described someone who could only be you, I think.*'

In Wilfred's state of mind, the letter could only add irritation to astonishment. Why didn't the man mind his own business?

He picked up one of the little books and examined it with a most unfriendly eye. The pages were yellowed and showed a good deal of marginal scoring and sometimes even exclamation marks. He chanced on a sentence that turned him to ice.

He closed the book, put it with its fellow, made a parcel of both volumes and placed it in the bottom of his closet, beside his shoes. Then he went to wash his hands and, as he rubbed the fingers that had touched the grubby objects, wondered what he was going to do with his securities. The time for dreaming was over: if he wanted to stop working in a store, he must act.

His decision was quickly taken: he wrote to his cousin and without hesitation told him about the gift Uncle Horace had handed over to him. Then, with exemplary preciseness he copied all the necessary numbers, figures and dates.

How could the total amount of the securities be cashed without leaving a trace? He was as frightened as though he had been guilty. For what he would not admit, even to himself, was that he was afraid of James Knight who, in his eyes, represented law, justice, society, all the Protestant churches in one, and the banks into the bargain. If James Knight had not spoken to him as he had, Wilfred would simply have gone to his bank with the securities in his pocket. 'He suspects me,' he thought. The young man also wrote this to his cousin. In a sudden outburst of feeling, he told him everything. If Angus loved him, what wouldn't he do to help him?

The letter grew and grew. It no longer dealt with securities, but with his despair. What other word could describe his state of mind? He didn't want to sell shirts any more and something in him broke down suddenly. His hand raced over the paper, never before so swift. 'I am one of those people who dash themselves to pieces against the crystal wall of perfection,' he wrote, as though the sentence had sprung from his heart. When he was about to embark upon his love affairs, his fingers

151

stiffened on the pen and he forced them to pause in a race that drove them from one side of the paper to the other. He would keep his affairs for another time.

'For another time,' he said aloud.

Signing the letter without reading it over, he slipped it into an envelope, left his room, ran to the end of the street and threw it into a post box, after which he thought over what he had just done.

You act first and think afterwards, when it is too late, otherwise you don't act. Hardly had the letter escaped his fingers than he had the impression of having written a lot of nonsense that would have been best kept to himself. In spite of this, he felt relieved and the sentence about the crystal wall would certainly dazzle his cousin. Wilfred admired that sentence so much that he actually imagined he had thought of it himself.

The post-office clock said ten. He went to a neighbouring drugstore where he drank a large glass of milk and ate a triple-decked sandwich. Everything was smiling on him again, and glancing furtively in a mirror, he found himself both ugly and graceful. Anyway, his handsome cousin was moping for love of him. And then, what he had in his drawer was enough to live on for several years without working; he could inform Mr Schoenhals that he was leaving the store for ever.

Such thoughts as these ran through his head only to disappear suddenly when the name of Schoenhals came back to him. No other part of the body possessed such singular beauty, to his mind, as the neck. A round, straight, smooth neck that both hands imprisoned gently, like a column. Breast, flanks, legs spoke of nothing but physical pleasure, even the head and above all the face – But the neck was chaste. Wilfred's neck was long and powerful and of a whiteness that withstood tan, a bar-barian's neck, someone had told him once and this expression stuck in his memory, although its meaning was not very clear

152

to him. The neck in itself was similar to a body, but an innocent one. As for the organs of pleasure, both men's and women's, it would be folly to consider them beautiful. Only a sort of madness instigated by desire could allow anyone to consider these regions leniently, regions which, in his eyes, remained suspicious. All of a sudden, the sentence he had read in the *Imitation* flashed through his brain: 'O wretched and foolish sinner, who sometimes fearest the countenance of an angry man, what answer wilt thou make to God who knoweth all thy wickedness!'

Putting down his glass, he paid and went out.

CHAPTER XXXII

That night, he wandered about the port without finding a woman quite to his liking and finally, in a mean, sinister bar, was obliged to fall back on a girl who had nothing but very fine grey eyes and a spontaneous gaiety that warmed the heart. Pretty, she would have proved overbearing and difficult but knowing herself ill-favoured, when Wilfred spoke to her, she looked at him with a mixture of gratitude and tenderness. This touched him, so deeply did he wish to be loved.

Returning to his room a few hours later, all his past fears overwhelmed him; he drenched his body in water as though to wash away all the caresses that might have contaminated his flesh. 'That's where God will strike you,' he thought. But he would have to wait for days and days before knowing whether he had caught something, and yet he felt incapable of asking God to spare him this once more: it seemed too easy and even a little disgraceful, so after making a big sign of the cross, that was not exempt from fear, he threw himself into sleep.

CHAPTER XXXIII

Several days went by. He waited for the first symptoms of a disease he dreaded even more than usual, and this time not without reason. At every opportunity he went and examined himself with mingled horror and curiosity: he could think of nothing else. The girl had aroused his suspicions. He knew, of course, that what terrified our forefathers is quite easily cured nowadays, yet certain words, certain terms made him intensely anxious. The taste for adventures left him, and with it his financial worries, and he no longer minded selling shirts. He no longer minded anything. 'I'm done for,' he said to himself. At the store, he withdrew to the toilet almost hourly to find out whether there was anything the matter with him. Nothing could be seen, but he thought he looked less well than usual.

One afternoon, at the height of his anxiety (for he felt each day bring him nearer to the loathsome discovery), a customer made overtures to him. There is no other way of expressing it. The man was middle-aged, very sprucely dressed and had a rather British appearance and accent. While he inspected shirts, he asked Wilfred's advice about the shape of a collar and, without giving him time to answer, wanted to know whether he had a taste for travelling. Would it amuse him to visit Europe?

Wilfred was used to this kind of situation: sometimes he

pretended not to understand, was all innocence and smiles (for it is so agreeable to be liked); sometimes, on the contrary, he turned gloomy and kept a threatening silence. That day he asked his customer why he asked such questions.

'Because,' said the customer in a low voice and not without a certain artlessness, 'I think you're attractive.'

'But you don't know me,' said Wilfred in the same tone.

'I am never mistaken about young men's faces.'

'And I'm never mistaken about what to think of certain compliments.'

'I see that you're used to them.'

He bent over the shirts.

'In a store like this,' said Wilfred gently, 'you see a little of everything.'

'You mean all sorts of people?'

'All sorts of people.'

'Do you dislike it?' asked the customer, feeling the silk of a shirt.

'Yes, sometimes.'

'Not always?'

'Most of the time I don't care. I'm not interested, you know.'

At this, the customer raised his eyes and the lined face of the man in his forties seemed sad and bitter to Wilfred, in spite of the smile that creased the corners of his eyelids.

'How,' he asked, 'can you spend the best years of your youth behind this counter?'

Wilfred remembered the disease with which he imagined he was threatened and his heart sank. Without quite knowing what he did, he took another type of shirt from a drawer and laid it before the customer. Mr Schoenhals went slowly by.

'I don't care much for these stripes,' said the customer.

'We have another model,' replied Wilfred, turning toward a fresh drawer.

155

Another shirt was added to the others on the counter. The customer examined it minutely.

'If you were free for dinner tonight,' he muttered, 'we could talk over your future to some advantage.'

'I'm sorry, but I'm not free.'

'What about tomorrow?'

'Neither tomorrow, nor any other day.'

'That's really a pity – I could do a lot for you.'

Wilfred drummed lightly on the counter without replying. The customer sighed and ordered five shirts among those he had been shown. At the desk, Wilfred heard him give a name that was very well-known in theatrical circles and the address of one of the best hotels in town. In an admirable manner, his precise voice detached each syllable without raising its tone and, when he had disappeared, the old lady at the desk looked at Wilfred with raised eyebrows.

'And now – a celebrity,' she said with an air of connivance.

Turning his back on her, he found himself face to face with Mr Schoenhals. The latter signed to the young man to follow him and led him into a corner of the store.

'I suppose you know who it is you sold those five shirts to?'

'I heard his name at the desk.'

'I'm under the impression that you and he talked together, Wilfred. Am I mistaken?'

'He was an awfully long time making up his mind what to choose.'

'I don't wish to insist, but the interest I take in you forces me to tell you the man is dangerous.'

'To others, perhaps,' said Wilfred, staring straight at Mr Schoenhals, 'but not to me.'

The shop walker had probably not expected that kind of answer, for the young salesman saw something flicker in his sea-

156

green eyes, and hunching his shoulders a little, Mr Schoenhals
walked away.

CHAPTER XXXIV

This banal incident faded almost at once from Wilfred's
memory. He had other worries on his mind, and after work that
same afternoon, went to the very heart of a remote quarter of
the city.

There stood a small chapel where he rarely set foot. Dating
from the time when America was still a mission country, it was
built of planks, without a steeple, and it cut a rather shabby
figure at the end of a dismal little street where the children of
Italian workmen played in the dust. The inside was clean and
unpretentious: carpeted with brown linoleum that muffled the
sound of footsteps, two rows of black pews and a tiny red lamp
burning before an altar decked with a few white flowers. The
setting sun poured through the gaudy stained-glass windows
in many-coloured shafts of light and somehow the effect
inspired sadness. They shone upon the statue of a holy woman
and her expressionless face as if upon some valuable object.
As Wilfred had hoped, there was no one but himself in the
chapel.

Going straight to the confessional, he knelt there behind a
heavy curtain that wrapped him in dense shadow. His heart
was beating fast. After pausing for a moment, he recited the
Confiteor and began to confess all his sins. In the silent chapel,
his hurried, breathless voice enumerated all his errors, all the
unchaste acts that had sullied his body, all the desires that

157

devastated his heart, all the graces unceasingly refused day in day out, all the love he had spurned.

He waited for the priest to say something, to ask questions, but heard nothing except the blood buzzing in his own head. Then, overwhelmed with shame, he confessed in a still more muffled voice his fear that a disease would be sent to him to punish his lustfulness.

That was not all. He also feared that inveterate wrong-doing would cause a kind of automatism and that this horrible mechanical process would lead him straight to hell.

His brow pressed to the grating, he felt tears of anguish roll down his cheeks, and could no longer speak. The confessional was empty and Wilfred knew it, yet he stayed on as though someone were there. When he grew calmer he began talking once more, but no longer had any idea of what he was saying. Disconnected words escaped his lips.

After a long time, he left the confessional and knelt in a pew. 'Closer,' said a secret voice. He drew nearer to the altar. 'Closer still. Come quite close,' said the voice. Wilfred went up to the Communion table and there, shutting his eyes, he threw his head back. When he rose to his feet it was almost dark.

On returning to his room he wondered what he was going to do. The idea of leaving the house to have supper seemed impossible after what had happened. To begin with, he was not hungry, he wanted nothing. Everything seemed different, although he was the same person and nothing in fact had any meaning now except what he had divined in the chapel, at the moment when he had closed his eyes. All he wanted at present was for someone to talk to him about God. He even forgot the threat of disease. Throwing himself on the bed, he tried to read his conscience, but it seemed to him that the single capacity for thought had been taken from him. After the agitation of the last few days, a feeling of deep security made him see his life in quite another light: nothing could assail or hurt him, but he would have wished someone to be with him, to talk to him about God, because he loved God. He was a child once more.

An hour later, he remembered the books that Max had given him, and jumping from bed opened the closet where he had placed them. With extraordinary eagerness, he read the first chapters of the *Imitation*.

From its pages rose a voice that seemed to come from beyond this earth of ours and it condemned the world. Wilfred had the confused impression of being lost and saved at one and the same time. If he could do everything the book said, he was snatched from evil, but he was judged at each successive page. Every word concerned him, concerned him personally. In sentences that rang like steel, he recognized the forebodings he had had in streets by night, in bars where the devil made enough noise to deafen him. This was a magic book. Wilfred was frightened but it seemed as though the book stuck to his fingers and, as he read on, that the pages turned of themselves. Thirty or so of them passed before his eyes without his finding strength enough to drop the terrible little volume. When he went to bed, he slipped it under his pillow and that night he said his prayers, he said them badly, but he said them all.

CHAPTER XXXV

Next morning he found a letter from Uncle Horace's solicitor in his mail. Wilfred was notified that the deceased's will would be read two days later at six-thirty p.m. The meeting was to take place three streets from Wilfred's house and it would not even be necessary to ask Mr Schoenhals for time off again, but why bother to go? Hadn't Uncle Horace told him that he was not much favoured in his will? He decided not to attend the meeting.

That day at the store, he sold a few shirts and some underwear, but had the impression of being there and not being there at the same time. All that remained of yesterday's emotion was a nostalgic but deep regret, for he had felt happy in the chapel and the idea was taking root in his mind that if this happiness was true, then the world was a delusion. There was no comparison possible between the two and one excluded the other. For the first time, he looked at the store around him wondering if it existed elsewhere than in his imagination.

He had lunch and supper alone in a very modest restaurant and went without bread and dessert to practise mortification, as in the *Imitation*; he wanted to be a saint. Never again would he sleep with women. When he got up from the table, he felt hungry still and this caused him peculiar satisfaction. Also in a spirit of mortification, he refrained all that day from examining parts of his body where the disease might appear, but yielding to curiosity when he went to bed, found nothing the matter. Nothing yet.

Next day after work he went to confession at the nearest church, but compared with his confession of the day before in an empty confessional, this seemed cold and soulless to him. He could not help it. What counted in his eyes was his sincere resolution never to yield again to lust. The priest who heard him seemed scarcely older than himself, almost a seminarist. Wilfred could see his slightly shiny cheekbone, his half closed eye; the priest listened with admirable attention and in the deepest silence, as though he were at a dying man's bedside.

When Wilfred had finished speaking, the confessor said nothing for a long time, for such a long time that the young man added:

'Perhaps the sins that I have just told hide others from me

that I have forgotten, but I really believe I have not omitted anything.'

The priest waited a little while longer, then turning his face slightly to Wilfred began to talk to him with such gentleness that tears rose to the penitent's eyes. Emotion prevented him from catching everything said by a voice that seemed to be whispering secrets, but suddenly he heard a sentence that sank deep into his being and filled him with extraordinary joy.

'Do as you like, no one in the world will ever love you as God loves you at this instant. You would have been lost if you had died in sin, but God is patient. He awaited you here. You are saved.'

He continued talking to him for a long time but Wilfred could not hear him very well. The word *love* alone stood out in a murmur of indistinct words and made the young man's heart beat fast, because all he wanted was love. He then recited his act of contrition, not without stammering, and received absolution. The penance he was given seemed a light one to him. He went and hid at the back of the church, face in hands so that no one could notice his flush and, it must be said, the tears that rolled endlessly down his cheeks. He could not have said, anyway, why he cried, since he felt perfectly happy, but his lower lip quivered.

After a few minutes, he grew calmer and went out. The air was soft and the sky, before turning quite dark, tinged with pink. In this becoming light, the walls of houses and even the faces of pedestrians seemed to reflect a vast and distant bonfire. A gentle breeze, laden with tenderness, brought with it an immense desire for happiness: this first gust of spring caught him full in the face and for a moment he felt an exhilaration that forced him to stop and then to sit on a bench. It was wonderful to be on this earth, to be on this earth at his age. Under other circumstances he would have thought of dissipation, but at present dissipation

161

appeared in the light of a fearful though remote danger. Absorbed in his new-found freedom, he was like a child once more and no longer enslaved by his body.

The evening was exemplary. Having eaten supper early and quickly, he returned to a room that he found less forbidding than usual. The crucifix was taken from its hiding-place and put back above the bed, after which Wilfred tried to say his prayers with exceptional attention, convinced that fervour would follow, for it had to be recognized, all fervour was proving absent that evening and he was unable to recapture the emotion that had shaken him in church.

Human beings behave so peculiarly when they are alone that they might be taken for lunatics if they could be seen, if their thoughts could be read. So it was that the young man went to look at himself in the bathroom, hoping secretly to discover some change in his features. When you were in a state of grace, did it show? In the purity of expression perhaps? But there was no difference in his eyes. The eye that was always noticed because it slanted up still looked tantalizing.

Of course that did not mean anything, as he had no bad thoughts. After standing a long time before the mirror, he had the impression that the outline of his face was growing blurred and that another face was replacing his. That was an experiment he had often made without letting it lead him too far, as there always came a time when he felt seized with a kind of panic. Never would he have dared to admit that what he perhaps feared was the devil's apparition. But the devil did not appear, the devil kept quiet. Was it not to his interest to lie low?

Wilfred suffered from being alone. He would almost have wished to hear someone knock at his door and see Max who wanted so much to talk to him about religion. That evening, a conversation would have been possible. Seated at the open window, he read a page and a half from the *Imitation*. There was

162

no doubt that he felt at peace, at peace with God. 'I could die,' he thought, 'everything is in order.' When all was said and done, you had to die, it always came to that, all the books said so, even those that did not mention the subject. Death was everywhere, at the street corner, in churches, at the store, in bars, in beds, in the bodies of men and women. He recalled Uncle Horace's eyes at the very end of their last conversation, they were the eyes of a man who was sinking like a stone. People sank like stones –

He threw himself on his knees and hid his face in the bedspread, he tried to hide himself in God. There alone you did not feel frightened. He threw himself at God, as one would let oneself drop from the top of a sky-scraper.

CHAPTER XXXVI

The following day proved difficult because Wilfred knew he would attend the solicitor's meeting although he did not wish to. What worried him was that he would go, in spite of himself, because of the people he expected to meet there. By tricking his conscience, he would finally convince himself that the appointment must be kept. What wrong could there be in that, anyway?

It seemed as though everybody in the store had leagued together to give him evil thoughts, particularly a young salesman of twenty who could talk of nothing but girls, those he had had and those he expected to have. Wilfred did not care much for him because he was rather unpleasantly ugly, with an oversized head on a stunted body and eyes that glowed unhealthily between pink lids. He was called Freddie. When Mr Schoenhals was nowhere about, Freddie would sidle up to Wilfred and allude to his adventures in obscene, schoolboyish terms, guessing, perhaps, that they were two of a kind. For all sorts of reasons, Wilfred strongly suspected him of being a virgin.

That day however, Freddie came up to him with something rapturous in his eyes that foretold a major event, and whispering like a conspirator, embarked on a narrative of his most recent feats. What atrocious little spree had given him the ecstatic expression that made him look nastier than usual? His nose shone in a pasty face. Seized with sudden disgust, Wilfred turned away with a muttered excuse but, as he leaned against his counter, immediately felt a little remorse for his brusqueness. He had offended the little man, and after some hesitation he went up to Freddie.

'You're being careful, I hope?'

Freddie raised his over-large eyes.

'Careful?'

'You haven't forgotten about diseases?'

Freddie turned red.

'Oh, I hope there was nothing the matter with her,' he said.

Wilfred leaned forward slightly and eyed him like a judge:

'It was the first time, wasn't it?'

At this, Freddie grew scarlet and mumbled:

'What do you mean, the first time? What first time?'

And suddenly, he inquired:

'How did you know that?'

'I guessed it, old fellow.'

The poor worried face turned from red to a waxy pallor and the following question was asked in an ashamed whisper:

'Do you think I ought to see a doctor? Do people see a doctor after – ?'

164

Wilfred hesitated, feeling as though he were destiny in person.

'No,' he said at last, 'but do be careful.'

'The first time – that would really be tough luck.'

'I wouldn't give it another thought, if I were you.'

Freddie came closer to him.

'You won't tell anyone it was the first time, will you?'

'It's a promise,' said Wilfred as he moved away.

'I've passed on my own fears to him,' he thought. These were to increase and flourish in the boy's wretched brain. Was Freddie a believer? How was he going to get out of this? Even now panic could be seen in his great black eyes and it occurred to Wilfred to go and say the first thing that came into his head, to soothe his troubled mind. For instance, that the most serious venereal diseases were easily cured, but these words would be sufficient to strike fresh terror in the lad's heart. Suddenly, Wilfred had the feeling that Freddie was watching him and he at once assumed an unconcerned attitude. He wondered what Christ would have done in his place, but how could anyone tell?

At that moment, Mr Schoenhals sailed majestically up to him.

'What about those securities?' he asked. 'Has your friend come to any decision on the subject?'

'I believe he's done what was necessary,' said Wilfred.

Mr Schoenhals smiled and nodded.

'I'm always there if you need any help,' he said.

The young man also smiled and kept silent. Mr Schoenhals stood there, eyes protruding, lips grinning. Perhaps he wished to add something. Wilfred always had the impression that he wished to add something to what he had said. Finally the shop-walker gave a little cough and left.

Of course, Christ would have gone to Freddie and forgiven him his sins: at the same time He would have warded off the disease. In this store, under these electric lights, with all those

165

salesmen and all those customers? Yes. 'But I'm not Christ,' thought Wilfred.

However, he went up to Freddie and said very quickly:

'Don't be scared. It's a thousand to one there's nothing the matter with you.'

Freddie looked at him like a hunted animal.

'I don't want to go mad. One of my uncles caught a disease and died a lunatic five years later.'

'Such things don't happen nowadays. When did your uncle die?'

'Before I was born.'

'Science has made great strides in the last twenty years.'

'Just the same, I think I'll go and see a doctor.'

'Yes, do, if you think it will reassure you.'

'Would you go if you were I?'

'No, I'd wait.'

'Wait for what? For the disease to break out?'

'Anyway, you can't do anything until you're sure. Are you a believer?'

Why had he asked that question? It made them both feel ill at ease. Freddie shrugged his shoulders slightly.

'A believer? I don't know. Those problems don't interest me much. I don't see the connexion –'

He turned away a little and looked toward one of the large windows.

'Do you read the Gospel?' asked Wilfred in a voice that was growing a little strangled.

'Oh, not very often.'

'If you read the Gospel,' said Wilfred, running a finger inside his collar, 'you must know that we receive what we ask for. There's no reason you shouldn't be given health, if you ask for it.'

'I don't believe in miracles.'

'You don't believe in the Gospel?'

166

'Oh, yes, a little, in a certain way. Generally speaking. But there aren't any miraculous healings now as there were at the time of the Gospel. I'm not a Catholic, see?'

He knew that Wilfred was a Catholic. Everyone knew it.

'I'm not saying that to hurt your feelings,' he added.

Wilfred cleared his throat.

'Protestants also believe that God answers prayers,' he said, 'otherwise they wouldn't pray.'

'That may be,' answered Freddie without looking at him, 'but I'm not a Protestant. I'm not against religion, but I'm nothing. My parents are nothing. God has never given me what I asked for. I've tried two or three times. Perhaps you're luckier than I am – Just the same, I think I'll go and see a doctor.'

'You could do both. You ought to –'

As he said this, he felt relieved to see a customer come up to them, for the conversation was getting more and more embarrassing and he was allowing himself to be carried away by something beyond his power.

The customer wished to buy a sports shirt and three or four were shown him, but he would have none of them. He was not only overbearing, red-faced and dressed like a man who spends most of his life outdoors, he was also pot-bellied and grizzled. Wilfred felt the man disliked him, for his great rough hands pushed away the shirts displayed for his benefit and he spoke in a voice that was both muffled and imperious and made one long to snub him. Model after model was submitted to this critical gentleman's judgment and Wilfred noticed with a sensation verging on horror his big, red, hairy ears. Was there anyone in the whole world, he asked himself, who could love such a hideous being? It occurred to him that God perhaps loved him. How was one to know? The thought disturbed Wilfred, as it did not tally with those he usually had in mind.

It seemed as though the stranger vaguely guessed something

167

of this, for he looked up at his salesman with tiny swinish eyes full of penetrating malice. In spite of his efforts, Wilfred could not manage to avoid his stare and the silence between them very soon became unbearable. If the man didn't want to buy anything, why didn't he go? After a moment that seemed endless, the customer asked:

'You have nothing else?'

'No, nothing,' said Wilfred, putting away the shirts.

'Then show me some gloves.'

'Oh, we don't keep gloves at this counter. You'll find them over there.'

The stranger breathed hard. Wilfred had never yet seen a man so much like an animal and wished with all his heart that Mr Schoenhals would come by, but he remained at the other end of the store.

'Over there, eh?' asked the customer.

He had probably been drinking. Wilfred put away the shirts without replying, but his hands shook slightly. Long forgotten childhood terrors rose from the depth of his memory: the devil sometimes assumed a human shape. True, for several weeks after he had begun working at the store, he had taken it into his head that Mr Schoenhals was the devil, because of his peculiar ugliness, but Mr Schoenhals was almost nice looking, compared with the wild boar who demanded gloves.

'Yes, over there,' he said at last in an expressionless voice.

The man gave a short grunt and hunching his massive shoulders trotted straight to the exit.

'No one would ever believe what a lot of lunatics and eccentrics wander in and out of stores,' thought Wilfred. No need to bring the devil into such things. Generally speaking, everyone was the devil. The young man was convinced of this, just as he believed, without being able to account for it clearly, that God was present in each being and that there were moments

168

when this showed. However, he preferred to keep such ideas to himself. Max was probably the only person who might have understood.

CHAPTER XXXVII

The next afternoon, he went to the solicitor's. His intention of going to Communion that Sunday made him careful to avoid committing the smallest fault, but to be present when a will was read provided no grounds for scruples. True, there was something that he would not admit, even to himself, and that his conscience told him over and over, with unflinching gentleness: 'You're going there for a certain reason. If you don't go, you'll be advised by letter of whatever has been left you. The solicitor has your address.' But he wanted to go.

The office was a cold, dull room with walls painted sea-green and armchairs covered in velvet of the same shade. The solicitor, a skinny old man whose large starched cuffs made quite a noise, sat behind a mahogany desk shuffling his papers with an important air. The heirs had assembled, a little as though they were in a chapel and a little as though they were in a death-chamber.

Wilfred looked around for his cousin, but Angus's mother had come without him and the young man sat down by her.

When Mrs Knight appeared, he felt his throat tighten a little. To his great surprise, she was alone and took a seat at some distance from his after greeting him with a nod. A great many other people were present that Wilfred did not know even by sight and he was a trifle ashamed of being there, for, he thought, everyone knew he was a salesman in a store. He was certainly the youngest and poorest of them all, son to a man who had not made a success of his life. If there were any mention of him in the will it would surely be an insignificant or absurd one. One way or the other he was laying himself open to some humiliation. Then what was he doing there? He refused to answer this question.

Elegantly dressed in black taffeta, his aunt talked in an undertone to her neighbour, a lady on the wrong side of fifty whose rather artificial inflections conjured up fashionable life, dining out and garden-parties. They laughed softly, politely, over some joke that Wilfred did not catch. With the most condescending benevolence, Mrs Howard then bent her queenly profile to Wilfred and asked news of his health, after which, without waiting for an answer, she began to speak of her son, who had been unable to come, she explained, on account of his work.

'He works too hard,' said Wilfred thoughtlessly.

Mrs Howard looked at him with an amused expression and said at last:

'Angus has enormous intellectual powers, but knows how to keep himself in good shape. He rides a couple of hours daily.'

'He rides? Where?'

'Oh, he takes his car and drives to Stanhope, where his groom meets him. The country is magnificent around there. He gallops in the meadows.'

The last sentence set Wilfred dreaming: he thought of his store.

'Angus is very careful not to gain weight,' continued Mrs Howard. 'He does what's necessary to keep his figure.'

Wilfred was on the point of asking whether he expected to marry some day, but the question seemed to him at once absurd and vaguely indecent. He remained silent.

'And what about you?' asked his aunt absently. 'Still behind your counter? Why, that's fine. Any job is a good job that keeps you going. Ah, here we are!'

170

The solicitor had just motioned for silence and then announced that he was about to open the deceased's will and read it out, which he immediately did.

This took barely fifteen minutes during which Wilfred saw many of those present change countenance. He did not quite know what they expected but almost everyone appeared disappointed. The house passed into James Knight's hands with most of the furniture excepting eight chairs, three armchairs and a small desk allotted to Mrs Howard, who gave a little shrug. What on earth could she do with that Victorian junk? As for Wilfred, he was left a portrait of Uncle Horace as a cavalry officer. Angus got nothing.

Lastly, quite a large sum was bequeathed to the Church, a clause greeted with deathly silence, while lips stretched into a sort of angry grin. Phoebe Knight's set face was the only one where nothing could be found but sadness. In a little black straw hat that made her look like a child, she had never seemed so pretty to Wilfred, nor so completely disarmed among all these grasping, disdainful people.

Much against his will, he looked towards her. The first time, he could put this down to absent-mindedness, but the following times, doubt was no longer possible. He wanted that woman with all his might. After a brief struggle, his throat dry, he gave in suddenly and allowed his covetousness a free hand. With violent, painful delight, he gazed at her innocent cheek, at her great light eye clouded with melancholy. No one took any notice of him: he could look his fill at her. The day of the funeral came back to him and the minute when that tiny, full mouth had brushed against his cheek, right and left of his own mouth, and the memory sent the blood rushing to his face.

Once the will had been read, everyone got up and Mrs Howard turned to Wilfred with a coaxing smile.

'The portrait that falls to you is in the big drawing-room at

171

Wormsloe,' she said. 'Perhaps you had never noticed it. You had? Anyway, Angus likes it for reasons that have nothing to do with sentiment, believe me. It's the period he's interested in, you understand, the uniforms of that time. He mentioned this to me only yesterday, precisely on account of that portrait which he longs to own. So, unless you're desperately fond of the painting – which, by the way, is valueless – we might make an exchange.'

'An exchange –'

'Oh, an exchange or a business arrangement,' she replied, thinking that she caught a hint of calculation in the young man's expression.

He asked to be allowed to think it over and said good-bye to her to go up to Phoebe Knight. Crossing the few yards between them, he felt an extraordinary freedom of movement. A smile greeted him, and with somewhat provincial artlessness Phoebe kissed him without the least embarrassment; once more her lips lightly touched his face, a little below the cheekbones.

'I hoped you would come,' she said, her hand on Wilfred's arm. 'Shall we go and sit over there for a little while?'

He followed her into a corner of the room and there, a little out of the way of possible listeners, she looked straight at him and he saw tears well up in her eyes.

'Wilfred,' she said, 'I'm afraid that something may happen. My husband is ill. Oh, not very ill, of course, but he couldn't be here today: the doctor wouldn't allow it.'

He squeezed her hand and she could not prevent two tears from rolling down her cheeks.

'Maybe it's nothing serious,' he whispered.

'Maybe, but I've had a scare. It's his heart. He had an attack last week. Yes, he's been looking after himself, he's been careful for years and last week –'

She put her handkerchief over her mouth as though to smother words she did not wish to utter. Wilfred stood in front

172

of her as much to hide her from prying glances as to keep her to himself. How was it that tears and anxiety made her even more attractive to him? He imagined her in his arms, with that expression on her face.

'How glad I am you're here!' she exclaimed in a subdued voice. 'All those unknown people around me – I hope this legacy business isn't going to make trouble for my poor James.'

'He's inheriting a fine house.'

She waved her hand vaguely.

'Won't you come downstairs with me?' she asked.

He was preparing to follow her when an old lady in a chinchilla coat and black gloves came towards him, wagging a finger in his direction.

'Now don't you run away, Wilfred Ingram. I knew your father.'

Pushing aside a chair that stood in the way, she reached the young man and pressed the same finger to his breast.

'I knew him when he was your age.'

Phoebe Knight moved quietly towards the door.

'You look a little like him,' continued the old lady, 'but he was taller than you, my boy. And what a way he had with women – We were all in love with him,' she added, shaking with laughter. 'But you're a very steady young man, it seems. Now that's fine, it's even very fine, but there's plenty of time for that, you know, when you're past youth.'

He bowed and before she even realized what he was about, reached the door with catlike agility.

A few seconds later, he overtook Phoebe Knight in the street. She heard him running behind her and turned with an anxious glance as though she were afraid of him, though she smiled with unconscious tenderness. At that moment, he felt sure that she was losing her head a little and that sooner or later, depending

173

on circumstances, she would belong to him. Today, a great deal of respect was necessary.

He asked if he could take her to her car. She gave a laugh, that rather irritating small girl laugh of hers; for with Phoebe sudden fits of joy followed anxiety, she forgot that she was unhappy.

'Oh,' she said, 'how ceremonious you've become! I can drive you home, if you like.'

He turned to see if they were being followed.

'What are you frightened of?' she asked. 'Is it forbidden to walk down the street together?'

Wilfred looked down at her. She probably imagined that she had shocked him, for her brow coloured suddenly and he remembered she believed him to be religious. Something in him felt grieved, but he laughed at once with such unconcern that his own easiness surprised him.

'Forbidden? By whom?'

A moment later, they were in a car that she drove with an expert hand. From time to time, she threw him a glance and talked unceasingly in her quick, soft voice, as though to prevent him from putting in a word. 'She's not very clever,' he thought, 'but I must be careful of her intuition. Like lots of other women, she guesses what goes on in your mind and if she doesn't yet know what I want of her, it's because she doesn't choose to know it.'

'Actually,' she said, 'James looks much fiercer than he really is. He's awfully plain-spoken and sincere, but he is good.'

It soothed her conscience, apparently, to talk to Wilfred about her husband, she wanted him to be present, in this manner, between them. 'How easy it is to read this woman's mind!' he thought. He inspected her more brazenly. She wore a dress of such a dark shade of green that it verged on black and enhanced the whiteness of her throat. She must have known this perfectly well, for it was certainly the colour best suited to the faintly

174

pearly quality of her skin: she had the makings of a flirt capable of turning the devil's own head, but knowing very little about herself, chose to think herself pure, faithful and religious. Wilfred attempted unsuccessfully to imagine her husband taking her in his arms. 'It's unimaginable,' he thought, 'therefore he can't possibly do it.'

'I hope you'll get to know us better some day,' she continued with that guilelessness of hers that went to Wilfred's head like a perfume. 'His is a most affectionate nature, but a sense of decency makes him hide his feelings. I'm afraid he talked to you gruffly when he met you at Uncle Horace's. You don't hold it against him, do you?'

'Not in the least.'

'He distrusts young men of your age because he credits them with intentions they don't have at all, I'm sure. I mean that some of them are serious, as you are, (she spoke a little too quickly then, and bent over the wheel). 'I told him you were very religious –'

Why had she used that word? Wilfred could not help shifting in his seat.

'Oh, forgive me if I've been tactless,' she continued with a smile so humble that it upset him. 'I didn't wish to – At heart, although he doesn't believe in the same things as you, I'm sure he has a respect for you. He has changed a lot since his illness. In a certain way, he's no longer the same. He probably had the feeling of having come close to something very serious, and so –'

He looked her straight in the eye. The car had just stopped at a red light and, at most, two hands' breadths separated her mouth from his. What laws, what conventions kept him from throwing himself on her? The blood thundered in Wilfred's head. She stared back at him both fascinated and alarmed. Now she knew. There was a pause that he would not break, because by keeping silent he held her in his power.

175

When they drove on again, she made some trifling little remarks about the difficulties of city traffic and stopped at the corner of the street where Wilfred lived. He thanked her with an icy politeness that cost him more than anything, and once more she smiled at him.

On closing the door of the car, he gave an involuntary exclamation, seized with a horrible and unaccountable fear that Phoebe's hand had been caught in it and crushed, but just then the car moved off.

CHAPTER XXXVIII

Instead of going home, he wandered about the streets. The word adultery settled in his mind and remained there the entire evening. You committed adultery in your heart with a woman when you looked at her with lust. Consequently, it was out of the question to go to Communion with such a sin on one's conscience, but with all his might he waved aside the idea of a possible Communion, he waved away the whole of religion. He did not want God to prevent his having that woman. For a quarter of an hour, he strode up and down talking to himself like a madman. Finally he went to a cinema and fell asleep there a few minutes afterwards. When the performance ended, the lights hit him suddenly, like a slap in the face. He got up and left.

Night was falling. He went to a drugstore and ate no matter what: in fact he did not really know what he was doing. He had never in his life desired a woman to that extent and stranger than anything else, he told himself, was the fact that so far he had not thought about her much, and suddenly he had to have her.

He walked to the park and sat on a bench to think about

Phoebe. In imagination, she was his already and he would have killed anyone who disturbed him in this amorous meditation. At one point, the memory of his visit to the church and his confession flitted through his mind and astounded him: so, you could very easily be two persons.

Face in hands, he talked to Phoebe in a gentle, beseeching voice pitched so low that he could scarcely hear it and his tender and obscene talk resembled a diabolical prayer. Two girls laughed as they passed by him and one said to the other: 'Drunk!' She was right: he was drunk with desire, at a loss what to do with himself, his body and the monstrous craving that possessed it. At about eleven, he went to a bar.

He wanted to tell somebody the whole story, Max for instance. No doubt there was something revolting about the man in Wilfred's eyes, but Max understood everything and that was why Wilfred would have liked to see him. Of course, he would not find Max in the bar, and yet, every time Wilfred thought of Max, he imagined him in this sinister and fascinating place.

There was not much of a crowd: a few rather fashionable men were talking among themselves with the severe, bored air so frequent in *habitués* of pleasure haunts, and two young women in an ill-lit corner were laughing softly with a sailor whose hair fell in a golden tumble over a face that alcohol wreathed in childlike smiles. The radio played a South-American tune in a subdued drone. Seated on a stool apart from the other customers, Wilfred felt himself slide all of a sudden into such a despair as no words could describe. It simply came to this: all was lost, nothing remained.

Nothing but a little bar where rows of bottles shone in a dubious pink light and where men and women stood talking low, awaiting the moment of their damnation. For reasons that Wilfred could not understand, his faith was roused by a setting which he hated all the more for its being necessary to him. At

177

church, on Sunday, he did not believe in the same manner, but here it seemed to him that communications were already established with the nether regions and the fiery lake. Here, everything was real, he could not deny that he himself existed, but he could lose his soul. Sooner or later someone would come and sit by him and it would be a woman who disgusted him, but whom he would end by finding desirable, if he drank enough. And so he would forget life, forget Phoebe and sink a little lower still.

Standing very straight in his white coat, the young bartender who faced him said something that he scarcely heard. The youth was about twenty and he tried to make an impertinent little face look manly by growing curly blond side-whiskers, shaped like yataghans, along each ear. Wilfred ordered a glass of gin.

The bartender returned a moment later and put down the glass.

'She left a letter,' he muttered. 'Do you want it?'

'Who left a letter?'

'The little brunette in a green sweater you went off with Tuesday evening.'

Wilfred had no recollection whatever of the woman.

'Give it to me,' he said.

Opening a drawer, the bartender handed him the letter with a contemptuous smile. His little curly whiskers seemed highly ridiculous to Wilfred and, at the same time, improper, although he could not have said why. The letter disappeared into his pocket.

'What are you smiling at?' he asked the bartender, puckering up his nose angrily.

Raising an eyebrow, the youth walked away. How delighted Wilfred would have been to tear out his pretty little whiskers, in gory tufts! He felt himself becoming spiteful. If Max had been there, it would have been nice to talk to him no doubt and

178

nicer still to send him sprawling with one blow of his fist, on account of several things he had said the other day and in particular that revolting business about sacrilege. To lay him out flat would have settled everything, after a certain fashion, and Wilfred could have loved him once more, for at the bottom of his heart, he loved everybody, but how could he hope to make himself clear? Max would have needed a good deal of Irish blood in his veins, like Wilfred.

Without even tasting his gin, he laid a coin, a silver coin, on the bar and left. A splendid moon overcame darkness in a completely black sky. The air was warm, filled with the soft tenderness that comes after rather hot days. 'A night for making love,' thought Wilfred. It even seemed idiotic to think of anything else: everything breathed desire.

Passers-by were rare after supper in that part of town. The port began at the end of the street and whiffs of tar and water roused a yearning for freedom and adventure in the young man's heart. His daily life seemed terribly second-rate and Mr Schoenhals' outline passing through his reverie, as though the shop walker were really there, in the port, made him grind his teeth with rage. Indeed he almost imagined seeing him. No, he was alone on a sidewalk bordered by tall grey houses. A few steps more and under his feet he could feel the rough cobblestones of wharves where street-lamps pierced the darkness at long intervals. Wilfred scarcely ever went that way. Such people as were never found elsewhere prowled about the place and rumour had it that a great many misdeeds were perpetrated there.

After a few minutes, he paused. Without being frightened, he felt some curiosity and, to tell the truth, disappointment in discovering nothing out of the ordinary. He stood on the very brink of the water whose powerful odour rose to his nostrils, and he was alone. Two or three yards away, the side of a ship rose like a huge black wall and hid the stars from him. One step

179

more and he would fall into the sea and certainly drown, as he could not swim. The weird idea of ending the whole thing right away attracted him, but what kept him back was the thought of all the happiness he would miss in crossing the short distance that separated him from an excruciating death, for sooner or later he would have the woman he wanted, and after her a countless number of others –

With a shiver and a short peal of laughter, he drew back a step, then another, and wheeling around, moved away from the waterfront. Hands thrust in pockets, he skirted the ship and almost ran into an empty crate on which he sat down, back turned to the sea. Faint whitish gleams from the street-lamp reached him and he could see, beyond a great heap of casks, the long black massive outline of shops in the port behind which the city lights formed a kind of halo. A more solitary spot could not be imagined. Yet, after a few minutes, Wilfred heard a murmur of voices and the shuffling of shoes on the cobbles, then a man and a woman emerged from the shadows and passed him so slowly that he felt sure they did not see him. A little further on, he saw the woman raise her face towards the man's and they stopped for a moment. Both seemed young and he could not help envying them.

Scarcely had they disappeared when a man in a waterproof went by, hands behind his back, somewhat like an actor crossing the stage of a theatre. Wilfred had unconsciously placed himself in a spot where he could not be noticed. The stranger stopped a little further on, looked around him, then turned off suddenly into the darkness that swallowed him up.

A motionless and apparently invisible onlooker, Wilfred waited. Behind him ropes creaked softly and the long drawn-out roar of the city reached his ears like the sound of a smothered voice. From sitting still so long it became more and more impossible for him to move. Wasn't this just as good a place as

180

any other in which to suffer? He loathed suffering. 'It will pass,' he thought. 'I've never desired a woman longer than a day.' But he also knew that this was no longer so.

All of a sudden, he forced himself to act. Getting up automatically, he crossed the gloomy stretch of cobblestones that separated him from the streets he had left a moment earlier, and in the brutal light of the first city lamp-posts, he suddenly saw Max coming towards him with a curious cat-like tread. Hadn't he recognized Wilfred? Perhaps the lights dazzled him. He stopped short and gave an exclamation of surprise.

'What are you doing here?'

'Probably the same thing as you.'

'Oh, that's not possible.'

He nudged Wilfred's elbow and the latter drew back imperceptibly. The two men looked at each other, then Max began to laugh.

'Why isn't it possible?' asked Wilfred. 'And what makes you laugh?'

'Oh, it would take too long to explain. Nothing is simple, you know, Wilfred. I certainly didn't expect to find you here. That's what made me laugh, among other things.'

He was not the same man as he had been the last time. Perhaps he had been drinking. The face remained unchanged but the expression was different. It was as though a stranger suddenly leaned from the window of a house where one knew every inhabitant. He shook his head.

'Let's go away from here,' he said.

'Why?'

'I think this place is sinister.'

'Then why do you come here?'

'A good many people come here for one reason or another. You, for instance –'

'Oh, I was just taking the air,' said Wilfred hastily.

181

'Of course. We're all taking the air. We all say we're taking the air. Come, let's not stay here. It's getting late. We're running the risk of getting into trouble.'

'What are you afraid of?'

'The port is always dangerous at night. Didn't you know it?'

His expression suddenly became so extremely sly and his eye so watchful that Wilfred looked away.

'No,' he answered dryly, 'I didn't know it.'

He lied. How could he be in ignorance of the rumours that went about concerning the port? But all that remained rather vague in his mind and, in any case, it was better to pretend not to know. Not without amazement, he recalled how, an hour ago, he had wished for the company of the man who stood before him, regarding him silently.

'I'm going,' he said, passing in front of Max.

'You're going home?'

'I'm going home.'

'I'll take you to your door.'

Without answering, Wilfred began walking a little faster and Max hopped along to keep up with him.

'Don't be afraid I'll be a bother to you,' he said. 'I won't go in with you. More's the pity, we might have talked things over.'

'I don't feel like talking things over.'

'Anything wrong?'

Wilfred kept silence. A sailor in a white uniform lurched uncertainly past them.

'He's going where we've just come from,' said Max.

'No doubt.'

'In a uniform designed, cut out and sewn by the devil,' added Max under his breath.

The young man did not challenge a statement which affected him unpleasantly. Almost everything that Max said that night had a meaning that Wilfred preferred not to go into. Yet he

182

wanted to talk to him. The urge was irresistible: he had to tell someone.

'You weren't wrong in thinking there was something the matter with me!' he cried. 'I'm in love.'

Max laid his hand on Wilfred's arm.

'Oh!' he exclaimed. 'I'm sorry for you. Of course it's –'

That was the moment Wilfred was waiting for.

'Of course, it's a woman,' he said cuttingly.

'Naturally,' said Max gently. 'Young?'

'Younger than I. And married.'

They walked silently down a deserted street where their footsteps rang out between tall black houses. Wilfred was grateful to his companion for keeping quiet, for being as mute as if he were at a funeral. In his way, the foreigner was not lacking in delicacy.

'Married,' he said finally. 'For a man with your ideas, it would be better to forget about it.'

'Ideas? What ideas?'

'Your principles.'

Wilfred stopped dead and looked him in the eye.

'A man in love has no principles,' he said quickly.

'Oh,' replied Max with a shake of the head, 'under all that, in your case, lies religion. Try as you may, religion lies underneath, it flows like a subterranean stream. Wherever you go, the stream is there, a hundred yards under your feet.'

'I've already told you that I didn't wish to talk about such things.'

'Very well, but when you take that woman in your arms, you're committing a tremendous sin.'

'There's been nothing between us so far.'

'Is she a believer?'

'Yes. She's a Protestant.'

He looked down at the tips of his shoes.

183

'Why don't you say something?' asked Wilfred.

'I don't want to irritate you. I would be too brutal.'

'Never mind. Tell me what you think.'

His heart beat fast, as though he expected a verdict. Max stood perfectly motionless, then raised his head.

'If I were you,' he said, 'I'd try to throw religion overboard for a time.'

'That has nothing to do with it –'

'Follow nature good and hard,' he said, stuffing his hands in his pockets. 'Religion distorts everything.'

'I tell you that has nothing to do with it,' replied Wilfred with the obstinacy of a man who can't find an answer.

'It has with a man like you. Your behaviour lacks firmness, and in the end, you're always ready to say yes to God. That's what's likely to make you bungle the affair. Believe me, I'm wise to all these dodges. I've gone through fits of religion.'

'Oh, hush, Max!'

'There, you see: you get angry if anyone meddles with religion.'

'I'm not angry. I only want you to give me some practical advice.'

'Please notice that I've been doing nothing else for the last five minutes, Wilfred. Have you glanced over the books I gave you?'

'Yes, a little.'

'You're intelligent, you must realize that all that is impossible, that it doesn't hold out in the face of passion. Such ethics make an enemy of our body, whereas it's with our body that we love – *The Imitation of Christ*!'

Wilfred drew back as though he had been struck.

'Excuse me,' said Max. 'I didn't mean to shock you. We won't mention all this again. I'm in one of my bad moods. Listen: if you can't contrive to have that woman, look elsewhere. With a physique like yours, you could have them all.'

184

'Not that one.'

'You could if you tried. She's a believer. She'll want to convert you. Allow yourself to be led – or pretend to.'

Wilfred crossed his arms.

'What a blackguard you are,' he said.

'Of course I am,' said Max in a polite tone. 'I'm a blackguard because of what I'm telling you. But what I say, you'll do, so the greater blackguard of the two is perhaps – you.'

A policeman passed slowly by them. Wilfred crossed the street followed by Max, who caught up with him in a single stride.

'You're angry with me, naturally,' he remarked when they reached the opposite pavement.

'I'm sorry I talked to you.'

'Why? Because I'm too clear-sighted? You think I'm the devil, eh?'

'Oh, no!'

'Let's go and have a drink.'

'No.'

They walked on for two or three minutes in silence, keeping step like a couple of soldiers. The street seemed interminable. Wilfred turned over in his mind all the things he could say to Phoebe if he were given an opportunity of seeing her again.

'Why don't you come with me to two hundred and thirteen and a half?' asked Max suddenly. 'It would amuse you. There are always four or five friends I can call up at any hour.'

Wilfred threw him a suspicious glance.

'Friends?' he asked.

'Oh, friends passing through town. In spite of your not having the same *Weltanschauung* as me, you'd find them delightful.'

Wilfred had not the least idea what a *Weltanschauung* could be, but he sniggered.

'I don't think so,' he said.

'Why do you say that?' asked Max giving his voice the sing-song modulations that made him seem even more foreign than usual to Wilfred. 'There is a whole world you know nothing about. The store, bars and church are your world.'

'If you don't stop, I'll send you rolling in the gutter.'

'I doubt your being able to do that,' said Max gently. 'Among other things, I've learnt wrestling – judo. It's worth more than knowing foreign languages. But to please you, I'll take back that sentence about the store, bars and church. You don't know yourself. That's where your real tragedy lies. I could have told you several important things on the subject. Then you would have been happier, but the first thing to do is to liquidate the supernatural. Come down to earth.'

They stood before Wilfred's house and the latter drew a key from his pocket. Max considered the object with an air of melancholy.

'It's a pity,' he said. 'The conversation promised to become interesting. But you don't understand.'

Without a word, Wilfred tossed his key up and down. A short silence ensued, then Max turned suddenly on his heel and departed.

CHAPTER XXXIX

As usual, much of what Max had said remained rather obscure to Wilfred. Pride prevented his asking for an explanation that would have certainly been furnished with zealous verbosity. 'He doesn't come from here,' thought Wilfred. And he was

186

ashamed, for that reason, of not understanding everything this disconcerting person said. The way he mouthed the word *Weltanschauung*, for instance, made Wilfred feel like hitting him. In fact, a longing to hit him never quite left the young man, yet he was always sorry to see him go. As he put the key in the lock of his door he experienced a curious sadness which increased the sadness he already felt because of Phoebe.

In the end he could think only of her, even when he said his prayers, for he said his prayers before going to bed, before going to bed like a good child who submits to doing without the cake it longs to bite into – How furious he was when this occurred to him! But he was tired and sleep overcame his anger.

The next day being Saturday, he was free: no Mr Schoenhals, no exacting or insolent customers. He could loll in bed and read the papers –

Like a long thrust, the thrust of a knife driven in slowly, everything that had happened the day before came back to him and he sighed with grief. Without hope or remedy, he was in love. The sun might shine and the air lightly caress his face, he wished he were dead. If Phoebe had been a girl, he could have married her, but she was already married and the mere fact of desiring her amounted to a kind of adultery. Why a kind of adultery? Adultery pure and simple. Such were his thoughts when he opened his eyes, and another thought immediately and forcefully occurred to him. It was one of Max's sentences: 'The first thing to do is to liquidate the supernatural.'

Couldn't one help being a Catholic? How did one go about getting rid of faith? Both hands went up to his eyes, he could have screamed with horror. Was he wrong in believing that Max was the devil? Was he wrong in believing that this passion for a married woman came to him from the devil? He had been taught that love came from God. Now, he would have died for Phoebe, to save her life, for instance. Well then was it his

187

fault if he had met her? Did he ask her to kiss his cheek?

He got up and dressed. At all costs, he must come down to earth, as Max said. He would go to Mass tomorrow, Sunday. That went without saying, but on the other hand he would seduce that woman or die. 'However,' he thought as he shaved, 'Knight could have another heart attack that might prove fatal. That's when you win. You don't want to win that way, but you win just the same. The thing will be to wait a little, and comfort Phoebe. You'll be tactful and then you'll end by having her. Why not even marry her?'

A little scarlet cut shone across his chin. Maybe he was going a bit quickly.

The day turned out a difficult one and despair went round and round his room, like a detective around a block of houses. Never before had Wilfred known what suffering could be. The mere idea of dissipation sickened him. He did not know what to do with his body, he could only wear it out by walking, by wandering in the neighbourhood to come home afterwards, sleep and go out again. The temptation to call up Phoebe was so strong that he shut himself into a telephone booth several times, dialled her number and then instinctively hung up the receiver at the first ring. Not to have known such heart-devastating moments was not to have lived at all. In the last twenty-four hours he had become a man.

Towards the end of the afternoon, he entered a little church that bore these words on its pediment: 'Come unto me, all ye who are weary.' He went in on account of that text, for if anyone was weary, he certainly was. But he felt very far removed from all religious fervour: he wanted to clasp Phoebe's body to him and wanted nothing else. Yet, in the shadowy silence, he hoped to find, if not peace, at least a respite, for though he thought himself incapable of praying, he dared not pursue in front of the altar the relentless erotic meditation that had enthralled him

188

for the last twenty-four hours and, as it happened, something came to stop, there was a sudden break: something gave way.

Around him, women and a few young men awaited their turn for confession. He rose suddenly and left the church.

On reaching home, he found two letters. On one of the envelopes he recognized Angus's writing and put the letter aside. The other was from Phoebe.

'*Dear Wilfred,*' she wrote, '*I talked about you at great length to my husband and he has expressed a wish to see you. I think what I said about you has changed his opinion where you are concerned. He is better, but I am still anxious. You can't refuse to lunch with us tomorrow. Don't answer, I'm counting on you. – Phoebe.*'

Putting down the letter, Wilfred started to laugh without being able to stop for several minutes, but his laughter would have frightened him a little had it come from anyone else, for it was totally devoid of cheerfulness. He felt the relief of a man who has been acquitted and who has dreaded death, he laughed too loudly. Tears rolled down his cheeks and, red with shame, he threw himself on his bed, sobbing.

CHAPTER XL

That night, he roamed around the Knights' house. It was located in one of those rather fashionable neighbourhoods where town becomes country with almost no transition. There was a long avenue lined with sycamores, then a small deserted street, and right at the end of it the house stood quietly in the middle of a big garden enclosed only by clumps of boxwood.

It was simpler than he had imagined. Of course the trees

189

around it made it look rather splendid and the lawns seemed immense, but the place only had one storey, if one excepted the tiny dormer windows just under the sloping roof. White and square as a box, it was in no way different from many other such little dwellings that escaped notice. To the right and left of the front door, he made out two slender columns with scrolled capitals the sole ornament of the almost childishly simple façade.

Wilfred looked more closely at the house; although he thought it commonplace, it suggested happiness, peace. That was perhaps because the trees partly overshadowed it in the moonlight. It was separate from the other houses, separate from the world. In a corner of the ground floor, a lighted window stood out in a golden rectangle. 'She's there,' he thought, he imagined her alone, without her husband who had perhaps gone to bed.

Three steps forward and he would have stood on the little path leading to the front door, but he dared not move. Standing motionless behind a wall of boxwood that he just topped, he whispered to Phoebe. 'You're going to belong to me,' he breathed, 'I'll do what's necessary, I'll fling everything overboard.'

A passer-by made him start and he walked off slowly, as thought he had been strolling by, then he returned to the house. 'I'm going to force her to think of me,' he thought. 'She'll end by feeling I'm here, twenty yards away from her.' His eyes were fixed on the lighted window, but he could distinguish nothing but a grey wall and half a piece of furniture that looked like a bookcase. After fifteen minutes he had the impression that his knees would give way from weariness. The temptation to walk up to the door harried him once more, but he was afraid of being seen from the street, and what sense did it make? In less than twelve hours, he would ring at that same door, walk into the house –

He went back to the long avenue and made his way home on foot.

CHAPTER XLI

Next day, a little before half past one, he crossed the little garden and rang at the Knights' door. By day, the house retained the air of innocence that had struck him the evening before. 'This could be such a happy place,' he thought sadly, 'if only –'

In the centre of the door shone a knocker, in the shape of a hand, a woman's pretty hand with bent fingers. He had time enough to consider it for the door was not opened at once and it flashed through his mind that he was being watched from a window, but he was in such a state of nervousness that he could have imagined anything.

A coloured servant led him into such a small drawing-room that it might have belonged to a doll, with its low ceiling and tiny windows. The light filtering through cream-coloured Venetian blinds showed armchairs with pink flowered loose covers bordered by little petticoat frills. On the walls hung old engravings that Wilfred did not have time to examine as, inexplicably, he could not take his eyes off the brass shovel, tongs and firedogs, all sparkling clean, and suddenly the door opened and he found himself face to face with James Knight when he was expecting to see Phoebe.

A horrifying suspicion darted through his mind that he had mistaken the day or that James Knight had not been informed of his wife's invitation, but a smile from the former reassured him.

Wilfred had never seen him smile. The man who stood before him took on the appearance of a stranger. The young man

191

looked vainly for the coldly regular face he remembered. What he found on the contrary, in James Knight's expression and even in his features, was something kind and wounded and, in the depth of his great black eyes, mingled with immense sadness, a sort of astonishment. That was what was most striking, even more so than the purplish tinge of his lips. In a dainty little room where everything seemed so frivolous, the impression made by a man touched by the finger of death was almost indescribable.

'Hello, Wilfred,' he said gently. 'Won't you sit down?'

The young man sat on the edge of an armchair. James Knight walked up and down from the window to the door.

'I'm glad my wife asked you here,' he said as he moved about. 'She'll be here in a moment. I'm happy to have an opportunity of talking to you alone. Oh, not that I have anything particular to say to you, but it seems to me we ought to know each other a little better. After all, we're related – My wife has talked to me about you: I don't want you to take me for a fanatic, Wilfred.'

He paused and glanced at his guest.

'Even though our beliefs differ,' he continued, 'what counts is that you and I take our religion seriously. Isn't that so?'

The answer was a nod and James Knight began walking up and down again. That morning Wilfred had gone to Mass. He could not have said that he would rather die than miss going to Mass, because such an idea conveyed nothing to his mind, but he would have missed the most wonderful of affairs rather than not go to church on a Sunday.

'You've been told of my illness?' asked James Knight.

'Yes.'

'I recovered rather quickly and now it's over. I can go up to my room just as fast as I did before this little heart attack and I can walk to my office. However, there came a time when I thought my illness rather serious, in fact, I had what is called a warning. You understand what I mean?'

'Yes, I do.'

'In such moments, Wilfred, you don't think about faith. Your one idea is to live.'

There was a silence. James Knight stood motionless.

'It's the body,' murmured Wilfred. 'The body putting up a fight.'

'I don't know – There's not a thought for God. I didn't think of God. I did later, when everything was ship-shape again, when disease loosened its grip. Now, that grip is God. It is God too. You'll see. One wants to live.'

Wilfred got up, suddenly moved with compassion.

'That heart attack is over,' he said, 'everything will be all right if you take care of yourself.'

'Everything will be all right,' repeated James Knight absently. 'Yes, of course. But it will come back. I mean that I'll have to go because of that or something else. I'll have to think of God, if I can. Some day, you'll see, you too will see.'

Wilfred cleared his throat.

'God knows very well that if we don't think about Him at such moments, it's because we can't,' he said. 'What He wants above all –'

James Knight looked at him with parted lips:

'How do you know what He wants?' he asked. 'You talk like someone who has faith. But you'll see.'

'You also have faith, Mr Knight.'

'Oh, yes, of course. I have faith now, but there was a time, there was that time – Since then, everything seems different. More beautiful, in a certain way. Light, for instance. Light is beautiful. I used to take it for something ordinary, but it's not: when you begin to watch it, to follow it hour by hour, you understand –'

193

He saw Wilfred's astonishment and continued:

'You understand that its task is to show us a great many things and that we simply must look and look –'

'That's a fine discovery,' thought Wilfred. 'His brain is affected.' But he was moved. It seemed as though the man read his mind. James Knight's eyes took on a sorrowful expression.

'I look for all I'm worth,' he said. 'In the garden, for instance, at every leaf. Even at night. Why, last night, I sat over there.'

He pointed to a lawn that could be seen through a window with a raised blind. Wilfred felt himself blush a little.

'Yes, I was there,' pursued James Knight, 'on a bench with my wife. She was talking about you. I've been mistaken about you, Wilfred. Human beings are better than I thought. That's something you finally realize, particularly when you draw nearer to the moment – to that difficult moment. You'll see.'

Once more he looked at Wilfred and there was a silence.

'I can't remember what I was talking to you about,' he said in an ashamed voice.

The young man waved his hand toward the window.

'Ah, yes,' said James Knight. 'We were sitting on the bench and at our feet was what seemed to be a pool of white light. I don't know why we can't find words to express what we feel at such moments. I was happy, at peace, do you see? But as soon as we attempt to express these things, the words don't sound right, don't sound right at all.'

Wilfred turned his head away to hide his confusion, but James Knight apparently no longer paid him any attention and talked as one talks to oneself, yet with rather unusual verbosity.

'Perhaps you have never been in that state of mind,' he said. 'Nothing has changed around you and yet you wonder how you could have given the least importance to this thing or that. No more anxiety, no more threats – But that doesn't last.'

At that moment the door opened and his wife came in.

Wilfred noticed at once that her eyelids were red, yet she smiled and said with rather artificial gaiety:

'So I've lured the bear from his den at last!'

Contrary to her habit, she did not kiss him and for a few minutes conversation took the playful insignificant turn that makes society the realm of boredom.

CHAPTER XLII

It was nearly two when they had lunch, but Wilfred's appetite failed him. Neuralgia had gripped his head in a band of pain for the last few minutes and although avocado pears were served – and he was particularly fond of them – eating proved an effort.

'You're not looking after him,' said James Knight to his wife with unconscious cruelty. 'His plate is empty.'

She laughed and helped Wilfred to food, in spite of protests that she mistook for politeness; she could not know it pained him to have her so near that by just moving his hand he might have touched hers. He thought her particularly attractive that day. Everything made her laugh and her limpid glance and childlike prattle added to her charm, a charm that affected him like a burn. What had made him think for a minute that she guessed his love? Quite obviously, she knew nothing.

The dining-room was the counterpart of the little parlour, with the sole difference that only one picture hung on the walls, the portrait of a minister in a white wig and starched bands, easily recognized as an ancestor of James Knight's. Wilfred looked absently at the picture and also at the dark mahogany sideboard where bits of old silver lent a prosperous air to that corner of the house. It was not difficult to guess that Phoebe

195

and her husband prized these things, as the setting of their life. This made Wilfred feel that he knew them both a little better, and James Knight, who had so deeply impressed him at Wormsloe, now turned into a most commonplace man, the man who owned the silver, the furniture, all the little family keepsakes that probably made him cling to this world. He was no longer the least bit terrifying. He was going to die. In his presence, Wilfred dared looked at his wife's face, her neck, her hands. She was smiling in a rather naïve way that delighted and disheartened him at the same time, for the woman's innocence seemed even greater than he had supposed, and it crossed his mind that no physical relations existed between the couple. That explained, said Wilfred to himself, why he could not imagine them in each other's arms. Of course, that was not a proof, but it took no more than a minute or two for this supposition to become a certainty. 'There's something, some obstacle,' he thought.

While he milled over these ideas in his head, James Knight laughed for the first time and asked what he was thinking about:

'You're awfully silent,' he said. 'Silent and reserved. Don't take this for a reproach, quite the opposite – Young men nowadays are such braggers – But still, we'd like you to tell us a little about yourself.'

And he asked him questions about his job that Wilfred was obliged to answer, and quite evidently James Knight spoke without malicious intent, but if he had wanted to humiliate the young man before his wife, he would not have gone about it differently. The guest had to give precise information about his working hours, to describe everything he was employed to sell – as if he were displaying the articles on the table – to give his hosts an idea of the various customers he dealt with.

Later, he remembered that they were eating vanilla ice-cream, and with every spoonful he felt as though he were pouring fire down his throat, when he suddenly noticed in Phoebe's eyes an

196

almost motherly tenderness. 'She loves me,' he thought. 'It's going to be easy.' And hope restoring his courage, he began talking modestly of ambitions he had had to renounce. And thus he regretted not having gone to one of the great colleges in that part of the country, but was trying to fill in gaps in his education by reading in the evening.

'What do you read?' asked James Knight whose attentive eyes never left his face.

What did he read? Wilfred flushed violently; for never indeed had a more impudent lie left his lips, and for a minute or two he stopped short. Not a single title came to his mind. He had nothing in his room but detective stories. No, he did own something else. A word shaped itself on his lips, as of itself:

'*The Imitation.*'

Why had he said that? He did not know. The title had certainly not been uttered with any calculation; on the contrary, Wilfred felt ready to die of shame as if he had said something improper. Phoebe and James Knight exchanged a glance, then the husband's voice said gently:

'There's no reason for you to feel flustered, my friend. It's the finest book in the world after the Bible. Phoebe and I used to read it every day.'

'Every day!' she exclaimed, her eyes glowing with enthusiasm.

Wilfred thought he saw tears glistening on her lashes and suddenly hated himself. He was deceiving two people in the cruelest possible way and he longed to take back what he had said, but that was impossible. This intolerable situation was like a machine whose functioning could not be modified. He was caught in a fiendishly solid and delicate trap. In spite of himself he was winning at a game where a more skilful man might perhaps have lost. Yet, he attempted to tell the truth.

'I also read far less serious books,' he stammered.

His hosts burst out laughing.

'If you only read the *Imitation* . . .' cried Phoebe.

She did not explain what she meant to say, but her husband nodded his approbation and all three left the table. Phoebe and James Knight appeared relieved for a reason that the young man did not at once guess at, for he was upset, and the agitation that showed in his face worked in his favour, although without his knowledge. He felt awkward, unhappy, but his clumsiness won him the confidence of this couple, reassured them about him. In a mirror, he saw James Knight give his wife a slight nod, as much as to say: 'You were right.'

CHAPTER XLIII

They all three strolled around the garden, then James Knight went to rest in the drawing-room while Phoebe and Wilfred remained under a small clump of trees; a rather short iron bench had been placed there, probably the very one mentioned before lunch.

'The doctor wants him to keep very quiet,' said Phoebe as she sat down, 'but he doesn't always obey. He does too much, just to convince himself he isn't ill.'

Wilfred sat on the bench, as far as possible from Phoebe, and one arm thrown over the back of the seat. 'So, if anyone sees us from the house –' he thought.

'He's better,' said Wilfred.

'Better, yes, but I'm frightened.'

For a minute or so, he tried to comfort her and she looked at him gratefully; once more, a tenderness in her expression stirred him. She smiled a trifle sadly but, in some indefinable way, seemed happier than her words led him to think, though she was certainly anxious. Yet how clear it was to Wilfred that they were made for one another! So fresh, so healthy in her pale blue dress, with her charming way of lowering her head and then raising it suddenly to look him full in the face, with eyes that spoke boldly. This time he was sure; his first intuition had been right. She was in love with him, but to what extent, and did she realize it?

Without moving or smiling, he said her name in a low voice. At the same moment he thought: 'Death is watching us from inside the house.'

Phoebe did not answer but stopped smiling. He felt vaguely that the spell would be broken if she spoke; a single word, no matter what, would be enough to make everything resume a normal course; but she kept silent. His heart beat violently: right then, he was losing his soul and hers along with his, under the motionless trees, in the heat of the afternoon.

'We must talk,' he said after a rather long pause. 'It will seem strange if we keep silent, as we can be heard from the house.'

'I'm frightened, Wilfred,' she whispered.

'Are you happy, Phoebe?'

'I don't know. I don't want to stay out here.'

A sunbeam shone through the leaves and rested on the upper part of Wilfred's face, but he did not attempt to avoid it. She was looking at his eyes and he guessed that to influence her, all he had to do was to look back at her.

'Why do you want to go in?' he asked in an undertone. 'What's the matter? We aren't doing anything wrong.'

She whispered:

'Yes, we are.'

'Are you frightened of me, Phoebe?'

'No. I'm frightened of myself.'

'That's impossible. It doesn't make sense.'

'I'm asking you to get up and go back to the house with me.'

'When shall we meet again?'

'I don't know. Some day.'

'Alone, Phoebe?'

'Alone as we are today? I don't know.'

'We aren't alone today.'

'Please don't say another word.'

She tried to get up and Wilfred made a gesture as though to help her, for he thought she was near fainting.

'Don't,' she said, 'everything can be seen.'

After another effort she left her seat, Wilfred also rose, and at that moment James Knight appeared in the doorway and came towards them. While the whole stretch of lawn still separated them from him, Phoebe murmured:

'Be kind to James. I think he's losing his faith.'

He came up to them, walking youthfully and smiling, and the sunlight showed up the furrows right and left of his mouth.

'Did you succeed in making him talk a little?' he asked his wife as he glanced at Wilfred.

She hesitated.

'I must admit I'm not very talkative,' said Wilfred with a laugh.

'So you're shy?' asked James Knight. 'I was too when I was your age. Come with me, I'll show you my little library, since you're fond of books. Phoebe, I'm taking him from you for a few minutes.'

The two men stood in a small room on the second floor, a little obscured by the branches of an elm that blocked out a corner of the sky. An intricately carved sofa filled the space beneath long rows of books sunk into the wall. A writing-table completed the furnishings of the study, which had a feeling of another age.

'You must think our house very simple,' said James Knight as he showed Wilfred to the sofa and himself took a chair facing it.

200

'But three months from now, at the latest, we'll be settled out there, in your Uncle Horace's place. Did my wife tell you about this?'

'No.'

'I believe she's grown very fond of this little cottage where we've lived since our marriage, but we'll be far better off out there. The air is more wholesome, we'll have far more room, and the view is wonderful. Phoebe is a little afraid of being lonely but I've promised to bring her to town now and then.'

'Your friends will come out to see you.'

'No.'

He said this so flatly that Wilfred dared not persist. A few moments went by, then James Knight added:

'Of course, you can come to see us. I wasn't thinking of you when I said that – But it's some distance if you haven't a car. However we'll manage about that – We must keep in contact – Your family doesn't pay you much attention.'

'You may be dead in three months,' thought Wilfred. 'You'll never live in that house on the river side.'

James Knight shuffled some papers on the table and said 'yes' as though in answer to some question. He visibly wished to talk about something else and was looking around for a change of subject. Then it was that Wilfred would have liked to go, for he vaguely guessed what was coming.

'You'll understand certain things when you get to be my age,' said James Knight suddenly.

With which, he got up at once and took up his stand by the window.

'You wouldn't believe how often I've looked at this branch that hides the sky from me. They wanted to cut it, but I won't allow them to touch it.'

'It's really a very fine branch.'

'Fine? Yes, it is, but above all, it's alive and grows stronger.

201

If no one cuts it down, the branch will still be here in another hundred years.'

'We won't be here to see it,' said Wilfred laughing.

'No, I won't be here, nor you. It will be as though we had never existed. Life in this world is so short that it must necessarily continue elsewhere. It would be too senseless –'

'Life only appears to cease.'

'Yes, one is sure of that, at your age, but after forty, something happens. You'll see. I felt like you until I was past forty. Until – Until last month. How is it that one man believes and that his neighbour does not? You, for instance, you believe, but the faith you have received might have been given to another, to someone who perhaps wanted it –'

Wilfred shifted his position on the sofa.

'Oh, to want faith means that you already have it, in a certain manner,' he answered impatiently.

'Don't say that. You can believe after a certain fashion, I don't know how, with your head, perhaps, but you can't be sure, to the core of your being, that what you believe is true. That is a gift from God.'

'Yes, a gift from God,' repeated Wilfred, rather weightily solemn, and to his own surprise, for as he said this he seemed to have become another person in his own eyes.

He wanted to add something to this, but found nothing. James Knight looked silently at him, and Wilfred felt uneasy. Phoebe's face suddenly came back to him. He had no desire to talk about religion, particularly with a Protestant, he wanted to leave.

'If ever you lost your faith,' said James Knight, 'you'd blow your brains out.'

Wilfred made a gesture and got up.

'Oh,' continued James Knight, 'you and I belong to the same kind. We can't do without faith: nothing has any meaning

202

without it. Without faith life just ends in a great black hole.'

'But we don't believe in the same things,' said Wilfred in a colourless voice for, much against his will, the fanatic in him stirred.

James Knight sat down.

'You believe in God?' he asked.

'Naturally.'

'You believe in the divinity of Christ?'

'Of course.'

'That's the main point. After that, we separate into Catholics and Protestants, but it's the main point that counts and it's the main point that saves us.'

Wilfred tried to remember a sentence from his catechism but irritation muddled his brain and he could find no answers to the man's arguments. Yet he felt there must be an answer.

'Something else is necessary,' he mumbled. 'If a man lives like a criminal – It would all be too easy, simply because he has faith –'

'But if he has faith, he lives like one of the elect. And if he lives like a reprobate, then he hasn't faith, even if he thinks he has.'

Wilfred lost his footing at one sweep. Everything that James Knight said appeared false to him, but how was he to argue with him? 'I was wrong to answer him,' he thought. 'No one ought ever to answer a Protestant.'

'You seem perturbed,' said James Knight gently. 'I didn't want to upset you, Wilfred. Please believe me to be sincere. Keep your faith and live in the fear of the Lord. In short, that's what will get you out of difficulties. Sit down.'

Instead of sitting down, the young man went to the door.

'I'm sorry, but I must go,' he murmured. 'Thank you, Mr Knight.'

James Knight waved his hand and the gesture seemed to have no particular meaning.

Wilfred found Phoebe at the foot of the stairs.

'Are you going already?'

She lifted her face to his with that expression of anxiety she must have had at the age of ten when she was scared of some misfortune. He walked down the last steps and silently kissed her cheek. She appeared not to notice this.

'How do you find him?' she asked.

'Well. Very well indeed.'

She gave a sigh and the lines in her brow disappeared.

'Yes, isn't he? He's better, but he talks more than he did. What did he say to you?'

'He spoke about the house on the river.'

'I don't like that house,' she said. 'To begin with, it's at the end of the world.'

There was something sensual and unappeased in her voice that stirred him to the heart.

'I'll be such a long way from you,' he said under his breath.

Once more, he kissed her cheek, but this time so near her mouth that their lips touched. She started as though she had been burned and fell back a step. At that moment, they heard a door open on the floor above.

'Wilfred,' said James Knight's voice softly.

'Yes, Mr Knight.'

'Think of me when you read the *Imitation* again.'

Phoebe turned deathly pale.

'My husband wants you to pray for him,' she said, moving back a little farther.

The door closed.

'He's going to die,' she said in a voice that no longer sounded like hers. 'He's afraid of not having faith. Don't come near me, Wilfred. I'll think of you, but I believe we must part now.'

She avoided looking at him. He planted himself before her.

'Phoebe –'

204

She said no with a shake of the head and went to the little drawing-room and from there to another room, the door of which she closed. After wavering he walked to the door leading into the garden, facing the street. For almost five minutes, he stood, his hand on the brass knob that he could not make up his mind to turn.

CHAPTER XLIV

His sadness was inexpressible when he reached home again and found himself in the room he had left three hours before with such a hopeful heart. He had believed then that Phoebe was his. How was it he had lost her? Perhaps on account of one word, a single word: the *Imitation*. He soon had an assurance of this, an assurance without proof, an interior assurance more powerful than any proofs. If he hadn't mentioned that book, everything would have taken a different turn, but what could one do against destiny and who was there to accuse? Max, who had given him the book? In a sudden gust of anger he began kicking one of the chairs, his usual scapegoat.

He spent that magnificent afternoon half naked on his bed, talking to himself like a madman. What had become of his well-known power over women? He had simply made himself ridiculous and played the part of a base hypocrite. James Knight had seen through his little game and his wife had run away from him. This humiliation wrested tears from Wilfred and he let them flow shamelessly, without even thinking of wiping them away with his fingers, and they ran right into his mouth.

A little later, when he went to look at himself in the bathroom

205

mirror, he saw a reflection of a man who has just had a basin of water flung in his face. His eyelids were red, and perhaps, if Phoebe had seen him then, she might have taken him into her arms. At that moment, he had the idea that she had run away because she loved him and was frightened of a love she could no longer master. His heart swelled as he remembered the look she had given him in the garden. As he grew calmer, he stared smiling at the mask of a pensive young ogre which looked out from the mirror. Sooner or later, Phoebe would surrender. And going from extreme melancholy to no less extreme joy, he began to sing.

His voice was true and clear with modulations that recalled those of children. Formerly, in church, it was he who sang solo, and years after, in moments of happiness, Latin hymns were what came back to him, in particular the *Lauda Sion*, of which he never tired. That day he probably did not realize how incongruous this was: he undressed, and as he soaped himself under the shower, filled the silence with these venerable strains. Life smiled at him once more.

Suddenly he remembered that Angus's letter had remained in a pocket of the suit he had worn the day before. It counted so little in comparison with Phoebe's note that he had not even opened it, but now he felt interested and, scarcely pausing to dry himself, ran to his closet and thrust a hand inside his coat.

'*Dear Wilfred,*' wrote Angus, '*Uncle Horace has treated you a little better than we thought, for the securities you describe have more than tripled in value since their date of issue. In case you don't wish to negotiate them yourself, I could do it for you, but it would be better not to mail them to me. I would have called for them in person if, for reasons you know, it did not seem preferable not to meet again, but if you can wait another ten days, someone will come for them. You can have the same confidence in him that you have in me. You will recognize him, no doubt – ANGUS.*'

206

'*P.S. Don't imagine you're as rich as Croesus. No foolishness, please.*'

Having read the letter, Wilfred sat on his bed to read it over, then opened the drawer in his desk and counted his securities again. The sum had to be multiplied by three, and the amount seemed enormous to him. He did his calculations all over again and tossing his pencil in the air, began walking around the room on his hands.

CHAPTER XLV

The morning after, he went to his work and glanced at himself in the store's mirrors as much as to say good morning to the new Wilfred. He thought himself extremely dashing and his *Weltanschauung* was not in the least the same. As the word came back to him, he roared with laughter. He intended to make that scoundrel Max a present and in fact, since the night before, he mentally gave everybody presents, including Mr Schoenhals. As it happened he had something to say to Mr Schoenhals.

Of course, Phoebe would have specially nice gifts and even James Knight a small token, but the greatest tact would be necessary! Angus, who was so intelligent, as well as subtle and cultivated, would have been the man to consult under the circumstances. Wilfred now saw him possessed of every virtue and some work of art would reward this strange fellow's kindness: then he would realize that his less fortunate cousin also had good taste.

Naturally, the poor would not be forgotten. On that score there was an account to be squared with Heaven, a rather tremendous one, thought Wilfred. All this whirled through his head as he went to his place in the shirt department.

Mr Schoenhals greeted him with the smile he kept for him personally and which differed, in some indefinable manner, from the smile reserved for customers. He asked Wilfred if he had had a nice Sunday. The dear fellow had no idea of what was to come.

'Horrible,' said Wilfred with a laugh.

Mr Schoenhals also laughed softly.

'What wouldn't I give for one of the horrible Sundays I spent when I was your age,' he answerd with a sigh. 'I'd be glad enough to have it now.'

'Why's that?' asked Wilfred solicitously. 'Aren't you happy, Mr Schoenhals?'

He felt kindly that morning and at the same time light, superficial, impertinent. Mr Schoenhals looked at him in surprise as though he had said something improper.

'There's no such thing as happiness at my age, let me tell you,' he said gravely.

'Nor at mine! I've been through a bad time.'

The shopwalker squeezed his elbow lightly with the tips of his fat pointed fingers.

'You're a child,' he said.

Wilfred noticed that something resembling emotion stole into those glaucous eyes of his, but just for an instant. He felt moved and watched Mr Schoenhals move away without being able to tell him what he had in mind.

The stout man had scarcely turned on his heel when Freddie came toward Wilfred, calling him in a low voice. Not a customer in sight. Wilfred, remembering Freddie's little tragedy, went up to him.

'Well, Freddie?'

Freddie threw him a terrified glance and remained speechless.

'Now then, speak up. Have you noticed anything wrong?'

'No.'

'Well then?'

208

'I can't go on living like this. I'm scared, see? I think I'd kill myself if there is anything the matter with me.'

'You must wait another few days to know.'

'That's impossible, I can't sleep.'

He looked, in fact, very white and even uglier than usual.

'Buck up! Even if you have caught something, it can be cured.'

'Oh, I can't buck up. I have no courage. I feel like going home to bed.'

'That's ridiculous. Probably you aren't sick at all. Try to think of something else.'

'I've tried it. I can't.'

He whispered beseechingly:

'Help me, will you?'

A customer parted them at that moment, but towards the end of the morning Wilfred told Freddie to meet him in front of the store at lunch-time, and once in the street, he suggested, although a little reluctantly, that they take their meal together. Freddie looked at him like a stray dog who had found a home.

Five minutes later they were in a drugstore, seated at a small table in a corner of the room. Freddie drank a little milk and nibbled his sandwich and Wilfred was afraid the wretched boy would burst into tears, for his cadaverous little face was undergoing strange contortions.

'Listen,' he said firmly. 'There's only one way out of this. I'm going to take you to a hospital and you can have a blood test made.'

Terror once more filled his great dark eyes.

'To a hospital!'

'I'll take charge of the whole business. We'll go there together tonight after work and your mind will be easy within three days. But next time, you've got to be careful.'

'Oh, that's all over, you can imagine. I'll never to it again.'

209

What Wilfred dreaded happened: tears flowed.

'Now, Freddie, be a man. People can see us.'

'I can't help it,' stammered Freddie, concealing as much as he could of his face in the glass of milk. 'Thank you – thank you –'

Wilfred had to undergo his gratitude.

When they returned to the store, he went to Mr Schoenhals. What a number of small happenings in one day! All this went to his head a little.

'Mr Schoenhals,' he said in a businesslike voice, 'I have something to say to you.'

'Very well, my boy. We'll see about that later, after work.'

Wilfred laid a hand on his hip:

'If you don't mind, I'll tell you right away. I'm leaving.'

The shopwalker seemed not to understand.

'I'm leaving this place,' specified Wilfred. 'I'd like to leave in a month's time. Will you let the management know a week beforehand?'

'Why?' asked Mr Schoenhals.

The habitual smile had vanished, his mouth remained half open and there was such confusion in his expression that Wilfred felt amazed, in spite of what he had vaguely guessed. Was it possible that such everyday words could bring so much dismay to a man of fifty? Letting his hand drop to his side, the young salesman tried to smile.

'Mr Schoenhals, I've taken this decision for personal reasons that I'll give you some other time. I'm sure you won't have any trouble in finding a substitute. It's a good job.'

'A substitute,' murmured Mr Schoenhals, his protruding eyes looking a little haggard.

He drew himself up suddenly and said without a glance at Wilfred:

'Very well, my boy. I'll inform the management.'

With which, he retired to the other end of the shop where the

210

young man saw him walking up and down as usual, hands behind his back. It was then that Wilfred regretted having spoken to him with so little consideration. He had been unnecessarily unkind. Well? Wasn't Mr Schoenhals twice his age? 'He must know I'm not going to drag on for ever in this store,' he thought. 'Of course he's nice to me but that's no reason –'

A voice cut short these reflections. Someone wanted a coloured shirt. Rather crossly, Wilfred displayed several models on the counter and then put his hand to his hip. The customer was young and did not quite know his own mind, for his taste leaned toward bright shades and at the same time, he wanted nothing too showy. Carefully dressed, he had the gestures of an old maid and the pretty face of a doll. Wilfred suddenly cleared the counter of coloured shirts and produced a white one.

'This will suit you perfectly,' he said peremptorily.

'White? Do you really think so?'

'That's just right, believe me.'

'I never would have thought of white. I –'

'People don't think often enough of white. Shall I give you two?'

Not daring to kick, the customer was led to the desk like a lamb.

'You certainly treat those customers of yours with a high hand,' said Mrs Splitpenny, the cashier. 'Young or old –'

She was insinuating something. Wilfred did not know what. She was always insinuating something. He looked at her without answering. For the first time since he had known her, he felt that she had no face, because she had the face of the mob. She was dull and unkind, and she was dying of boredom.

'We can only do our best, Mrs Splitpenny,' he said.

'You know, most men adore being treated like that,' she continued in a sexless, nasal voice. 'Every woman knows that. Still, the other salesmen haven't got your – nerve.'

211

'My nerve?'

'Call it your charm, if you like. Everybody knows you have charm,' she said, putting away a voucher.

'You've never told me about my charm, Mrs Splitpenny,' he replied with his most captivating smile.

She suddenly raised her mud coloured eyes and he thought her hideous.

'Don't you try that little game on me, it won't work,' she said.

He gave her a wink and retreated a few steps.

'Keep that for the others,' she whispered leaning toward Wilfred.

What she meant by that he understood perfectly, and was on the point of answering, but something prevented him and he made his way back to the end of the counter where he resumed his place arms crossed, in an attitude of supreme indifference. 'What does it matter?' he thought. 'I'm leaving.'

CHAPTER XLVI

At about six-thirty, he went to the hospital with Freddie. The latter followed him down one passage and up another as though he wanted to hide behind him and Wilfred was ashamed of his cowardice. Yet he himself had never dared have a blood test taken, for fear of learning something unpleasant. This did not prevent his looking important that evening.

'You have no guts,' he told Freddie.

'I know it,' replied his companion humbly.

They walked soundlessly over the linoleum like a couple of

ghosts. Finally, Wilfred pushed open the door they had been directed to and a young intern met them.

'I called up a few minutes ago,' said Wilfred.

He gave his name. The intern made Freddie sit on a high stool, his right shirt sleeve rolled up.

Everything happened so quickly that the patient did not have time to be frightened, but nevertheless, Wilfred looked away. Freddie smiled at him as he buttoned his cuff and whispered:

'It was nothing at all.'

By a sudden inspiration, Wilfred removed his coat and turned up his shirt sleeve.

'I'll have it done too,' he said to the intern.

The latter returned from the end of the room where he had gone to put the test-tube of blood.

'Have you eaten anything since lunch?' he asked.

'No.'

The intern motioned him to the stool and took his name and address. Wilfred felt his heart beat fast. He thought of Phoebe. If ever – The idea that he should give Phoebe a disease was intolerable. The needle's tiny prick did not make him turn a hair, but when he saw the test-tube full of bright red blood, what he considered above all things ridiculous happened: he fainted.

'The intern swears it even happens to soldiers,' said Freddie as they left the hospital. 'It's just reflex action.'

Wilfred said nothing and walked a little faster down a long avenue bordered with trees riddled by the setting sun's beams. From time to time Freddie quickened his pace to catch up with his companion.

'He said it didn't mean a thing, you know, Wilfred,' he continued.

'Why, of course. What could it mean? It's about as unintentional as sneezing.'

They were silent for a moment. Wilfred was furious.

213

'He said we'd know in four days,' said Freddie.

'In three days.'

'Well, yes, Thursday evening. I wish it was Thursday now. And then after all, I don't: it's better in a way not to know. You aren't worried, are you?'

'Worried?' Wilfred's eye swept contemptuously over Freddie. 'Why should I be worried? I wanted a blood test, just on principle. It's always a good thing to have a check up now and then.'

'You have nothing to fear, whereas I –'

'You aren't going through all that again, Freddie?'

They had reached a bus stop.

'I'll leave you here,' said Wilfred. 'I'm walking home.'

'Don't you want me to come with you?'

'No, I have my own reasons for wishing to be alone.'

How harshly he had said that meaningless sentence! To be alone? Why? Because Freddie irritated him: he was ugly, sickly, shabby and there was something embarrassing about his expression: it was that of a pauper or an invalid. Freddie would never be a success and no doubt something in him sensed it vaguely. His eyes raised to Wilfred's, he implored silently but Wilfred did not move.

'Wilfred –'

'Well, good-bye, see you tomorrow morning.'

Freddie touched his hand with the tips of his fingers.

'Do you think there's anything the matter with me?'

'No, for the twentieth time, no.'

A kind word would probably have comforted Freddie, but Wilfred could not find it in him to say it. 'I'm not kind,' he thought. 'I don't know how to do good properly. All I know how to do properly is to do evil, what's called evil.' This sudden idea horrified him and at the same time made him laugh.

'Why do you laugh, Wilfred?'

'I don't know. It's your expression –'

214

'You're a Catholic,' said Freddie suddenly. 'You're a believer. You ask for something and get it.'

Wilfred started.

'Oh, it's not as easy as all that,' he replied.

'Nevertheless, you believe. You ask for something and get it.'

'Sometimes, yes.'

'Won't you ask for me?'

He said this all in one breath and added timidly:

'You might ask for me not to be ill, and that nothing's wrong in the test-tube with my name on it.'

'Why don't you ask yourself?'

'Because I haven't got enough faith.'

'Aren't you a Protestant?'

'I've already told you that I'm nothing. My parents are nothing. I haven't been baptized in any church.'

'If you don't believe, why do you want me to ask?'

'Because there's something in it, maybe –'

Freddie stopped as a man and a woman passed them. Once they were alone again, he continued:

'There may be something in it after all. I'm not denying it. If you ask for me not to be ill, perhaps things will turn out all right.'

Wilfred looked at him for a moment without answering, suddenly and unaccountably moved, then, scarcely knowing what he did, leaned towards Freddie and his lips quickly touched his cheek.

'I'll try,' he whispered in his ear.

Freddie grew scarlet and glanced right and left as though he were afraid they had been seen. Wilfred strode off and almost immediately heard Freddie running behind him:

'Thanks, Wilfred!' he cried. 'Thanks!'

215

CHAPTER XLVII

Instead of going straight home, Wilfred took refuge in the little church frequented by Italians where he wished to carry out his promise. To take refuge was the term that occurred to him, but why take refuge? Because his heart was ravaged by passion? Who could say?

Inside the church, gold glittered freely and painted statues smiled on their pedestals. The general effect could be considered a little childlike, a little barbaric – James Knight would have said pagan – but amid so much colour and tinsel a dark massive object stood in the chancel and startled Wilfred who had not expected to see a catafalque.

He and death were alone in the church. Perhaps this meant something, but what, he wondered. Did it mean two dead persons, dead as the one lying in the coffin, or two living beings, alive as the one who stood near the door? Wilfred's first impulse was to leave, to go to another church, instead of which he stood there motionless, eyes fixed on the black drapery where he saw, shining like ice, a big 'I': the dead man's name and his had the same initial. 'It means nothing,' he thought, but he felt disturbed, as though it were a bad omen.

After some hesitation, he knelt as far away as possible from the coffin and prayed for the deceased, but as usual he prayed badly, never having known exactly what it was to pray well. He asked that the dead man should pass quickly from the fires of Purgatory to Paradise. At the bottom of his soul, in its most obscure part, he was frightened of the dead man who stood in his way, for, after his own fashion, the dead man was speaking to him and Wilfred dreaded the dialogue that began between them.

'Look at me,' said the dead man.

'I can't. You're in that box.'

'Your soul sees perfectly well through drapery and wood. I'm frightful, aren't I? How do you know I'm saved? Why did you say the word Purgatory?'

'I don't know. I don't know anything. I'm praying for you, poor soul.'

'The prayer of a man in a state of mortal sin – What's that worth?'

'I don't know. I hope that God listens to it.'

'Don't talk about God. You'll be under a tightly screwed down lid, some day, like me. I led a gay life, like you. I had hands for grasping, a body for enjoyment, a mouth – You should see it now, you should see it with your eyes of flesh. I sinned with my mouth, like you.'

Wilfred crossed himself and rose. The blood pounded at his temples, in his throat, in his breast, life beat furiously against the very casings of his body, as though to remind him of its presence. As he stood up, he remembered his promise and whispered: 'Lord, have mercy on little Freddie.' That was all he could say. He genuflected and went out.

In the street, he leaned against the walls of houses. It seemed to him that he prayed better outside than within the church. 'Lord,' he said under his breath, 'grant that he hasn't caught the disease he dreads so.' And almost at once, he added: 'Nor me either, I beseech You.'

Having said this, he paused. Uncle Horace's remark came back to him: 'That doesn't sound like a prayer.' No doubt. To begin with, it was not long enough, but he could find nothing else. He made a vague sign of the cross that was like the gestures

217

of someone washing his face, for people might be watching him. At the end of the street, children shouted as they played, little Italians with eyes that were almost too large and expressions unlike those of young Americans. 'Well, there's nothing the matter with them, at any rate,' he thought as he watched them. 'They aren't diseased.' The nightmare was about to begin.

He had had a blood test made because something in him warned him of danger, otherwise the idea would not have occurred to him. Like Freddie, he was frightened, with this difference, that Freddie had someone to comfort him. 'And who is there to comfort me?'

The reply was easy: he had God. But God did not answer his questions. God was there and looked at him, but said nothing. Yet, He could cure him, He could grant that the test-tube contained no bacilli. But perhaps to obtain this grace he must promise never to touch a woman again.

Particularly one woman, that woman more than any other, said a voice in his innermost being. Wilfred stopped dead. You couldn't trick that voice. A moment earlier he had said to himself that God never spoke, but now, someone was speaking. 'Thou shalt not covet thy neighbour's wife, thou shalt not commit adultery.' Books, plays, films were all of them full of stories about adultery. It wasn't his fault if he had fallen in love with Phoebe. It had taken him some time. She had been the first to lose her heart, she had gone after him. 'You must not touch that woman,' said the voice.

He went home in the subway and, when he saw the buff coloured walls of his room again, felt furious with everything, with life, with himself, with what prevented him from being happy, but being half dead with fatigue, he threw himself on his bed without undressing and slept through the evening. It was about eleven when he woke.

218

CHAPTER XLVIII

Leaving his room, he went prowling on Sherman Avenue at some
distance from two hundred and thirteen and a half. He would
have liked to meet Max, as it were by chance and without seeming to be looking for him, and for some time he strolled about,
one hand in his trouser pocket, whistling away. Usually he did
not whistle, but that night he needed to appear unconcerned.
He crossed over several times and gradually drew near to the
house.

What he saw gave him a sort of shock. The same window was
lighted as last time and the same old man in shirtsleeves was
there, leaning his arms on a long red cushion fitted over the
stone window-sill. There was nothing really very surprising
in that after all, but Wilfred had the impression of turning back
the pages of a book. Head raised, he looked at the man whose
skull silvered a bit above the ears.

'Good evening,' said the old man in a colourless voice.

'Good evening.'

'Fine weather for strolling around.'

'Yes.'

'Specially for a youngster, eh?'

'Is Max there?'

The old man laughed softly.

'Yes, Max is there.'

Once more he laughed in a knowing way that irritated Wilfred.

'Are you keen on seeing Max?'

No. Wilfred did not care to see him. Suddenly, he no longer

wanted to. Without replying, he walked away and as had happened the last time, in the lighted room, he could hear the sound of talking that was like animals yelping.

A few seconds later, Max ran after him and took him brusquely by the shoulder.

'Don't play the fool, Wilfred,' he said, a little out of breath. 'Come, we'll go up there for a while.'

'Who's the old boy who talked to me?'

'You won't see him again. He's gone. I'll explain. There's no one at present.'

His hand under Wilfred's arm, he led him to the house. In the steep narrow staircase lighted by a single electric bulb, he seemed taller, heavier, with something disorderly and over-excited about him that Wilfred did not recognize. With an indescribable air of embarrassment Max turned and said with obsequious politeness:

'I'll go first. You'll forgive me, won't you?'

'Stop being so courteous. It's too silly.'

Max burst out laughing.

'Things are awfully simple up there you know. It really makes me quite shy to see you here.'

'You're drunk.'

'Just a little, but it doesn't matter. I'm sometimes most agreeable when I've been drinking.'

Drawing a key from his pocket, he handed it to Wilfred when they reached the door.

'Would you mind?' he asked laughing. 'I can't manage to fit it in the lock when I've had a drink too many.'

Wilfred snatched the key and opened the door. Max went in ahead of him, glancing about to make sure everything was tidy.

The room was high-ceilinged and so long that it suggested a corridor with a window at the far end and, on its stone sill, Wilfred recognized the long worn red velvet cushion where

220

traces of two elbows were still visible. Near the window, a scarlet plush armchair: overstuffed, rotund and edged with a fringe, it reminded one of a monstrous molar freshly extracted. Looking at this hideous and comfortable bit of furniture, Wilfred fancied that the old man he had caught sight of, rested there in its arms, waiting for the end of his life.

Along one wall, a sofa with a flowered loose cover was half buried under cushions of all shades of the rainbow; the room was decorated with a few coloured reproductions of landscapes and lighted by a lamp whose pretentious pleated and furbelowed shade belonged to another period than ours. What was more, everything in the place was foreign to Wilfred's habitual surroundings.

As he entered after his companion, a door he had not noticed at first closed and he heard the sound of retreating footsteps. A newspaper littered the theadbare rug. Max picked it up, folded it and threw it on the mahogany radio, then dropped into the red armchair and motioned Wilfred to the sofa.

'Stretch out, if you like. Take off your coat and make yourself comfortable.'

He then collapsed, arms dangling over the elbow-rests, legs extended. His head thrown back on the lace antimacassar that protected the back of the plush armchair, he lay for an instant with closed eyes and parted lips. Wilfred was struck by the whiteness of his neck and a curious idea occurred to him: how easy it would be to cut his throat with a razor.

'I feel tired,' said Max, 'but happy, happy you're here. If you only knew –'

Wilfred sat down on the sofa. Max suddenly raised his head:

'That's where I sleep, sometimes,' he said. 'On that sofa. The springs are broken because it's been used by too many people, but you sleep well there. In the daytime, it has a loose cover, the one that's on it now, and the place becomes a sitting-room, although a bit bare. Humble but respectable. It has to look respectable. The old man says so from morning till night. Would you like to hear a little music, Wilfred? Turned down very low to serve as a background for conversation. Right now, they're playing a double concerto by some one or other. You're right, I'm tipsy, you know.'

'I don't want to hear any music.'

Max stretched a hand toward the radio and switched it on with a broad smile that showed his wonderfully white teeth.

'Yes, you do,' he said. 'No one comes in here when there's music. It means there's company. I'll explain, I'll explain everything. Are you still in love?'

At that moment a vast murmuring swept into the room and Wilfred remained silent. Without knowing much about it, he had always had a feeling for music and for what it said, and this music talked to him of his love. He bent his head for tears rose to his eyes.

'Too loud?' asked Max toning down the radio a little. 'But it's got to be heard on the other side of the door. Now then, Wilfred, what about your love affair?'

'I don't want to talk about it.'

He had come here for that very reason, but the music altered everything.

'Please stop that radio,' he said getting up. 'What does it matter if anyone comes in?'

'Oh, it doesn't matter, but I don't wish the old man to return: he's inquisitive.'

'Now, who is that old man?'

'Something like my boss. We're slightly related into the bargain. For the last two years we've been working together at the office.'

'What office?'

222

'This one here. I'll explain everything later. Won't you have a little whisky?'

'No, I'm going.'

Too much mystery hung about the room to suit Wilfred and he felt ill at ease there. What he disliked most was the fact that there were people behind the door facing him. Max probably guessed his thoughts for he rose and turned the key in the lock.

'There,' he said. 'Like that, you have nothing to worry about and can stay.'

He staggered very slightly and dropped on the sofa, on his back by Wilfred.

'I feel happy,' he said very low and his eyes closed.

The blood glowed in his cheeks and gave his whole face extraordinary radiance. For the first time, Wilfred noticed that Max was handsome and this unaccountably embarrassed him.

'You've had too much to drink,' he said, moving away slightly.

'Not really. I just feel happy, that's all. Happy and holy. I can guess that sounds strange to you, but you couldn't possibly understand. I've just had a terribly good time and now I'm remorseful. It's most agreeable – If anyone notices that I've locked the door, I'll be bawled out good and proper, but I don't care. Tonight, I don't care. Tell me if you're happy, Wilfred.'

'Not precisely. I'd rather talk of something else.'

'Just as you like. They say walls have ears. What wouldn't they tell, if they had mouths too? These, for instance – You have no idea – I don't know why I'm talking to you about this. I shouldn't –'

'Oh, tell about it just the same,' said Wilfred, suddenly curious.

'Oh no. Not yet. Not like that. You're much too proper. Yes, you are. Even though you do run after girls, certain kinds of girls, I'd shock you –'

223

His soft, even voice could scarcely be heard above the music's loud murmur.

'You're a queer fish,' he continued, 'but I can understand you: a pious rake.'

'Don't call me pious, or I'll hit you,' said Wilfred suddenly.

Max did not move, did not even open his eyes. Wilfred went on, in a calmer tone:

'There's a woman I want, see? The woman I told you about. So when people say I'm pious, it puts me in a rage.'

'I adore people flying into rages.'

'What on earth have you been drinking to say such idiotic things?' asked Wilfred with a shrug. 'I wonder how I can talk to you.'

'Because I'm the only person who can really understand you,' said Max without moving. 'And then, you intrigue me.'

Wilfred did not reply. The music swept over the silence with a kind of violent and savage tenderness.

'Give me something to drink,' said Wilfred.

Max half opened his eyelids and glanced sideways at him. In three seconds he was on his feet, looking in a cupboard for a bottle.

'Here,' he said, handing Wilfred a glass.

The latter took it silently. He had to talk about Phoebe. By talking about her, he obliged her to be near him. He drank a few swallows.

'What's this filthy stuff, Max?'

'A mixture,' replied Max going back to the sofa. 'My own mixture.'

He clasped his hands behind his neck.

'I need her,' continued Wilfred. 'Even if nothing happens between us, I want her near me, do you understand?'

'A child would understand. But you'll have her and things will go as they usually do in such cases. Look – you're not

224

awfully handsome, but you have a good figure and something in your eyes that's just right. A woman will never say no
to you. So you'll end by having that one, like the others, with
patience.'

'I have no patience.'

'Yet it's so amusing to wait, to exercise your imagination,
when you're sure of winning. It's even agreeable.'

'There are too many difficulties in the way, too many obstacles.
I'm not at all sure of succeeding.'

The music stopped and the sound of applause filled the room.

'Hear that?' asked Max. 'You'd think it was the sea. The
sound is the same. There should be another movement –'

'I've told you that she is married.'

Max hummed the first bars as an accompaniment to the
orchestra.

'Don't be silly,' he said finally, in his sing-song voice. 'You'll
get your sweetheart, even if you have to burn some day.'

'Burn?'

'Oh,' said Max gently, 'we'll all have to burn. We're lost, you,
I and the others.'

'I've told you I didn't want to talk about such things.'

'What does it matter to you? You still have forty years ahead
of you. It will only happen in forty years, that is, never.'

He murmured several other sentences that Wilfred could not
catch. His head was swimming.

'All that should be thrown overboard,' he said violently. 'The
whole business ought to be liquidated.'

Max looked at him and began laughing.

'That can't be done, you know. Strangely enough, it can't
be done.'

'You thought differently the other day. I'm only repeating
your own words.'

'We must make a pretense,' explained Max. 'That's what I

225

meant. Live as though there was nothing. Nothing on the other side. Have a good time. When you have something that bothers you in your room, you put it in the bottom of a cupboard and think no more about it. That's what I mean. But you open the cupboard all the time to have a look inside it. So do I, as it happens. But it's a mistake.'

Wilfred thought of his crucifix in the drawer of his desk.

'Will you give me a drink?' he asked.

'In a little while. If you drink too fast, you'll be knocked out. Then the effect is lost. How do you feel?'

'Pretty well.'

He dropped back, his neck buried in the cushions. As he listened to the music, he had the impression that it swept through him, like the wind through a tree. 'Tomorrow,' he thought, 'I'll buy myself a radio. That will be one of the first things I'll treat myself to.'

'Do you think it would be a good idea to write to her?' he asked.

'It would be idiotic, on account of her husband.'

'Her husband is going to die,' said Wilfred. 'He is very ill.'

He waited for a moment, then a sentence he had not expected escaped him:

'It's a dirty business.'

'She'll just slip into your arms, when he's dead,' said Max in a calm voice.

'I can't wait. I'm in love.'

'Don't be offended by what I'm about to say, but personally I think people in love are terribly boring. Forgive me.'

'You haven't offended me. I think just the way you do, but what else can I talk to you about? I only came here for that.'

'So you see,' remarked Max in a voice as thin and smooth as a metal blade, 'faith doesn't hold its ground before desire.'

'Oh, you make me tired! If you talk like that, I'm going.'

'You aren't thirsty, by any chance?'

'Yes, I am,' said Wilfred, laughing in spite of himself, 'but I don't know what I've done with my glass.'

As through a mist, he saw his companion get to his feet with a litheness like that of some wild animal, and a sudden benevolence came over him.

'You're a good fellow,' he said while Max busied himself at the cupboard.

'I knew you'd become more agreeable,' replied Max without turning. 'It always works, after a while. How do you feel? Better?'

'Yes. I even feel very well.'

Max came up to him and handed him a glass.

'You aren't going to talk about her any more, eh?'

'Well, as you don't want me to –'

He raised himself up a little and leaned on his elbow, glass in hand.

'That music is wonderful, don't you think?' asked Max.

'Wonderful,' agreed Wilfred obediently.

Strictly speaking, what he heard was a hurricane of sound rolling toward them from beyond great empty spaces.

'It expresses everything I feel,' he whispered sadly.

They listened for a moment, then Max sat down by him.

'I'm going to introduce a friend to you,' he said.

'Who is it?'

'The Angel. That's what he is called for several reasons. I met him three days ago. He's a soldier.'

'A soldier?'

'He's not in uniform tonight. He reminds me a little of you, because he's Irish. Yesterday, quite by chance, I discovered he had a rosary in his pocket.'

'You mean that you went through his pockets.'

227

'No, I didn't. I'm not a detective. But he had put his coat on a chair.'

'You're a rotter, Max.'

'That's funny. You're the third person to call me that today. And yet, it's not true. Not quite true.'

'Ah?'

'The Angel has faith. It doesn't prevent his going on the razzle dazzle, but he has faith. He doesn't have it in his head, like me, or even in his heart. He's got it in his guts, see?'

'I don't care for that way of speaking.'

'There's no other way of saying it. In his guts. I was sure of it, the moment I laid eyes on him. I nose these things out. When I found the rosary in his pocket after –'

'After what?'

'Oh, nothing. After he had put his coat on the chair. I laughed to myself when I felt the beads and little cross with my fingers. I know, there wasn't anything to laugh about, but I wasn't making fun of this, I was simply delighted not to have been mistaken.'

Wilfred tried to give him a blow with his fist, but lacked the necessary strength.

'Please stop talking that way,' he murmured.

'I'll go and fetch the Angel,' said Max, getting up. 'He's a very simple fellow, you know. Fond of athletics –'

Wilfred's head fell back and he closed his eyes. Max took his glass away from him and roaring with laughter, said something.

'Yes,' answered Wilfred at random.

'You should have said no,' remarked Max, still laughing, 'but it doesn't matter.'

He left the room and closed the door. Wilfred remained perfectly motionless, almost asleep. The music had ceased and from the radio came a small continuous sound, like the humming of some insect.

228

Wilfred did not know how many minutes had slipped by when the door opened again and Max appeared, alone.

'I've been rather long,' he said. 'He's busy for the moment, but will come in by and by. Are you all right?'

'What stuff was that you made me drink, Max?'

'Nothing very bad. My own mixture. I wanted to make you forget your troubles.'

'Oh, you make me sick!'

'You say that because you're still a little tight. So am I, as it happens. I've been drinking next door with the Angel.'

'You make me sick,' repeated Wilfred. 'With your filthy goings-on – If you think I don't understand –'

'Naturally you take me for a skunk, but I'm not completely one. I'm vicious, granted, because I'm young and can't get the better of that damned temperament of mine, but there's also something else. I share your beliefs, I've been marked and the mark can't be erased, a deluge of fire wouldn't erase it. You aren't listening?'

'No, I'm dozing.'

'That doesn't matter. I talk more freely when I feel I'm not being listened to. It's enough for you to be here. I'm talking to you just the same. Nothing in the world can prevent a man from speaking, if he has a drop of Slav blood in his veins – If you knew what I've done to my wretched body, you'd refuse to see me. You're no saint, but in your case, it's not quite the same thing. One is obliged to respect you, in a way, not to take advantage –' (he sniffed). 'You rank with ordinary sinners, you do. At the bottom of your heart, you love Him. You love the One I don't wish to name in this place. Not in this room, not on this sofa. On this sofa! I love Him too, in my way. Otherwise I wouldn't force Him to get down in the mud, against His will. I used to be frightened. But no longer. He puts Himself into my hands. I feel like laughing when I hear about certain people's

229

humility. His is terrifying. It frightens me – afterwards. It's His Passion beginning all over again, continuing in the midst of sacrilege: insults, spitting, soldiers' blows. You can make Him reel with a slap in the face, and steady Him with another, and He says nothing, He never says anything to me, but I need Him. I've never said this to anyone but you, Wilfred, I could never say it to anyone, but I had to say it to someone and having said it, I have to say it again. That's why I wanted to be alone with you, and not for any other reason, no matter what you may have thought, but the Angel mustn't know all this, you understand?'

'The Angel?'

'The man I told you about a little while ago.'

'Why do you want me to see him?'

'Just to see. To see what will happen.'

He turned over suddenly and, his face buried in the sofa, stifled a cry. Wilfred jumped up, sobered all at once.

'Max, I'm going.'

Max also rose and took Wilfred's hand.

'Don't go! I've been lying to you. You know very well that I always lie. I was an actor at twenty. Actors play a part from morning to night, all day and every day till they die. They can't help it. What I told you was false. I've never told you the truth.'

Wilfred did not believe him. Something was true in what Max had said, and he felt it so keenly that, in a fit of anger, he freed his hand and, without knowing why, slapped his face and, as Max did not budge, slapped it again and again for about a couple of minutes. At every blow the face quivered slightly, turning right, then left, with a sort of horrible and fascinating docility, while the set eyes stared blankly into those of his tormentor. Suddenly, he fell like a log at Wilfred's feet. The latter took fright and, running to the door, disappeared down the staircase.

CHAPTER XLIX

He walked faster and faster down the avenue and turned several times to see if he was being followed. Plunging into a little side street he ran with a swiftness of which he would not have believed himself capable. The tips of his shoes scarcely touched the pavement and made a little whispering noise that echoed through the stillness of the night. After a new minutes, he slackened his pace and walked unhurriedly to the next street.

That was the last time he would go to two hundred and thirteen and a half. He had struck Max with such energy that his palm still burned and he was haunted by the picture of a tortured face that made no attempt to escape his anger. 'He's mad,' thought Wilfred, 'the poor wretch is unbalanced, I won't see him again.' But for all that, he was ashamed and frightened, frightened of his own ungovernable rage. 'I had to make him stop talking,' he told himself in justification, 'make him stop at any cost, I couldn't listen a moment longer to that blasphemous talk –'

A taxi went by just then. Wilfred signed to the driver and threw himself into the car after giving his address. He felt calmer now. What had perturbed him above anything else, a few minutes ago, was the man's passiveness, he had let himself be struck without so much as opening his mouth. But he didn't want to think about Max any longer.

Entering his room, he threw his hat on the bed and at that very instant resolved to find another room as quickly as possible. He had suffered too much within these walls, suffered too much from boredom, and he hated the view from his window. Now that he had the means, he would find a place to live in more suited to his tastes.

For one long hour, he *left* his room, he mentally emptied it of all his belongings and then *returned* there to put out his tongue at the brass bed and oak desk. Someone else could sleep and suffer on that mattress, some other fool who would also hide his little secrets in those drawers, his papers, his photographs – his crucifix, perhaps. In his new room, no cross would hang on the wall. That would put an end to awkward predicaments, to lengthy deliberations as to whether the cross could or could not remain above the bed – Wilfred pictured flowered wall paper and a rather springy carpet. Supposing there were no carpet, he would buy one, at a pinch. He had had enough of severe simplicity, what he wanted was a gay, smiling setting, the kind that Phoebe would like, for of course she would come to his room.

He read over her little note, it never left him, he treasured it. Although so very commonplace, Phoebe's hand had touched that bit of paper and he kissed it several times. He didn't want to go to bed. Sleep was a waste of time when he could be thinking of her. Seated at his desk, he wrote her one of those crazy letters that are never mailed. To begin with, there was James Knight (but James Knight was going to die –). And then, the idea that Phoebe might read such sentences made Wilfred blush to the ears. The sentences resembled those he had read in Alicia's and Uncle Horace's letters.

Tearing up the letter, he took Alicia's photograph from the drawer. Beyond doubt there was a likeness to Phoebe, particularly in the poise of the head, the neck, what could be guessed of the body and throat, but also in the expression. Like Phoebe, Alicia had the expression of a little girl, but that innocence meant nothing, at least not in Alicia's case, for after all there were those letters – Or perhaps physical passion left a certain purity of soul apparently intact. He dreamed over these things for a long time and at the back of all such reveries skulked an idea that always came forward, although he impatiently brushed it away. For hours now, it had unceasingly been in his mind, even while Max was talking to him in the horrible sitting-room of two hundred and thirteen and a half. Wilfred recalled the ruby coloured test-tube in the intern's hand. In that little glass tube, fate slowly prepared an answer that would be yes or no.

Instinctively, he made a sign of the cross and went to bed.

CHAPTER L

At the store next day, he glanced around for Freddie and did not see him. After hesitating, he went to Mr Schoenhals and, for the first time, the man was not smiling.

'I've had a telephone call from his father,' he said. 'Freddie is ill. Probably appendicitis or something of the kind. He was taken to the hospital this morning.'

'What hospital?'

Mr Schoenhals told him and added:

'I doubt if we'll be allowed to see him for several days.'

He paused a moment, then asked:

'What about you, Wilfred?'

'Me?'

'Don't look so terrified,' said Mr Schoenhals with a sad little smile. 'I only wanted to know if you had reconsidered your decision.'

'My decision? No. I'm leaving, Mr Schoenhals.'

'You probably have another job in view. I might perhaps manage to have your salary raised, if you stayed on.'

Shaking his head negatively, Wilfred walked away feeling violently sick. A moment later he was in one of the white enamelled toilets that the store reserved for its staff and, two fingers down his throat, was trying to vomit, but nothing happened. He leaned against the wall, gasping, his face streaming with perspiration. The mirror pitilessly reflected his drawn features and he thought bitterly of how Phoebe would have felt if she had seen him in that condition.

When he returned to his department, he asked Mr Schoenhals to allow him to go home and the shopwalker immediately acquiesced and not without the most solicitous inquiries about his health.

Once outside, Wilfred threw himself into a taxi after giving the hospital's address. He was not acting solely from charitable motives. Distracted with fear, his brain established a connexion between his fate and Freddie's. If Freddie was ill, he was too and he saw a sort of omen in the fact that both of them had had a blood test made on the same day, by the same person. Such reasoning was of course absurd, but that is the way fear reasons, with nightmarish logic.

The hospital was located at a short distance from town and birds sang in the trees around it. Their carolling wrung Wilfred's heart. As in a dream (what was he doing there instead of selling shirts in the store?) he went to an office where he asked to see the patient. His name was taken, then he was sent to the floor above where he walked down a sinister milk-white passage. Rubber carpeting suppressed the sound of his footsteps and it seemed to him that he moved forward like a ghost.

Notebook in hand, a young nurse awaited him at the end of the passage and in spite of his confused state, Wilfred could not help thinking her pretty: she had pink cheeks and smoke grey

234

eyes. 'She must be rather attractive,' he thought. 'What a pity her youth should be so sadly wasted in a hospital!' Almost in spite of himself he smiled faintly, but her answering look had something chilling. She wished to know if he were related to Freddie and he said no. A friend?

'Yes, but I don't know him very well. A friend is saying a good deal.'

How he disowned Freddie and his disease, particularly his disease!

'Yet,' said the nurse, 'he's been asking persistently to see you as soon as possible and alone. We telephoned to the address he gave us but you had just left. His parents are with him at present. I'll go and inquire whether you can see him for a few minutes.'

'Is he in pain?'

'He has some trouble in breathing.'

'Is his illness serious?'

'We'll keep you informed, if it's necessary.'

She took Wilfred's address, then asked him to follow her to a clean, white, empty room with three metal chairs lined up against one of the walls.

'Wait here, please.'

Once alone, he went to a window with a view over the lawns where trees planted in a haphazard fashion stirred faintly in the breeze. Wilfred thought one great maple so majestically beautiful that he could not stop looking at it, although his heart was full of despair as he admired the sturdy limbs that so delicately bore masses of dark and light green foliage. What good would life be to him if he was ill? He loathed the idea of suffering. And now, he suffered and looked at that tree through the eyes of suffering. He had lost Phoebe.

Nearly fifteen minutes went by before the nurse returned. Her limpid expression was the same, but Wilfred detected a hint of emotion in her voice.

'You can stay for ten minutes with the patient,' she said. 'His parents consent to your seeing him alone, but please don't ask him anything that might upset him.'

Leaving the waiting-room, they crossed the passage and she showed him into Freddie's room. Wilfred could feel his heart thumping and without quite knowing what to expect he stopped short, three paces from the bed, while the door closed gently.

Freddie turned towards him: his face was swollen and coloured an unhealthy pink.

'I knew you'd come,' he said in a voice that could scarcely pass his lips. 'They've told you how things are?'

He gasped.

'No,' replied Wilfred sitting down by him.

'I couldn't live through those three days of waiting, so I took something. I didn't want to kill myself, I just wanted to suppress those three days.'

'Don't speak if it tires you, Freddie.'

'I must. You've got to know. I thought I'd sleep for three days.'

He stammered a little but his eyes never left Wilfred.

'You'll be all right,' said the latter.

'No, I won't.'

'Now, Freddie, what are you dreaming up?'

'I know what's going to happen, but I'm not scared. I was only scared of the disease, nothing else. I should have gone yesterday. I suffered less. I'm choking.'

His eyes peered into Wilfred's.

'Did you pray for me?' he asked.

'Yes.'

'They say Catholics light candles when they pray.'

'Not always, Freddie.'

'Will you light one for me?'

236

'Yes.'

'I'd like to see a priest, but my parents won't allow it.'

'Why? I could ask one to come.'

'It's no use. You don't know them. And they're in such a state – Mamma's almost crazy, Wilfred –'

He waved his hands like a baby.

'What is it, Freddie?'

'What do you have to do to be a Catholic?'

Wilfred's throat grew so tight that he could not answer. For a few seconds, he had the feeling, one that was so familiar to him, of having been overtaken by someone more powerful than he. Within the white walls of this banal little room, he had just fallen into a trap and realized he was trembling.

'Why do you ask me that?' he said, leaning slightly towards the sick man.

Freddie looked at him without answering. In a voice he scarcely recognized, Wilfred said all of a sudden:

'You have to believe that Christ is God.'

'I believe it. I believe everything you do.'

In a low, halting voice, he added:

'I want to be like you, Wilfred. A Catholic.'

'You've not been baptized?'

'No. They wouldn't have it done.'

Wilfred rose brusquely and hid his face in his hands.

'Freddie,' he said with an effort, 'every Christian has the power to baptize. Will you receive baptism?'

Tears rolled down Freddie's face. He nodded.

Wilfred went to the wash-stand and ran some water into a glass, then came back to the bed. Freddie smiled. If ever Wilfred had seen happiness in a human face, it was on that of the dying lad. Bending over him, Wilfred wet his brow, made the sign of the cross with his thumb, pronouncing clearly as possible words of which each syllable rang out in an extraordinary silence:

237

'Frederick, I baptize you in the name of the Father, and of the Son, and of the Holy Ghost.'

Having said this, he put down the glass and said to the patient:

'You are saved. There is nothing else – I can do nothing else. You are going to Heaven.'

Freddie began gasping again. The water ran down his brow.

'Will you kiss me?' he asked in a low voice.

Wilfred bent and laid his lips against his cheek.

When he left the hospital, his strength failed him suddenly and he had barely time to reach a bench and drop on to it. It was only at that moment that he realized he had acted for someone else, during his entire visit to Freddie.

The rest of the day passed without further incident. He went back to his work and sold a few shirts, much as an automaton might have done, and it seemed to him that Mr Schoenhals avoided him, and how little he cared! Everything seemed indescribably dull, and from time to time, under the bright glass globes, he looked around for the unobtrusive little being who would never return.

CHAPTER LI

That evening, he went home early, as it was quite out of the question to roam the streets and have a good time. He no longer felt the same and any remembrance of his past life only filled him with shame and boredom. For several hours now, the conviction had grown: he was about to turn his whole life into a failure and, if such words make sense, to pass himself by.

Such were his thoughts in the lift, but a surprise awaited him

238

at his door. A large package carefully wrapped in yellow paper stood against the wall and it only took him a second to guess what it was as its shape and size told everything. 'Life is such a practical joker,' he thought. Was this the day for Uncle Horace's portrait? A week earlier, it might have amused him, but after a tragic morning and in his present serious mood, why should he be burdened with this rather absurd object?

A letter came with it and was from Phoebe. He opened it at once, on the landing. '*Dear Wilfred*,' she wrote, '*We went to Wormsloe this morning and I had this work of art wrapped up as it belongs to you! The air was so pure by the riverside and the birds sang so beautifully that I began believing in happiness again. We talked about you and your future: it worries us a little. Will you come and see us when we are settled? It will take me some time to get used to this big melancholy house. – PHOEBE.*'

He pushed his hat back and said aloud:

'Well, I never!'

Then he read the letter over attentively, weighing each word. How could you guess what took place in a woman's head? Didn't perversion and innocence often use the same language? If Phoebe had wished to rouse hope in his heart, she would not have written otherwise. In the same way, supposing she had not guessed his feelings for her – And so, whether she was in love or indifferent, she managed to write a note that could be taken any way you liked – but psychology bored Wilfred. Holding the brief letter in his hand, he felt suddenly overwhelmed by the rapture of an impossible passion. That, at any rate, was true. Poor Freddie was probably going to die, but he, Wilfred Ingram, was very much alive and the blood ran hot in his veins.

In the act of turning the key in the lock, his hand stopped. His blood – he had left a little of it in a test-tube, a little that did not run, it was settling and would have something to tell, tomorrow.

Sobering down suddenly, he entered the room and laid Uncle

239

Horace's portrait on the desk. Everything had changed in a flash. Freddie had wished to escape the threat that hung over him and was going to die. In vain, he told himself every word he knew about the improved methods that mastered the loathsome disease in a few days. That nightmare was coming to an end, in our times, but the disease was one thing and the dread of the disease another. Its very name terrified you, made you ill.

For several minutes, he felt incapable of moving, then the sound of a car in the street roused him suddenly from his torpor and he began unwrapping the picture.

The paper crackled noisily as he tore it and Uncle Horace appeared fresh as a daisy, spick and span, triumphant. With both hands, Wilfred stood him against the wall. A more charming face, a better figure could not be imagined. Actually, the portrait was not that of a man but rather of a toy, a toy in the hands of the devil, for the use of anyone who wanted it. A great many women had lost their souls on his account, that was certain, because they wanted him to turn that little round head of his towards them, because they wanted a smile from that pretty mouth. At present all that rotted in a box, in the peaceful light of the moon. How often had Uncle Horace raved in the moonlight! Now he was doing something else.

Wilfred could not look at him enough. A rather fancy military jacket showed the shape of his figure in a slightly immodest fashion and there was something about the oval of that happy face, something satiated and impertinent that would have justified a hail of blows. Had he ever had that disease? No, of course not. He was the kind that life treats kindly and fondles because of pleasing looks. People said he had kept his youth and attractiveness until he reached fifty and even later, as he approached old age, and at the end, at the very end, he had remembered his faith, so that the dirty, lucky old dog had had an edifying death. But after? After?

240

Wilfred flew into a sudden rage and shrugged his shoulders as he looked at the smug little second-lieutenant. 'It's not possible,' he muttered, addressing the portrait, 'you've made a hash of things and now you know it, in your box –' Max was right. From bed to bed you finally landed in everlasting fire, in the fire that is not quenched.

Seizing the wrapping paper, he rolled it into a ball and with his heel stuffed it into the waste-paper basket. He, Wilfred, would not burn. Something would happen and he would escape. At that moment, a curious thought crossed his mind: perhaps there was a rosary in the pocket of that fancy military jacket. A rosary! It seemed as though a voice had said that to him, a gentle precise voice. 'Well,' he said aloud, 'and what does that prove? Nothing.' 'Nothing,' echoed the voice.

He undressed and stood under the shower to wash from head to foot, but did not glance in the mirror or look at his body because there might be something horrible there and he did not want to see it, he simply wanted to be clean. He would go to the hospital next day in the afternoon. Then he would know. Meanwhile, a sort of happiness remained to him, the happiness of uncertainty, since he was not sure of being stricken by death. Indeed, wasn't it all a mere question of death, death that stalked behind him? With every step he took, it took one too. If he stopped, it stopped and waited. Some day, it would lay its finger on him. Now Freddie had grown tired of being followed. He had turned and gone to meet death, but Freddie's case was a particular one. Freddie was saved.

Putting on his dark blue linen pyjamas, he leaned out of the window. On the other side of the street, little low houses were lined up, good as gold, all very much alike with their white stone steps and brass knockers. Here and there, a window lighted up, but there wasn't a sound. As a rule, Wilfred was far afield at that time of night, having a good time, forgetting the

241

very existence of a little street that offered such a cruelly precise picture of boredom. In spite of himself, he looked on, bewitched by the magic of monotony, of regularity, of emptiness when, all of a sudden, a ring of the bell made him start.

Someone had rung at his door. Without quite knowing what he was doing, he put on a dressing-gown and stood perfectly motionless in the middle of the room. The absurd idea occurred to him that Freddie was there, on the other side of the door, then he wondered if it was not Max. He would have liked it to be Max, to make his peace with him.

The bell rang again, but this time more softly.

'Is that you, Max?' he asked aloud.

'No,' replied a voice he did not recognize.

He waited a moment.

'Wilfred,' pursued the voice that became majestic, 'it's Mr Schoenhals.'

'Mr Schoenhals!'

Another silence. He could not receive Mr Schoenhals in a dressing-gown, the very idea was impossible.

'Forgive me for coming so late,' said the voice on the other side of the door, 'but I must speak to you.'

Wilfred explained that he was about to go to bed.

'Well, slip something on, my boy,' said the voice with a certain impatience as though the fact of keeping Mr Schoenhals waiting was a breach of professional etiquette.

He added in a slightly offended tone:

'You don't suppose I'd come out of my way without serious reason?'

Out of pure meanness, Wilfred waited another few seconds, then opened and though he knew it beforehand it seemed stupefying to see Mr Schoenhals on the landing, Mr Schoenhals without the store around him.

The shopwalker was not smiling. He had removed his smile

as one removes a mask. Wilfred stood aside and the stout man entered, going straight to a chair where he sat with such authority that it turned the young salesman into a small boy.

'I've had a telephone call,' he said when Wilfred had closed the door.

'A telephone call?'

'You must prepare for a sad piece of news.'

'I think I know what it is, Mr Schoenhals.'

The latter stared fixedly at the wall.

'Freddie,' he said.

In the ensuing silence, Wilfred noticed that he puffed a little, his mouth half open. Perhaps he was more moved than the young man himself, who could not be surprised at the news.

'A friend of his father's called me, a moment ago,' continued Mr Schoenhals without moving. 'I wouldn't have thought I'd feel so badly about it. Pneumonia. Very strange. You're a believer, Wilfred. I've even been given to understand that you are a Catholic.'

Wilfred had just seated himself on the edge of the bed, and as he heard this last sentence, he instinctively turned his head to the nail in the wall above his bed. He imagined that Mr Schoenhals looked up at it.

'Yes, a Roman Catholic,' he said a little mechanically.

'Why did God strike a boy who had never done anyone harm?'

'That's something we don't know, Mr Schoenhals. I don't think we have any right to ask ourselves such questions.'

'I'm not a believer, Wilfred. I wish I were, but things like that would prevent me from believing.'

'Sooner of later,' thought Wilfred, 'he's going to ask the meaning or that nail: he can't keep his eyes from it.' He felt ill at ease. Far better than at the store, he could see the weight of years of sorrow in Mr Schoenhals' heavy face, doubtless because his smile had disappeared. Right behind the visitor, the second-lieutenant threw his shoulders back and turned up the corners of his pretty mouth.

'I used to believe,' said Mr Schoenhals suddenly. 'Or I imagined I believed, like so many men who have had very little experience of life. I was brought up by very religious parents. My father was –'

He stopped short and stared at Wilfred from eyes full of heartbreaking melancholy. All of a sudden, he looked a thousand years old.

'You have nothing against Jews, have you, Wilfred?'

'Absolutely nothing.'

'My father was a rabbi. A very good, a very honest man. I had his opinions, his faith, then all that went, with the years. I regret it. I like people to have faith and nothing in the world would make me wish to shake yours. It's a very good thing to be a Catholic, if you really believe.'

Wilfred stood still, waiting for that sentence about the nail.

'It must surprise you,' continued Mr Schoenhals, 'to hear me speak of such things. It's because of little Freddie. He had such a short life. I wonder what it all means. Why was he born? Forgive me, I'm upset and just saying what comes into my head. However, I wanted to talk to you about something else.'

The man who stared at Wilfred did not in the least resemble the affable, quietly imperious shop walker at the store. In a certain manner that words cannot describe, he looked like a pauper, he looked ruined. In the lamp light, the wrinkles on his great bald forehead and somewhat flabby cheeks seemed drawn in strokes of charcoal.

'I wanted to ask you not to leave, in the interest of the store and yours also. The manager promised me this morning that your salary would be raised. You can change departments, if you like: stay on the same floor but in the jewellery section.'

For several minutes, he talked with surprising glibness,

considering that his speech was usually slow and solemn, and began making gestures with his small, round hands. Wilfred was not listening. He was thinking of what he would say when Mr Schoenhals stopped, a sentence he gloated over beforehand because it avenged him for long months of boredom. At last came a pause and he covered his knees with a fold of his dressing-gown.

'I'm awfully sorry, Mr Schoenhals, but my decision is final. You will have to inform the manager I'm leaving, when the time comes.'

A thrill of pleasure ran down his spine as the words shaped themselves on his lips. Particularly 'my decision' – He looked a little cocky as he said this and his pride was quickened in all its breadth and depth: it occurred to Wilfred that if the cross had hung behind him, above his head, he would have talked differently.

Mr Schoenhals stared at him, open-mouthed.

Inform the manager –' he repeated, like a child.

All of a sudden, with visible effort, he rose and walked about, stopping in front of Uncle Horace's portrait.

'Your father ?' he asked.

'No, my uncle. The one who died some time ago.'

'Ah, yes. Fine looking man. Fine uniform.'

For a moment he stood motionless, arms dangling, with something rather heavy and rather dazed in his attitude. Wilfred jumped nimbly from the bed and stuffed both hands in the pockets of his dressing-gown. In spite of himself, he felt sorry for Mr Schoenhals. He had nothing against Mr Schoenhals. To revenge himself on the store was what he wanted, on the store and on life.

Mr Schoenhals shook his head.

'I was pretty sure you'd say no,' he said in an undertone. 'As far as we're concerned, we always expect the worst.'

Wilfred did not inquire about what he meant by *we*.

245

'You'll find someone else,' he said good-naturedly.

'Of course, but that's not the point. I can't explain, unfortunately. Not that I care for the store any more than you do, but your presence there made everything easier.'

'Thank you, Mr Schoenhals.'

'Have you found another job?'

'Not yet.'

'You acted impulsively, Wilfred. It's not too late to reconsider your decision.'

'I never go back on a decision.'

Mr Schoenhals gave a sort of moan and clapped his hands to his head as though someone had struck him. Wilfred's foolishness no doubt appalled him.

'In a few years from now,' he continued, 'you'll remember this conversation and see it in a different light. You'll understand things better.'

'I don't have to wait,' thought Wilfred, 'I understand everything perfectly, Mr Schoenhals.'

However, he assumed his most candid expression:

'In a few years from now?'

Mr Schoenhals waved his hand without replying and recovering his professional dignity went to the door.

'See you tomorrow. Nine o'clock,' he said.

'See you tomorrow, Mr Schoenhals.'

The door closed, and after a few seconds Wilfred heard the sound of the lift. He began laughing to himself, as he would have laughed at a good joke. At that moment, the inner voice said clearly: 'You have behaved unkindly.' He laughed once more. 'Unkindly,' said the voice.

CHAPTER LII

Well, how should he have behaved? Kindly? Talked charitably to a man who was visibly grieved? But he did not believe himself kind. He had shown no compassion and had laughed, as once before, on the road to Wormsloe. The impulse that sends a real Christian to a brother in distress was something he never felt, or felt too late. Baptism was not sufficient to make a good Christian of you and insure your salvation, or else you had to die right away and take your baptism to Heaven with you, as little Freddie had just done. Freddie was saved. 'You and I are lost,' Max had said. Try as he might to persuade himself that Max did not know what he was talking about, Wilfred slept badly that night.

Next morning, he went straight to Mr Schoenhals. His smile once more glued to his face, the shopwalker stood erect and sleek like an idol, thought Wilfred as he neared him.

He continued to smile when he saw the young salesman, but puffed slightly, his mouth half open.

'Good morning, Wilfred.'

'Mr Schoenhals –'

How ugly he looked suddenly, with his protruding eyes! Wilfred could not remember what he had planned to say.

'Mr Schoenhals, I shouldn't have talked to you the way I did last night. I apologize. I didn't mean to offend you. I didn't mean –'

His voice choked. Mr Schoenhals' expression changed suddenly. Stretching out his hand, he squeezed Wilfred's arm without a word, then turned and walked off. The young man felt greatly relieved, something akin to happiness swept over him, but the thought of what he had to do in the afternoon turned him gloomy again.

At half past six he was at the hospital and asked to see the intern who had attended to Freddie and himself. He was made to wait in a small empty room. In his distress, he kept the cross of his rosary in his hand at the bottom of a pocket as he tried mentally to pray. He promised God several things, without daring to say he would not do some of them again, he merely bound himself to make an effort, not to follow women in the street, not to go to bars, and his promise was worthless, he knew, because it cost him nothing. What he would not promise was quite another matter.

'Phoebe,' he thought, grasping the little metal cross so tightly in the hollow of his hand that the flesh was bruised. 'Lord,' he said to himself, 'it's terrible that there should be this woman. You know that I never tried to see her. It was she –'

The door opened, the intern came in smiling.

'Negative,' he said. 'You can be perfectly easy in your mind.'

Wilfred all but embraced him.

'Thanks.'

'Thanks for what? I have nothing to do with it.'

Wilfred's face had such an odd expression that the intern began to laugh.

'If you can't be good, be careful,' he said.

'What about Freddie?' thought Wilfred. He reminded the intern that they had come to the hospital together.

'I remember. You can tell your friend there's nothing the matter with him either. Just look at this, anyway –'

248

He handed Wilfred two sheets of green paper with the results of the analyses.

In the avenue, Wilfred waited for the bus at the stop where he had left Freddie, a few days earlier. Freddie had died, for nothing, for absolutely nothing. So said the green sheet of paper, but Wilfred was under the impression that he stood by him laughing as he would certainly have laughed. 'I'll go and burn a taper for you,' said the young man looking off into space, 'as you asked me to –' – 'I'll come with you,' said the dead man.

'If only you could have waited,' said Wilfred in a low voice, 'you'd be here now, but you lacked courage.'

'Lacked courage,' repeated Freddie with a laugh, somewhere in Wilfred's head.

The latter could have sworn that just then a hand took his arm and brusquely he glanced sideways, but of course he was alone. What surprised him more than anything else was that he should have glanced to one side.

At nightfall, he went to the Polish church. Benediction was just over, an odour of incense floated around the altar awakening in Wilfred the fervour of spotless childhood. That was what he wanted, childhood. Gold glittered faintly here and there, statues smiled and the tapers' little flames quivered like leaves. He felt safe there, sheltered from evil, sheltered from the street and its terrifying diseases. He could thank God and the Blessed Virgin. The devil wouldn't be able to find him within these walls.

Three or four old women knelt praying, the three or four old women who can be found in every church in the world, the old women on whom Heaven depends, he thought, but he would not look at them. Old age was repulsive to him. He looked at the high altar, the little golden gates of the tabernacle and the great bunches of white flowers. It was enough to kneel and say a prayer or two, and in the same manner he got up with a choir-boy's alacrity and lit a big taper for Freddie in the Lady chapel. He wished that he could have had him near him then, as he had in an avenue a short time earlier, but he no longer felt his presence and as he watched his taper's flame leaning a little to the right, he said to himself that the flame was like a prayer.

'I must write to Phoebe and thank her for the portrait,' he thought and almost immediately left the church.

CHAPTER LIII

The air was warm outside the church and a gust of longing sent the blood rushing to Wilfred's face. His body was healthy, he could love Phoebe and he wanted her, not in the way he had wanted so many women in former days, and had them: he needed her tenderness, her arms around his shoulders; her cheek against his. The idea of laying his head on her breast came back to him again and again.

On reaching home, he took out a sheet of paper and wondered what he was going to say. Finding nothing suitable, he looked at Uncle Horace's portrait and sentences from his letters returned to his mind. In a sudden burst of irritation, he found Alicia's picture in the drawer and pressed it to the second-lieutenant's face: 'Now then, kiss your sweetheart!' he cried. After which, filled with shame, he kissed Alicia's photograph himself. 'Anyone who saw me would take me for a lunatic,' he thought. Yet that was nothing compared with what followed.

He wrote Phoebe a letter and in three pages and a half he explained what he wished to obtain from her. This calmed him and he was then able to concoct a quiet, polite little note with just enough respect, flavoured with a touch of lawful affection. Both letters were then folded and slipped into two similar envelopes which he sealed; after which he wrote Phoebe's address in his best hand (he was proud of his handwriting).

As in each case one sheet of folded paper had been used, both letters had the same thickness, although one contained a single page of writing. It was no longer possible now to distinguish one from the other, to know which should be posted and which thrown in the sewer that seemed its natural destination. He stamped both and put them in his pocket.

A frenzy of love no doubt was responsible for his singular behaviour, which was so unlike the image he had of himself. 'I'll just pick one of the letters and put it in the box,' he said to himself. 'Fate will decide which.'

A few seconds later, he had left the house. There was a post office on his street, three houses away from his. Taking up one of the two letters, he held it in his fingers for almost a minute, close to the slit in the mail box. Finally, his hand opened and the letter slipped in. Nothing could be done to recover it, but perhaps it was the very proper letter that now lay in the bottom of the box. There was only one way of finding that out, namely to open the letter he still kept in his pocket, but that he would not do. Walking to the end of the street, he began looking in the window of a bookstore that was still lit up. Very attentively, he read the titles of all the books displayed in their gay many-coloured jackets. 'If the proper letter is in the mail box, you can sleep peacefully,' he said to himself. 'It's insignificant and won't change anything in the situation. If it's the other one –'

Afraid of the letter he fingered in his pocket, he dared not open it and yet felt tempted to destroy it, to destroy it unread. Then he could always hope the proper letter was on its way to Phoebe. There was one chance out of two – Never did he quite understand

251

why he strolled back nonchalantly, reached the post office, and there, with a quick and expert hand, sent the second letter to join the first. It all happened so rapidly that he had the impression that someone else had done it. The street was empty. Leaning against the post office wall, he made the sign of the cross.

CHAPTER LIV

Five days went by without bringing anything new into his life. Phoebe thought it best not to see him again, no doubt, and whose fault was it? He did not even have the consolation of accusing what he vaguely called fate. A boy of fifteen would not have acted more foolishly.

The store looked more sinister than usual to Wilfred because he could see a cloudless blue sky above the bookseller's black house. Mr Schoenhals rarely spoke to him. A big red-headed boy whom no one liked replaced little Freddie. The newcomer, from shyness perhaps, seemed to keep everyone at arm's length, although he fawned on the customers.

'Three weeks more,' thought Wilfred, 'I'll be free in three weeks.' Yet he had heard nothing from his cousin, and his financial situation would soon depend on what Angus would do to help him. All these worries depressed him and it would have been a relief to vent his ill-humour on Max, but there was no sign of him. Nothing very surprising in that, when you came to think of it.

Fear of having lost Phoebe sent Wilfred each day a little farther down the dark steps of despair. Never had life appeared so gloomy or so completely useless and there was nothing in the world he wanted. Had he asked to be born? Why was it absolutely impossible to avoid suffering? What did it all mean?

On the following Sunday, he went to the Jesuits' church where he was sure not to meet anyone he knew. The choir there was celebrated for the crystal clear quality of its children's voices as they rose to the vaulting with surprising buoyancy. It was all marble and gold, a testimony to the parish's wealth. Wilfred found a seat at the back of this magnificent building and said his prayers perfunctorily.

A garnet coloured velvet cushion kept his knees from bruising, but he felt listless and dared not own, even to himself, that he was bored among smart people who came to church as to a concert and had to have very subtle, delicate music to make them accept Mass. Music was necessary to Wilfred too that Sunday for, strange as it may seem, it prevented him from thinking of God. On the other hand, nothing could have induced him to miss Holy Mass.

In the afternoon, he wanted to walk in the park, but there were too many people, too many children there and something advised him to go home. Yet, if there was a time when he loathed his room, it was on a day like this when an exultant sun shone in the clear and empty sky. A longing to lose himself in the country oppressed him. He remembered the house on the river and the place where he had stretched out on the grass. Oh, to lie there on his back, his hand in Phoebe's – They wouldn't do anything wrong, they would say rather silly things, those things people say when they look up at the sky. Perhaps she would have a blade of grass between her lips.

When he saw the light coffee coloured walls again, he could not resist kicking one of the chairs, then he opened the drawer to make sure that his securities were in their place. Everything was in order. He was a long time closing the drawer and turned the little key in the lock with great care; boredom slowed down

253

each of his gestures to the point when he finally stood motionless.

No one went by in the street and he had nothing to do. Time must be allowed to wear on. Removing his coat and tie, he threw himself on the bed, hands clasped behind his head and mind adrift.

It was hot, he dozed off, but suddenly gave a start. Someone had knocked at his door, not rung but knocked. He did not move. It was probably Max and he had no desire to see him now. Three hours earlier, perhaps, but not now – There was another knock and Wilfred smiled sarcastically, without stirring: 'Knock on,' he thought, 'I won't open. Excuse me.' A minute went by in the deepest silence and he waited in vain for the sound of the lift. Suddenly a voice on the other side of the door said his name:

'Wilfred, I know you're there. Open.'

Wilfred jumped to the floor with a cry of surprise. It was Angus. Without quite knowing why, he turned Uncle Horace's portrait to the wall before opening. He saw at once that his cousin had changed.

'Angus, something's happened to you!'

Angus came in, and turning his great dark eyes toward Wilfred looked at him with astonishment.

'Why, no. Nothing. I decided to fetch your securities myself, that's all.'

He walked by Wilfred and took one of the chairs.

'Close the door,' he said.

Wilfred obeyed, and taking advantage of the fact that his back was turned to the visitor, buttoned his shirt collar. He watched Angus from the corner of his eye. The latter sat motionless, hands on knees and head a little bowed. Against his will and not without a trace of envy, he admired his cousin's face and its singularly white complexion. 'His features are more delicate than mine,' he thought and once again felt himself a country bumpkin compared with Angus whose light grey summer suit made him years younger: he looked like a student on holiday.

'You're right, Wilfred,' said Angus without moving. 'I've made a fool of myself.'

'Made a fool of yourself, you?'

'I had decided to send someone here in my place. My mother's chauffeur, a man I trust completely. You know him, anyway. Do you remember the young fellow who met you at the station in a cart?'

'Why, yes. I don't understand, Angus.'

'Yet it's simple enough. He lost his job at Wormsloe when our uncle died. I persuaded my mother to engage him as a chauffeur.'

'I would never have given him those securities.'

Angus raised his head suddenly and looked at him like a man with a great load taken off his mind.

'You wouldn't? That's just what I thought. So I was right to come here, after all.'

'Now how could you imagine I would give such important papers to –'

Angus interrupted him.

'The man is perfectly honest.'

This was said in such a definite manner that Wilfred held his tongue. There was a short pause.

'Will you show me the securities?' asked Angus. 'We'll look at them together.'

Wilfred took the bundle of securities from the drawer and handed it silently to his cousin who examined each share, counted the lot and slipped everything into the envelope again, serious as a businessman.

'What are you going to do with that money, Wilfred?'

'Oh, I don't know. I'll think about it.'

'You must invest it,' said Angus.

He glanced shrewdly at Wilfred and suddenly looked like his mother when she talked about financial transactions.

'Invest it? We haven't got that far!' cried Wilfred laughing.

'Almost that far. I'll have collected the money for you in a couple of days.'

There followed a little speech on how to lay out to best advantage a sum Wilfred was fully determined to spend as pleasantly as possible.

'I hope you don't imagine you're rich,' concluded Angus anxiously.

Nothing would have induced Wilfred to tell his cousin he was leaving the store and yet the words rose to his lips of themselves.

'I've decided to give my boss notice.'

As he said this, he stuffed both hands in his pockets, and looking at his astounded cousin burst out laughing, but at heart, he felt frightened. For the first time he realized that he was frightened of Angus. The latter put the securities on the table and simply said:

'I congratulate you.'

Suddenly he bit his lip and looked down. His fair hair curled a little, like a child's, over a milk white neck. Wilfred could not help looking at it and thinking: 'A skin they're so proud of in his family –' His desire for Angus to leave increased, as he guessed vaguely that his cousin was about to say things best unsaid.

A great patch of sunlight widened around their feet. Wilfred got up to draw down the green blind, thus plunging the room into semi-darkness. He then sat on a corner of the desk and faced Angus, playing all the while with his keys dangling from a chain, twirling them in space with a little jarring noise.

256

'Wilfred,' he began, 'I said just now I'd made a fool of myself and that's exactly so. I shouldn't have come here. We could have managed things differently.'

Wilfred dreaded another declaration and, at the same time, expected it.

'Differently? Why?' he asked, to his own surprise, in a calm, natural voice. 'It's very simple. Everything is settled. You'll take the securities with you.'

He replaced the keys in his pocket.

'The securities? Yes, of course, Wilfred. But there's something else. I've been walking round this house for over an hour. Instead of ringing I knocked, very softly at first, because I hoped you wouldn't hear, then louder, still hoping you wouldn't hear and yet wanting you to. Can you understand such a thing?'

He waited for an answer that never came, then said at a breath: 'I came here yesterday.'

'Yesterday?'

'Yes. I've been in town for two days. This may seem extraordinary to you, but it's on your account. During all these past weeks, I've been thinking of you – far too much.'

He stopped for a moment and once more Wilfred felt tempted to make for the door and run away. As though he had guessed this, Angus got up.

'Can you imagine how hard it is for me to be saying such things to you?' he asked.

Wilfred did not answer. They stared into each other's eyes.

'You need not be afraid of me,' said Angus.

He shrugged his shoulders with such a sad smile as he said this that Wilfred felt like hugging him.

'Please, Angus, let's not talk about that any more.'

'Why do you want to prevent me from telling you the truth? You are the only person I wish to say it to. The others would not be able to bear it. I can't destroy the opinion they have of me, because it would hurt them too much. How do I know how it all began ?'

Wilfred blushed.

'If my mother knew the truth,' continued Angus, 'it would kill her. She has no idea of anything. She never will. You must judge me very severely.'

'Oh, I don't judge you at all!'

'When I think of what you are, of your way of thinking –'

'You're mistaken about me, as people are about you,' said Wilfred with a gesture.

'No, because you have your faith. I have none at all but am forced to let people think I believe. I suppose you already fancy me in hell ?'

The last remark was accompanied by a nervous laugh.

'Don't be so silly, Angus.'

'Silly, why ? Does any possible salvation exist for people like me in your system ?'

'In my system ?' asked Wilfred in a low voice.

'Maybe the term shocks you. Forgive me. I'll put the question differently. Does the Church of Rome teach that men of my kind are damned ?'

'Men of your kind ?'

'Don't you understand what I'm talking about, Wilfred ? Men who are born with tastes like mine . . .'

'I understand,' said Wilfred. His face was covered with perspiration.

'And what then ?'

In the semi-darkness Angus's face looked waxy white and his eyes so dark and so sorrowful that Wilfred bent his head rather than meet such an unbearably sad gaze.

'I'm sure the Church teaches nothing of the sort,' he said at last. 'God forgives everything. That's what we're taught.'

'But how was it God's will that I should be made the way I

258

am? What does it mean? I didn't ask for anything, I wasn't given a choice. Then why? Why are things so?'

He asked this with such violence that Wilfred felt a shock go through him as though each question were a blow. Suddenly Angus took his wrist and shook it.

'Why don't you say something? Why don't you answer?'

'I can't talk about religion, Angus. I never could.'

'Then who will if men like you are silent?' he asked, dropping his cousin's arm. 'You have no right to keep silence. You have faith, a believer speaks up in such a case. There are millions of men like me on earth and you who have faith content yourselves with sighing as you think of us.'

'That's not so. The Church prays for everybody.'

'The Church! But you, Wilfred, have you ever prayed for me?'

Wilfred dared not tell Angus that it had never occurred to him to do so.

'How can it matter to you if people pray for you,' he asked, 'as long as you don't believe in anything?'

'How do I know? Let me tell you something. One night, I did pray. I prayed because of you. That's a surprise to you. It surprised me too. Here's the whole story. I was leaving that young man's room, the young man my mother had just engaged, and was passing through the quiet house. All of a sudden, I was overwhelmed by the most horrible sadness, a deadly unaccountable sadness. I thought of you, of your life – a life I had judged so humdrum and that suddenly seemed extraordinarily beautiful, because of your faith.'

'Oh no!' cried Wilfred. 'My life is not beautiful.'

'I had a sudden loathing then for what I had done,' continued Angus without seeming to notice the interruption. 'It could not be called remorse, it was the terror of feeling myself in abysmal solitude. You don't know what that means. You are never alone. I tried to pray so as not to be alone, because when you

259

pray, you're talking to someone. I even went down on my knees. I asked, but nobody came. If someone had come, I would have felt it. There was no one there.'

'How do you know?'

'There was no one there for me. Not for me, Wilfred. Heaven is for those who believe in it. The rest of us remain in what you call outer darkness. We are cast out. It's a harsh word, but it's in the Gospel. I've heard it many a time in the church where I go with my mother not only to please her but because I can't tell her I don't believe in anything, any more than I own up to the rest with her.'

He stopped brusquely and sat on a chair, his back to the window, apparently exhausted. Wilfred raised the blind a little, for the room was too warm and needed ventilation. On the other side of the street, he noticed a well-dressed young man who stood smoking a cigarette as he waited.

'If you want to believe, how do you go about it?' asked Angus suddenly.

'You must ask, pray.'

'Pray when you're sure there's no one there?'

Wilfred thought for a moment, then, scarcely knowing what he said, answered hesitantly:

'You can imagine there's someone.'

'And what then?' asked Angus without moving. 'By dint of imagination, you force Him to come?'

'That's not quite it. He's there, you understand? What you imagined was true.'

'You believe He is here?'

'Yes, I do,' answered Wilfred with a sudden energy tinged with exasperation. 'I believe He is here with us, in this room and that if you and I are together, facing one another, it's because He wishes it.'

'Why doesn't He let us know it beyond any doubt?'

260

'I don't know. He hides. He talks in His own way.'

'What are you looking at?' asked Angus without turning.

'Me? Nothing.'

'Yes, you are. A man is strolling about, isn't he? On the opposite sidewalk. Don't you recognize him?'

'No.'

'That's because of the way he's dressed. When I first saw him, he looked like a real country boy. There was something wild about him that affected me.'

Wilfred promptly drew down the blind as far as it could go.

'Angus! It's the young man who drove the cart?'

'Of course,' said Angus as he got up. 'I've changed the man's fortune completely. Now you know the main part of what there is to know about me. At any rate you know the worst. Give me those securities.'

With an impulsive gesture, Wilfred grasped him violently by both arms.

'You shan't go before I tell you the truth!' he cried.

'What's the use? I know you better than you think.'

'No. I've lied to you. I've lied to you by holding my tongue.'

'Do you really take me for such a simpleton? Let me go, Wilfred.' (Wilfred at once obeyed.) 'Don't imagine you can take me in. Your face tells me all I want to know. I'm accustomed to men's faces, particularly men of your age. You are consumed by passions, but have kept your faith in spite of it. That's what surprises me most and what I envy you. Faith is stronger than everything else in you. Give me those papers.'

Wilfred mechanically handed him the bundle of securities.

'Listen, Angus, we can't part like this.'

'Yes, we can. I must go.'

He opened the door as he said this and seeing Wilfred stretch out a hand to detain him, moved aside.

'Please –' he said. 'We've said everything we had to say to

each other. I'll make the necessary transactions and send you a cheque within the week.'

Did he take pleasure in leaving after that rapidly spoken sentence? Wilfred remembered the scene on the road and the way he had moved away from his cousin when he tried to kiss him. 'He's taking his revenge,' he thought, 'or else he's trying to protect himself because he's afraid.' For a second or two Angus stared at him and there was a gleam in his dark eyes that made him look furious. His lips parted, he seemed about to say something, but with a sudden change of mind, disappeared.

The door closed, Wilfred covered his ears with his hands so as not to hear the sound of the lift, but heard it nevertheless. He felt like throwing himself on his knees in front of the bare wall where the nail cast a little shadow that was clear as a pencil stroke. Disconnected, incoherent sentences escaped him.

'YOU did that!' he cried several times.

Whom was the remark intended for and what did it mean? He gradually calmed down.

'Everthing passed off very well, on the whole,' he murmured. 'Yes, on the whole.'

Putting his face close to the bathroom mirror, he thought himself rather nice-looking, but Angus was right: his passions showed – 'My passions,' he thought and smiled indulgently at his reflection.

CHAPTER LV

His spare time next day was spent in looking for another room, but he tired himself to no purpose. Everything offered was depressing or beyond his means, for Angus's remark stuck in his mind: 'Don't imagine you're rich.' He most reluctantly refused a small flat where the prettiest of three rooms looked out on a garden: he could have been happy there. He pictured himself sitting on the big chintz sofa with Phoebe on a fine June night, gazing at the stars and holding her hand by the open window. These childish dreams consumed him. It was impossible to live with Phoebe as long as her husband was above ground. Now, what use was Mr Knight? He didn't make her happy and was going to die anyway. Wilfred had started thinking about him almost as often as he did of his wife, but for widely differing reasons that he dared not quite own to, even to himself, because it was not in him to hate another human being.

Three days later, he received the cheque that Angus had promised him. The amount was far larger than anticipated, but Angus in a rather short note pointed out that his cousin had been mistaken in his caclulations. From sheer excitement, Wilfred dropped sitting on his bed. If the little three room flat was still free, he would rent it. A great extravagance, no doubt, but his heart leapt for joy in his breast, at the idea of leaving that light coffee-coloured room for ever –

At the risk of getting to his work late (but what did that matter now?) he rushed to a drug-store to make a telephone call.

The flat had been let. Wilfred hung up and the whole world appeared unbearably sad. He went to the store looking like a man taken back to jail after an unsuccessful break-away.

A surprise lay in store for him at the end of the morning. A quarter of an hour before lunchtime, he saw someone coming up to him and almost cried out on recognizing James Knight. Among all the thoughts that flashed through the young man's mind, the most terrifying was 'He's come here to create a scandal on account of that letter –'

263

Wilfred was singularly wrong. James Knight came up to him smiling and said with apparently unfeigned breeziness:

'Young man, show me some shirts with stiff collars.'

'What size collar?' asked Wilfred choking.

'Fifteen.'

Wilfred displayed several types of stiff collared shirts.

'I bet you didn't expect to see me,' said James Knight bending over the counter. And he added: 'My wife was delighted with your little note.'

'She didn't show him the awful letter,' said Wilfred to himself. 'She's in love with me.'

'It was just to thank her,' he stammered.

James Knight raised his eyes and looked at him so gravely and so gently that Wilfred was filled with dreadful remorse for a few seconds. 'Perhaps God looks that way at men,' he thought. And it seemed as though God were gazing at him through the eyes of this man he had offended.

'I wanted to see the store where you work,' continued James Knight. 'I happened to be passing this way with Phoebe. She's down below.'

'Down below!' cried Wilfred involuntarily.

'She's waiting in the car. She hasn't been well recently ,but she wants you to come and see us.'

His pale mauvish lips scarcely moved as he spoke.

'I hope she isn't ill,' said Wilfred.

'Oh, no, she's simply tired from shopping in town.'

He added with a smile that pained Wilfred:

'I'm the one who does the waiting usually because I have to take care of my health, but I wanted to buy my shirts here, to see you.'

He took several that Wilfred immediately wrapped up.

'Will you have supper with us on the twenty-third?' asked James Knight when he had paid.

264

That was the following Saturday. Wilfred accepted.

'Come early. Come at six.'

His cheeks afire, the young man watched him moving away with measured rather weary steps, the pace he had adopted since his heart attack; and Wilfred wondered if he had seen him blush and what he thought.

At all events he knew nothing and Wilfred could rest easy on that score. And then, Phoebe wanted to see him. He felt tears well up in his eyes, loving, happy tears. Unconsciously, he smiled at the cashier who threw him a glance of contempt, but this was not enough to depress him. An outburst of fellow-feeling for the whole of humanity swept over him. He went to say something kindly to the disagreeable red-head who had taken Freddie's place and who raised his eyebrows with a shade of scorn:

'I see you're feeling pretty good,' he said.

Wilfred lost his head.

'Will you have lunch with me?' he asked.

'Sorry. I have a date.'

Just then, the clock struck and Wilfred left the store with the other salesmen.

CHAPTER LVI

Something kept him from depositing his cheque in the bank, although it was an easy enough matter as Mr Schoenhals would certainly have excused his being a few minutes late, but Wilfred kept the precious green slip in his wallet, though he could not have given a reason for his behaviour. On returning home that afternoon, he found another letter from his cousin, one that he thought peculiar.

'*Dear Wilfred,*' wrote Angus, '*if you haven't deposited the cheque I sent you yesterday, keep it another few days, because I can bring you the amount in banknotes. That would be a simplification and you could then be sure that no one will ever ask awkward questions.*'

Angus knew his cousin's wariness as well as his fears, and Wilfred thanked him mentally as he went on with the letter.

'*You'd be mistaken in thinking this a trick, an excuse to see you again. However, truth compels me to say that although it grieves me to be with you, yet this very grief is accompanied by a kind of happiness, a happiness that brings pain with it. It hurts my pride to write you such things. As a rule I master my feelings better, but you saw me as I am, the other day –*'

'Poor Angus,' thought Wilfred, 'he really is in love, like me.' However, his compassion was tempered by a faint satisfaction, as he was fond of attention.

'*Pleasure apart,*' continued Angus, '*my life is strangely like some descriptions of hell, for love has no place in it. At certain times, at certain most precise moments; those that come afterwards, do you understand, I hate my chosen companion who holds me down as never a planter held down his slaves before the Civil War. The hardened sinner you think me can't hope to be understood by a man of your kind. You believe from top to bottom of your soul, and the sins you may commit are washed away as soon as you confess them –*'

Wilfred put down the letter. The tone of religious indifference was no longer to be found in what his cousin said, but was replaced by one of veiled anxiety. He thought this over for a moment and then continued the letter.

'*Personally, I don't like what I have become. With the exception of one person, alas, I can attract anyone I please, but loathe my own*

266

ability. My mother thinks me chaste. I've always believed that parents recover a certain innocence and that marriage seems to wipe out all memories of their past life. Wilfred, what my body wants is not what I want, for I too have known a life that was chaste and untroubled by desire, and in early youth had an inkling of what faith could be. When I was a child and read the Gospel, I wanted to be like the One whose name I have not the courage to write here. In a certain fashion I think He is still with us on earth, although I can't believe in God. If the door of the room where I am writing opened and He came in and sat down, I could speak to Him. This dream has never left me, even in the darkest hours. I could have told Him what I can't tell anyone, because He would not have judged me and it's because He is not here that I am alone. He will not come and the other is waiting for me.'

Wilfred looked vainly for a signature. The letter had apparently been slipped hurriedly into an envelope, for it was folded crooked. For almost a quarter of an hour, he held the letter in his hand, reading it over and over again. The last of its strange sentences stirred him, for they echoed his own aspirations; and his turn of mind induced him to take them for a sign, a sort of warning, but the warning did not come from his cousin.

Going to look at himself in a mirror later, he attempted to see himself as Angus saw him. To judge Angus would have seemed ludicrous, if not hateful. To be fit to judge a man on his physical tastes you would have to be chaste, chaste as a saint, and anyway, saints judged no one, but Wilfred was trying to understand. Angus could certainly not think him handsome. No one thought him handsome and yet there was something else that escaped him.

He looked at himself so long that he grew dizzy.

267

CHAPTER LVII

The following Saturday, as he left the house to go to the Knights',
he was joined by Max. The latter wore his yellow waterproof in
spite of a cloudless sky, but this doubtful garment was intended
to conceal the shabbiness of a suit Wilfred knew only too well.
He waved Max aside emphatically.

'Sorry, Max, I haven't got the time today.'

'You're in a hurry,' said Max falling into step with him. 'A
rendezvous, no doubt. I can tell that by your tie.'

'Max,' answered Wilfred, stopping suddenly to look him in
the eye, 'if you want us to remain friends, you'll leave me right
away, for as it happens, I do have an appointment.'

Smiling broadly, Max showed his teeth; as usual, Wilfred
was astonished at their whiteness and once more fell a victim
to the charm of a man he secretly called a scoundrel; most
unwillingly, he smiled too.

'You must admit,' he said, 'that this is enough to make a man
furious, when he's in a hurry.'

'Oh, I'm only asking to go along with you for three minutes.
You can spare me three minutes.'

'What have you got to say?'

'Well, here in the street, nothing much. We can hardly talk
about religion.'

'I should say not.'

'Or sexuality.'

'Still less. I've already told you that I loathe the word.'

'What you really loathe is what it stands for. Platonic love
is what you want.'

268

'Don't be absurd. What use would the body be?'

'For suffering.'

'I haven't the least intention of making my body suffer.'

'Have you got your rosary on you?'

'That's none of your business.'

'Well, when I have a date, I leave mine at two hundred and thirteen and a half, in a drawer, because I'm afraid of its messing up things.'

'So you have a rosary?'

Max's only answer was to thrust a hand into his pocket, bring out a little rosary with red glass beads and flourish it in the sunlight: his hand seemed to drip blood.

'Put that away, Max,' said Wilfred.

With the tips of forefinger and thumb he made sure that his own rosary was in his pocket.

'I'm not ashamed of my religion,' said Max lifting the tiny cross to his lips before putting the rosary away.

'You're drunk, aren't you?'

'Hardly at all. Just enough. But I have no intention of going on a spree. I feel – now how can I explain it? Holy.'

'Really?'

'Yes, really. That's why I forgive you that shabby behaviour of yours the other night and your blows. I forgive you everything. I feel kindly, see?'

'You've already told me that. Max, this is where we're going to part.'

They had reached the street corner where Wilfred's bus stopped.

'I'll wait here with you,' said Max. 'You're good, too. Everybody is good, but you and I should have been saints, real ones. We have the makings of saints.'

Wilfred listened, a little unwillingly.

'But you've just told me that you felt holy, Max.'

269

'Oh, that doesn't mean one is saved. There are men and women in hell who felt the presence of God when they lived on earth.'

'That's impossible.'

'No, it's not. God follows us step by step. You don't realize it. Sometimes He has to be told to go away to make Him leave us – just as we would do to a beggar – and still He comes back.'

His eyes glistened.

'On certain days,' he continued, 'He just won't be driven away. He returns, Wilfred. "Go away, Lord, let me have a good time. I want to go and caress a body I long for, even if I must burn later. You bother me, Lord. Leave me alone." But he stays there. He is used to insults. The Roman soldiers struck Him again and again. When He staggered under one blow, they gave Him another to steady Him. Can you imagine that? Those men in armour who talked Latin, the Latin used in Mass, as a matter of fact.'

Instinctively, Wilfred laid his hand on Max's arm and, to his surprise, noticed that the hand shook.

'Now listen, Max, stop it. We'll meet some other time, but please go away now.'

'Go away! That's what I tell Him. You're saying go away to God.'

Two women passed them at that moment and Wilfred felt himself grow red with shame, for they were both of them young and, seeing Max's excited state, quickened their pace in order to have a good laugh a little farther on. Wilfred cast a despairing glance down the street: no bus in sight.

'Max,' he suggested in a most reasonable voice, 'let's make a date. What about tomorrow at ten, at this very spot?'

'No. It won't be the same tomorrow, I won't be the same person. I won't say the same things.'

'Do calm down.'

270

'I'm perfectly calm but I'm bringing out what's at the bottom of my heart. I'm afraid of what God is doing at present. After being rejected and driven away over and over again, He goes away. There comes a day when He draws close to you for the last time, only you don't know it's the last time. Suddenly you are completely peaceful because He is no longer there. I'm thinking of Him at this moment, because He is thinking of me.'

Wilfred was silent.

'There are times when I don't love Him, when I rebel and refuse to let Him love me.'

Another few seconds passed.

'Answer!' cried Max shaking Wilfred's arm.

'Answer what?' asked the young man suddenly furious. 'You bore me to death.'

Meanwhile, the bus arrived. Wilfred jumped on to the platform and waved good-bye to his companion.

'See you tomorrow!'

'Sure!' cried Max bounding into the bus as it moved away.

Hurriedly climbing the little staircase that led to the top of the bus, Wilfred went and sat in a corner right in front. Max sat down by him almost immediately. Fortunately, or unfortunately, they were alone.

'Max,' said Wilfred controlling himself, 'I lied to you just now. I told you I had an appointment. It's not so. I said so out of vanity, just to brag. There's no appointment. I'm going to have supper with a lady and a gentleman, both very staid, and I'm doing it on account of my future. It's important, see? I haven't the least intention of playing the fool. You asked me a little while ago if I had my rosary with me. Here it is.'

He showed him a rosary made up of black beads.

'Let's have a look,' said Max. 'Is it indulgenced? Mine is indulgenced.'

'Mine is not, but its cross is indulgenced for a holy death.'

271

And he replaced it in his pocket.

'Are you easier in your mind about me?' he asked, adopting the soothing voice reserved usually for quietening lunatics. 'Do I look like someone going on a spree?'

'Yes, you always have that look, but that you can't help. At the same time, there's something else about you –'

'Won't you leave me alone? If you'll get down at the next stop, I'll give you enough to go home in a taxi.'

'I don't need your money. You're ashamed of me because I'm badly dressed.'

'Not at all. I swear I'm not.'

'My profession has been imposed on me by circumstances.'

'Oh,' said Wilfred, suddenly interested, 'there's nothing discreditable about that.'

'You really think so?'

Wilfred wondered if he was at last to discover how Max earned his living.

'I have no prejudices of any kind whatever, I assure you. That you can understand, considering the sort of life I lead –'

Max looked at him slyly.

'Did I talk much the other night?'

'A little, yes.'

Max was about to say something when the bus conductor appeared and held out his little metal box; Wilfred slipped two silver coins into it.

'You don't have to worry about that in the least,' added Wilfred when they were alone again. 'I never give away a secret.'

'Then you must understand how painful all this is for me at certain times, Wilfred, because I'm a believer. I'm sure, in the very marrow of my bones, that what the Church teaches is true. This didn't prevent my glutting myself last night with dissipation, like an animal, do you hear, like an animal. I was besotted with physical pleasure.'

272

He waited a second or two and then, looking straight ahead, said suddenly:

'I had the feeling of leaving my body, of floating above my body in space. That's the devil's work. You know what I mean? You've had that experience?'

'No, and I don't want you to talk to me about such things.'

'He's walking round you, but he hasn't reached your heart yet. It takes some time to batter down a Christian soul, for all that.'

Almost unwittingly, these words acted on Wilfred like a powerful electric shock. He was up suddenly and passed Max to reach the little staircase. As he went down the top steps he heard the foreign voice crying out in its raucous but musical accents:

'Some day you'll have to account for your desertion!'

Jumping from the platform before the bus came to a stop, he found himself on the sidewalk, stunned and much relieved that Max had not tried to join him again.

'He's drunk, drunk and unbalanced,' he thought as he went along, for rather than wait for the next bus, he preferred to walk the rest of the way. It would take him a good quarter of an hour, but by then he was almost in the country and the light grew softer. Along the road huge sycamores fluttered their large serrated leaves under a pale blue sky. Carefully clipped hedges surrounded gardens, where flowers shone in the sun, and small white houses that seemed to spell happiness. There was such peaceful simplicity about the landscape and something so curiously childlike that it impressed Wilfred although he had been familiar with the sight for a long time. He looked around him as if he had never been there. Boys on roller skates passed him, calling out as they went, and he envied them their light hearts and wild animal eyes.

'Max talks too much foolishness,' he thought. 'He's crazy. I

273

won't see him any more.' But his heart was still beating fast and he had had the feeling of being somebody else for several minutes. He sat down on a bench to calm himself, to recover and find himself again. He should have been happy, but he no longer was.

CHAPTER LVIII

It was Phoebe who opened the door and she must have seen at once that something had gone wrong for the schoolgirl smile froze on her little face.

'Oh, Wilfred, what's the matter with you?'

He laughed rather foolishly.

'Why, nothing. Nothing at all. I hope I'm on time.'

She took him to the little drawing-room and sat on the pink and green flowered sofa while he dropped into an armchair.

'James will be here in a minute,' she said. 'He's resting in his room.'

Through the open window, Wilfred could see the small clump of trees under which he had talked to Phoebe a few days earlier. Why didn't she take him there now, instead of staying in such a warm room? Perhaps she had unpleasant memories of their conversation under the trees that first afternoon? Yet she smiled. She smiled too much. He would have preferred her to reproach him with his behaviour and particularly to scold him for certain sentences he had dared to write her.

'Phoebe –'

'Yes, Wilfred?'

'I hope you aren't angry about that letter.'

'That little note of yours? It was charming. A trifle stiff but nice. James couldn't help smiling as he handed it to me. He had just left his study where the mail is brought him. I was struck by his expression. I think he likes you much better than he did.'

'Phoebe, why did you say he smiled as he handed you my letter? Had he read it?'

'James reads all my letters. I myself asked him to do so, the day we were married. He opens my mail and gives me my letters. What's the matter with you?'

Wilfred fell back in the armchair and closed his eyes. She got up at once.

'Why, what is it, Wilfred?'

'Absolutely nothing. I feel a little tired, that's all.'

Phoebe went to a small table, picked up a glass of orange juice in which floated a little ice and handed it to Wilfred.

'This will do you good,' she said, peremptory as a nurse.

Something delicate and perfectly intact pervaded her whole being, so much so that for a second or two Wilfred had a strange longing to get up and go. He looked at the slender well-shaped hand that held a glass full of violently coloured liquid. Certain terms in his letter came back to him.

'Take it,' she said.

He took the glass and swallowed a little orange juice.

'Has your husband talked to you about me since I wrote you?' he asked.

'What a funny question!' she exclaimed laughing.

'He doesn't like me, Phoebe.'

'Don't be so silly. I've already told you his attitude towards you has changed completely. He thinks you ought to have a more interesting job. He'll help you to find one, if you like. He's so kind, you know –' (her eyes moistened suddenly) ' – particularly since his illness.'

Wilfred wanted to say something but stopped dead. James

275

Knight had read that letter, had read that shameless declaration of love, almost obscene in its simplicity, and had kept it to himself. Far from being angry with its author apparently, he had gone to see him at the store and asked him to supper. 'What horrible and complicated trap does this conceal?' thought Wilfred.

He finished his drink at a gulp and looked at Phoebe.

'Why doesn't he come?'

'How strange you are today! He'll be here in a moment. Haven't you anything to say to me?'

In spite of himself, he looked towards the door. Suddenly Phoebe leaned towards him and kissed his cheek, then sat back on the sofa.

'We're going to take you to Wormsloe after supper,' she said smiling. 'James is there almost every day. He's restless and has to move around constantly, and then he's crazy about that old house. I must say the place is wonderful on a fine summer night, but it's too big for my taste. It's too much like a rich man's estate – When we're settled out there, you must come and see us. You mustn't desert me.'

'Desert you!'

'Oh, I was only joking. If you're alone with him this evening, try to talk to him about serious things. I don't dare to any longer.'

'What do you mean?'

'I'm thinking of religion. It's a subject he never broaches any more. He has an expression at times that grieves me, Wilfred. Formerly he was so sure of his faith and salvation. Now he keeps all that to himself. Won't you talk to him?'

'That's impossible, Phoebe.'

'Because you're a Catholic?'

'No. I find it embarrassing even with Catholics.'

'You have nothing to fear, I assure you. Yesterday, when we were talking about you, he looked me straight in the eye and said

276

he wondered you had kept your faith when so many men lose it just at your age. It is really very rare, you know – We're not fanatics. We try to understand you Catholics, but our effort isn't always reciprocated.'

She said this with childlike sweetness and a little pout that made Wilfred long to throw himself on her and bite her mouth. He felt his heart beat faster and peered through the window at the shady depth of the little grove where they had sat. Phoebe followed his glance.

'Remember what we said to each other out there?' he asked rather hoarsely.

'When you came to lunch? Yes. It was frightfully hot that day.'

'Well, didn't you guess something?'

'No. Was there anything to guess?'

She looked at him with the eyes of a woman who has never lied and he was obliged to hang his head.

At that moment, the door opened and James Knight came in. He did not seem in any way changed. At most something more peaceful could be seen in his face, and his voice, when he began speaking, was certainly gentler. Laying a hand on Wilfred's shoulder, he talked to him for a little while as though they had met the day before. At supper the conversation was as common-place as possible and several times the guest wondered if he had not dreamt that business of the love letter. James Knight asked him a number of questions about his work and Wilfred met his calm glance with a good deal of difficulty.

'We don't see each other often enough,' declared James Knight suddenly.

'You must remember we live a little far away,' said Phoebe. 'And we're going to live farther still,' she added.

'Oh, Wilfred will have a car of his own some day.'

The guest could not help laughing. Indeed he would have one

277

and soon, out of his money, but he said nothing about that, any more than he spoke of leaving the store.

'That's the first time I've ever heard you laugh,' remarked James Knight.

After supper, as Phoebe had foreseen, it was decided they should spend a little while at Wormsloe. Wilfred offered to drive.

'I didn't know you knew how to drive,' said Phoebe.

'Wilfred's not the dreamer you think he is,' said James Knight with a good-natured little laugh. 'I'm sure he drives very well.'

'I've had a licence for the last three years,' said Wilfred.

'There, you see,' said James Knight, seating himself in the back of the car. 'Come next to me, Phoebe, and let Wilfred take the wheel.'

This was said so jovially that Wilfred felt unaccountably uneasy but he took his appointed place and drove off.

The sweetness of that night irresistibly turned his thoughts to love. The warm air caressed his face, his hands, and in a cloudless sky the moon shed a sad and pensive light that inclined Wilfred to the rather foolish tenderness peculiar to youths of his age, one that made him forget his troubles.

Some desultory talk went on between the three, then gradually they dropped into a silence that no one apparently wished to break. Wilfred's misgivings were now accompanied by increasing curiosity that made him accept the prospect of falling into a trap. It seemed only too natural to him that James Knight should be thinking of revenge, but what would it be?

They reached the house in about half an hour and when the noise of the car had ceased, all around him, in the summer night's deep stillness, Wilfred heard the tree-frogs' mysterious song. Thousands of tiny, clear, liquid notes melted into a single, melancholy, sweet voice. Childhood memories came back to him. Instinctively, he sought for Phoebe's hand as they went

278

up the veranda steps. James Knight who walked ahead of them opened the door with a key and lit the lamp in the entrance.

Wilfred immediately recognized the naked woman bearing a frosted glass torch at the foot of the staircase. He was conscious of a faint smell of dust and stared with a kind of amazement at a place where he had the impression of not having been for many years. As James Knight went into the library, Phoebe plucked at Wilfred's sleeve and whispered:

'He's going to walk around in the house, as he always does. Follow him. I'll stay on the veranda. Try to talk to him.'

'Why is he so anxious to come here?'

'He comes here almost every day, even after supper, like this evening. It's the beginning of a new life for him. He makes all sorts of plans – Please go in –'

Much against his will, Wilfred joined James Knight who went from room to room, turning on the lights. In the great drawing-room with the plum-coloured velvet curtains, the young man saw him look around as though he were alone, with an absorbed expression.

'Where is my wife?' he asked on seeing Wilfred.

'On the veranda.'

James Knight sat in a big tufted leather armchair near which a lamp stood on a little mahogany table. The light fell on his narrow hands as they lay on his knees and he looked up at Wilfred with an air of attention. With a little less gentleness in his expression he would have resembled a judge.

'As we're alone,' he said, 'we might have a little talk.'

'Why, certainly, Mr Knight.'

With a beating heart Wilfred sat on a chair facing him.

'Have you nothing to say to me?' asked James Knight.

'Why – no, nothing in particular. I think – I think you'll be very comfortable in this house.'

'Yes, won't we? This will be my bedroom. The library will be

279

next to it. I don't want to climb stairs. Phoebe will sleep on the second floor. The whole of the second floor will be hers.'

He rose, putting his hands in his pockets.

'I'll have the morning sun here,' he said. 'Of course all the wallpapers and furnishings must be changed. Everything around me must be modern. In this house you'd fancy yourself in the last century, don't you think?'

'Yes, indeed. In the last century.'

Going up to one of the great carved oak bookcases, James Knight bent over a row of books and suddenly, without turning, asked:

'Are you still as religious, Wilfred, still as much of a believer?'

Wilfred felt himself blush.

'Why, yes,' he answered. 'Certainly.'

'And you still say your prayers in Latin?'

'In Latin? Sometimes. There are certain prayers that can be said in Latin –'

James Knight picked up a book bound in black leather, returned to the centre of the room and laid the volume on a long table.

'Faith is a very great thing, isn't it, Wilfred?'

This was said in such a serious, quiet voice that in some inexpressible fashion, the words seem to blend with the silence.

'Yes,' whispered the young man.

James Knight motioned him to come nearer and taking a key from his waistcoat pocket opened the table drawer wide. Wilfred lowered his eyes and raised them immediately. A single object lay in the drawer, conspicuously: a revolver. The two men stared silently at each other for a few seconds. Wilfred heard the blood buzzing in his ears, then James asked:

'What is its name, in Latin?'

Wilfred did not reply. James Knight closed the drawer and said:

'I want to be alone, now. I have a few little things to do here. Go and keep my wife company on the veranda. We'll return to town after a while. I'll call you.'

Wilfred left the room. 'He wants to kill me,' he thought. 'He'll kill me if I lay a finger on Phoebe.'

Suddenly overcome by nausea, he closed his eyes and leaned against some piece of furniture in the dark room he was crossing to reach the hall. His face was bathed in perspiration and he could feel drops of it rolling down his neck. He did not want to die. So that was the trap. He had been lured here to be murdered. The idea seemed absurd and was replaced by another: 'He wants to kill himself. He wants to kill himself as people do when they're afraid of dying. He no longer has faith and the doctors have given him up –'

He joined Phoebe on the veranda and took a rocking-chair next to hers. Contrary to what he expected, she seemed very calm.

'You didn't stay with him very long,' she said. 'Did you talk to him a little?'

'Yes, a little.'

'But what did you talk about, Wilfred? You're so silent. What's the matter with you?'

'Nothing is the matter – He talked about the way he expected to arrange the house –'

'He likes it so much – I don't know why. It does him good to come here. He looks at the books and takes measurements. He has already drawn up a plan of the ground floor. Sometimes, when we come here in the evening, he has a nap in the leather armchair, then gets up and walks to and fro in those big rooms.'

She allowed a few seconds to go by.

'Didn't you talk about anything else?' she asked. 'I mean, more serious things –'

'No, we didn't have time. He wanted to be alone.'

281

'Did he seem peaceful?'

'Peaceful? Yes. I've never seen him more peaceful.'

'Nor I. I think he's better. What you say makes me feel happy, Wilfred.'

Their conversation scarcely rose above a whisper and soon ceased as they listened to the tree-frogs whose little voices seemed to come from all directions in a vast soft murmur ascending to the deep blue sky. On the long stretch of grass that ran down to the river, oaks planted here and there reared immense outlines heavy with their first summer foliage. By dint of looking at them, one had the impression of giants coming in procession towards the house, but stopped for ever, each one in his place.

Wilfred's heart beat more slowly in his breast now, but his face still dripped with perspiration. He unfastened his shirt collar.

'What are you thinking about, Phoebe?' he asked after some time.

'I don't know,' she answered in a low voice. 'About all sorts of things – He's not making a sound. If he's asleep, our voices will wake him.'

'Do you think he can hear us?'

'I don't know.'

She said this like a child. His hand tried to take hers but she freed herself at once.'

'Come out on the lawn with me,' he whispered.

'No.'

Suddenly, he stood before her. An unexpected dizziness made him shut his eyes and he felt as though someone were hitting the middle of his chest with great blows of the first. The young woman remained motionless.

'Phoebe,' he said opening his eyes, 'I have something to tell you. Please.'

She waited for almost a minute, then stood up suddenly. He

282

stopped the rocking of the armchair she had just left for the sound might have betrayed them. Slowly she went down the veranda steps. He cleared them at a leap to join her and silently they crossed the lawn.

Everything in Phoebe's behaviour surprised Wilfred. She appeared to be acting on a sudden decision and walked without hesitating to the little winding path above the river. It was there that he seized her hand once more and this time she did not take it away. They walked a little way together until they reached a row of sycamores whose limbs shut out the sky. From where they stood, they could see the surface of the water shine in the moonlight and the penetrating odour that came up from the river filled their nostrils. Wilfred shook.

'Phoebe,' he murmured.

She did not answer. Then, with sudden violence he took her in his arms and she said: 'No!' in a muffled voice, but immediately surrendered. With blended happiness and terror, he held her tightly to him as though he wanted to crush her and she panted against his neck.

'We must go in,' he said.

'Not now, not yet,' she whispered.

He kissed her. Limp and unresisting she lay in his arms and knotting her hands behind Wilfred's neck, she clung to him in such a way that the image of a drowning woman came into his mind.

Very gently, he parted her hands and held them in his.

'Will you love me always?' she asked.

Her head rolled on his breast and he guessed that she was crying.

'Love you? What else can I do? I loved you from the very first.'

Instinctively, they turned and looked at the house where a light in a single window shone through the trees.

She murmured:

'Let's stay here a little longer. Perhaps there will never be another moment like this one.'

'Yes, there will be. We'll meet again.'

'Not here, not at night by the river. When I'm alone and hear the tree-frogs sing, I'll think of you.'

He put his arms around her and laid his cheek against hers.

'We'll see each other again, Phoebe.'

She put her hand on his breast and whispered:

'How your heart beats! It frightens me to hear it beat so fast,

He guessed what she was thinking about.

'Don't be frightened. I'm not ill.'

The words had scarcely escaped him when he regretted them.

'It's love,' he said violently.

'Don't leave me,' she stammered. 'Don't forsake me. Nothing has any importance. There's no one in the world but us.'

She added in a halting voice:

'This is the first time I've ever been in love. I didn't know. I didn't even know it yesterday. I liked to think about you, but I didn't know I loved you. I only understood that tonight.'

She talked as though she were delirious. Laying his lips on hers he stopped her voice and for several minutes they remained motionless. She broke away suddenly.

'I am lost,' she said.

He clasped her in his arms once more.

'Hush!' he said.

She did not struggle but leaned her head on his shoulder and, in a lower tone, added as though she were talking to herself:

'It doesn't matter.'

He allowed a long while to go by without speaking. They both looked at the little square of light between the trees and almost unconsciously, walked back to the house again.

A little way from the veranda, she whispered in his ear:

'Go and talk to him. Perhaps he's still asleep. I'll wait here in an armchair. I couldn't bear to see him just now.'

'Don't be frightened,' he said in a low voice.

'I'm not frightened, but I don't want to see him right away.' She asked under her breath:

'How long were we out there?'

He answered that he did not know and helped her up the veranda steps, for she leaned against him and he felt her weakness. Suddenly her knees gave way. He held her up and carried her in his arms to an armchair.

'Come back quickly,' she said almost aloud.

Wilfred walked across the veranda and stopped before the open front door. The entrance and drawing-room were in darkness but he could see the gleam of a lamp in the library. He mechanically tied his tie again and smoothed his hair with one hand. It seemed as though his flesh was one huge burn, the heat of the body he had clasped to his, and suddenly he noticed he was trembling. In the semi-darkness, he listened for a moment to the song of the tree-frogs as it quickened the silence. He had heard it a little while before, by the river, a song that said the same thing unceasingly, a thing that had no meaning, but for Wilfred it was already filled with meaning.

He entered the drawing-room and leaned against the back of a big sofa; under the palms of his hands he could feel its carved roses. If James Knight had called him at that moment, it would have been a relief, but not a sound came from the library. With a lump in his throat, he said aloud:

'Mr Knight!'

There was no reply. Wilfred waited a few seconds, then went to the library door and saw James Knight seated in his armchair, eyes closed.

There was no answer. 'He is dead,' thought Wilfred at once and with the slow rather stiff movements of an automaton, he made a big sign of the cross, but at the bottom of his heart, he did not believe that Mr Knight was dead, nor did he hope it.

Crossing the drawing-room again, he joined Phoebe and sat down by her.

'He's asleep,' he whispered.

'He's asleep,' she repeated in a voice full of quiet despair. And almost in one breath, she added:

'Wilfred, I'll never be able to look him in the face again. He knows my thoughts only too well and I don't know how to lie.'

'The only thing to do is simply to keep silent.'

Then she let her head roll on Wilfred's arm and moaned like a child:

'It's all my fault. I loved you from the first minute, when I knelt behind you. My heart went out to you. That's what I felt I must tell you tonight. I belong to you, I want to belong to you. I was too unhappy with him.'

'Unhappy?'

He bent over her, over a head that talked in the shadows.

'Oh, he's very good, but he should not have married me. I often wonder if he didn't marry me so I wouldn't belong to another man, so I wouldn't belong to anyone – His ideas about right and wrong are terrible. The thought of certain things horrifies him, and yet he loves me.'

'Why did he bring us out here, Phoebe? Why did he leave us here alone?'

'I don't know. I never know what he thinks.'

'Do you believe he has any suspicions?'

'What suspicions could he have? He thinks me incapable of certain things.'

Freeing herself suddenly, she got up and held out her arms to him.

286

'Kill me,' she said gently, 'kill me.'

She repeated this several times and the words hovered on her lips like a moan of love.

He clasped her to him with his whole strength and for a moment thought she had fainted, but she spoke once more:

'I should never have married him. I am not his wife. I should have been your wife.'

'And supposing he was dead,' he said to himself, 'if he was dead right now –'

As though she had read his mind, she murmured after a time:

'Go and see if he's still asleep. I'll wait for you here.'

'Don't be frightened, Phoebe.'

'I'm not frightened.'

He left her and went in. Crossing the entrance, he stopped with a beating heart in the drawing-room where everything seemed to be listening. 'He is dead,' he thought, 'he died while we were out there.' He realized suddenly that he was gasping, and to recover sat on one of the little ballroom chairs he had always thought pretty and a trifle absurd with their flame-coloured satin seats. In a flash, he saw himself again in this very room, with his father and Uncle Horace. That was fifteen years ago nothing had changed in the house, but now, James Knight was in the next room. After a few minutes, he rose and went to the library. As he crossed the threshold, he felt a hissing in his ears and a shiver ran down his spine. Exercising all his power of will he walked around the armchair and stopped suddenly.

'Well, my boy,' said Mr Knight in a calm voice.

Seated a little to one side in the armchair, he held a small black Bible, one finger slipped between the pages. Wilfred pretended to laugh.

'Oh, Mr Knight, I thought you were asleep.'

'I *did* sleep for a little while but have been awake some time. Will you sit down?'

Wilfred took a chair and sat down facing Mr Knight.

'What's the time? asked the latter.

'I don't know. I imagine it must be a little after ten.'

Mr Knight drew a watch from his waistcoat pocket.

'It's twenty past eleven,' he said gently.

'Twenty past eleven!'

'Yes, my boy. Where is Phoebe?'

'Mrs Knight is on the veranda.'

James Knight smiled and said, after a pause.

'I was thinking about you a few minutes ago, thinking about you two, Wilfred. You don't know her very well yet. She seems a little childlike, but she doesn't confide in anyone, not even completely in me. I am still trying to guess what she can be. You're surprised to hear all this, aren't you?'

'Yes, a little, I must admit.'

'Yet it's the truth. There's something untouched in her. She is undefiled, her faith is undefiled. Sin would make her lose it, but sin is unknown to her. She is not like us. If there is someone in the world I believe in, it's she.'

He stopped and looked at Wilfred, whose eyes met his with an effort; but very soon the young man felt as though a fog lay in front of him, behind which Mr Knight's face retreated then advanced.

'Why don't you say something?' asked the latter finally.

'I'm listening,' replied Wilfred rather hoarsely.

'Do you hear the tree-frogs' song? There are a great many in the trees by the river. This evening will remain in your memory, Wilfred. It will be like a before and an after in your life. Before this evening and after this evening. Do you understand?'

'Not very well, Mr Knight.'

'You will understand in the end or I'm much mistaken in you. A little while ago, I surprised you by showing you that unpleasant object in the drawer. Isn't that so?'

288

Wilfred was speechless. He felt drops of sweat roll lazily down his cheeks and dared not wipe them, as though the faintest gesture or the least word would be enough to ruin him.

'Of course,' continued Mr Knight, 'that object was empty. It is only there to be a little frightening, when need be. I have no desire to kill anyone, much less you. Maybe you'll be astonished to hear that I've always wished you well. On that point, my feelings are unchanged.'

'Thank you,' said Wilfred running the tips of his fingers over his jaw.

James Knight smiled without speaking. The lamp near him lit up the lower part of his face, his long thin mouth and bluish lips, but his great sad eyes remained in the shadow.

'You don't much care for people to talk to you about religion,' he continued. 'Particularly those who don't belong to *your* religion. Now you and I don't believe the same things, but we've been fostered by the same Gospel. I'm not going to talk to you about religion, but I'm going to read you four verses and I'm quite sure they will stick in your memory when I'm gone, as it's probable I shall go first. As it happens, the passage is one that is not often noticed because people think they know it by heart.'

He opened the Bible and read:

'Now the names of the twelve apostles are these; The first, Simon, who is called Peter, and Andrew his brother; James the son of Zebedee, and John his brother; Philip and Bartholomew; Thomas, and Matthew the publican; James the son of Alphaeus, and Lebbaeus, whose surname was Thaddaeus; Simon the Canaanite – and James Knight, who also betrayed Him.'

Wilfred started.

'What makes you say that?' he asked.

'Doesn't it seem likely to you that James Knight should have betrayed Jesus?' He lowered his book. 'Well then, let's use another name instead: 'And the twelfth was called Wilfred, who betrayed him.'

Wilfred got up and opened his mouth without finding strength enough to say a word.

'Mark you,' said Mr Knight, 'any one of us could put his name down instead of Judas. Have you never thought of all this?'

'Yes, I have.'

'Then why are you surprised? Jesus loved Judas. Now, if it was a great sin to betray Jesus, it was nevertheless a forgivable one. Judas' error lay in believing that it was not forgivable and in hanging himself. Imagine that everything took place differently, Judas running up to Jesus as He stumbled and tottered under the weight of the cross. The traitor falls to his knees, crying out, weeping, catches hold of the hem of His garment and beseeches Him, in spite of Roman soldiers' kicks. How would the Lord regard him? With hate? I don't think so. He would look at him with love, Wilfred, with love. During the Passion there was one minute where Judas alone could have comforted Jesus by asking His forgiveness. What is really shocking is that this minute should have gone by and that Judas should not have been there. That's the way I see things.'

Putting down the book, he got up and said:

'We must go, it's late. I'll close the windows and turn off the lights. Go and tell Phoebe we're leaving.'

Phoebe stood waiting on the veranda. He could see her little face, her motionless eyes fixed on him in the transparent night. 'She's not the same,' he thought. She did not move.

'It's my fault,' she whispered. 'I loved you too much.'

'He's coming. Try to pull yourself together.'

'What do you suppose he'll do?' she asked suddenly.

'Nothing. He's very calm. He talked about religion.'

She turned her head away and in such a low voice that he could scarcely hear, said breathlessly:

'I wasn't thinking of him.'

A few minutes later, they left Wormsloe. Wilfred drove and, after a few insignificant remarks, silence settled between the three of them, as a curtain drops. In an effort to control his emotion, the young man set his jaw and the idea of a possible accident occurred to him several times. 'What a release it would be!' he thought. However, the car drove straight into the night on an empty road and the gleaming head-lights cut the darkness, as scissors snip through material. For the first time in his life he called for death with all his might, but he knew that it would not come, because things never happened in such a simple fashion. The woman he had held in his arms under that black yet luminous sky, what he had said as he clasped her to him, and later on, Mr Knight's strange speech in the watchful library, all that was only a beginning. Something else would follow. He remembered Phoebe's question: 'What do you suppose he'll do?' Finally, he dimly guessed what it meant.

CHAPTER LIX

Following Mr Knight's instructions, he stopped the car only when he reached his own door. Phoebe then took his seat at the wheel and Wilfred thanked them and said good night in a rather subdued voice. He stood on the sidewalk, his head swimming a little, wondering whether he was about to faint in the presence of a man whose thoughts he could not guess, but this shame was spared him and he watched the car disappear with as much relief as despair.

In his room, he found a letter that had been slipped under the door and recognized his cousin's writing on the unstamped envelope. Angus had probably been to see him during the afternoon. This seemed so futile that he dropped the letter on the floor, and flinging himself flat on the bed, head in hands, he began crying with a sudden, uncontrollable violence that surprised him. He cried from sadness and he cried from anger because he felt worsted and wounded in his pride. Never yet had he behaved so awkwardly with a woman. How she must have despised him at the bottom of her heart, for she loved him with a deep love, of the kind that disconcerts sensual men, because physical desire plays such a small part in it, and yet, she must have expected something else. It seemed as though he heard her voice: 'Let's stay a little longer – There will never be another minute like this one by the river at night, this spring night –' He it was who had wanted to go in because he was frightened, not she. She would have boldly embarked on sin. And afterwards came that humiliating conversation with Mr Knight in the library.

Suddenly, he got up and went to the bathroom. There, he filled the basin with cold water and plunged his face into it, as though to wipe the memory of that odious evening out of his mind, his whole being. And so, never again would he wear the clothes he had worn then; he tore them off in a sort of fury, as though he were fighting with someone and, stark naked, kicked them away in a heap to a corner of his little room. Tomorrow, he could make them into a parcel for the poor. If he could have rid himself of his flesh in the same manner he would have done so.

Feeling calmer then, he chose a suit that was a little less shabby than the rest and dressed to go out, for sleep was out of the question. The one reasonable thing to do, he thought, was to walk the streets, to go down one street, then another and then another. There were enough of them in the town to exhaust the most tenacious despair.

As he was about to open the door, he saw the letter on the floor, and picking it up, removed it from its envelope with a shrug.

'*Wilfred*,' wrote Angus, '*I'll wait for you this evening, from six o'clock on, at the park entrance. I'll wait until eight, if necessary. In case you don't read this note in time to see me today, I'll wait for you tomorrow, at the same hour and the same place. – ANGUS.*'

The letter was immediately tossed into the wastepaper basket and Wilfred went out.

Apparently everyone was asleep in this part of town, as the streets were deserted and not a light shone in the windows, but Wilfred walked along briskly and in a few minutes reached a long crowded avenue that led to the heart of the huge city. As a rule Wilfred avoided this section of the town where he stood a chance of running into people he did not care to see. From nightfall to dawn, it was the meeting-place of pleasure-seekers who mingled with the crowd and among them, fellow salesmen less careful of their reputation than Wilfred. However, he threw all prudence to the winds that night, because nothing seemed to him worth troubling about.

Soon, he reached a large square lined with movie theatres, restaurants and hotels whose brutal electric signs tore the face from the night and replaced it with a kind of daylight that hurt the eyes, much as a scream splits the ear. Above this girdle of dazzling light, the irregular black outlines of skyscrapers faded into an inaccessibly serene firmament while passers-by wandered like stray sheep in this hell of electricity and looked up at

293

illuminated advertisements with faces where boredom obliterated all traces of pleasure.

There was a little of everything: people coming out of theatres, loafers who would not or could not go home to sleep and who, dreading solitude, sought the anonymous companionship of the crowd, sailors in search of women, provincials stunned with fatigue and surprise, and lastly, a respectable number of pickpockets distinguished by their intelligent, attentive expression.

A continuous murmuring of voices rose from this multitude as it moved this way and that, pushed here and there by vague despair while radios bellowed, sometimes jocular, sometimes sentimental.

Wilfred slipped into the crowd at once. Here, Phoebe no longer existed, Mr Knight no longer existed. He himself lost all consciousness of what had brought a lump to his throat a moment before; he did not feel quite like Wilfred and with a hazy sensation of release gradually became part of everybody else. Coloured posters held his glance for two or three seconds, then a face that vanished almost at once, then another, and yet another, all this in a sort of collective and brutish stupor that affected him like laudanum a wounded man.

For ten minutes or so he followed the movements of the crowd, letting himself be driven this way and that, scarcely conscious that people laughed occasionally, thinking he was drunk. Suddenly a hand took his arm, timidly at first and then imperiously, while a voice insistently repeated his name over and over again. Wilfred turned his head and started as he recognized the light eyes that stared at him so gayly.

'Tommy! What are you doing here at this time of night?'

'I'll go into that another time,' said Tommy laughing. 'What about having a beer? Look, we can go to the bar at the corner.'

Taking his elbow with a peremptory gesture, he guided him almost forcibly to a bar where cigarette smoke floated

294

like an intangible scarf on a level with the customers' heads.

'There,' said Tommy pointing to a table in a corner, 'we'll be more comfortable to have a talk.'

Wilfred sat down, speechless with surprise.

'Tommy!' he cried at last.

'What's the matter with you? Have you had a drink too many?'

'This can't be you, it's not possible – How you've changed – It's fantastic.'

'That's what everyone tells me. Will you have a beer? Two beers,' he said to the waiter.

Raising his eyebrows and looking superior, he asked Wilfred:

'Why do you look at my suit? I suppose you don't think it's well-cut.'

'On the contrary, I've never seen you so smart. That's just it –'

Tommy glanced down at the sleeves of a grey coat with narrow black stripes and burst out laughing as he ran his finger tips over his carefully groomed fair hair. There was such an air of unconcern and assurance in Tommy's appearance, in each of his movements, that Wilfred felt amazed, remembering him as a shy, easily silenced boy.

'Now I come to think of it,' said Tommy offering Wilfred a cigarette, which he refused, 'we haven't met since that memorable evening.'

'What memorable evening? Forgive me, Tommy, I've had a hard day.'

'Poor Wilfred, are you in trouble?'

Wilfred waved his hand as though to drive something away.

'Let's not talk about me,' he said. 'What do you call that memorable evening?'

'Memorable for me, although you didn't realize it. Remember now: supper on the second floor of that restaurant.'

'I remember perfectly. It was only six weeks ago.'

'You said the most outrageous things, old fellow. About love–'

295

'Oh, forget it. I probably shocked you.'

'You bet you did!' cried Tommy throwing himself back. 'But don't be sorry for it. On the contrary, you did me an awfully good turn, rest assured of that. You opened my eyes, in a sense –'

At that moment the waiter put two glasses of beer on the table. Tommy quickly took a coin from his pocket.

'If you don't mind,' said Wilfred when they were alone once more, alone in a crowd that did not hear them, 'we won't mention that evening again.'

'Just as you like,' said Tommy holding his glass in a long, narrow, well-shaped hand that Wilfred admired in spite of himself. 'Perhaps it may amuse you to know that I've left the bookstore where I worked.'

'The Catholic bookstore?'

'Yes. The place with its atmosphere of nuns and seminarists finally got on my nerves, see? And the books on marriage –' (He laughed softly.) 'You were perfectly right. One fine day I received an interesting offer and am now working at a picture dealer's. Do you know the Daub Gallery?'

'No.'

'Oh, we only sell the most advanced type of painting. I don't know if you're interested in all that.'

'How did you meet your picture-dealer?'

'By chance. In the street. I'll tell you about it some day.'

'Why not now? I'm awfully interested.'

Tommy turned a little red.

'It's rather a long story. And then this isn't the place – I'll introduce you to my boss, if you like. He's charming, you know. Very highly cultured.'

'How old is he?'

'Why, I've never thought of asking him. Old enough to be a boss. Forty, perhaps. Why do you want to know?'

'I think you ought to have stayed at the Catholic bookstore.'

'You're joking. To begin with, my opinions have changed.'

'What do you mean?'

'I mean,' said Tommy, looking important, 'that there's a certain amount of stuff and nonsense in which I can no longer believe.'

'What stuff and nonsense?'

'My turn to say I'd rather talk of something else. Why do you look at me like that?'

'Tommy, I simply want you to tell me what you call stuff and nonsense.'

'Well, if you really wish to know: almost everything we were taught at the catechism classes. However, I do admit there's a certain beauty about some of the symbols.'

'Whom did you borrow that sentence from? From your picture dealer?'

'Why, not at all! I assure you I'm quite capable of forming my own opinions. Say, what's got into you? Last time I saw you, you told me you made love every night. Well, I do too, at present. When I began, I suddenly understood a whole lot of things at one go. It seemed to me that I was discovering the world around me. In the bookstore, I might have been living undergound, in a mole-hill. That's exactly it: a mole-hill.'

'Answer yes or no to what I'm going to ask: do you still go to Mass?'

'That's none of your business. It's a purely personal matter. I simply can't understand your attitude, Wilfred. If I'd only known, I wouldn't have come up to you, just now.'

Wilfred drank a little beer without answering and Tommy did the same. Silently they appeared to listen to the noise of conversation around them, but both their hearts beat fast and Tommy pretended to be watching the other customers.

'I was wrong,' said Wilfred suddenly as he got up. 'Let's leave this place. I have something to say to you. Well, are you coming?'

297

He leaned towards Tommy whose light eyes stared distrustfully at him.

'We aren't going to argue, are we, Wilfred? I warn you I've got to go home soon, Someone is waiting for me.'

'It's a promise. We won't argue.'

They left the bar and stood on the sidewalk where the crowd was now a little thinner. Passing through the square, they walked to a neighbouring street and strolled down it until the town's vast murmur had subsided, and then Wilfred stopped and in a voice that he tried to make as gentle as he could, said:

'Listen, Tommy. It's all over. I want to die.'

Tommy's head turned suddenly towards him.

'What do you mean?'

'I mean that I'm losing my soul, that I'm losing my soul at this very minute. Up to now I always managed to get out of it when I had committed a sin. This time, it's no longer possible. I've fallen into a trap. When you've lost your heart to someone, there's nothing to be done about it.'

'I don't understand. You're in love, that's all.'

'In people like us desire kills faith. Now in your case, you want to get rid of faith because it prevents you from enjoying yourself.'

Tommy looked him in the eye.

'Wilfred, I no longer believe at all and I'm perfectly happy.'

'I'm sure you're happy and that's what frightens me.'

'You don't have to be frightened on my account. I'm absolutely convinced that there's nothing.'

'In spite of that, I'm frightened about you as I am about me. We're detaching ourselves from God right now. You know what that means.'

'I don't believe in God.'

As he said this, he leaned against a wall and Wilfred gently laid both hands flat on the stonework, on either side of Tommy's head, so as to keep him prisoner. Their two faces almost touched. A queer smile shaped itself on Tommy's lips.

'You know what being detached from God means. It means going to hell.'

'There's no such place as hell. You know it as well as I do. What proof could we have of it, to begin with?'

'Don't talk like a fool, Tommy. You and I have been baptized. Millions of men don't know, but we know, you and I know what is true. We have all that in our blood. Such things are not believed in the mind. Proofs are useless.'

'But you make love every night, Wilfred.'

'What makes you say that?'

Tommy looked sly.

'Isn't it true?' he asked in a slightly lower tone.

Wilfred straightened up suddenly and let his arms drop to his sides. He longed to slap that smiling, mocking face, but controlled himself, and in a voice made a little shrill by emotion, said:

'It's no longer true, do you hear, it will never be true again. It's over.'

Surprised by what he had said, he added:

'I've changed.'

'Ah? Since when?'

'Since this minute.'

Tommy slipped to one side and took a leap that removed him several feet.

'Congratulations,' he said. 'You'll have to excuse me. I have a date.'

'Tommy!' cried Wilfred.

But Tommy ran off at top speed and Wilfred stood motionless, feeling deeply ridiculous.

CHAPTER LX

Next morning found him at his place behind the counter displaying three different kinds of shirts for the inspection of a customer who fingered the poplin and looked both bored and distrustful. The same or almost the same customer that Wilfred saw every day. Life prescribed identical circumstances in an unchangeable setting and what took place in the heart remained invisible.

'What size collar?'

'Fifteen and a half.'

A little as though he were dreaming, Wilfred's hands wrapped up the two shirts that had been selected, then went to the desk with them and returned to his place. He wondered what he was thinking about, but he was not thinking of anything in particular. He was simply in pain and his heart tightened in his breast.

If he could only see her once more, talk to her alone – but if he saw her again, he would really fall in love. At present he only stood on the brink of love. On the brink of love, what could that mean? Very little. Yet one could believe that this had a meaning.

'What do you suppose he's going to do?' Phoebe's question came back to him for the hundredth time. Her expression had been so strange as she said that and her eyes had seemed immense.

Suddenly, Mr Schoenhals stood by him.

'Anything wrong, Wilfred? You don't look yourself.'

'Nothing's the matter with me, Mr Schoenhals.'

'It's going to be terribly warm today. We'll have some new

300

ventilators in a few days. Tuesday week, to be precise. As a matter of fact, Tuesday week –'

'Tuesday week,' repeated Wilfred mechanically.

'You won't be here.'

'That's true. I'm leaving on Thursday.'

Mr Schoenhals bent his head and his double chin bulged over his collar.

'You haven't changed your mind, Wilfred?'

'No.'

'A more important position would be given you, as I've already said, with a substantial raise.'

'I know, Mr Schoenhals. I'm sorry, but it's impossible.'

Mr Schoenhals stayed there for fully two minutes as though he meant to say something, but he sighed without adding a word and finally walked away.

Toward the end of the afternoon, he came up to Wilfred again and took an envelope from his wallet.

'I forgot to tell you,' he said gravely, 'that this letter came for you a little while ago. The management does not favour its employees' private mail getting mixed up with the firm's business letters, but seeing that you are leaving it consents to pass over such an irregular proceeding.'

Wilfred turned pale. 'Phoebe,' he thought, 'she wanted to reach me more quickly by writing here.'

But the writing was not Phoebe's. He turned aside when Mr Schoenhals had gone and tore open the envelope. The letter was from Lovejoy, the country boy to whom he had sold shirts a few months before. The disappointment was so sharp that Wilfred had to steady himself against the counter.

'*Dear old Wilfred,*' wrote Lovejoy, '*I'm married and there's a baby on the way. If it's a boy, as I hope, do you know what his name*

301

will be? Can't you guess? You aren't very smart! His name will be
Wilfred! That's the surprise I had for you. First my wife said no,
and then I talked about you so much that she finally said yes. So,
if you think its all right –'

Without reading the letter to the end, he slipped it into a
pocket and bit his lips. Suddenly he wanted to cry. to cry like a
child, but he forced back these shameful tears.

That evening, a little before eight, he was at the park entrance
waiting for Angus with an impatience that surprised him. If ever
he could have foreseen an appointment with Angus – Of course,
there was one important thing: that sum of money. Having
given notice at the store, he was going to run short of cash, but
that was not all: he wanted to talk to his cousin although he did
did not quite know what he meant to tell him. Angus had suffered
perhaps. Therefore he must say something to soothe his pain,
show himself compassionate.

He did not wait long. Angus suddenly appeared. Electric
light shining through the trees fell on his handsome face
devoured by anxiety; his great dark eyes stared into Wilfred's
light ones.

'I only have a minute,' said Angus so rapidly that his words
seemed rolled into one. 'I'll come to your house tomorrow. I'll
explain. Have you still got the cheque I sent you?'

'Yes. Do you want it?'

'No. You must cash it tomorrow morning as early as possible.
I couldn't bring you the money. Someone is watching me. At
this very moment – I've fallen into a terrible trap. I could not
resist certain temptations, Wilfred. I was caught red-handed
in a house – It was a put-up job. Ghéza's doing – Now three of
them threaten to inform the police about me. There were
witnesses. If my mother hears of all this, it will kill her.'

'What's that? I don't understand.'

'It doesn't matter. Don't put your hand on mine. We're being

302

watched. Burn all my letters, will you? I assure you that if I believed in God, I would throw myself into His arms.'

He mumbled this, turned his head sharply and looked over his shoulder as he added:

'I'm going. Pray for me. Pray, Wilfred.'

His lips stretched slightly in a smile that was more like a wince of pain. He looked at Wilfred for a second with extreme intensity and moved away without another word. Lost in astonishment, Wilfred saw him cross the avenue to reach a little side street. At that moment a quiet voice murmured in the stillness:

'Good evening.'

Wheeling around, Wilfred recognized Ghéza, Angus's chauffeur. He was dressed in a pale grey linen suit worn with deliberate but unobtrusive elegance. His dark eyes shone softly through the smoke of his cigarette. He smiled pleasantly and repeated:

'Good evening – Wilfred.'

'Good evening,' said Wilfred falling back a little.

'Are you running away already? Am I in your way? You have a date, perhaps –'

The awkward, studied politeness in Ghéza's foreign voice was somehow counterfieit and sudden curiosity held Wilfred motionless.

'No,' he answered.

Ghéza surveyed him from top to toe and said:

'So we're taking advantage of the fine weather to stroll around the neighbourhood.'

By slow degrees, he came nearer and puffed at his cigarette.

'My car is close at hand. Wouldn't you like a short drive in the country?'

'No, thanks. I'm going home.'

'That's a pity,' said Ghéza.

303

He smiled and added, passing on to another subject:

'By the way, Angus told me about the glove you lost on the road. You ought to have said something – I would have stopped with pleasure. You are shy.'

Wilfred felt the blood rush to his cheeks.

'The glove? I'd forgotten about it. It's of no importance. My cousin shouldn't have mentioned it to you –

'Oh, he tells me everything. He seemed in a hurry this evening, don't you think?'

The question affected Wilfred so unpleasantly that he turned his eyes away.

'I don't feel like answering you,' he said dryly.

'Of course you don't,' replied Ghéza calmly, 'but I have to watch over him a little, see? I don't want him to get into trouble. It would grieve his mother.'

'Where does he live?' asked Wilfred shortly.

'Here? At an hotel, naturally.'

'Which hotel?'

'What can it matter to you? Didn't he tell you? He spent some time with you, just now. Are you really so anxious to see him again?'

He began whistling a popular tune under his breath and suddenly winked very faintly. Wilfred blushed and walked away without a word but Ghéza's rather sarcastic voice followed him:

'See you soon, Wilfred!'

Without answering, he hastened across the avenue and as he reached the street that Angus had taken, forced himself to walk slowly, so as not to seem to be running away. It was only five minutes later that he asked himself: 'Why did I hurry off?' That, he really could not say, but he remembered what Ghéza had said a moment earlier about the glove, and that was as good as an answer: 'You ought to have said something – I would have stopped with pleasure –'

304

CHAPTER LXI

A letter was waiting for him at home. It was not a surprise, he was sure it would be there and with a beating heart, read it standing up:

'*Wilfred, I am alone in my room, but I feel as though I was making my way into yours by writing this, and that by shaping the letters of your name on the paper, I am with you. I don't know what I'm going to say to you. I've often dreamt that we were alone together, holding hands like children and that was all, we did nothing wrong. When I returned here a little while ago and found myself in my room again, I thought I was going mad, because nothing had changed, but I was another person and things looked at me as if I was a stranger, the walls, the bed. I told myself that it wasn't true, that you had not held me so closely in your arms, that you had not touched me, that nothing had happened – James is sleeping in another part of the house, as he always has since our marriage. Everything is the way it was around me, everything is the way it was yesterday and I have finally calmed down. I wanted what took place out there to happen. Each time I saw you here, I used to think that it was impossible, that your lips would never touch mine, and a voice said: "Yes, this will come about." I don't know why I behaved the way I did. I loved you, that's all. When you told me to get up and follow you, I obeyed, obeyed heart and soul. I wanted your love. The rest was of no interest, I mean what the body does. I would have consented to anything for love of you, I had no feeling of having committed a serious offence. Perhaps I have no moral sense. But I don't want James to suffer. He must not know that we love each other. He is already beginning to frighten me, because what he says applies to you and me without his realizing it. It seems to me that he talks of nothing but us. I have never really known what kind of man he was, nor exactly what he thought. At one time I imagined that he had lost his faith, but that night, when we were alone in the car, he talked to me about you –'*

Wilfred dropped the letter on his bed and sat near it, as you would sit by a person. In the warm breeze that blew from the window, the white curtains swelled out, then hollowed into eddies that fascinated the eye. It seemed as though invisible hands waved them about silently and, by looking long enough, you could imagine that there was nothing real in the world but those curtains. 'I'm losing my mind,' thought Wilfred. 'That's the way people go mad.' Shaking off his immobility with an effort, he continued the letter.

'He said: "To interfere with his faith would mean his destruction, Phoebe." I don't know why he said that to me at that moment. You had just left us. I had the impression that he guessed something, but he trusts me. I'm not ashamed, Wilfred. I want to feel ashamed but can't because I love you. I was frightened by what James said. I don't want anyone to meddle with you, with what you are, with your faith. I'm frightened by what James said, as if his words brought bad luck. My love, we must keep our faith. We must not meet for a little while and God will perhaps forget what we did. Nothing wrong will happen. I hate evil, that is, what people call evil. The body must be left alone –'

Once more, he paused. In spite of obscureness and incoherence there were sentences him the letter that struck in full in the heart. The body must be left alone. That was really what he wanted too. What he longed for most desperately filled him with horror.

'– horror,' he said under his breath, as if he were talking to someone.

'I beg you to burn this letter,' continued Phoebe. *'I ask you to.*

306

And so the evil longing will be consumed and love will remain and we will keep our faith, yours and mine that meet in the heart of the same God. Then you will be able to kneel and so will I, behind you, as it happened on that first day at Wormsloe. I loved you right away, I loved you before you loved me, at that very minute, just as I saw you, with your child's hair on your white neck, and your little ears —'

The letter ended there. Wilfred turned over the sheet, looking for another sentence, a signature, but there was nothing and the last half of the page was blank. He stared at it for a moment as though that empty space still said something, then getting up, he burnt the two little sheets over an ashtray. The flame danced in the air for a second or two and he let go when it almost reached his fingers. The charred fragments scattered over the desk. All that was left was a small corner of a page on which he read: '— *love will rem* —'

CHAPTER LXII

Next morning, he telephoned Mr Schoenhals to say he would be late and went immediately to his bank where he deposited Angus's cheque. The clerk who attended to him was a young man of his own age. Wilfred always dealt with him in preference to the others because he thought him less stern. When he saw the figure on the green slip, the clerk raised his eyebrows and said with a smile:

'Congratulations!'

'It's a legacy,' explained Wilfred and he added breathlessly: 'I'd like to know if it's possible for me to cash part of the amount today.'

307

'In the ordinary course, you'd have to wait until the cheque had been collected. How much do you want?'

Wilfred named a figure.

The clerk pondered for a moment.

'Would you like to talk to the manager about it?' he asked.

Wilfred had not expected the conversation to take this turn. He had hoped that everything would be simpler and, without knowing why, felt guilty. Perhaps the cheque did not inspire confidence.

'Talk to the manager?' he repeated doubtfully.

'Oh, I don't think there will be any difficulty about it,' said the clerk, seeing his disturbance. 'We know you, and the signature on the cheque is more than sufficient security. It's just a formality.'

Another smile and he disappeared with the cheque. Wilfred began looking around him with as much assurance as he could muster. He felt uncomfortable in banks. This one with its white marble columns and glittering brass railings offered every appearance of solid prosperity, but he had heard of banks that went broke and in any case, eveything to do with money made him a little uneasy. One of his most curious traits was the fact that money frightened him because of the expression it gave people when they talked about it. He did not want any such expression ever to be seen on his face.

After a while, the clerk returned with the sub-manager, a slim little man, still young but balding.

'Mr Ingram,' he said cordially, 'we could only wish for your own sake that you might often bring us cheques of that size. I'm sorry however that a bereavement should be its cause. Would a thousand dollars be enough for you today?'

This was a little less than Wilfred had asked for.

'A thousand dollars, yes,' he said.

'Then kindly endorse Mr Howard's cheque, and if you have

308

your cheque-book on you, write out a cheque for a thousand dollars that you can cash immediately.'

This transaction took a few minutes and Wilfred found himself in the street again, his wallet swollen with banknotes. 'You're like the rich,' he thought. And for the first time in his life he had a weird feeling of beginning to exist in a new way, of being able to do almost anything he liked.

As he went back to the store, he heard someone calling his name and, turning his head, recognized the old lady who had spoken to him in the solicitor's office. She was dressed in black and walked as fast as her years would allow, but there was something energetic about her that suggested youth.

'Hello there Wilfred!' she cried, gayly waving her hand.

He walked back a few steps to meet her.

'Young man,' she said with a smile that bared teeth that were too white, 'you shan't escape me this time. You ran away when I tried to speak to you at Mr Starkweather's. Don't say it's not so. I know men.'

He looked at her curiously. She panted a little like a dog and her small pale blue eyes fastened on Wilfred's smooth face. It was impossible to know what her looks had been in youth, but as present, in the pitiless street light, her poor, flabby, bruised features seemed to have been punched by death.

'Are you in a terrible hurry, Wilfred?'

'Well, you see, I have my work.'

'I'll only take five minutes of your time. Now come with me to my car. It's just a few yards away.'

There was such good-natured authority in the way she said this that he found no excuse to refuse.

'You know,' she continued as they walked along the sidewalk, 'Your father and I were great friends. He wasn't as serious-minded as you. He was what's called a charmer, like your uncle. I knew your uncle still better. Didn't he leave you anything interesting?'

'Er –'

'I know. I was there when the will was read. A few keepsakes, that's all. He was wrong. The family knew your circumstances. I hadn't seen anything of him for a long time. Stupid people had caused a misunderstanding between us. The world is so unkind. Oh, Wilfred –'

She stopped, her mouth half open, and once more he noticed that she panted.

'I've had an idea,' she said. 'About those souvenirs – Now, you must have that portrait –'

'That portrait?'

'The famous portrait of that rascal Horace in uniform. I say famous because ladies often asked to see it – certain ladies. you have it?'

'Why, yes. It's mine.'

'Do you really care for it much? Because I wanted to suggest an exchange – or a transaction.'

A transaction. That was the word Angus's mother had used.

'Come,' she went on, laying the tips of her fingers on his arm: 'let me persuade you. It would amuse me to own that portrait. It has no artistic value, but it would amuse me. Do say yes.'

'I don't know –'

'What don't you know? I can imagine it seems difficult to you to settle the business in the middle of the street, with all those people going by. Won't you come to my house? I give a little cocktail party every Thursday. You'll meet some charming young people – But come early. Come at six-thirty. I'll manage to see you alone. Do say yes. I'm sure we'll agree perfectly.'

'If it can give you any pleasure –'

'Just hear the way he said that!' she exclaimed laughing.

Although you look so innocent, you're a real wheedler. Just like your father. I'm going to give you my card with my address –'

Opening her bag, she took out a card and handed it to him.

'– because I'm sure you don't even know my name!'

'Oh, Mrs Beauchamp!' he said glancing at the card.

She bent her head very slightly to one side and smiled.

'Call me Alicia,' she said.

In the store, Mr Schoenhals walked straight up to Wilfred and taking him by the arm led him behind the counter to a recess in one of the large windows.

'Wilfred,' he said in an undertone, 'has anything happened?'

'No. Nothing.'

'I'm not asking you to confide in me. I just want to know if anything is the matter.'

An outburst of compassion made a tear shine in his big attentive eyes.

'Yes, something is the matter, Mr Schoenhals,' murmured Wilfred.

'Can I help you?'

'No.'

'You don't want to talk to me about what's worrying you?'

'Not now. Not here.'

'Everything wears itself out, even grief, Wilfred, everything.'

'Not this. I'll never be the same as I was yesterday. I realized that a moment ago.'

'I'm going to send you home, Wilfred. I'll explain things to the management. If you need anything, let me know and I'll come.'

Wilfred thanked him and left.

He went back to his room and throwing himself on his bed

fully dressed, fell into a deep sleep. First he dreamt that he was lying at the bottom of a long boat, both hands behind his head, and that he sailed very slowly down a river whose muddy waters stretched as far as the eye could reach. Not a cloud crossed the pale blue sky, but by staring at it a long time, he felt a sort of dizziness. A vague happiness mingled with this contemplation but, as though he wanted to retain such exquisite bliss, Wilfred closed his eyes and slept. He then dreamt that Phoebe was bending over him, not the whole of Phoebe, but just her head, and the head said: 'Look, my love, I am dead.' Her pallor was indeed unmistakable. Then he cried out and found himself in the boat again, but each time he closed his eyes to sleep, the head spoke once more and uttered the same words.

With a violent effort, he woke. The setting sun drew a big golden square on the wall. Wilfred bounded up and stood for a second in the middle of the room, motionless, haggard, trying to remember the dream that escaped him. After a few minutes, thought, he opened the drawer in his desk from which he took Alicia's and Uncle Horace's letters; they were torn up one by one into small pieces, then torn into even smaller fragments with a sort of furious patience, but when he saw Alicia's photograph at the bottom of the drawer, Wilfred hesitated. The tender, sensuous little face seemed to be smiling at him, asking for mercy. 'You'll have others just as pretty,' said a voice inside him. 'Life is full of pretty women. Hundreds of them are waiting for you.' And he thought: 'I must have been dreaming of her or of Phoebe.' Then he tore up the photograph with a quick movement of his two big hands. The gesture was not a difficult one, although he had believed it impossible, but Wilfred had made it and looked at the tiny bits of cardboard in sorrowful amazement. A moment went by and a grip around his heart seemed to loosen.

Supper time passed without his thinking of food. He was

thirsty and in the bathroom drank two large glasses of water. In the mirror he looked at himself as though he saw a stranger. His cheeks were white. 'I'm not the same,' he said to himself and smiled, but his smiled seemed to him like a grimace.

At nightfall, he left his room and in the street hailed a taxi. He hesitated for a moment over what address to give, told the driver to take him down-town and half-way there, thought better of it.

'I've changed my mind,' he said laughing.

And he gave Phoebe's address.

Fifteen minutes later, he was alone in the peaceful little empty street lined with gardens hemmed in only by green hedges. It had been a warm day, the air smelt of dust and watered grass and night's sweetness rose in the transparent sky. He walked along the sidewalk to the Knights' house and looked under the trees. Not a light in the windows and he thought at first: 'They have gone to Wormsloe,' when a murmur of voices drew him to a part of the garden that was sheltered from the street by a clump of ashes and sycamores.

Passing swiftly by a street-lamp whose light glimmered through the foliage, he paused in a more shadowy spot where he stood no chance of being seen, although he was closer to the group of trees. There he waited motionless. The murmur was more distinct. Wilfred recognized Mr Knight's rather monotonous voice but could not catch what he said. Looking all around him first, Wilfred stepped over the hedge, nimble as an animal, and stretched out on the grass. To discover his presence from the street, it would have been necessary to lean over the hedge, for the garden was in deep darkness. Nevertheless, Wilfred felt his heart thump and for almost a minute could not fix his attention on Mr Knight's remarks.

313

'There's no cause for hurry,' said the quiet voice. 'We have all summer.'

'I wish everything was over and done with,' said Phoebe.

As he heard her voice, Wilfred was seized with a longing to call out, and bit his lip. Phoebe's voice was like a physical body.

'You're a little girl,' said Mr Knight.

'You keep saying that, James.'

'You're just right the way you are.'

A few seconds went by, then he added so softly that Wilfred could scarcely hear:

'Last week, you didn't want to go out there. Now you want to go there immediately. Have you changed your mind about Wormsloe?'

'A little.'

'Why, Phoebe?'

'I don't know. I took a dislike to this house when I understood that we were really going to leave it.'

'You're not fond of it any more?'

'Not in the way I was. Now I feel as though we were no longer here. And then, it's better for us to live a long way out of town.'

'The air is better out there.'

'Yes, the air is better.'

James Knight murmured something that Wilfred did not hear and then was silent for a long time. The young man was under the impression that Mr Knight had taken his wife's hand. Finally the deep soft voice sounded once more:

'I've never wanted anything but Phoebe's happiness.'

There came another pause. Wilfred felt as though he had glued his ear to a door and shame sent the blood rushing to his cheeks, but he dared not move. Several minutes went by.

'Do you want to go in?' asked Mr Knight.

'Just as you like.'

They got up and Wilfred saw them slowly cross the lawn.

314

Phoebe leaned on her husband's arm and bent her head sideways as she sometimes did when she was thinking. What had she told him? What did she know? The young man waited until they had disappeared inside the house, then rose and stepped over the hedge again. Standing in the prim little street, he looked at a window that had lighted up at that moment on the ground floor of the Knight's house. Some time went by and another lighted up on the floor above.

'Phoebe!' he called in a low voice. 'Phoebe!'

Suddenly, a cry burst from his throat, an almost inhuman cry that rent the night. Wilfred was terrified to hear that unearthly shout. 'It's not I,' he thought. 'I didn't cry out.' He hesitated a moment, crossed the street and went quickly to the great avenue where the giant sycamores guarded the solitude. There he walked faster and faster until he reached a bench where he sat down.

Almost at once a man sat down by him. Thin and middle-aged, neatly dressed in navy blue alpaca, he stared searchingly at Wilfred and after a moment of indecision, plucked up courage and asked:

'Didn't you hear someone call out just now?'

'Call out?' repeated Wilfred.

He was about to add something when the stranger's rather slow voice went on quietly:

'It was probably one of those boys that carry on like lunatics and have a good time scaring the neighbourhood with Indian war whoops. Marvellous evening, isn't it?'

'Marvellous,' agreed Wilfred as he got up.

He hailed a cruising taxi and told the driver to take him down-town.

A vast confused uproar betrayed the presence of a great

railway station near the street where Wilfred got out of the taxi. He walked a little way past big, silent, black houses and then into a wider street where a line of wretchedly dressed men waited silently before a church. It was a Franciscan convent where the poor were fed every evening. Most of the men kept their hands in their pockets and talked among themselves in a low voice as they advanced step by step with the utmost slowness. None entered the church where the door stood ajar. They went a little farther on, to a long building topped by a cross. There, they walked up a couple of steps, entered, and after a short time, could be seen leaving one after the other by a door a few yards distant.

Wilfred passed behind the poor and walked up the short flight of steps that led to the church door. Eyes turned and looked at him. He could feel unkindly glances surrounding his head, his body, or so he thought, as since that morning he imagined everyone believed him to be rich and guessed that he carried a large sum of money on him.

He took refuge in the church where a single electric bulb lighted the great cradle-vault supported by massive columns scarcely taller than a man. Here and there, on long black benches, women prayed, motionless, a scarf tied over their heads. The small red lamp that shone before the altar looked like a tiny spark in the semi-dark chancel, and a rather sickly odour of incense and wax floated in the air.

Wilfred dipped the tips of his fingers in the holy water font and crossed himself. For a moment he looked at the altar then at the women's outlines. Not a sound reached the church and time seemed to have come to an end. Unconsciously he knelt in a corner, but could not pray. 'What am I to do?' he wondered.

He was in a neighbourhood and a church which he knew well, for a definite reason. The church bore the name of Saint Francis, and like Saint Francis, he wanted to give his possessions to the

316

poor. His possessions, that is, the money he had collected at the bank. Now, the poor were there, in front of the church, but they made him feel shy and he didn't know how to talk to them. The simplest thing to do, as he was in that mood, was to put all that money in the hands of a monk who would allocate it to a charitable institution, but that would not be at all the same. The gesture would no longer be the same. Once more everything would go through banks. It would be a banking transaction and he would not see God smiling at him through the eyes of the poor. No doubt if anyone knew, he would be taken for a lunatic. You had to be mad or drunk to give banknotes to the poor in the street. That was not the way to give alms. It was done formerly perhaps, in barbarous times. Now everthing was organized. You gave to the poor without seeing them. The inconvenience of being face to face with them no longer existed.

With a moan that he immediately stifled, he hid his face in his hands. To see God in the eyes of the poor, you should not be frightened of the poor, nor of God. Unfortunately, he was frightened. Since the night before, he was trembling, not in his body, but at the core of his heart, because in the innermost part of him, a very simple sentence took shape, became more precise, a sentence made up of three words, and it was as though a tiny deafening voice repeated from time to time: 'You are lost.' Each time he heard it, he shook his head and whispered: 'No.' But the voice would not be silent.

A short distance from him stood a confessional, a huge piece of furniture, made of dark wood, provided with thick black curtains. Wilfred was familiar with that type of confessional. You parted the black curtain, and once inside, it enclosed you to the heels and you were in total blackness, you saw nothing, and in this complete darkness there were only two voices that sought each other out blindly: the priest's and the penitent's.

'I can't tonight,' he thought. 'No one is there, to begin with.

But tomorrow, tomorrow morning.' Suddenly he remembered his first confession, his throbbing heart, his confusion and then the sudden joy that came over him when the priest absolved him. At that age he had very little to confess, but now he could imagine around and almost over him the heavy black drapery that cut him off from the world and delivered him to his inflexible conscience. He would have to search his memory, bring everything to that strange interior light where human happiness so often assumed a criminal aspect.

He saw himself once more by the river with Phoebe, in the extreme sweetness of that spring night. All the smells of the earth blended with the scent of Phoebe's hair as she sank in his arms and the memory of that instant filled his heart with tenderness. Drops of sweat ran down his brow and he clasped his hands so hard that his finger-joints cracked. 'I could not,' he said to himself, 'I could not give her up.' – 'No,' said the voice in a reasonable tone, 'and that's why you are lost.'

Leaving his seat he silently drew closer to one of the praying women, as though to rob her of a little fervour, a little trust. Tomorrow morning – He looked toward the altar and thought: 'I promise You.' He would kneel behind that dreadful black curtain and tell everything. He would hear his choking voice, pausing suddenly, telling the whole story of his relations with Phoebe from the moment when he first saw her to that when he had held her to him under the trees. Was that all? No. There was all the rest, unchastity, the fixed idea of pleasure, the chance encounters, the sole and continual gnawing desire to possess another being. Was there nothing else? Bent in two, sitting with his head almost touching his knees, he racked his brains. Suddenly, he thought of Max. He had behaved uncharitably to that wretched madman. 'I lost my temper with him,' he said inwardly, as though he was already speaking to someone. 'I've been wanting in –' He hesitated: 'I've been wanting in love.' He meant to say: in charity, but the word seemed weak. Charity was not what people wished for.

'I've been wanting in love,' he repeated very low in the hollow of his hands.

The words burst from him violently, but as he whispered them, seemed ridiculous, almost shocking, because after all they concerned Max. Never could he say such a thing behind the black curtain.

Any more than he could ever talk of Phoebe, reduce to a few mean, paltry sentences the ecstasy of frenzied passion, a night teeming with song, Phoebe's body as it yielded, words breathed in her hair, her neck. She yielded, she surrendered, she was in his arms; there, in the church, he lived over all this, he needed only to close his eyes, cover his face with his big hands, he looked as though he were praying, but he was not praying, he was on the riverside and he loved a woman with the delirious infatuation of first love. She had said: 'Let's stay here a little longer – There will never be another moment like this one –'

For a long time, he remained bent double, his hair tumbling over his brow, bowed so low that the blood pounded in the arteries of his neck. Seized with dizziness, he all but fell sideways and got up. Three rows ahead of him, the praying women had not moved and he looked around him like a man who has just awakened. The pillars, the devotional pictures, the altar, the ruby-coloured lamp, nothing moved, everything remained steadfast in faith, everything believed. In him alone there was this tumult.

He wondered why he was there, what he was doing there. An hour earlier, he had shouted like a lunatic in that little deserted street, shouted with love, and now he was in this church, with women who were looking at the altar, one here, one here and two others over there. What did this mean? He had come here to give his possessions to the poor. What did that mean? Like

319

Saint Francis. What connexion with him? He had once been told the story of Saint Francis and now he, poor fool, wanted to behave like the saint. To begin with, there weren't any saints in the world, nowadays, any saints like Francis of Assisi, or people would know it. And then he wanted to buy a whole lot of things, a radio like Max's, a suit, several suits, some ties. He wanted to be well-dressed, smart. Naturally, he would look for a room. A little flat where he could see Phoebe. It would have a view of one of those small, narrow gardens lined with trees that formed a lane. At that moment, he remembered a sentence from Phoebe's letter: 'He said: "To interfere with his faith would mean his destruction".' With a violent effort, he knelt and wanted to recite the Lord's prayer, but could not shape a single sound. His lips remained parted and the tip of his tongue motionless against his teeth. Taking his rosary from his pocket, he signed himself with the little cross and kissed it. That was all he could do. He thought: 'It's because I'm upset –', '– and because I'm lost,' added the voice, but very gently.

Wilfred shrugged his shoulders and left after a genuflection. As he was about to open the church door, he stopped suddenly. 'Maybe this is the last time I shall cross the threshold of a church,' he thought. That meant he was about to be rid of everything that stood in the way of his love. He had often been told such tales. Because of a woman, one lost faith, because of a passion that carried away everything, but that could never happen to him. He could run after girls, never have the same one twice, and one day, smitten with remorse, he would go to a priest. He counted on that remorse as he counted on that priest. What priests could not put up with was a liaison and, above all, adultery. Now that was what he was implicated in, at this very moment. Faith was about to be taken from him, as it had been from so many others. That was the price. 'It's impossible,' he said to himself. 'I believe as I did before.' He remembered his

320

little speech to that simpleton Tommy last evening. Like Tommy, he was going to become an ag – an agnos – The ridiculous word escaped him, but it meant that you no longer ever went to Mass. 'You know what it means to be detached from God, Tommy? It means going to hell.' He had dared to say such things.

'My God,' he begged inwardly, 'stay with me!' What did that mean? Under his breath, he continued: 'Stay with me until the end.' The sentence quieted him. Turning back, he went to a big rack where tapers of all sizes were stacked according to height. By it was a collecting-box. Wilfred put in a silver coin, chose what he thought was the finest taper, and holding it at arm's length with a reverential air, went and placed it on an iron taper-hearse before an altar dedicated to the Blessed Virgin, first lighting the wick. The flame wavered, fluttered for a second, then caught and shone with those of all the tapers that made up a great blazing nosegay at the foot of the painted plaster statue. Wilfred watched his taper for a moment, raised his eyes to the pink and white face smiling above the altar and he said the first words only of a prayer he reserved for the darkest hours: 'Remember, O most gracious Virgin Mary –' After which he genuflected, head bent, and crossing himself, went out.

Just before leaving the church, he folded his hat in two and hid it in his coat, then he turned his collar up, rumpled his hair and, hands in pockets, walked down the steps and took his place at the end of the line. For a few minutes, he became the object of silent examination and at first he kept his eyes down. 'When they get used to my presence,' he thought, 'I'll talk to them, I'll smile at them.' Smiling was his most effective weapon and he knew it at last, but at present dared not use it.

The man who stood next to him was about sixty and smelt very bad. Stocky and heavy-shouldered, in a tattered overcoat, he raised a face to Wilfred's that craft, distrust and above all sadness had furrowed seemingly with strokes of charcoal;

grey stubble covered his cheeks to the swollen-lidded eyes.

'What are you doing here?' he asked.

'I'm waiting, like you.'

'Yes, but I'm hungry, I am.'

Wilfred tried to smile.

'How do you know I'm not hungry too?'

'You!'

The old man nudged his neighbour who then gazed fixedly at Wilfred. The man was tall and youngish; a shapeless cap pulled down over a long bony face, his light grey eyes seemed to peer at the world through the slats in a Venetian blind. Scarcely moving his lips he said to Wilfred:

'Guys dressed like you go somewheres else to eat.'

'I've lost my job,' replied Wilfred with a blush.

'What kind of a job?'

'That's my business.'

The old man came a little closer to Wilfred and whispered:

'Trouble with the police?'

'Could be,' said Wilfred, scarlet to the ears because he did not know how to lie.

'If that's so –' said the old man with a shade of respect.

And his mouth stretched into a smile, then he exchanged a few words in a low voice with the man ahead of him: a third man turned and gave a little whistle of sarcastic admiration as he stared Wilfred up and down. His small pallid face assumed a scoffing expression and he said in a flat voice that made one think of the blade of a knife:

'I'd like to be there when the priest sees you. He'll think he's seeing things.'

'Don't pay him no mind,' said the old man laying a hand like the paw of some huge animal on Wilfred's arm.

Wilfred did not move.

'Does the monk ask questions?' he muttered.

322

'Questions? Never. But the old fellow's a hard nut to crack and he stares at you good. Doesn't matter to him if you're Catholic, Protestant or Jew. What's important is to look like the real stuff.'

Wilfred was about to ask: 'What's the real stuff?' but refrained. Quite obviously, he did not look like a pauper. His heart beat fast. If he wished to begin distributing his possessions, the time had come. It might have been wiser perhap to drink a few glasses of whisky first to nerve himself and catch the right tone for a holy young man about to renounce the world.

The line moved slowly on. He thought: 'It's too much for me. I'll come back tomorrow in other clothes. Tonight, I can't do it. All these men hate me because they think I'm rich.' 'Because they know I'm rich,' corrected the voice.

Letting a short time go by, he took a small silver coin from his pocket and slipped it into the hand of the old man who had spoken to him. The latter looked at him in surprise.

'Thank you, prince,' he said.

'Are you here every evening?' asked Wilfred.

'Every evening.'

'Where do you live?'

This question was greeted by a roar of laughter and several heads turned with sudden attention.

'You can ask for me at the Waldorf. If I'm not there, just look in at the Saint Regis.'

Wilfred left the line immediately, crossed the street and walked away quickly. He had made himself ridiculous because he didn't know how to talk to the poor.

After another few yards, he reached the corner of a more dimly lit street where he took cover. There, at least, they could not see him. Turning down his coat collar, he ran a comb through his tumbled hair and put on his hat. The experiment had been made. He had intended to give the poor the money drawn out of the bank. In actual fact, he had given ten cents to the old man who smelt so bad, ten cents, that is, the ten thousandth part of what he had on him, a bus fare. But why get rid of all that money? The answer was simple: to disarm divine justice. The question he wanted to know was whether, having appeased Heaven, he could see Phoebe again. There again, the answer was simple: no. 'I'm a fool,' he thought. 'All men are fools at some time or other. I can't solve a problem, not that one, at any rate. I hate problems. I want to be happy.'

To go home, find himself in that horrible little room again, seemed impossible. He did not want to be alone. Above all, he wanted to talk to someone. As he passed a taxi-rank, he suddenly opened the door of the first in the line and sat down. His first idea was to give the address of a familiar bar, but in a flash he had a vision of ending a gloomy evening with a woman he did not want and going home at dawn, in the height of anguish, through these inhuman streets that gave solitude a diabolical character.

'Sherman Avenue,' he said suddenly.

'What number?'

'I don't know. I'll stop you.'

The last thing in the world to do was to see Max, but the address came of itself to Wilfred's lips. 'After all,' he thought, 'I don't have to see him. I'll stroll about in that direction.' Yet he knew that this had no meaning. He had nothing to do in Sherman Avenue if he did not want to see Max. 'I'll get out long before reaching his house,' he thought.

The car ran through the quiet streets with a muffled, even noise and Wilfred's thoughts were becoming a little confused, as though, through fatigue, he might fall asleep, but the same image came back ceaselessly: he held Phoebe's body to his by the water, in a thick darkness filled with tiny silvery cries. She bent, both heavy and light, and with a hand like a child's caressed his burning face as it lay close to hers. His thoughts went to other

324

things, then returned to her. He remembered Mr Knight's slow, clear voice reading the list of the twelve apostles in the library, then the terrifying little sermon about Judas, and once again he hugged the frail young woman to him and she gently said: 'Kill me!' She pressed her lips to Wilfred's and the name of the twelfth was Wilfred, who was Judas, who was also the son of perdition. Who began all that?

'She did,' he murmured.

'What number?' asked the driver.

'I didn't say anything,' said Wilfred.

'But we're on Sherman Avenue.'

'Then stop.'

Now he was alone and walking up Sherman Avenue. One hundred numbers separated him from the house he loathed and in which he was fully determined never to set foot again. He only wanted to walk around the neighbourhood and, if he happened on Max, they might have a talk in the street. Max was the only person to whom he could say certain things. With all his vices and extravagances, Max knew a lot more then the rest of them. He was both repulsive and terrifying, but Wilfred thought of him with a compassion he had never felt for anyone, not even Angus.

'I've offended him,' he said to himself, 'I'll beg his pardon.' And almost immediately he added: 'At any rate, I'll try.' To apologize was always horribly difficult and the idea of apologizing to Max seemed ridiculous and degrading into the bargain.

'I'll manage,' he said aloud. 'I'll make it clear to him that I'm sorry.'

He walked noiselessly down the long quiet avenue. If he thought it necessary to apologize to an individual such as Max (the word individual, the meaning of which he did not quite grasp, seemed the right expression to him), it was in order to talk to him afterwards of something else and to free himself

from a burden. Some human being must listen to him, even
without understanding what he said, even without answering.
This time, he, who was usually so reserved, was going to tell
everything that had been torturing him for weeks. Words already
rose from his heart like a flood. He had felt it in church. If a
priest had been there at that moment to touch him on the
shoulder, smile at him, Wilfred would have told him all, even
behind the frightening black curtain. That night, the priest
would be Max.

He stopped dead. There was something sacrilegious in the
idea that frightened him and he wondered if he weren't losing
his mind. Raising his eyes, he found that he had unconsciously
passed two hundred and thirteen and a half by twelve numbers.

Slowly he walked back. The window on the third floor was
lighted, but no one was there. After a long hesitation, Wilfred
called softly:

'Max!'

No answer.

'Max!' he called a little louder in the watchful stillness.

A few seconds elapsed, then the bald old man appeared.
Leaning his elbows on the red cushion that covered the window-
sill, he stared at the young man and gave an amused laugh.

'Max!' he called, imitating Wilfred's voice.

'Is he there, yes or no?'

'How impatient we are!' he laughed coarsely and added:
'Max is there, but he's busy. Do you want to see him?'

'I have something to say to him. I want to see him here, in the
street.'

'In the street! What an idea! It's impossible.'

'Why?'

'Because –'

They stared at each other in silence for a few seconds. Wilfred
did not know what to say. The old man smiled and waited.

'Just stroll around for five or ten minutes,' he said at last. 'Return then and you can come up.'

'I have no time to lose. It's now or never.'

'In a hurry, eh? So was I, when I was your age.'

Hideously, he smiled a tender smile.

'I'm going,' said Wilfred.

'No.'

Straightening up, the old man turned towards the room and uttered a few curt sounds in a foreign tongue, then leaning in Wilfred's direction made what he doubtless thought to be a captivating face:

'Count up to ten,' he said, 'and come up here.'

Wilfred allowed a few minutes to pass. It bothered him to go into that peculiar house with all his money on him, but who knew about it? – Max thought he was poor. He ran and the door opened. With great care he closed it noiselessly after him and at that moment, through an unaccountable freak of memory, he recalled the name of the priest who had spoken to him the day his uncle died. 'I'll go and see him tomorrow,' he thought. 'I'll tell him everything. I prefer that to the black curtain –'

He went up. On the third floor, the door was ajar, he had only to push it open.

Max stood in the middle of the room, his hair tousled. He knotted his tie, looking more serious than usual.

'What do you want?' he asked.

'Am I disturbing you?'

'Hardly. What have you come here for?'

'To talk to you for a moment, if it doesn't bore you.'

'Will you be long?'

'I can come back another time,' said Wilfred gently as he went towards the door.

Max caught him by the arm.

'Don't be an idiot. Well, as you're here, you're here. You've

327

finally roused my curiosity. Have you done anything foolish?'

He closed the door and leaned against it with both shoulders.

'I was almost sure we'd never meet again,' he said without waiting for an answer to his question. 'In a way, it would have been better so. Don't turn your eyes away. It happens that I want to look you in the eye. Your face –'

He panted a little. Wilfred smelt the odour of his breath.

'What's the matter with you, Max? Have you been drinking?'

'A little, but I'm not drunk. Just wicked.'

'Wicked!' cried Wilfred with a forced laugh.

'You don't know me. When I've drunk a little, it's a bad thing. When I'm drunk as a fiddler and have painted the town red, I feel holy. Now sit down and let me look at you.'

He pushed Wilfred on to the sofa and sat facing him in the red armchair.

'Smile,' he commanded.

Wilfred obeyed mechanically.

'You smile badly. It really bores you to be here. You hate me too.'

'Why, Max, what are you thinking of? Would I have come here –'

'Did the old man tell you to come up?'

'The old man at the window? Yes.'

'He and I will have an account to settle one of these days. Will you have a drink?'

'No thanks. What has the old man done to you?'

'The old man is the boss. It happens that he's my uncle. It is he who's so anxious we should go to Mass together and that I should do my Easter duty. Yet, if anyone is in the know, it's he. Three years ago the swine had me locked up, thirty miles from here.'

'They put you in jail?'

'In jail!' repeated Max with a jeering laugh. 'Jail would be

328

paradise compared with what I went through out there. Tied hand and foot for a month. Watched over for another four. They call that watching. They make you sleep on straw. They hit you over the head with keys.'

'Why?'

'Why? Don't ask silly questions. You know too much already, but I've been drinking. Come, don't look at me like that. Will you have a drink? No? I will.'

Getting up, he crossed the sitting-room and opened the cupboard. At the same moment, Wilfred left his seat and went towards the door.

'No use,' said Max without even turning. 'I locked it just now. Didn't you notice I had my hands behind my back?'

He filled a glass and returned to the armchair. Wilfred remained standing.

'Sit down,' said Max. 'Do you hear me?'

Wilfred hesitated, then sat down.

'What did you come here for?' asked Max.

'Nothing. To talk to you.'

'At this time of night? What did you want to talk to me about?'

Hanging his head a little, Wilfred made an effort to control himself and said quickly:

'I'm sorry I struck you, here, the other evening.'

'Is that what you came to tell me?' asked Max, laughing contemptuously. 'You might just as well have kept your regrets to yourself, for all the good they do me – I thought you were going to talk about your sweetheart. Have you had her?'

'That's not the point.'

'Have you had her, yes or no?'

'I forbid you to talk about her.'

'Then what are you doing here?'

'I've said all I had to say. I want to go.'

'Not right away. You'd better wait now.'

329

'Wait for what?'

'Wait till I feel a little less wicked. I've scarcely begun to drink. You look like a choir boy. You've been to confession.'

'Open that door, Max.'

'What strikes me most about you is that you always look as though you were making eyes at someone. You look like a choir boy, but like a choir boy who has gone wrong and who makes eyes.'

Wilfred leapt to his feet.

'I insist on your taking back what you've just said.'

'How do you expect me to take my words back?' asked Max disdainfully. 'Do you imagine they're floating around the room like streamers? Don't be ridiculous. You aren't going to slap me as you did last time, are you? Did you go to confession?'

'I haven't been to confession. And it's none of your business, anyway.'

'It's a pity you haven't been to confession,' said Max, taking a swallow. 'I know a priest who understands everything. He lives by himself at the other end of town in a little wooden house, with the Russians. He wears a black robe with long floating sleeves and nobody can talk about religion as he does. He looks after the Catholic Slav colony.'

'I don't feel like seeing him.'

'I had no intention of suggesting it,' said Max with sudden gentleness. 'I'm only sorry you've never met him. Don't go on standing, Wilfred. I know you feel like hitting me, but you mustn't. That's bad, you know. That's dangerous. I'm going to explain why. Will you sit down? Will you listen to me?'

Wilfred resumed his seat on the edge of the sofa. Now he knew that Max was insane. He had had a very vague suspicion of this on his first meeting with the foreigner, but had brushed aside the warning. Tonight, he was certain – Max himself had let slip a few words about his confinement in a mental hospital. He

330

wondered what to do: talk quietly, say nothing that might cause irritation? But his heart thumped.

As though he guessed this, Max smiled with the inscrutable air peculiar to people with deranged minds.

'You're frightened, Wilfred?' he asked.

'Frightened of whom?'

Max put down his glass on a table by his armchair and threw his head back.

'Frightened of me,' he replied calmly.

Thrusting one hand in his trouser pocket, he continued:

'Men of my type are wrongly judged, you know. Judge not. That's in the Gospel. Now, *you* judged me by striking me the other evening. Eight times. I counted them. You struck me eight times. I dropped to your feet to put an end to such violence. Note that I might have gone about it differently, but you would have suffered, and more than suffered. You probably thought I had fainted. Didn't you?'

'Why, yes,' murmured Wilfred. 'I've already told you I was sorry –'

'Sorry!' Max shrugged his shoulders. 'That's too easy. Well, I hadn't fainted. I just pretended to. You roused something terrible in me by those blows. But even then I was overwhelmed by tenderness. You can't understand. In short, I wanted you to go and go you did.'

He paused for a second and looked towards the window.

'Well?' asked Wilfred.

'When I heard you going down the stairs, I rose to my feet and went to the window with a certain object in my pocket, an object that never leaves me. Say, Wilfred, do you want to see it? Do you?'

Wilfred did not answer.

'It's in my pocket,' continued Max, looking both crafty and boastful. 'Now listen! I've been humiliated enough since I came

331

into this world. Right here and next door, in the room where things take place. What things?' he asked suddenly. 'Do you know?'

'No.'

'Do you want to know?'

'No.'

'Just the same, you've got to know that this place is the office, that this is a curious house and you aren't the first to have struck me. So in my pocket I keep a small object reserved for all useful purposes, for the time when I have it out with the old man. He's the one who is responsible. Some people are going to hell, but he's there already. You really don't care to see the little object? No? Admit you're feeling uncomfortable.'

He laughed, and crossing his legs, moved a foot as though to beat time.

'So, at that window with the red cushion that prevents the old man from bruising his elbows as he watches what goes on in the street, I stood waiting for you to come out. I saw you at last. You walked so gracefully – Hasn't anyone ever told you that you have a curious walk? It's light, a little shy, yes, like that of a young animal, like that of a boy. That's what saved you.'

He allowed a few moments to pass and added gloomily:

'You looked so beautiful that I couldn't fire. That night, I couldn't stop a life, end a life – I was in one of my good moods. I was overcome with tenderness when I saw you at my mercy. Yet, it would have been so simple, you would have leapt and tumbled like a rabbit, but I'd been drinking heavily and dropped my weapon. Afterwards, I cried with rage – but that doesn't concern you. Next day I went to the priest with the long sleeves in his little wooden house and made a confession that was full of lies, but just for the sake of tenderness you understand?'

'Max, I'm going,' said Wilfred rising.

332

As he stood, he realized that his legs shook a little and feared that Max might notice it.

'Going?' Max repeated.

'Yes. Open that door, Max. We'll meet again some other time.'

'I wouldn't be too sure of that, if I were you. Things won't be the same, tonight.'

'What do you mean?'

'We have an account to settle.'

'You're crazy!'

Max rose.

'Why do you say that?' he asked.

'We haven't got an account to settle, Max. That's what I meant to say.'

'You're frightened.'

'I'm not.'

Max suddenly took his hand from his pocket with such a rapid, unexpected movement that Wilfred could not help starting.

'Here,' said Max, giving him a key. 'Open the door yourself.'

Wilfred took the key. They stared at each other in silence.

'You hate me,' said Max, after a few seconds.

'Not at all. On the contrary. I came here with the best of intentions, I –'

Max eyed him coldly.

'How you bore me with your good intentions! If you want to go, why don't you open the door?'

After some hesitation, Wilfred walked to the door. He had the impression of throwing himself against it and when he tried to put the key in the lock, he went about it so clumsily that the little metal instrument all but slipped through his fingers. Finally, he opened the door and swung round to face Max who watched him without moving.

'I have something to tell you,' said Wilfred.

'I haven't time to listen. I advise you to go.'

'Now, be reasonable. You talked just now about something I'm familiar with, that I feel. Yes, that tenderness, that –'

'There's no tenderness tonight,' said Max calmly. 'Tenderness comes later, comes afterwards.'

'Comes after what?'

'After the regrettable act. Then comes repentance.'

'Won't you come down with me, walk about the street a little? There's something I want to give you, right here, in my pocket.'

'Go away.'

'Let's have a talk, Max. I didn't behave to you the way I should.'

'Did you hear me?'

'We can't part as enemies. I've never had an enemy in my life.'

'Did you hear me, Wilfred?' asked Max taking a step towards him.

Wilfred did not move. Max stretched out his arm and grasping the door, made it turn on its hinges. At that moment, Wilfred drew back and found himself on the landing. The door closed softly.

Wilfred groped in the darkness for the staircase switch and, having found it, pressed the button. The light went on. Wilfred walked downstairs immediately. The one thing to do, he thought, was to leave that cursed house as quickly as possible, but he had not gone down ten steps when he stopped. The idea that Max was watching for him at the window struck him with paralysing violence. To leave the house at present would be dangerous.

'Dangerous,' he whispered like a child, and looked around him.

The walls painted a light brown, the black metal banisters: nothing could be more ordinary. The uncarpeted steps showed signs of wear. There was no lift. A long time passed and suddenly the light went out, but there was something comforting about the darkness. Wilfred felt that it concealed him, as an object is concealed at the bottom of a pocket, and it was some time before he realized that he was suffering cruelly from fear, and had done so since the moment when Max had alluded to having been confined in a mental hospital. Once more in the darkness he saw the ashen face and staring, glowing eyes. 'What can he have against me?' he asked himself. 'I struck him, but that's not why he hates me, there's something else.' Insanity is a labyrinth. If one could retrace the progress of an idea in a lunatic's mind, the answer that would release him from his madness might perhaps be found. So Wilfred thought. Maybe he should have asked Max very simple questions, but Max always muddled things up at once with words that seemed to have a meaning and had none. And then, there were questions best unasked and to which Wilfred knew the answer perfectly.

He leaned against the wall and thought. Why did Max hate him? The question was absurd. Wilfred knew very well why. Nothing was easier to read in the foreigner's glance than a mute entreaty that so quickly changed to anger, because Wilfred's eyes invariably answered no. Between the two, and for weeks, since the moment they met, that tacit dialogue was each time resumed, no matter what their lips said. Max was willing and Wilfred was not. Max wanted to kill Wilfred for that reason. That was not difficult to grasp, but a whole part of Wilfred refused to understand it. Now he understood. 'He wants to kill me,' he said to himself, and as he turned it over in his mind the sentence seemed extraordinary to him. To die was something that might happen to other people, but not to him. To die in that way, above all. That was all right for people the papers talked about. He wasn't going to be killed in this sinister stair-case, he, Wilfred, full of life and strength.

He went up the steps softly and pressed his ear to Max's door, but he heard nothing. 'He's watching,' he thought, 'he's waiting. If needs be, he'll wait all night.'

What could he do? Go up to the fourth floor, ring, say a lunatic had designs on his life and that the police must be called in? This seemed to him the only solution. Yet, to have someone arrested without proof – How could one be sure that Max had a revolver in his pocket, that the whole story was not a fabrication, including the confinement in a mental home? Max was not mad, he had no weapon in his pocket, he simply wished to make fun of him, take his revenge that way, frighten him. He wasn't a bad fellow, but just a weird, fantastic foreigner.

He went down to the ground floor and pressed the switch button. The light once more showed him the staircase in all its unyielding ugliness. The steps, the banisters, the walls spelt reality, an everyday reality that was beyond argument. There was nothing there that the hand could not touch, the eye could not see. The rest did not exist, the rest was nothing but a dream. 'The rest – ' he thought, fingering his rosary's little cross as it lay in his pocket. Such thoughts had never entered his head, but they developed in his mind, like a tune that could not be driven away. 'The reality of wood and iron, the reality of brick walls, the reality of three steps forward and into the street, the reality of a revolver bullet.'

Quite obviously, he must climb to the fourth floor, ring at the door, explain the situation, and if he had been mistaken no one would snap his head off. Anything was better than waiting and trembling irresolutely. So he went up noiselessly. In front of Max's door he stopped once again, strained his ear, but not a sound came from the room he had left a little while before. That was the very thing that worried him most. A little noise would have reassured him. What had become of the old man, as Max called him?

Climbing the steps to the fourth floor, he thought over what he

336

would say and rang. To ring at that time of night, you had to have plenty of good reasons ready. He would say that he had been threatened with murder, but first he would apologize most politely, most – If a man opened the door, it would be difficult. The man would be furious. When he came to think of it there was something rather amusing about all this. He would make light of it, tomorrow.

No one answered. He must ring again. He pressed the button and heard the sound made by the bell in a room that he fancied hung in blue silk, with Oriental lamps and a large mirror slanting over the sofa. On the sofa – No one answered. No one sat on the sofa. The flat was empty. Perhaps it was an office or there was someone there too frightened to open at that late hour, an old maid who was pulling the sheet up over her ears.

Below were Max and the dreadful old man. But no doubt Max was alone at the window, like a hunter in a lookout. Wilfred imagined him glancing right, then left, waiting, watching the door.

He rang once more, ran his hands over his face to wipe away the sweat, then rang again with furious urgency, pressing the button as hard as he could, never taking his finger from it, but the door stayed shut.

There might be someone above, on the top storey. He went up and found himself before a door exactly like the other two: painted brown, with a small brass button in a white marble circle. Laying the tip of one finger on the button, he waited a few seconds and then pressed it rather furtively. At that moment the light went out.

Almost at the same time, Wilfred heard the door on the third floor open, Max's door. He leaned over the banisters and could see nothing but the reflection of a big square of light. Nearly a minute passed, then the door was closed with a brusqueness that betrayed a great deal of impatience.

337

Once again he rang at the fourth floor door. Leaning his brow on it, he tried to pray, but a certainty that the door would not open terrified him suddenly and his entreaties were mingled with a faint murmur much like the wailing of a dying man. Never before had he felt the kind of fear that grips a man at the pit of his stomach, and flattening against the door, he glued his cheek to it, as though hoping to press his way through the thickness of the wood. Suddenly ashamed, he flung himself away from the door.

One hand on the banisters, he walked down one flight, then another, with quick, silent steps. On the ground floor, he very slightly opened the door leading to Sherman Avenue and peeped out cautiously: the banal aspect of the nocturnal scene reassured him. Facing him stood a row of tall, brick houses begrimed by the city's smoke, caught in the garish light of street lamps that left the top storeys in the shadows. He felt that all those windows looked at him with unutterable indifference. At that moment light sprang up around him and he heard Max's soft, precise voice from the second floor landing:

'If you move, I'll shoot.'

The voice seemed to strike at the back of his neck. For a few seconds he remained perfectly still, holding his breath. 'I'm going to die,' he thought. The idea of praying did not even occur to him, although he had always imagined that certain prayers would come back to him, when he came to die. What rose within him, as if from the depths of an abyss, was an immense desire to live.

'You thought I wouldn't hear you come down,' remarked Max in the silence, 'but I followed you.'

Wilfred did not reply. Through a crack in the door, he caught sight of the street: empty and quiet, as mysterious as it was commonplace, yet irresistibly attractive. He could steal out. He planned his movements, and in his imagination he pictured himself on the other side of the door, in a flash. The tips of his feet would scarcely touch the ground, he would scarcely hear the sound of his shoes on the pavement. His heart thumped violently.

'Max,' he said in a rather shaky voice, 'you see I'm not moving. Put that revolver in your pocket and tell me what you want.'

'I want you to obey me.'

'Well, you see I'm obeying you. I'm not moving.'

'Close the door and turn round.'

'All right,' said Wilfred.

He kicked the door open with his foot and bounded forward. The shot went off. Wilfred fell on his face without a sound.

He was curled up on the sidewalk in the attitude of a sleeping child, but he was moaning softly. On his knees by him, Max cried:

'Why did you come here tonight? Say something! Say just anything!'

Bending double suddenly, he brought his lips to Wilfred's ear:

'Say you forgive me,' he begged. 'Don't go without saying you forgive me! Just say yes. Say yes for the love of Christ!'

Then, with a terrible effort, Wilfred's glance turned slowly towards the murderer, but his eyes rolled back almost immediately. One word was uttered, however, a word that wiped everything away, that redeemed everything because it expressed the greatest love of all. So faintly that Max could scarcely hear, his lips murmured:

'Yes –'

At that moment Wilfred lost consciousness and two policemen ran up from opposite directions.

CHAPTER LXIII

He was taken to a hospital and given the room occupied a few weeks before by little Freddie, but no one knew that. The pretty grey-eyed nurse would probably have noticed the coincidence, but she was on leave. God alone knew how to describe things exactly as they were. On the bed where the little salesman had died after being baptized by Wilfred, Wilfred himself now lay. He had no idea of this, he had no idea of anything.

If he could have recovered consciousness for a moment and opened his eyes he would have seen one of the trees he had admired through the window, a young acacia whose flexible branches bent lightly beneath the weight of flame-coloured birds as they swung there, chirping. Other trees filled with song surrounded the hospital and a very pale blue sky shone through the leaves. No young man in love with life could have hoped for a more intoxicating day.

So thought Mr Knight as he turned his head towards the garden. For over an hour he had been sitting at the foot of Wilfred's bed, looking at him silently, but at times the bird calls made him glance at the window and a resentful expression stole over a face devastated by sadness and lack of sleep.

Wilfred lay on his back, his hands at his sides, above the sheet. Nothing could be read in his face, and he had the absorbed, absent expression of sleepers who seem to pursue a secret meditation. There were dark rings around his closed eyes, and although his cheeks and forehead were excessively pale, no trace of suffering could be detected in his perfectly still features.

He had been washed and his freshly smoothed hair made a great dark, glossy patch on the white pillow. His breast rose very lightly, at regular intervals.

'He's breathing,' thought Mr Knight, surprised. 'Why must that stop?' In the morning, after the operation, they had said: 'There's one chance in a thousand of his recovering. What's pretty well certain is that he'll be spared all suffering until the end.' Until the end – The end would come. Life could not be kept in his body, breath in his lungs. Mr Knight rose and did what he had already done several times: he picked up the rosary on the little bedside table and examined it. So many beads, so many prayers, that he vaguely knew, but what prayers? This was one of the mysterious Roman superstitions to which Catholics were so deeply attached and that formerly shocked him, but now he looked at the object in his palm and had a sudden temptation to pocket it. He dared not give in to it and put the rosary down.

Going back to his seat, he leaned both elbows on his knees and bent double, head in hands, gave a moan that was like a long-drawn-out cry of horror. 'Why?' he asked. 'Why? Why?' If the shot had been aimed a hair's breadth higher, Wilfred would have been up and about in a few hours, but the course of that small bit of metal had been determined with faultless accuracy. Who had determined it? Who had allowed it? The lunatic had fired, the bullet might have struck elsewhere. 'Just a hair's breadth higher!' he said mentally, as one says a prayer in an attempt to alter the normal sequence of things.

For several minutes, he sat still, deep in thought, then started as the door opened and a young nurse came in, one he had never seen before. She went straight to the bed and felt the patient's pulse.

'Are you his father?' she asked Mr Knight.

'No. His cousin.'

He added almost at once:

'Why do you ask?'

'The priest will be here in a moment.'

'But the patient is unconscious.'

'Question the priest about that. Are you a Catholic?'

'No.'

'Do you care to stay?'

Mr Knight shook his head and went out.

CHAPTER LXIV

The little church was the one where, a few weeks earlier, Wilfred had seen the coffin draped in black. Now, that morning, he himself lay under the same drapery used for one and all, and a few people sat in pews to right and left of the coffin. At the left, Mr Schoenhals and the manager of the firm that had employed Wilfred. At the right, Mr Knight, Angus and Angus's mother.

That made five of them when the priest came in to say Mass, but when the service reached the Offertory, Tommy stole in shyly behind the family. He was the only one who knelt for the Elevation. All the others remained standing, and suddenly a scandalous thing happened: Tommy sobbed. Heads turned in his direction. His face buried in his forearms, his grief burst out brazenly in a silence only broken so far by the murmur of Latin prayers. Finally, he grew calmer but kept a flushed, ashamed face in his hands.

Mr Schoenhals, on the other hand, smiled. He smiled as he did at the store, with this difference that his brow and cheeks were livid, his protruding eyes devoid of thought. However, the corners of his mouth turned up slightly and this professional grimace enabled him to preserve what he considered a fitting attitude.

On the other side of the nave, Mr Knight stood completely motionless and only Tommy – who did not notice – could have seen him hold Angus firmly by the arm, for now and then the young man reeled as though he had been drinking. His waxen face fell on his breast at times and his eyes with swollen lids had black rings that looked like bruises. His mouth half open, he seemed lost in astonishment and never ceased staring at the white tiled pavement with its pale blue design.

On Angus's right hand, his mother looked around her with quiet curiosity, apparently unaware that her son could scarcely stand on his feet. Dressed in black, she gave an impression of great dignity, although once or twice she looked stealthily at a little wrist-watch set in diamonds.

Towards the end of the ceremony, the church door opened so softly that no one heard it and Ghéza entered in his chauffeur's uniform: black with leather leggings that shone like bronze and a stiff military looking cap held in the fingers of the left hand. He stared for a moment at the coffin, then turned a watchful eye on Angus and Mrs Howard. Although his face reflected no emotion whatever, he seemed interested in the scene and allowed a minute or two to pass before leaving as quietly as he had come.

Outside, the sun shone in a sky so pale as to be almost white. On the pavement facing the church, a few women and street-boys waited to see the coffin lifted into the hearse.

The first to come out of the church was Mr Schoenhals, accompanied by the manager. The shopwalker moved like an automaton and smiled in a pitiless light that carefully stressed and deepened the new lines in his face, those of his most recent grief, as though to show them to the onlookers. After a short

343

time, he went away with the manager and both men got into a small salad-green car.

Next appeared, one after the other, Mrs Howard, Angus and Mr Knight. Long and black, very smart but in a way a trifle funereal, the Howards' car was drawn up at the kerb, and by the open door, cap in hand, stood Ghéza, motionless and respectful. But Tommy did not leave the church.

'I hope Phoebe isn't ill,' said Mrs Howard to James Knight.

'No, but she's sensitive and I wanted to spare her a painful experience.'

'Dear Phoebe –' said Mrs Howard with what she imagined to be an angelic smile, and added at once: 'Don't you think it extraordinary that Wilfred should have had enough money on him to pay for his hospital expenses and funeral? There's something about it that's – how can I put it – providential.'

She was visibly in a talkative mood and regretted that time should be so short, as she had her own car and Mr Knight his, but she hoped to make up for this at the cemetery, after the burial.

'Poor Wilfred had no future,' she said, getting into her car, 'but I'd be curious to know where that money came from.'

Angus was about to follow her. At that moment, Mr Knight intervened.

'I'm taking your son with me,' he said in a tone that brooked no contradiction. 'I have something to say to him. You shall have him back in a little while.'

Closing the door of the car on Mrs Howard, whose amazement was only equalled by Ghéza's, Mr Knight grasped Angus by the arm and took him to his car.

Angus offered no resistance and dropped rather than sat on the seat by Mr Knight.

'Don't look,' said the latter gently. 'Close your eyes.'

At that moment the coffin was being put in the hearse which

344

drove off at once. Both cars followed, first Mrs Howard's, then Mr Knight's.

'Angus,' said Mr Knight, 'I can see that you're very much grieved, and I can easily guess why. This is hard to bear. I would cry, if I were you, without the least shame.'

Angus shook his head without answering. His handsome face was terribly white and his eyes enlarged, as though some vision enthralled him.

'God took him away at the best moment,' said Mr Knight. 'A moment He alone knows and the one He always chooses. We will probably never find out what poor Wilfred was doing in that street, nor why that lunatic fired at him. It's been impossible to drag anything coherent out of the murderer.'

The little funeral procession entered a quiet street lined with gardens.

'I hope you believe in God,' said Mr Knight.

'I can't,' whispered Angus hoarsely.

'What keeps you from believing?'

After a pause, Angus replied simply:

'This.'

Mr Knight was silent. It took a good fifteen minutes to reach the cemetery and the funeral procession, as it left town, now drove through a large avenue where the houses stood farther and farther apart, hidden among trees, a sign that the country was close at hand. The shadows of sycamores stirred faintly over façades with slender white columns, and flowers gleamed on lawns. From time to time, a passer-by paused to see the hearse go by in the dazzling sunshine.

'I was with him at the end, you know,' said Mr Knight suddenly in a low voice. 'I think it would comfort you to hear what I'm going to tell you. Will you allow me to tell you?'

Angus nodded.

'First came a sort of ceremony they call extreme unction. I

345

refused to be present. It's not that I'm hostile to these rites, but I did not wish to hamper the priest. I went to see him afterwards in an office that is set apart for him. He is an insignificant looking little man, something like an official. That, at any rate, was my first impression. Spectacles and a round face, a well-fed air. After having told him who I was, I asked him about extreme unction and what benefit it could be to a dying man. I must admit there was a sort of trap in my questions, but you can't catch these people unawares, even the simplest among them. He answered very accurately. I asked him to tell me how he expected to come into contact with the soul of a dying man who had been drugged into unconsciousness. He looked at me a moment, then stated very calmly: "I have never assisted a dying man whose soul seemed to me more present or more attentive." "That," said I, "was an impression, for the fact is that he heard nothing." Once again, he looked at me. "Shall we go and look at him?" he asked. I followed him into the room.'

'Well?' asked Angus in a muffled voice.

'Well, Angus, I'm not a man to give in too quickly to my emotions. When I found myself in that little room again I had to catch hold of the bed's metal bars with both hands, to make sure of standing up straight. I've lived a long time. Never yet have I seen such an expression of happiness on any human face as that which lit up Wilfred's. Applied to him, the word death had no meaning. He was alive, he lived! For a minute I stood plunged in a sort of amazement, then heard myself ask the priest: "Is it over?" He answered: "Yes, it is over if you mean that the heart has stopped beating." I don't know what I said. It is of no importance. I could not keep my eyes from Wilfred. It seemed as though he smiled at my surprise and that he knew secrets and was keeping them to himself. As though he had played a trick on us by going, a boy's prank, and that he was watching us from afar, from a region of light, in spite of the fact

346

that his eyelids were shut. I came closer to him and kissed him twice, three times. I felt a little embarrassed on account of the priest who had dropped on his knees. I think that if I had been alone with Wilfred, I would have talked to him, I would have talked to him for you, if I had known what I know now, I would have talked to him for myself, and for Phoebe too, because he was there, Angus, he was far away and he was near, very near –'

Angus doubled up and clasped his brow with both hands.

'Hush,' he begged. 'I can bear nothing more, nothing, nothing.'